THE
BURNING
TOWER

Chick & Adolph,
With fond memories
of our travels around
downstate New York
in the late 1970s

THE
BURNING
TOWER

BOOK 1 OF THE SECRET JOURNEY

COLIN GLASSEY

This is a work of fiction. All the characters, organizations, and events portrayed in this
novel are products of the author's imagination.

The Burning Tower
Book 1 of The Secret Journey

Print ISBN: 9780998578309
Ebook ISBN: 780998578316

For Gene Wolfe,
Roger Zelazny,
J. R. R. Tolkien,
and Lord Dunsany

*If I had seen one miracle fail, I had witnessed another; and even
a seemingly purposeless miracle is an inexhaustible source of hope,
because it proves to us that since we do not understand everything, our
defeats—so much more numerous than our few and empty victories—
may be equally specious.*

~Gene Wolfe, *The Sword of the Lictor*

TABLE OF CONTENTS

ACKNOWLEDGMENTS

My love and thanks to my children, to my family, to Mia, and to the land of California, which I have walked across and driven over for many, many years.

MAPS

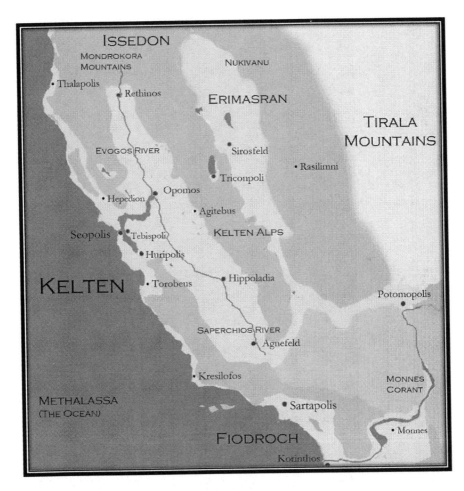

ISSEDON

MONDROKORA
MOUNTAINS

NUKIVANU

• Thalapolis

• Rethinos

ERIMASRAN

TIRALA
MOUNTAINS

EVOGOS RIVER

• Sirosfeld

• Rasilimni

• Triconpoli

Opomos

• Hepedion

• Agitebus

KELTEN ALPS

Seopolis •   • Tebispoli

• Huripolis

KELTEN

• Torobeus

• Hippoladia

Potomopolis

SAPERCHIOS RIVER

• Agnefeld

• Kresilofos

MONNES
CORANT

METHALASSA
(THE OCEAN)

• Sartapolis

FIODROCH

• Monnes

Kotinthos

kelten

iii

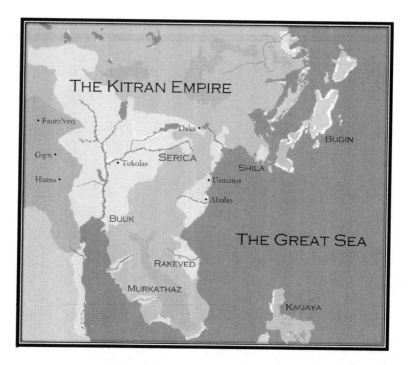

Serica and Surrounding Lands

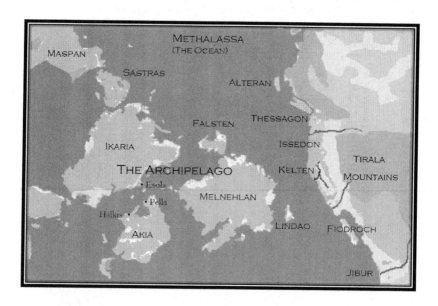

The Archipelago

Central Serica

PART ONE

Kelten

In the beginning, there was the map. Folded twice over, stained brown with age, in places unreadable, marked by long-evaporated water, the aged paper fell from the book Sandun Eiger held and onto his lap.

Sandun expertly unfolded the sheet despite his thick fingers and gazed with increasing wonder at the thin, faded lines. As one of the royal archivists, he was supposed to know every chart, sketch, tracing, and plan in the collection. He loved maps—had loved them ever since he was a boy—and he really did know all the drawings in the king's collection.

His love of depictions of the world could be dated to the hour he had entered his father's workroom and found, spread out on the drawing table, a large vellum map of Hepedion. In that hour, he felt like a seagull over the town. Every building and every street through which he had run while chasing cats or other small boys or being chased by larger boys—all this was revealed to him in a rising tide of simple joy. There was the temple, and out of the main market circle was Fish Street, crossing the old stone bridge and headed west toward the sea. And there was Sun Street, and if you turned left onto Newt's Tail and then right on Ironmonger Row, his house. Sandun never forgot his first map.

A new chart, even poorly drawn, could provide an hour's entertainment, so he set aside the annals of King Stepos the Rash and took up the magnifying glass standing in its place of honor at the top of the desk; he studied long and thoughtfully as the ink gave way to vistas of places he had never before seen.

"By the Spear of Sho'Ash, I find you hard to trust. And yet, if you are what you claim to be…" Sandun half breathed this to the map, his heart beating hard, his faced flushed.

"Anyone looking at you would say you'd found an illumination of the Lady Maormos, all ready for her bath," said Master Eulogo. "Come, what are you bent over? I was about to call you to lunch," Still a vigorous man despite his years, in his black robes he looked a bit like a crow eyeing a shiny pebble.

"My dear sir, I am trying to decide if this is the new lodestone of the map collection or if it should be turned to ash for fear it will lead the young and impressionable to their certain doom." Sandun respected the old man, but they had sparred often enough, most recently over a very confusing battle plan left by General Anandus, one of the least educated of King Pandion's warlords. It had been a victory but, by terrible luck, the very last officer who served with the old warrior had died in battle with the Issedonians just one month before they had realized they needed his explanation of events.

"And may I, the master of the king's records, be allowed to see this engine of ambiguous effect?" Picking up the book Sandun had been reading, he continued, "Korun's teeth, this book has been gathering dust as long as I have toiled here."

"I found this sketch tucked within the pages." Sandun handed Eulogo the map and the magnifying glass.

The old man bent over the aged sheepskin and began to mutter to himself, "Stigia was ruined nearly two hundred years ago, and yet here it is."

Sandun interjected, "Look how the Evgos River bends to the west of the Vasten Hills. The great flood of 485 changed its path to lie on the eastern side, as it is still."

"I noticed that," said Master Eulogo dryly, yet as he studied it, rising excitement could be heard in the timbre of his voice. "I think, I think, my boy, you have found a nova—a new star for our collection." He pointed his long, twiglike finger at the top right corner of the map. "This must be investigated." He nodded his head, as if his mind needed to concur with his tongue. "If this map is speaking the truth to us over the centuries, then there was, at one time, a road to Serica."

A road to Serica! No man from Kelten had gone to Serica and returned in many centuries. A thousand years ago, during the Third Trimarch of the Archipelago Empire, there had been trade over the far northern plains and through the nearly endless pine forests. The reliable explorers who had made the journey claimed it took almost a year to go from Wallbard to the first major Serice city.

Vases and goblets of Serice glass were highly prized in Kelten, indeed throughout the Archipelago. Kings and earls vied with each other to own them and display them. Serice glass had colors that could not be duplicated, and the glass itself was of astonishing strength. Other artwork from Serica commanded high prices: polished and intricately carved stones, wood of an unknown tree that was dense and held a strange luster, and more.

Despite the value of the goods, trade with Serica had died away like the fading howls of a wolf pack running toward the hills in the night. Sandun had once read the journal of the last known Kelten trader: Herek, younger brother of Tindares, the Island King. Herek vividly described snowfalls in the middle of summer and partially frozen rivers with blocks of ice that smashed many of the rafts his men made. Since the days of Herek, the Sogands had taken full control over the north, and they killed almost anyone who entered their lands. The northern route had been closed for hundreds of years.

"Let us study this more, but I believe a meeting with our king is necessary." Master Eulogo pursed his lips as he considered the implications. "I will make inquiries from my friends on the king's council as to which way the winds of royal favor are blowing this month."

"Who would oppose us investigating this old map? A path to Serica could only be beneficial, yes?"

"My boy, there are always opponents of any change, and the atmosphere in court has been like a miasma to many unwary advisors, nobles, and even ministers. To bring an issue requiring royal approval before the king without first sounding out the current favorites and advisors is unwise and even dangerous."

Sandun digested this and then offered a new tack. "Could we speak to the king privately? Invite him to visit? He was last here, what, two years this last Highsunday, as I recall?"

"We could do that, but it would take time to arrange, and when word came out about this map, this discovery, my enemies might spread the lie that I concealed this news from the king for reasons of self-interest. No, we cannot wait on this. I must plan the presentation of this map with both care and haste."

Master Eulogo paced a circuit around the shelves holding the records; his hand brushed against some of the volumes of aged leather, as if seeking comfort from touching the tools of his trade. "Since your contacts with the king are less influential than mine own, you must authenticate this map— find out who created it and why it has lain forgotten for so many years. If we are wrong, it will harm us, and if we are right, there may be more than a few who would see this news as a threat to their schemes."

"But surely none but our enemies would see this knowledge as harmful?"

"No, no. Everyone walks on a knife edge, and the closer one is to the king, the greater the risk if one should fall. These days, any change can upset the balance of power in the court. The lord exchequer could bring in a report of a poor wine harvest from Nemiada, and three men could be removed from office the next day. All news is dangerous."

Sandun's frustration broke his usual reticence at discussing matters of politics with his superior. "How long can this state continue? How can the king make wise decisions if every advisor must first weigh his views on the scales of personal risk and reward before speaking openly? Is the king only to hear what his councillors deem safe for them to tell him? How can he make good choices if all he hears are half-truths, or distortions, or self-serving platitudes? I remember the days of Oniktes, when no man spoke openly, when in closed rooms by candlelight we whispered rumors about the missing queen, but upon the streets everyone greeted one another with false smiles and spoke only about the low clouds and the chance of rain. And did we overthrow that false king with fire and sword only to have the same fears descend on us? Are we not free men, not Keltens? Sho'Ash save us all." With his invocation of Sho'Ash, Sandun struck the quill pen on his desk and knocked its ink bottle to the floor; the black ink poured out. Embarrassed and uncertain of Eulogo's reaction, he took a rag and cleaned up the dark pool from the smooth wooden boards.

Eulogo perched on a small stool usually used for standing to reach the high shelves. He looked at Sandun with a piercing eye. "I first apprenticed under Master Tomlima in the last years of King Kranus. He once told me about his life years before, when Pandion the Great ruled. After the battle of Rohyla, Pandion was unchallenged at court. Everyone loved him; all his ministers felt free to give him the unvarnished truth without fear of reprisals. The king was wise, and his councillors were well chosen for their knowledge and honesty. Those were golden years. Which is why we were able to conquer Fiodroch and hold it against Jibur and Melnehlan. So Master Tomlima taught me." He sighed.

"Seventy years ago. Followed by evil days, unwise regents, decades of civil war. All my life has been spent in twilight. As you say, it was worse under Oniktes II. He was a man no one could trust, a man who'd smile and flatter you one day and have you murdered on the street the next." He closed his eyes; his voice grew fainter. "Master Isambar's blood ran between my fingers as I tried to stanch the wounds inflicted by Oniktes's assassins. They laughed and jested as they walked away, the daggers in their hands dripping blood onto the cobblestones. All my words died in my throat."

Master Eulogo stood up and cleared his throat. "Our king, Pandion, Third of his Name, is a good man, and he keeps the flatterers to a minimum. He is both prudent and thoughtful, and not overly fond of anyone, as a king should be. And we have need of his prudence; dark clouds are gathering to the north in Issedon and the west in Melnehlan. Peace with Fiodroch is welcome after our long war, but who can say if it will last beyond the reign of their King Langaras? But do not be overly concerned. If the map holds up to further scrutiny, be certain to make a copy."

Eulogo walked to the door. "I shall spend this afternoon catching up on court gossip. This evening, we shall subject the document to a most pressing cross-examination. If it be not falsified, I shall cross the great estuary and pay visits to friends on the morrow. I leave you to your task."

All thought of lunch driven from his mind by the task ahead, Sandun brought the map over to the light streaming in through the narrow south window.

Two weeks later, Sandun accompanied Master Eulogo to meet with King Pandion in his palace. They crossed the great estuary in one of the many sailboats that spent every day crossing the salty waters from east to west, north to south, leaving wakes of white foam as they beat against the wind. The day was fair, though low clouds covered the Pelikrisi and a stiff sea air blew east from the Great Sea. At the main pier, they disembarked and joined the throng of merchants and laborers and visitors to Seopolis, the capital city of Kelten.

When he had first been appointed to work in the Royal Archive, a year after the victory at Agnefeld, Sandun had taken every opportunity to visit Seopolis. He had grown up in Hepedion, where it took four days of steady walking to reach the northern end of the Helioada River and from there, depending on the tide, several hours sailing down the river and across the estuary to reach the capital. As a young man, he'd made the trip to see Oniktes II crowned, even though at the time of the coronation there were already rumors of rebellion and the day of the ceremony was dreary, with low clouds covering the parade route. Nowadays, Sandun came less often to the city, preferring instead to while away his free time in the forested and sunny hills, just east of the Archives, that climbed up a thousand feet and more.

Today, the city was as it always seemed to be: different in details but essentially unchanging. Several teams of men were erecting new stone buildings right on the waterfront across from the docks. A nobleman in his finery strolled down the pier in front of them, flanked by two large men with gloved hands on their swords. Working men and women carried baskets of goods and food up from boats tied to the creaking pier. The familiar smell of smoke, from thousands of cooking fires, drifted to them along with the odors of horse urine and manure.

Master Eulogo and Sandun wore their robes, decorated with the heraldry denoting the Archives: a round shield in the old Imperial style with three rolled scrolls in the center. Walking to the palace was out of the question given the distance. Since there were two of them, it was cheaper to rent a carriage rather than horses.

"Two silvers," said the coachman.

"We can add this to the heating bill." A nervous joke, from Sandun—the Archives were generally not heated since the vellum and parchment lasted longer with a constant temperature. "What is going to happen?"

"Watch and learn. If my little plot turns out, I shall explain it all afterward." Master Eulogo seemed jovial, but Sandun thought he detected a false note in the old man's smile.

"As a fellow Archivist, you might let me know so I can prepare."

"You play your part, I shall play mine, and we will get along like the seagull and the eel."

After this mysterious reference, presumably to an obscure folk expression, Sandun ventured no further questions. He gripped his stiff satchel, also emblazoned with the shield and the scrolls, and looked out the window.

As the carriage climbed up the first hill, the houses, city residences of the lesser nobility, became fancier. This was the Dromo Thalas, the main road from the port to the palace. A mile farther on, the land leveled and large oaks spread their branches over the road. The great estates of the most powerful nobles came into view, protected by tall iron fences and, behind them, the household warriors dressed in the distinctive liveries of their masters. Unlike common soldiers, these men bore two-handed swords and wide-bladed spears with blades carefully covered with decorative cloth sheaths.

At last, the great stairs of the Sita Elaf or "New Palace" came into view. The name "New Palace" was a source of amusement to the locals; it was both accurate, since it was newer than the old castle, and completely misleading as it was also one of the oldest buildings in the city. Like many buildings in Seopolis, the New Palace was both very old and in the process of being rebuilt, as windows and facades were torn apart and replaced so as to take advantage of improvements in the art of glass making. The steps, made of shining white granite with veins of quartz running through it, were crowded with people from all over the kingdom and even some from the other nations of the Archipelago. By long tradition, the steps were free to everyone, though the foolish and the disrespectful were swiftly removed and taught not to repeat their mistakes by the hard fists of the huge men who made up the king's guard.

Most who came here just wanted to see the palace and watch the parade of elegant women and men who daily passed in and out of the gilded gateway. Often enough, the king or the queen or one of the princes would come out and extend greetings to the visitors, sometimes with gifts for the obviously needy.

Queen Joaris was of noble birth and generally liked for her good grace and her daily worship at the temple. Married to the king at a young age, she had stood with him through times of deadly peril and had borne him two sons, the Princes Proklos and Leonos, both fine young men. Nothing more could be asked of her.

The queen's handmaidens were all young and pretty women from among the aristocracy. One or more of them could be seen throughout the day, sauntering on some errand of the queen's or simply collecting admiring looks from the crowd. A few years back, Sandun had fallen under the spell of one of these girls, a golden-haired beauty and the daughter of a lesser lord near Betholferry. Sandun spent many weekend hours on the steps, seeking more views of this demigoddess. But inquiry and research had revealed that a queen's handmaiden nearly always married far above Sandun's station in life. Despite his official robes and respectable office, he was just a commoner and not likely to advance even to the lowest ranks of the nobility.

A year after Sandun first laid eyes on her, the girl married the third son of the Earl of Agnefeld, a young man who now commanded one of the best cavalry regiments patrolling the disputed border with Fiodroch. All this information was recorded in the Archives, as the genealogies of every noble family were very carefully tracked.

Master Eulogo and Sandun's carriage, with permission from the street captain, rolled up the steep gravel path. They exited the carriage and walked into the palace from the side entrance. The palace floors were white stone, like the great steps, and the walls were rich yellow pine with many tapestries and paintings depicting scenes both historical and religious.

They waited in the antechamber for a few minutes before they were joined by three men. Sandun knew them by sight: the Earl of Torobeus, the Count of Opomos, and the king's younger brother, the minister of war, the Duke of Huripolis. Master Eulogo made deft inquiries as to the families of each of the men and complimented them on their successes.

The Earl of Torobeus was polite but cold. The Count of Opomos shook hands gladly, with a big smile. He said he well remembered his days at the Archives ten years ago, looking for geological reports, hoping to find more wonder rocks like the one that had been discovered in his marshlands. He said that his prospectors had found many strange rocks in the Kelten Alps to the east, but nothing like the wonder stone.

The duke, though he looked like the king, was a different sort of man: bigger, weightier, with a curly beard that covered half his face. While the king's hair was already gray at the temples, the duke's hair appeared untouched by age. In temperament they differed as well; where the king was quick, with a sharp mind and a sharp tongue, the duke was solid, loyal, and happy to defer to his older brother, save for matters of horseflesh and battle. While Pandion had recruited good men and kept them well fed and well paid, it was the duke who had charged with reckless fury into King Oniktes's guard and struck down the king's champion in single combat.

Sandun had been part of Pandion's army that day, which was now famous as the Battle of Agnefeld. In the battle, he commanded five war machines and some thirty men to operate them. His battery had fired giant bolts at the massed formation of the enemy archers, causing much carnage. In the final hour, he looked through his farseer with a glee mixed with horror as the duke's footmen surged past their lord, overwhelmed the royal guard of Oniktes, and butchered the evil king in a mad, bestial fury. Axes and greatswords rose and fell, turning horses and men into nothing more than piles of red meat. To his dying day, Sandun would remember seeing Oniktes in his golden armor disappear from view. He would remember shouting, "The king is dead! The king is dead! Victory!" The cry spread through the whole army, and suddenly men who had been fighting for Oniktes began laying down their weapons and crying for mercy. Though won ten years ago, the battle was as vivid in Sandun's mind as this morning's trip across the water.

The door opened, King Pandion III was sitting at the round table of state. They all bowed and then took seats.

"Master Eulogo, good to see you. You are looking unchanged," said the king. "The years and stacks of dusty tomes have not turned you into a wight."

Master Eulogo bowed his head. "Not yet, my lord. That transformation may yet occur, and if it does, I suppose I will have to keep my position for eternity, until the Glorious Battle."

"Good to see you too, Master Sandun. The care of our royal records has not aged you overmuch; you seem as fit as you did a decade ago."

Sandun bowed, but as no witty repartee came to mind, he thought it best to remain silent.

The king waved to his footman. "Would you gentlemen care for some wine? As my brother knows, we have recently been gifted with a fine white wine from the Lord Arkoamplo's vineyards."

"Indeed," answered the duke, "I enjoy this new white, and I urge you all to try it, despite the weighty matters we are here to discuss. A glass of wine may smooth the debate."

After sipping the wine, Master Eulogo made his prepared speech:

"Your Highness, my lords, the matter before us is not so weighty, at least not yet. My colleague, Master Sandun, has discovered an old map, concealed in a set of land deeds from the days of King Stepos. The map purports to show a path that travels through the impassable Tirala Mountains and leads, ultimately, to the border of Serica. The map was made by a previously unknown Kelten explorer named Jon of Stenston, who appears to have returned to his home village of Stenston in the year 495. It is the considered opinion of the Archives that an effort should be made to ascertain the truth of this."

"Stuff me with feathers and call the cat!" said the Earl of Torobeus. "First, if there was such a route, it would be used today—everyone desires the glassware and craftworks of Serica. Second, if a route had been discovered, it would never have been forgotten."

"My lord, we share your skepticism—to a degree," Master Eulogo said soothingly. "This is why I say the matter before us is not so serious. At least, not yet. As you say, what are the odds that a route to Serica would not be in use today? They are low. And what are the odds that the discovery of a route, even three hundred years ago, would be forgotten? Equally low. However, despite the poor odds, we think this map slipped through the cracks of time. Master Sandun shall explain our case to you, as briefly as he can."

Sandun drew from his satchel the map, now placed on a stiff leather backing, and the old folio of land deeds in which the map had been found; both were passed around.

Sandun laid out the support for map's validity: the use of names that had long gone out of style, the changes in geography, and then the reason why the knowledge could have been lost. He made his points carefully, buttressed by facts commonly understood by the lords.

"As you all know, the later years of Stepos the Rash were a time of troubles the likes of which this land has rarely seen, though I daresay many men would speak worse of the recent misrule by the usurper Oniktes. In any event, the chaos was so great that the years 495 and 496 are missing from the Seopolis records. What I have here is a folio, a local copy of land deed transactions, made in Stenston and brought back to the Royal Archive as part of the resurvey project at your highness's direction. We believe no one had reason to look at this folio because the Viscount of Stenston has been succeeded by eldest son to eldest son for nearly four hundred years, until the late Viscount Stenston died without a legitimate heir earlier this year. So, with no reason to examine the land deeds, it seems likely that no one looked at this folio."

Sandun took a sip of wine and continued. "As to why this news could have been lost, suppose a traveler were to have returned from Serica in the year 495? Is it not likely that he would have been swept up in the great revolt that saw many of the nobles allied against the king? If that man had perished in the fighting, which lasted for more than a year, would anyone have remembered that man's story of a path to Serica at that time? We cannot say for a certainty, but it seems moderately plausible."

At Sandun's conclusion, even the earl was nodding his head slowly, as though to a hidden beat in the wooden room. But the Count of Opomos objected, "Lord King, my river farmers have a saying: 'All seems good when the rains fall, but woe betide when the summer o'er stays its welcome.' The meaning of this is simple: Sho'Ash is still at war with the Black Terror, a slow war but an ever-present one. We live in a world constantly in struggle, and the very land changes year by year as generations of men march on and do battle with the darkness in his name. Even if there was a route that one man followed three hundred years ago, the land has changed. On my borders, the woodsmen of the Kelten Alps suffer from landslides and avalanches during the fierce winter months each year. To the north, Sho'Ash caused Mount Inessa to explode, which unleashed a massive rockfall that in turn blocked a river, and now there is a lake where once lay a fertile valley."

Opomos continued, "It seems to me a fool's errand to seek something lost for three centuries and which might never have existed in the first place.

We must needs worry about the Issedonians to the north, the Melnehlans to the west, and Fiodroch to the south before we spend crowns chasing a marshlight into the bog."

Sandun was dismayed by Lord Opomos's vigorous attack. He could tell that the other lords were puzzled.

The Earl of Torobeus spoke up. "Unusually, I find myself in agreement with my Lord Opomos. It seems a fool's errand…and yet, in my port I have seen traders from distant Maspan bring to market small yet terribly expensive vases and plates from Serica. A route that once existed still may be possible for a few hardy men, and but a sackful of Serice glass vases would make a man rich. It is hard to always see the hand of Sho'Ash in day-to-day events, yet would it not be strange to wall Serica away from his words of salvation for all time? Though it costs us some coin, mayhap it is our duty to make the attempt?"

The king gestured to his brother. "What say you, my lord duke?"

The duke spoke slowly but with force. "I am reluctant to see the Spear of Sho'Ash in this potential discovery. But we Keltens have long taken pride in our ability to make profitable trades with almost all nations. If there is a chance to trade with Serica, I say we seize the chance. As Opomos says, we have pressing claims on the royal purse. So I suggest a cheap expedition but a swift one."

The king now gave his pronouncement. "My lords, I thank you for your thoughts on this. I deem that an effort must be made to find out the truth of this matter. Trade with Serica would be most beneficial. Even a few strong men every year bearing loads on their backs would improve our purse and raise our status with the other nations of the Archipelago. As Lord Torobeus observed, small things from Serica command great prices in all markets of the Archipelago. If pack trains of mules could make the journey, our treasure chests might one day groan from being overstuffed—whereas now, being ill fed, they are silent."

The king paused and looked up at the tall windows through which sunlight entered, illuminating the paneled room. "Who among us has not dreamed of visiting Serica? So inaccessible and yet, if the stories be true, a great nation with many wise men and with not a few craftsmen who remain unsurpassed in all the world. It was the kingdom with the largest cities and the mightiest rivers. The palace in Kemek was said to have spread across miles, filled with gardens and elegant halls, music and song. As a young boy, living in exile in Fiodroch, I contemplated making the journey myself."

The king finished his wine and sat in silence for moment. Then he said, "My lords Huripolis and Opomos have the truth of it; our efforts must be economical. To that end, I wish a small party of outdoorsmen who are skilled and yet schooled and of good character. Mine old tutor once told me Serica's leaders set a great store on virtue and at times refused dealings with coarse traders and discourteous diplomats."

Now the king stared at Sandun and Master Eulogo with piercing eyes. "This investigation I delegate to the Royal Archives. I command you to be discreet. The public purpose must be as dry as bone; no word of this possible route must reach Issedon or Fiodroch. Submit a proposed budget with an uninteresting story to the royal exchequer. The King of Kelten gives you eight hundred crowns and a squadron of cavalry as escort. Report to me personally when your expedition is ready to depart."

The king rose to his feet; the audience was over. Sandun found it difficult to stand, as the blood seemed to have drained from his head. The idea that this task would fall to the Royal Archives and that he would almost certainly be responsible for leading it had come like a bolt from Naktam.

As they were walking out of the room, the king patted Sandun on his back. "Don't worry yourself overmuch, Sandun. The route is likely impossible, and northern Erimasran has been mostly safe since last summer. The royal collectors have had so few complaints that it may be time to raise the taxes on the free folk who live therein." The king chuckled at the thought of raising taxes. "I'm counting on your safe return, and I daresay the books will gather only a bit more dust whilst you are away."

The king stopped them before they left the chambers. "Remember, not a word of this to anyone. I am looking forward to seeing the chancellor of the exchequer come storming in when he receives your expense request—he will be livid! I suppose I should warn him ahead of time; it is unmannerly to tweak him so. But must a king deny himself all pleasure in pursuit of his royal duty? I think not!" At this, the king laughed, and the nobles and the archivists bowed themselves out.

Outside the room, Master Eulogo and Sandun exchanged glances. "Let us summon a light refreshment and rest a while in the palace gardens before we head back across the water," said Master Eulogo. "The next few weeks will be busy."

✤

The Venerable Hine wrote in his *Discourse of Chronos and Eros*: "There are two ways to lie effectively. First is to tell only a part of the truth, leaving out what is most important to conceal. The second way involves telling the truth but so unconvincingly that your listener is sure you are lying."

Seven days passed in a flurry of behind-the-scenes activity. Master Eulogo and Sandun came up with a plausible proposal and a budget for the expedition. As a starting point, they consulted old writs from the exchequer's office documenting two overland expeditions conducted during the reign of King Pandion II: one to Potomopolis, the other to eastern Issedon in what turned out to be a successful effort to make common cause with a clan that hated the then-king of Issedon. The expedition to Potomopolis, more reconnaissance than conquest, traveled roughly the same distance as Sandun expected to travel and involved less than seventy-five men.

Prices were higher now than they had been twenty years ago, and so the eight hundred crowns, which seemed more than enough at first hearing, was half the amount they requested in the writ they sent over to the exchequer.

"Don't worry, my boy," Master Eulogo said expansively. "His Majesty expects us to ask for more money than he stated. It's an unwritten law of government: an important task takes double the time and twice the money allocated."

Sandun knew from his readings that the growth in prices was inescapable; it had been well documented by several masters of the Archives over the last century. The reasons for the steady rise in prices remained baffling, and it was a source of continual frustration to every recent Kelten monarch.

With the cover story complete, they began to spread news of the upcoming expedition to those who needed to know. First, the apprentices at the Archive were told, and then it was mentioned in the local Tebispoli tavern. Sandun also put out the word at the Koryfog livery that they were in the market for some sturdy horses and strong mules for a long journey out to the far eastern frontier.

Since the Duke of Huripolis was going to summon a squad of mounted scouts to provide escort, the two archivists settled on a group of three men to lead the expedition.

Sandun was the obvious choice to go, so obvious it was barely discussed. Sandun himself would have preferred to be asked if he wanted to go, rather than Master Eulogo and the king assuming he would. Late one night, he thought about the trip, considering the pros and cons. He was unmarried, and no woman or small children depended on him. Like all young men who'd come of age during the War of the Nobles, he had trained in the bow and the dagger, the spear and the sword. As a young man living on his own in Seopolis, he exchanged blows with rival gang members on several occasions. The battle of Agnefeld was the largest battle he had been part of but was not the only one. Since those rough days of easy violence had come to an end, he now enjoyed fencing. For years, he had been a regular at the Tebispoli fencing club and was considered good. Physically he was fit; every Shoday he hiked in the hills ten miles or more. Clearly, Master Eulogo was not capable of the journey because of his age, so if someone from the Archives were to lead the expedition, Sandun was the man for the job.

But why had this job been given to the Archive? Surely there were professional diplomats who were capable or young knights who were eager to gain fame. Even if they did not find the path, it was dangerous to travel to the edge of the kingdom. And if they did find the path, the journey through the Tirala Mountains was a leap into the unknown, scarcely less dangerous than jumping off a cliff into the swirling waters of the Krisopeli. Finally, the most recent stories or rumors about the state of Serica were bad: there seemed to have been a long war and many supernatural disasters, and some reported that great cities had been utterly destroyed.

Despite the dangers, Sandun had to admit to himself that he was bored and restless at the Archives. He longed to travel to the edge of the known maps and explore further. He could have taken a wife and started a family, but hadn't. Why hadn't he married the baker's daughter last year, when she so clearly fancied him? Perhaps the Earl of Torobeus was right; perhaps Sandun had a destiny, a road, which Sho'Ash had set down for him to follow—if he had the courage.

The next evening, he went to the temple and prayed to Sho'Ash. The temple was simple—in comparison to the great temple across the estuary in Seopolis—an octagon with a large statue of Sho'Ash in the center, holding a spear in his right hand, his massive left foot stepping on the twisted form of the Black Terror. Other, smaller statues of various saints stood along the walls, looking at Sho'Ash. Sandun took the sacred stairs that led down to the large underground chamber below. Here, most worshippers gathered, on their knees and looking up through the iron grate to the lights at the top of the temple, just as Sho'Ash did when he was imprisoned in the deadly dungeons of the Black Terror.

The priest was there; he knew Sandun by sight and came over after a short time. "You are going on a long journey soon, I hear."

"Yes, holy one."

"You are afraid to go, and yet your duty requires you go."

"Yes, holy one."

"Take comfort. Our lord Sho'Ash, once a prince in his own lands, left his wife, his home, his family. He traveled a year and a day to put an end to the evil of the Black Terror. Now and forever he guides and guards those who go forth in his name to do good deeds." What the priest said was well known to Sandun: these were core elements of the story of Sho'Ash, which Sandun had heard every year during Holy Week when the sacred rituals of Sho'Ash were acted out.

Sandun wondered if everyone who was going on a journey into the unknown felt the same fears. Sho'Ash had left his native land, gone into the unknown, and challenged the greatest evil the world had seen—but he was a god, the son of Dyus, destined for glorious victory. Sho'Ash was never afraid; he'd had unshakable confidence. Sandun didn't think he had much choice, but if he were offered the choice freely, would he take it? He didn't know.

He climbed the stairs up to the light. Before leaving the temple, he stopped to pray before two of the saints: Hurin and Pellar. Hurin held his long sword up to the sky, pledging his every victory to the glory of Sho'Ash. Saint Pellar had her book open in her hands, but her face was lifted to stare at the face of her lord.

Sandun returned to his dark house and lit a lamp before going to bed. The journey seemed no less impossible, but miracles had occurred in the past; despite his many faults and his many sins, Sandun now felt hope. After all, what was the passage of centuries or millenniums to a god? An eyeblink? An hour spent staring at the sun?

Sandun's second-in-command was selected from the journeymen of the Archives. The most physically gifted of the young men was Maklin Leo. Maklin had grown up on an orange farm in Miloalos. Maklin had the arms of an oak tree, and he was skilled with a wood axe. He also had a prodigious memory; he had named every tree on his family's farm and had counted every orange on every tree for two years running. The priest of the local temple had recommended him to the exchequer, and he had worked there for a year. Then he requested a transfer to Archives, and they had been happy to have him as memorization was a crucial talent for those who worked inside the Royal Archives. Maklin also chopped the firewood not only for the Archives but for all the other official agencies clustered in

Tebispoli: the Royal Astronomers, the Herb Masters, the newly relocated Navy Department, and the College of Natural Philosophers. He was paid for this work, but he told anyone who asked that it was only when he was cutting logs that his mind was quiet.

Sandun doubted that skill in handling a wood axe would be very useful on the expedition, but Master Eulogo insisted that Maklin's strength and farming background made him the best choice. Sandun did get his pick for the third man: the mapmaker, Basil Vono.

Like Sandun, Basil was from Hepedion; he and Sandun had been friends while they were young boys. But then Basil's father, a surveyor of land borders, had run afoul of the Viscount of Helioada, and so Basil's family was forced to leave town and flee north to the forests outside of Thalapolis, where they had relatives who could protect them. Sandun heard little of his friend for the next ten years, during which time Basil became an expert hunter and one of the finest bowmen of the northlands. When he was not out hunting, he was tutored by his father in the art of surveying. Since the Viscount of Helioada was loyal to King Oniktes, Basil joined Pandion's rebel army more for a chance to avenge his family than for any great love of the would-be king. There, he and Sandun were reunited, and they became blood brothers during the campaign that ended in the great victory of Agnefeld.

After the war, Basil was able to profitably combine his skills as a hunter and surveyor working for the king and for newly installed lords who wished their recently granted domains to be carefully delineated. Every three months or so, he would return to the Archives with one or two hand-drawn maps—for which he was paid handsomely—and some excellent venison or boar steaks. Basil and Sandun would usually eat at the local tavern, where Basil could be convinced to tell humorous hunting stories.

Soon after the meeting with the king, Sandun visited the hunter's hall in the old part of Seopolis. There he left a message with the door warden, offering a reward of ten crowns to any man who could get a message to Basil Vono. He did the same at the bowyer's guild hall, the fletcher's guild, and the currier's guild. The message was simple: come to Tebispoli as soon as possible.

One hunter who sold a bale of animal skins at the currier's hall the next day knew Basil's location and went to deliver the message. Nine days after, Basil showed up at the Royal Archives, dusty and curious, his hunting dog by his side. That very day he was asked to join the expedition at a lieutenant's pay, six months guaranteed, ninety crowns. In the evening at Sandun's house, over a fine bottle of fortified wine, Sandun told him the whole story.

Basil looked at a duplicate copy of the map, which Sandun carefully unrolled from a narrow copper tube. "I've travelled up and down Kelten and gone deep into the Kelten Alps, but I have not gone to this part of Erimasran," Basil said thoughtfully. "I do know the hunting becomes very poor on the other side of the Alps. Also, the people are so scattered that no lord has need of carefully marked borders, so there has been no work for me there."

He picked up another, larger map that purported to show the geography of the known world and brought it over to the light. He stared at it and marked out distances with his folding metal yardstick. He was silent for a long time as the hearth fire cracked and burned, slowly turning the wood into glowing orange embers.

"Even if we can find this path, the distance is too great. It seems impossible unless we find unknown help on the route. It is said by everyone that the mountains go on and on for several thousand miles, monstrously tall, barren peaks, and dry valleys between them."

Basil continued, "In good land with plenty of game, I can travel twenty miles a day, hunting animals at every camp. Assuming this map is correct, it would take me at least four months of steady travel. The longer it takes to hunt, the fewer miles I can manage per day. If the land is like Erimasran, the trip would take me six months. If the land is worse, perhaps seven or eight months. I must believe the Tiralas are impassible in the winter; all accounts insist on their great height. If the snows come and we can't find people who will shelter us, we will die."

"But we are bringing food with us, on mules, for exactly this purpose," replied Sandun.

"Good travel food can allow us to go faster, perhaps twenty-five miles a day for several months. I don't travel with mules myself; their braying drives most game into hiding." Basil stared at the map, playing out distances in his mind. "All right, perhaps even without finding an undiscovered nation in the middle of the Tiralas, it might be possible to cross in four months. If we find the path two weeks before midsummer, we might get through before the snows trap us."

Sandun smiled at Basil's reluctant concession. "You don't have to go with me. You can back out now and no one will think anything of it. You have a woman and a youngster."

Basil let out a low, mirthless laugh. "I'm a wanderer, gone for months at a time. Ezeil is happy to see me when I show up on her doorstep, but she knows what I am. There are few old hunters: a slip in a steep canyon, a tusk gash that starts to weep pus, and we are never heard from again. You have to go on this trip, right? The king's command?"

Sandun nodded slowly.

"Then that's it. We stick together, you and I. Besides, if we make it back, I'll be the most famous hunter in all of Kelten. They will put a portrait of me in the hunting lodge, right behind the main table. A hundred years from now, men will say, 'Basil Vono, the greatest guide in history.'" He laughed at the thought of it. Sandun doubted Basil had set foot in the Seopolis lodge more than a dozen times, but he nodded in agreement.

"What about me?"

"You aren't a member. Is there a guild of explorers? If we make it back, you can start one."

Three weeks later, the Archive Expedition was on a boat, sailing slowly east through the marsh toward Opomos and the mountains beyond. The preceding days had been a blur of continual decisions, frustrations, and second-guessing by everyone from Master Eulogo to King Pandion himself.

To Sandun's surprise and bemusement, their military escort had ridden into town a week earlier, and the commander was none other than the dashing third son of the Earl of Agnefeld: Sir Ako, a knight of Kelten, the same man who had married the queen's golden-haired handmaiden years before. Sir Ako was very tall and very handsome, with sandy hair. Despite his size, he was quick on his feet, and his hands had a grip like a vise. He practiced every day without fail with all weapons but mostly bow and sword. In speech he was affable, able to speak with perfect courtesy to his social equals—and then half an hour later, you could find him cursing and belting out orders to his scouts like the most ill-tempered mule driver.

The eleven scouts under his command were experienced professionals, a hand-picked group of soldiers used to days of hard riding and nights spent in lonely vigil looking out across the border to Fiodroch, watching for spies or signs of military forces massing. Relations between Fiodroch and Kelten were unusually cordial under King Pandion, so the border was largely untroubled for the first time in more than a hundred years—all to the good, since the northern border with Issedon had become bloody, with nearly constant raids and punitive counterstrikes. War with the northern kingdom was openly talked about in Seopolis.

Sandun wondered why a knight was in command of so small a detachment, but in several carefully worded conversations, Sir Ako indicated that he was aware of the true purpose of the expedition and had expressly asked for the command. Later, from Master Eulogo, Sandun learned that Sir Ako was only billed to the Archives at a captain's rate—a good thing indeed since a knight at full pay would have greatly exceeded their budget. Even so, when all was bought and paid for, the budget for the expedition came to 2,300 crowns, nearly triple what the king had authorized in their first meeting.

Despite the cover story and the vociferous complaints from the chancellor of the exchequer as to the pointlessness of the expedition, Sandun suspected that Issedon's spies were going to ferret out the truth sooner rather than later. The haste with which the trip was organized, the presence of a knight of the realm in command of elite scouts, and the fact that the king had taken a personal interest in the Archives—all these things suggested something more interesting than a search for an ancient library of the Pellian Empire was afoot. Sandun hoped that no enemies knew where they were going; as a precaution, the map had been seen by fewer than ten men.

It was late afternoon, and as they sat on the deck of the sailboat, the wind hardly seemed to move, yet the tall marsh reeds bent and swayed in the breeze blowing up from the Great Sea. Their sails were full and the boats, guided by men native to the river, tacked back and forth among the islands, always in the deep water, steadily beating upstream.

Several of the scouts attached long, thin lines to their arrows and ventured shots at waterfowl, who flew out of cover as the boat passed their resting places. The lines pulled the arrows off target and reduced their range. But the scouts made adjustments, and a lifetime of archery paid off with two fat ducks being squarely struck and hauled back to the boat.

Basil silently strung his large bow and gave a low whistle. His dog, one of the hunting breeds imported from Akia centuries ago, went to the edge of the boat and stood there, all coiled muscle, as tense as spring iron, looking back and forth between his master's bow and the reeds. Several birds burst from the thick green stalks, and Basil released his arrow. With a soft flutter of feathers, the largest bird plummeted from the orange-tinted sky. His dog leapt into the water, swam over to where the bird had splashed, and retrieved it. Back on the boat, the dog dropped the bird at Basil's feet and shook himself, making sure everyone around was aware that he had just been in the water and had come back with a fine catch. The other men nodded.

Sir Ako, resting after his combat practice for the day, came over and sat by Basil and Sandun. "I believe you hunted with my father some years back," he said to Basil. "He said that had been a good hunt and he had learned something of the habits of wild boar from you. At the time I was serving under Lord Tamiril; otherwise, I would have able to join in the fun."

"Your father handles a boar spear with as great courage as any man I have known," said Basil, who then added, "I rather doubt he learned anything about boars from me. His lordship has been hunting game animals since before I was born."

"He does not hunt nearly as often has he would like. The duties of a marcher lord are many and toilsome. As a knight in the king's army, I have more free time than he does. Usually when he left the castle it was to inspect the frontier defenses, not hunt. My eldest brother, ensnared by the same duties, complains to me at our every meeting." Sir Ako stretched out his long legs and smiled in contentment, looking up at the sky. "I am but a simple knight, but I get to ride all day, and when we are not chasing fools attempting to sneak across the border, we are culling the land of surplus deer and destructive boar. That they taste good when cooked over an open fire in the warm summer evenings is but a happy accident." This last was directed to his men, who chuckled with amusement.

The three boats with the men, the horses and mules, and the supplies moored next to one another at a decaying wooden dock loosely connected to one of the soft marsh islands. On the high point of the land, some ambitious boatmen had built a temporary shelter out of stranded branches and rotted boats. Nearby in the fire pit, the expedition cooked their meal as the light faded from the sky.

From the bank of the muddy isle, Sandun looked out across the land. To the east, far beyond the marshlands, the snowcapped high peaks of the Kelten Alps shone dimly. To the north were lines of lights, some of which appeared to be moving. Taking out his farseeing glass, he could tell that men were working…but on what? Coming down to the fire, he asked the boat master about the lights.

"That would be the mine of the great swamp rock. Mining does not cease day or night, 'cept on the Holy Week of Sun's Rebirth. We steer well clear o' that place; the guards be mighty quick with their arrows to warn away all but select cargo boats."

Sandun, like most people in the region, knew of the wonder rock. Discovered shortly after King Pandion III was crowned, it was later seen as divine favor bestowed on the new king. The place where the rock had been found had for centuries been nothing more than one of the larger islands of the marshland. But strong, shifting currents on one side had washed away the accumulated mud of uncounted years and revealed an underlying metallic stone of extraordinary composition, harder than iron and very slow to rust. Swords made from it were sharper and held their edge longer than nearly all others made in the Archipelago. The rock went far into the earth, some said like a dragon's tooth growing from subterranean depths. Others argued that it had fallen out of the sky like the famous "star stones" that had been found but rarely over the centuries.

Sir Ako boasted, "I have a sword made from that stone, though in truth, many knights of Kelten carry one these days." He drew the blade; Sandun, Basil, and several boatmen came close to admire the weapon. "We call them Fine Blades. King Pandion gifts some each year as tournament prizes or for heroic deeds. A few are sold, though never to foreigners. This one was given to me as a wedding present by the queen." Sir Ako slashed the air with some quick strokes.

Sandun thought about the gifts locked in a pouch that he carried close to him at all hours. King Pandion had traveled over to Tebispoli in his royal barge the day before their journey began. He inspected the soldiers and their equipment, checked the mules, and reviewed the ledger sheets. Sandun noted that neither the chancellor nor the lord exchequer accompanied the king. After commenting on how the prices had risen since the days he had organized his own army of invasion twelve years ago, he accompanied Master Eulogo and Master Sandun back to the Royal Archives.

King Pandion said, "I have given much thought to a fitting gift for the King of Serica, if the expedition succeeds, as I hope and pray that it will. The gift needs to be small and yet rare. Mere gold or gems I dismiss as unworthy of our great kingdom. Happily, a solution came to mind. Some months past, an alchemist named Moure from the town of Erithofeld invented remarkable glass spheres. He made a present of some to me, and I now entrust twelve of them to you to be given to the King of Serica and others of that land whom you deem will be friendly toward our kingdom and desire beneficial trade."

He'd summoned his champion, Sir Ekston, who produced a small bag, cunningly made of interlocking metal chains over a very tough leather pouch and locked with a small key. The king opened the lock and poured out twelve orbs onto the table. They were made of semitranslucent glass with a yellow-gold tint. One was as large as a cow's eye, the others a bit smaller. At first glance they seemed pretty enough but no more.

"Close the blinds, please," commanded the king. As soon as the blinds were drawn, the Archive room darkened, and the orbs now glowed with an eerie and unexpected green light.

"Master Moure assures me that he made glass spheres like these a year ago, and they are glowing just as brightly. They always give out light, night or day, no matter what you do to them: place them in water, lock them in a sealed box, or hold them in the sunlight."

Master Eulogo exclaimed, "Truly, these are a wonderment and a fitting present to the King of Serica. You said these can be manufactured? How? I have never heard of such things." At a nod of approval from the king, both he and Sandun picked up one of the orbs for close examination. Sandun saw that at the center of his orb there was a small black node. The others had it as well.

"Yes, they can be made, though Master Moure has not revealed the exact formula. Two years gone, the alchemists of Erithofeld discovered that a small portion of the wondrous rock is made of a different metal entirely, undescribed by any text. At first it was called Black Gold, but Master Moure has changed its name to Heliosium, or Sun Stone. He also discovered that one type of colored glass glows when placed in proximity to Heliosium. As you noticed, there is a small black eye in the center of each orb. That eye is a piece of Heliosium."

The king sighed, "These are quite rare, gentlemen. If, or perhaps when, the wondrous rock is mined out, the supply of Heliosium will be exhausted as well. As you can well understand, what I have told you must remain a secret, but you need to know we can make more. If these meet with approval by the King of Serica, then there is a basis for trade in these goods, at least for several decades and hopefully longer."

The king placed the stones back in the pouch and gave it to Sandun, along with the key. "If you do not reach Serica, I command that you bring the orbs back to me or see to it that they are returned by any means possible. No one knows what price these would bring in the great market of Pella, due to their remarkable nature and rarity, but I daresay you could sell one and, with the proceeds, buy a castle. Do not betray my trust."

On the muddy island, Sandun shuddered in the darkness. He did not want to carry the orb pouch and so draw attention to it, nor did he wish to not carry it and so lose it to a sneak thief who searched his bags. He did not want to think about the consequences of incurring the king's anger by losing the glowing orbs in an accident or from highway robbery, but his mind would not stop thinking about all the steps he should take to avoid losing them in every scenario. After half an hour of playing out ever-more fanciful circumstances and strategies in his mind, Sandun steeled himself and resolved to cease thinking about the glowing orbs.

That night, Sandun made his bed near Basil and his dog. As he drifted into the land of sleep, he resolved to tell Basil about the gift for Serica if they ever found the path into the Tirala Mountains.

Sandun's duty, other than finding the path and following it across the Tiralas, was to create a record of the expedition. Every day he updated his log with miles traveled, weather, and notable events, if any. He also made it a point to learn something of his new traveling companions.

Sergeant Torn, Age: 39. Served in the king's army more than 20 years. From his accent, he is from the north coast. Taciturn and with a melancholic disposition. Enjoys singing sad songs in the evening about faithless women and fishing boats that fail to return from storms at sea. He has a good voice, deep and soulful.

Padan, man-at-arms. Age: 31. A tall man, brown hair, with a ready laugh. Joined King Pandion's rebellion and fought at Agnefeld. Born in the foothills near Mount Lefkoati. Rarely misses with his longbow.

Damar, scout. Age: 26. Born and raised in Sun House Valley. Light-brown hair and a lean build. A cowherd who grew tired of herding cows. Curiously, he knew me by sight from the year I spent as a scribe working for Baron Griflen, though I had only a vague recollection of seeing the young man. Said he regretted not following me and some of the other men that left in the night to join Pandion's rebellion.

Olef, scout. Age: looks about 18. Very thin and boyish in looks, short dark hair, dark complexion. Talks rarely and then with a strong southern accent. Said to be good at hiding unnoticed amid the trees, which I can well believe.

Farrel, man-at-arms. Age: 28. Average height, stocky build, reddish hair. Born in Betholferry. Says he worked for two years as one of the king's messengers. Claims to have won an archery competition in Hippoliada, and judging from the fact that I have never seen him miss a target's bull's-eye, it is likely no more than truth.

Wiyat, scout. Age: 21. Brown hair, tall, and handy with weapons. Born on the estate of the Earl of Agnefeld, the son of one of his lordship's guards. Clearly idolizes Sir Ako. Says he joined the scouts to "see the world."

Gloval, scout. Age: 25. Born near Stenston. Like Damar, a cowherd. Would not explain why he joined the scouts other than mentioning "trouble" at home. A good singer of "cowherd laments."

Jon, scout. Age: 24. Born near the border of Fiodroch. Average height and build. A typical Kelten man; friendly, honest face. Appears to be the only man that Olef enjoys talking with.

Kinot, scout. Age: 23. Says he was born near Hepedion, but I place his accent as from Zanthos. Good looking, light-colored hair, and friendly but unusually skilled at cards.

Norris, scout. Age 25. Dark hair, average height. Solid build. Born in a small town called Coalton (which I've never heard of—he says it lies due west of Miloalos on the other side of the great valley). Another cowherd who says he "got sick one night after spending two days in the cold rain and vowed he'd never herd an animal again for the rest of his life." I'm not sure if the life of a scout is much of an improvement, but he is a cheerful fellow and well liked by everyone.

Eki, scout. Age 22. Brown hair, tall. Grew up in a small village just north of Agnefeld. Won a local archery competition and was recruited into the scouts. An excellent shot, though not as good as Farrel.

Days of travel brought the Archives Expedition into the foothills of the Kelten Alps; they took the king's road, which followed the Stradom River. A day had been spent in Opomos unloading the boats, making sure the horses and mules were packed and ready for the trip, replacing a couple of worn horseshoes.

Navigable waters went north and south from Opomos. Their destination was north and east, but to act their part of looking for an old library east of Sirosfeld, Sandun choose to follow the king's road to Triconpoli and thence to Sirosfeld.

Not even the most agile canoe could go up the Stradom River, where they were on this day, in early Triomon, the third month of the year. Snowmelt was starting to fill the riverbed, but huge boulders studded the river's course like iron bolts set in a castle's door. At whiles, the water careened past the stones in smooth, glassy sheets of pale green. In other places, the main force of the current ran straight at huge stones, throwing white spray up and about, covering the surface of the water with swiftly dissolving foam.

They had passed Agitebus the day before, and now as they climbed ever higher, the trees changed from great twisted oaks to a sea of tall pines. No trace of snow could be found on the ground, but the wind blowing above them through the thin green needles was chill and sounded like rain, though no clouds could be seen in the narrow sky between the looming peaks.

A shrill bird screamed like a red-tailed hawk, and it put Basil on alert. He asked Sir Ako to halt the company and send out scouts. Four men dismounted and went off into the woods on either side.

"A good place for an ambush, Sir Ako," said Basil quietly as he strung his carefully wrapped bow.

"I was thinking the same thing, but who would attack fifteen well-armed men this close to town?"

"If they thought they could distract us while spooking away some of our well-laden mules, they might count the candle worth the risk of burn," replied Basil.

At a word, all dismounted and readied their weapons, and the remaining scouts took up positions in a large circle about the horses. Sandun, Basil, Sir Ako, and Sergeant Torn took up positions in an inner ring. Scribe Maklin held his axe in one hand and the lines to all the mules in the other.

Sandun had practiced archery as a young man, but he had no great love for the bow. Of late, he had taken it up, when time allowed, as very little food would be gained with swordplay, and his life might well depend on shooting rabbits and other small mountain game. He had not fought in a battle since Agnefeld ten years past, but war is not something you forget. He rubbed his sweaty palms on his leather chaps and inspected his sword and dagger.

One scout, Farrel, returned and reported, "A large group, at least fifteen bows, three spears, up the slope to the left." The slope Farrel pointed at was sunny, but the trees climbed all the way to the top of the ridge, casting deep shadows. A hundred men could easily stand under the greenery, unnoticed by travelers on the road below.

"Should we attack?" Sir Ako asked the sergeant.

"I want hear the news from behind us," Torn replied. The sergeant was an old campaigner; scars on his face and arms and chest gave proof of a life spent in the company of sharp iron.

They waited in silence. The delay before a battle was maddening; Sandun hated it almost as much as the actual fighting. Sometimes one or even both commanders would find the enemy overstrong or decide the weather was against them and so order a retreat. But sometimes the battle call would sound, and then there was little time for reflection or even thought until after the fighting was over.

Scout Padan returned and reported from the road behind them: "Four or five young men we found. No weapons 'cept knives. Hidden at the stream side by the rocks. Very agile I guess, but I doubt they can dodge arrows. We'll stick them when they come out of the riverbed."

"So!" Sir Ako had his plan ready. "Standard flanking maneuver. Damar, go with Padan and put some feathers in the knife men behind us. Eki, Wiyat, and Farrel, follow me. Sergeant Torn, in fifteen minutes, make a deal of noise and get their attention. The ambushers will come to you, we hit them from the rear, and it will be all be over in half an hour. Questions? No? Then let's ride."

With that, Sir Ako and three scouts armed with bows and swords disappeared into the forest. Padan and Damar went back down the road and out of sight. The remaining six men, now under Sergeant Torn, took up positions close together but under cover.

"How do you suggest we draw their attention, Master Sandun? We don't want to frighten them away. I doubt they would rush to greet us if we raise our battle cry, though it be common practice between armies." Sergeant Torn was very respectful of the chain of command; he believed that Sandun was now in charge.

Sandun thought about what could lure bandits from an ambush. The usual enticements—wine, women, money—were not ready at hand. "Shame we did not bring a few of last night's women from the Golden Horn of Agitebus on this day's journey. Sending them to bathe by the river would do the trick."

The men all laughed at that thought, breaking a little of the tension they felt.

"I think a good rousing song will work. Our forest friends won't expect it, and natural curiosity will draw them in close. What about 'Don Dory'?

We will all join in on the rounds. If that doesn't bait our hook, we can try 'Saint Hurin's Drums.'"

With that agreed, they made deceptive small talk about the tavern while keeping on high alert. At the appointed time, Sergeant Torn began an old drinking song that every Kelten man knew.

> *As it fell on the Holy Week, and on the holy tide,*
> *Don Dory brought his ambling nag to Lygos for to ride.*
> *When Don Dory to Lygos came a little before the gate,*
> *Don Dory was fitted, the porter was witted to let him in thereat.*
> *The first lord that Don Dory did meet was King Ago of Pell.*
> *Don Dory did slip he tripped and spit and King Ago was wroth.*

> *{All} And King Ago was wroth!*

> *A pardon, a pardon, my liege and my king, favor me one more time.*
> *And all the churls of Kelten I'll bring them bound to thee.*

> *{All} I'll bring them bound to thee!*

> *Sir Nichol was a fisherman, a little beside Batide,*
> *and he manned a good black bark with fifty oars a side.*

> *{All} With fifty oars a side!*

> *Run up, my boy, unto the maintop, and look what thou canst spy.*
> *Who ho, who ho, a ship I see; I trow it to be Don Dory.*

> *{All} I trow it be Don Dory!*

> *They hoist the sails both top and top, the mizzen an' flag were tied*
> *And every man stood to his lot, whatever should betide.*

> *{All, with real gusto} Whatever should betide!*

> *The fiery arrows then were plied, and dum and dum went the drum.*

> *{All} And dum and dum went the drum!*

> *The braying trumpets loud they cried to courage all nearby.*
> *The grappling hooks were brought to bear, the oaken spear and sword.*
> *Don Dory at length, for all his strength, was clapped fast under board!*

> *{All} Clapped fast under board! Hey ho!*

With the last echo of the song, a voice cried out from the nearby trees: "Stand and deliver your goods to us. We are robbers, and we are many. You are surrounded!"

Sergeant Torn shouted back, "You'll get naught from us but cold iron in your bellies and arrows in your backs. We are scouts of Lord Arris's Mounted Company. If you surrender to us, we may spare your worthless lives!"

This provoked murmurs from the hidden robbers. After a minute, the leader of the robbers shouted again, "You lie! Everyone knows that Arris's company still patrols the southern border." A small trumpet sounded three short notes; apparently, this was some signal from the robber leader. He then continued, "You surrender! You have entered our land, and your goods are forfeit."

He was about to say more when his voice choked. There were several cries of pain, and shouts came from the bandits. Then Sir Ako's whistle blew, and the sergeant ran forward swiftly but cautiously, a sword in one hand and a small shield on his arm. The others advanced into the forest, drawn to the sounds of confusion and growing panic from the bandits.

Sandun passed by one robber, dead or dying with an arrow in his back. Another man stepped from behind a lodgepole pine with an arrow ready in his small hunting bow. He looked nervous, and Sandun used his command voice to call out, "Here is one—kill him!" He waved imaginary soldiers to the attack. The would-be bowman glanced nervously from side to side, and Sandun ran toward him, rapidly closing the distance. The robber looked half-starved, and his clothing was a mass of patches, poorly stitched. He turned and ran up the slope. Sandun followed him a short way and then, convinced he was not coming back, he turned and headed to the sound of metal clashing.

He arrived to see the final moments of a fight between Sir Ako and a large man, likely the leader judging from his unpatched clothing and the trumpet hanging from his neck. Sir Ako hammered at the man's guard, beating down his defenses with a mix of power and skill. In a move too swift to see, Sir Ako twisted the other man's blade to one side and, with his iron gauntlet, struck the robber below the man's metal cap, a stunning blow that knocked him to his knees. The other bandits were either on the ground or fled. The big man grunted, "I yield, spare me."

"There is no quarter for robbers on the king's highway. As knight of the realm, I carry the king's justice, and your sentence is death!" The bandit leader cried out and tried to struggle to his feet, but Sir Ako hit him again with his full strength, right on the man's forehead. The bandit leader fell prone to the ground, as if struck by a thunderbolt. Suddenly, all was quiet save for panting and low groans.

"He should have surrendered when he had the chance. Now he will swing if he does not expire on the way back to Agitebus." Sir Ako sheathed his sword as all sounds of battle faded. "Battle report, soldiers."

One after the other, the men told of how they had fared during the fight. The three scouts who had gone back down the road came and joined them. The final tally: five of the bandits dead, three gravely wounded and not likely to live a day. Three prisoners, including the bandit leader. The rest fled. The expedition's own injuries were of little note: several cuts, two twisted ankles. It was Scribe Maklin's first battle; he had chopped one robber's arm clean off, and the man bled to death while the battle continued.

"We could hang this ruffian now, but it would be better if we brought him back to Agitebus and let the local lord deal with him. However, it would delay us by two days." Sir Ako offered the decision up to Sandun. "As leader of the expedition, the decision is yours."

Basil commented that the high passes ahead of them were likely covered with snow and a delay of two days would not delay their arrival at the south lake much.

Sandun said, "You can take the prisoners back to Agitebus. Scribe Maklin can go with you. The rest of us will stay here and wait for your return."

After Sir Ako and his party departed downstream, Sergeant Torn set about gathering information from the wounded bandits. One older man, who had received an arrow that pierced his body below his ribs, proved quite talkative. Certain that the wound was fatal, he wanted to share his life's grievances with the sergeant before he passed on to face the judgment of Sho'Ash. Sergeant Torn, about the same age as the bandit, listened without judgment, taking notes slowly on cheap, military-issue paper. Sandun, curious almost despite himself, listened to the man's justifications for taking up life as a robber.

"Farmer, I was. Farmed on poor lands east of Rethinos. Lost my ox to the 'collectors' of King Oniktes just before he were killed by the new king. Lost my wife and eldest son to milk fever five years later. Two months on, me daughter, the only sweet thing in me life, she walked away one morn, said she be going to town. Never saw her agin. I searched, oh I searched. Some said they saw a girl fitted her description but going by another name, traveling south with a group of thieving actors. I believed it; she were a pretty lass."

Torn said, "Rethinos…that's a long way from here."

The injured man coughed. "I be getting to that. One day, the priest comes by, said he's sorry an' all but I got to pay my tithe to the temple. I says to him, I got no money to pay. Then he says, this land belongs to the temple, and the tithe is a rent and I must pay. He says to me, 'Rothgar, you've not been farming these last six months, you've been drinking and lying about.' Well, that were true enough, but I were in no mind to hear it. I got it in my head that I were going to find my girl, bring her back home, and then we'd make a go of the farm again."

"You headed south, following her trail."

"Aye, that I did. Weren't no trail to follow, though. Too much time passed. Should'a gone right quick, 'stead of drowning my woes in ale. I did odd jobs, slept in fields, gleaned fruit from orchards, heading south. Fell in with some traveling field hands last summer. They had a leader, a big man, you seen him, went by the name of Lelex. Fancy name for a farmhand."

Rothgar tried to laugh, but all the came out was a sickening, wheezing cough.

"We called him Red. End of last harvest season, Red says to us, he says he knows a hideout, up in the Alps, near a road. Says he we can tax the travelers, hunt bear and deer, live good and free. I followed him, we all did. We had money enough to buy bows an' arrows. Merchant caravans come up the trail, we'd tax them, send them on. We'd never have come within a mile of you lot had we known you was in the king's damn army. Red, he had big dreams, and they got bigger every month. He said you were just hired guards and'd turn tail as soon as the horns blew."

Rothgar's voice had sunk to nearly a whisper. Sandun, Basil, and two other scouts drew close. "Here I am, breathing out my last on this earth. Never found my darling Sally. If the Black Terror don't grab my spirit, Sho'Ash, aid me…aid me…"

The men around him all made the sign of the spear. Rothgar breathed weakly for a time and then died.

"I wonder how much of that story was true," Basil said as he and Sandun walked by the riverside while the scouts dug a grave.

"Do people actually lie with their final words?"

"He lied about his daughter. Acting troupes cannot take women with them. It's the law, and it is enforced in almost every town. On my journeys,

I've spent the night with several traveling players over the last decade. They loved sharing tales of young women begging to run away with them. Actors have creative ways to shame the girls and send them packing. Seems there are always new ones in every town with stars in their eyes and nary a thought in their pretty heads. For the players, its far better to move on to a new town unencumbered than risk being convicted for traveling with an unmarried woman."

Sandun protested, "I've seen plays with women in them, and it was no illusion of paint either."

"Ah, Sandun, you should get out more. Things are different in the big cities. Seopolis has professional acting companies. Actors are allowed to marry and settle down if they can make enough money. The licensed companies you find in Seopolis or Opomos often have the wives of actors playing roles. But if the company goes out to the countryside to perform, the women cannot go with them. My younger brother took up acting for several years, even joined a professional troupe in Thalapolis for a spell. Now he is a priest and a married man. I see him when I go north to hunt elk in the Modrokora Mountains."

Two days passed. Once the dead were properly buried, they fished by the river, and Sandun practiced archery under Basil's direction. As the sun was heading down the sky to the west on the third day, Sir Ako's party returned.

Maklin, leading the mules, was looking rather hangdog. He hid under his straw hat, but eventually it became clear that he had taken several blows to the head. Sandun asked him about his face, but Maklin only grunted. Sandun caught a meaningful look from Sir Ako, and so he did not press the issue further. After they ate dinner, Sandun had a private word with the knight. "Any trouble on the road?"

"None going, none coming back," Sir Ako replied cautiously.

"And in the town?"

"The Lord of Agitebus was off riding, but the shire reeve was happy to take custody of the prisoners. If the bandit leader lives, he will assuredly hang at the next assizes. The others can look forward to some hard years in chains, building roads."

"And?" pressed Sandun.

Sir Ako took a deep breath. "Last night, at the Golden Horn...well, there was a bit of drinking. People standing us rounds, more than a few as a matter of fact. They were expressing their gratitude for our swift elimination of an apparently notorious group that had been harassing travelers and merchants for some months starting last fall."

"But not sufficiently notorious for anyone to mention them to us when we passed their town four days ago. Do I detect a smell of guilt mixed with relief wafting up the road?"

"Could be. In any event, Scribe Maklin had more than enough drink, and when one comely lass, who was sitting in his lap, asked him where he was going and when he was coming back, he told her that he was going on a long journey to Serica and that he might die on the road before seeing another maiden so fair..." Sir Ako trailed off, his expression a mixture of dismay and combativeness. "Master Sandun, I tried to make amends, I told them the fellow was drunk and that we were going to collect old records from a library near Sirosfeld. This morning, I added to the misery of Scribe Maklin's hangover with some hard knocks and harsh words. He will not make that mistake again."

Sandun swore violently, "Sho'Ash's shit! I cannot believe what you tell me. By King Pandion's beard! I wish the fool had never come." He took up a fallen branch and smashed it to pieces against a tree.

After breathing hard for a minute, Sandun regained a measure of calm. "It cannot be helped. The rat has slipped the sack, and there is no way to tempt it back. I guess I am partly to blame. I should have come with you instead of sitting here on my posterior, shooting at birds. I'll talk to the young man. And do not blame yourself overmuch; no doubt you were distracted by a pretty lass with big blue eyes."

Sir Ako smiled ruefully but said nothing.

Sandun went over to Maklin. The young man was lying down but staring up into the darkening sky. The first stars were coming into view.

"Yes, I know," said Sandun. "I am angry with you, Maklin. Your words have placed us all in greater danger than we were in before. You swore by Saint Hurin's sword that you would not reveal the truth of the expedition to any man unless I gave you leave. And now, not a month later, you broke your oath. You are forsworn before Saint Hurin and Sho'Ash. But although you let drink cloud your mind, I am not sending you back to Tebispoli. You will share in the increased danger you brought on all of us. I hope we outlive your stupidity."

Looking both relieved and ashamed, Maklin started to cry. He covered his face with his hands, but strangled sobs forced their way out.

Sandun continued, gently: "I remember what it was like, after a battle, drinking in a village square, young girls at our sides filling our mugs. There are no words to describe how happy you are, because you and your comrades came through the fighting alive. You lived, while other men ran and some died. Victory is a heady wine, strong and seductive. It makes you feel like you are someone new." He slapped the young man on his arm. "Don't let this happen again, yes?"

"Yes, Master Sandun. Thank you."

Sandun wrapped himself in his blanket near Basil. He quietly explained the news.

Basil was not worried. "We are almost as far from Issedon as we are from Fiodroch. It was a drunken boast in a small tavern in an unimportant town."

"Consider this, my friend. If I were a spy, and I heard of an unusual expedition sent by the Royal Archives, maybe I would follow, days behind, perhaps a week. I arrive at Agitebus, and where do I go? The Golden Horn, of course. I'm a traveler, a peddler of tin cups maybe, I naturally ask about the road ahead. Locals talk of bandits killed, the leader waiting for execution. It's the talk of the town. And where are the heroes going? How long before someone repeats what Maklin said? Thirty minutes? An hour? It's a juicy rumor, probably no one believes it, but a tale worth telling, worth repeating. Going to Serica? Incredible."

Basil grunted, "Then what?"

"Hopefully nothing. It is, as you say, a long way to Issedon. And only you and I know where the map directs us. Erimasran is a vast land. Would King Tutaos of Issedon send a thousand wild horsemen into Erimasran on a rumor?"

"You speak of matters beyond my ken. I think we have much more to fear from Kelten's bandits than wild riders coming out of Issedon. Good night, brother."

For an hour, Sandun could find no rest as his mind spun around myriad possibilities. Finally, he put another log on the embers of the campfire and then fell asleep.

A week later, they reached the Kelten Alps' summit, and although it was covered in snow, the path was plainly marked with piles of stones and wooden poles topped with colored flags. The trail markers were placed at every bend, often less than five hundred feet apart. Despite the altitude and the snows that usually covered the pass from Dyusmon (the eleventh month) until

Ostarmon (the fourth month) people traveled the route almost year round. Now that spring was coming, it seemed every day they met a group of travelers heading downhill toward Agitebus or Opomos beyond.

A freezing wind blew snowflakes on them as they stood gazing in all directions. Looking down the steep, east-facing slope, they could see stone walls marking off farmland in the valley. In the distance, smoke was rising from many places—that was the town of Triconpoli. Through the haze, they could see one end of Lake Tricon.

Farther to the east, another line of mountains, the Arrokar Range, ascended rock on rock to meet the sky. Beyond those snowy peaks was Erimasran. Far, far beyond those peaks and invisible even from this great height, the mighty Tirala Mountains marked the eastern edge of Erimasran.

Looking back the way they'd come, they saw the great forest covering the land: a blanket of green with snowy fields peeking through clearings.

The horses began to stamp on the snow, expressing their unhappiness with this standing about and looking at scenery. Basil made quick sketches of the landscape but had no time to do more than guess at the heights of the nearby mountains. Most of the mountains near the road had been climbed; of late, men had lost their fear of the heights. The old stories of giants and dragons and Piksies had lost at least some of their power to frighten.

Taking out his farseer glass, Sandun looked at the tallest peak, south of them. He followed what looked like an easy path, up and up until, in his vision, he reached the top, and there was nothing but the endless blue beyond it.

As they followed the path down toward Triconpoli, the lake sometimes appeared between the trees to the north. It was a large lake, fully sixty miles long and fifteen miles at its widest. The path was not hard going down, though in one place an avalanche from the mountain above them had passed over the trail, which forced them to go around the broken chunks of snow and ice and take a steeper route down to the valley. It was nearly sunset when they finally reached the first farm, but everyone was eager to spend the night at the famous Bearskin Inn. So they rode along on a path that snaked between farmsteads, heading north as the pale sky became the color of rose petals. Dogs barked at them, and children came out of wooden cottages to wave at them as they passed by. The scent of burning pine logs filled the air. It seemed peaceful, and everyone breathed easier now that they were back among men and no longer alone in the wilderness.

As the night drew down upon them, the houses grew closer together and then streets appeared, paved with large pieces of granite more like slabs of stone than cobbles. Men and women, thickly bundled in furs or many layers of wool, were out walking. Most carried lantern candles; some servants carried torches for their masters, who followed them.

Sandun asked for directions to the inn and was told it was straight ahead of them. Soon it appeared out of the darkness, a tall building with a great sloped roof on both sides. The men of the expedition dismounted, left their horses and mules in the stables, and walked up the large stone stairs and into the heat of the inn.

Inside, the men of the expedition lost no time in ordering beer and roast meat. The beer they were promptly served was dark and had an unusual flavor.

"We make it w'th our own recipe. We roast the malt an' do add barley and corn in the mash," said the innkeeper, a large fellow with thick arms and a full beard. Sandun and Basil exchanged glances, but whatever strange grains were in the beer, it tasted fine at the end of a long journey. The roasted meat came hot off the fire on skewers of wrought iron. Sandun, as hungry as the proverbial wolf when he started eating, found he was curiously full after the first skewer was devoured. Either the beer or the exertion of the day blurred his vision.

"Aye, we have room enough for all," said the innkeeper. "Up the stairs, the large room in the back is fer you."

Sandun shook his head and asked with a suddenly clumsy tongue, "How did you know we were coming? None passed us on the trail."

The innkeeper looked pleased with himself. "Och, none cross the pass without our hearing word o' it afore long. It's the king's road, but it be our pass. You made no secret of your traveling, and it were most likely you were of the king's army an' heading to Sirosfeld. None that saw ye mistook ye for merchants." At this, the big man laughed as though this was a very funny joke.

Sandun felt too lightheaded to attempt to explain their journey, so he left it to the others to explain their presence and went to bed.

A day's rest in Triconpoli left all of them feeling much better. The lake was icy cold to the touch, but fishermen, seemingly heedless of the water's wintery grasp, waded into the shallows to cast nets and haul out fish. It was beautiful, Sandun thought to himself as he sat near the lakeshore in the calm afternoon. A vast expanse of water, flat and barely moving, so different from the Great Sea with its unending waves, its ever-shifting surface flecked with foam at whiles. Down by the lake, the mountains seemed less threatening, the snowy peaks reflected in the water like shafts of light.

Two of the scouts, Olef and Damar, tried fishing, without much success. Sir Ako left them to spend the afternoon with Sir Ledlam, the town's military commander, a friend who'd once served in the southern army. Basil took his bow and his dog out hunting after the midday meal. Sandun wrote a report, updated his journal, and figured expenses. Soon they would be leaving Kelten proper and traveling through the wilderness of Erimasran. The thought worried him like a dog worries a rat. To calm his mind, he borrowed a pole from Damar and fished for an hour. But his thoughts would not leave the road ahead.

Erimasran had been for centuries the frontier of Kelten. Dry and sparsely populated, for several hundred years it had suffered from a lack of rain, and several towns had been abandoned. In the north, the border with Issedon was disputed; in the south, Fiodroch and Kelten had taken and retaken the fort town of Potomopolis from each other at least six times over the last three centuries. For all these reasons and more, people from Kelten rarely traveled to Erimasran. When he was young and wild, Sandun had shared a room with a young man from Erimasran by the name of Kagne. They had gone separate ways in a night filled with sudden danger, and Sandun had never seen Kagne since.

That evening, they ate the fine buck that Basil had felled up at the snow's edge just south of the town. The beer still tasted odd, but it quenched the thirst. Many local men came to the inn to hear the latest news from Seopolis and sing songs. Sergeant Torn was persuaded to sing "Don Dory" again after the scouts described their battle with the bandits.

Upon leaving the Bearskin Inn, they rode in easy stages along the road near the lakeshore. They found it a fertile land, watered by many small streams that flowed into the lake. Smoke drifted up from cottages hidden amid the trees. High above them, cattle could be seen grazing in the alpine meadows of the Arrokars. Spring had put forth its green fingers in this land, the snows reduced to patches on north-facing slopes. New grass on the ground matched tender needles on the pines. The air smelled fresh. The expedition found small villages spaced at a half-day's walk on the road. Out on the deep-blue lake, every morning and evening fishing boats put out and then returned with long silver fish in buckets.

Across the lake, the Kelten Alps fell in sheer cliffs right down to the water's edge. Some of the deep valleys on the western side were accessible only by boat, though they offered wonderful vistas of snowy slopes that reached up and up the top of high, sharp peaks.

Despite the harsh winters and the avalanches from snows on high ridges, the lands around Lake Tricon felt peaceful, removed from the tumult in the cities and towns along the coast. Tricon had rarely known war, as it was equally far from Issedon in the north and Fiodroch to the south. The few passes were easily defended during the summer; during the winter, no raiders could cross with any hope of retreat while loaded down with booty. Regardless of their peaceful history, the men of Tricon could often be seen practicing in groups with large bows. Gleaming war axes, long hafted and sharp, were proudly displayed along the walls of every inn. "He who would know peace must prepare for war" was an adage the people of Tricon lived by.

At one small inn, an old man spent the evening telling Sandun and Basil stories about the lake and the people who lived around it. He told them that when the Pellian Empire had first explored this part of Kelten—more than a thousand years ago—there were a small people already living here. The Piksies, they were called. Before they vanished, the Piksies told the Pellian explorers that a great dragon lived at the bottom of the lake, and the dragon kept the lake from freezing. They said it was death to take a boat out to the middle of the lake because the dragon would wake and swallow every boat that dared.

"I don't hold no truck with the fishermen who go out near the center o' the lake," the old man told them solemnly. "T'aint respectful. Someday the dragon will wake and bring doom to us all. I hope I never live to see that day." Sandun bought the garrulous man a beer and thanked him warmly when he made to leave.

It was common knowledge that Lake Tricon never froze, even in the coldest winters, but aside from that curiosity, there had been no sign of a dragon anywhere in Kelten for hundreds of years. Nor had any man seen the Piksies since the days of Kelten's founding, though the small people lived on in stories told to every child. Some tales had it that on dark and windy nights, the Piksies came out from their secret lairs and traveled to the sea and then vanished under the waves. This was the first time Sandun had heard that they once lived around Lake Tricon.

As the expedition rode north the next day, scudding clouds cast great shadows across the waters, turning the lake from deep blue to near black and then back again to blue.

"Even the alpine lakes of Melnehlan cannot be more fair than this," Sandun commented to Basil.

"Perhaps that is so. I have never seen them," replied Basil. "But several years ago, the eldest son of the Count of Orobeus asked a few hunters to join him on a hunt in the Melnehlan Alps."

"To bring back some of the famous glacier goats?" Sandun asked.

"Just that. I considered the offer, but I had agreed to lead a deer hunt north of Kresilofos. A year or so later, I met the young lord again in Seopolis. He praised the hunting in Melnehlan to the skies and was proudly wearing a white cloak made from their good wool. Then I was filled with regret."

"There is more than one way to get to Melnehlan."

"What do you mean?"

"From Serica we could go east across a great lake to the land of Shila, thence across the sea to Budin, and then board one of the yearly trade expeditions to Ari'Maspan and then to Melnehlan."

"Travel all the way around the world? What, has the full moon risen early? You lunatic! Who will teach my boy how to shoot a bow or track a mountain lion? I do need to return home someday. Honestly, Sandun, my dog talks more sense than you."

PART TWO

Erimasran

They finally turned east, leaving Lake Tricon behind and winding their way through a narrow, twisting valley. The trees thinned out mile by mile as they went. Soon great bushes had wrested the land entirely away from the trees. Above the path, acres of high mountain slopes came into view, barren and rocky. Great boulders appeared in the valley every mile or so; several were a brilliant white when seen from a distance, the sunlight gleaming off their vast bulk.

Four more days of travel brought the expedition through the Arrokar Range and down to Sirosfeld, the last significant town before they took to the wilderness in search of the lost path to Serica.

Sirosfeld was a town of some size, with a low earthen wall around it and a high stone castle standing right in the middle of a flock of townhouses, at the top of a modest hill. The expedition stayed at a large and well-appointed inn near the river, which they had followed the last two days and which flowed down in a white rush, bringing snow water from the Arrokar Range to the plains of Erimasran.

Aside from the dress of many of the men, Sandun thought they might have been back in Opomos, what with all the carts and people hurrying through the streets. In Sirosfeld, many men and some women were dressed in leather, a rustic style not seen much in the more civilized parts of Kelten.

The day after they arrived, Sandun had a private audience with the Mark of Erimasran. The mark, an older, weathered man, looked like he had spent his life on horseback; there was the unmistakable look of sun and wind carved into his face. The mark's family had ruled in Erimasran since the days of the great king Agites. The Mark of Erimasran had stayed out of most of the civil wars of the last thirty years, being separated by distance and the need to maintain a strong military force to ward off Issedon and Fiodroch.

Sandun presented his document and seal from King Pandion. The mark looked them over and then addressed Sandun gravely.

"My steward tells me you have fourteen men with you. A knight and eleven soldiers, as well as two others from the Royal Archives. Your expedition is very small. The area you are going to search is not so far from the border with Issedon. The folk who live in the north are scattered, and they rely more on hiding and less on vigorous defense for their protection. When raiders from Issedon cross the border, my warriors head north. Sometimes the Issedonians retreat without a fight; other times blood is shed. This has been true for years beyond count. Of late, the raids have become more numerous than in earlier years."

"My lord, we hope to evade any Issedonians through stealth," replied Sandun.

"I can see that, young man, but while I understand what you are trying to do, I fear you have little understanding of the landscape here in Erimasran. Hiding in the forests of Kelten is very different from remaining hidden in the wild plains. For example, the air is often as clear as the eyes of Sho'Ash, and campfires can be seen from as far as thirty miles away, unless you take precautions. Another example: some trackers native to this land can smell human camps if the wind blows their way, even when the camps are hidden in gullies. Perhaps you don't believe me. Perhaps you think fifteen men cannot be found in the vast expanse of Erimasran. Perhaps you are right and Saint Hurin will protect you from harm, but I do not want King Pandion to learn that your heads are being carried to Issedon as war prizes. He would be wroth with me, and rightly so."

"What do you suggest, my lord? The Archive's expedition has not funds to hire fifty or even ten extra guards."

"No doubt, no doubt. Even if I sent my best, Duncan's Regiment, it might not keep you safe. Issedon would likely learn of Duncan's deployment near their border, and they might view this as an opportunity to destroy a key part of my strength and so send an even larger army to hunt it—and by extension, you."

The mark thought for a bit and then continued. "Here then is my counsel: Take one or two experts born and bred in Erimasran. Heed their advice, and treat every mile north of here as a mile inside a no-man's land, where danger increases with every day. Heading into the Tirala Mountains is a great risk, but while the mountains will kill you with supreme indifference, the raiders from Issedon take a sick pleasure in capturing my people and torturing them to death. They want this land, and we stand in their way.

"Talk to my steward. He knows better than I who is in town and who can help you. Before you go, let me say that I hope you succeed. If we became the western terminus to a trade route to Serica, Erimasran would prosper greatly. We feel rather isolated out here, at the edge of the kingdom. We have much land, and the rains have been good these last winters. We would welcome more settlers, and more taxes would allow us to build forts along our northern border. My scouts will keep careful watch on Issedon, and my soldiers will be ready to respond if we get news of a raid."

The mark's seneschal was brought in and given instructions. He promised that he would get in contact with Sandun's expedition in a day or two with some suitable guides.

Sandun spent the rest of the day at the market, buying food suited for long journeys. By chance he ran into Sir Ako, who was bent on the same task. As they inspected the dried beef jerky, Sandun recounted the conversation with the mark.

"A trusty guide would be a welcome addition. Special knowledge of the land is more valuable than half a dozen veteran soldiers. Still, I know from experience that the loyalty of some of these wanderers is up for debate. At least in the southlands, where I have been campaigning, more than a few of the men we captured sneaking over the border hailed from the lands around Potomopolis."

"But, Sir Ako, you know full well that Potomopolis has been neither fully Kelten nor fully of Fiodroch for many centuries past. Given how many times the fort has changed hands, it is little wonder than the men have no strong allegiance to either kingdom. Surely no man in his right mind would see Issedon in the same way. Fiodroch is a grand kingdom with many fair towns, while Issedon is a land of brigands and worse."

Sir Ako did not look convinced. "I have never been to the northern marches, and so you may have the right of it. My point is moot if the Mark of Sirosfeld can select a guide for us. I'll give him a fair shake. In any event, we must all be on our guard once we leave Sirosfeld. The road north will be dangerous, and more so as we draw near the border with Issedon."

Two days later, the marcher lord's seneschal found Sandun in the library. The lord's maps were more detailed than the maps that Sandun had examined in the Archive, a fact that he found disturbing, though he had to admit, it made sense that the people closest to the need would have the better knowledge.

"Master Sandun, forgive the interruption. I have found a man who fits my Lord Sirosfeld's description of the job: a man born and raised in northern Erimasran, one skilled in hiding and in finding paths."

"I'm pleased to hear this news. Where can I meet him?"

"He is in town, Master, but there is a problem…"

Sandun remained silent, his hands gently resting upon the parchment map he had been examining.

"He is being held by the bishop. It is a delicate matter, one that involves a dispute between the temple and some villages in the north."

"What sort of dispute? The tithe? The performance of rites?"

"Perhaps you have heard of *nerio sanion*, or as it is commonly known, dream weed?" The seneschal was showing off his learning; nearly everyone in Kelten knew of dream weed.

Sandun tried to suppress a grin. Laughter nearly burst forth, but with an effort he mastered his mirth and replied, "Yes, I am aware of dream weed and of the temple's doctrine regarding its use."

"Ah, good. Then I do not need to explain the details. Suffice it to say, my Lord Sirosfeld finds it politic to take no position on this issue, nor does he wish to offend the bishop."

"But I can?"

"Well, as the king's agent, you may intervene without upsetting deeply entrenched factions here."

"I see. I'll meet the fellow. What is his name?"

"Kagne Areka of Tokivanu."

At this, Sandun really did laugh. At the mention of dream weed, in the back of his mind he'd had a feeling that Kagne's name would appear.

"My lord?"

"Perhaps you will not credit this, but I know this Kagne, or rather knew him, twelve—no, thirteen—summers past."

The seneschal's expression of disbelief was so comical and the coincidence was so unlikely that Sandun laughed again. "I must go and see him at once. You can provide a page to guide me?"

An hour later, Sandun was at the temple annex. The page presented the hastily written note from the seneschal to the junior priest at the entrance.

The junior priest read the paper slowly. He was an older man with a noticeable limp when he paced back and forth. Sandun guessed from his looks that before his injury, he was a travelling priest. The travelers were men who spent years walking from hamlet to hamlet, bringing the words of the temple to the scattered peoples of Erimasran. After some thought and reexamination of the documents, including Sandun's letter from King Pandion, he said, "The bishop is out now, but I see no harm in letting you talk to the prisoner." He led Sandun and the page down to the lower level; no doubt it had once been the original temple, as the stonework was old but of good workmanship.

In a darkened alcove separated from the main hall by iron bars that went from floor to ceiling, a man was sitting on a wooden bed. He sprang to his feet as they approached.

"Good day, Taragat! You have brought visitors for me? You are too kind by far." Kagne's voice and manner were just as Sandun remembered, though the years had tempered a little of his exuberance.

Sandun went up to the bars and stuck his hand through them. "Kagne! So good to see you again."

"Sandun, it's a long way from Seopolis," Kagne replied with hardly a trace of surprise. "It's good to see you too. I trust you are here to get me out of this…place?"

"As a matter of fact, I am. Though when I came to Sirosfeld, I did not know you were here."

"Music to my ears, sweet music. The stars have aligned, as I knew they would."

At this, the priest took offense. "No stars have aligned for you, wretch! The will of Sho'Ash brooks no opposition from stars or spirits or what have you. The supreme prelate of Erimasran has given no command to free you, and the mark has no authority inside this temple."

"And I tell you, the stars guide our footsteps—even yours, Taragat, though you refuse to see it. I am free already, as surely as water falls from the clouds and flows down to the sea."

Sandun sighed at the sacrilegious views Kagne proclaimed, here inside the temple prison. This was going to be trickier than he'd first thought.

"Kagne, I'm afraid the priest is correct. I have no direct authority to compel the bishop to aid me in my expedition. I hope to convince the bishop to release you, but I'll need to know the particulars of your situation to make my argument. I thought you were here because of dream weed?"

"I'll be happy to explain my situation to you. Take a chair and listen. I'm sure good Taragat will be equally happy to hear my story again." Kagne gestured to a small wooden chair near the barred door. The priest grumbled something about not needing to hear this again and went back upstairs. The page also begged leave to depart, and soon Kagne and Sandun were by themselves in the dimly lit room.

"As you know, for many years, my people in northern Erimasran have grown dream weed. It is a hardy plant, and it sells for good coin throughout Kelten and Fiodroch."

"Aye, Kagne, I remember well our escapades in Seopolis. Hauling our cart covered with carrots up and down the streets of the city. Being chased by…well, you know."

Kagne smiled. For the next hour, the two men reminisced about old adventures and caught up on news. Sandun talked, in general terms, about why he was in Sirosfeld. Kagne, after some prodding, described his troubles as resulting from an attempt to "adjust" new temple rules about local priests.

"My clan asked me to talk to the bishop directly. So I came here, and he threw me in his special jail for heresy! It's an overreaction to a perfectly reasonable request from the northern clans. We still follow the temple on most things; we haven't changed. Why does the temple suddenly act like we are terrible deviants? Yes, we grow dream weed; yes, we watch the stars and follow their guidance. We have been doing this since the days of my father's father. The temple priests didn't object then. Why now?"

"I don't know, Kagne. The temple hasn't changed in Seopolis, at least not that I've noticed. But we hear stories about heretics and awful crusades in Ikaria and Sastras." In a whisper, Sandun said, "I dare not repeat some of the rumors I've heard about foul deeds supposedly done by the Central Synod in Pella."

He reached through the bars of the cell and took Kagne's hand. "The sooner we can get you out of here, the better. The mark wants you out, and I need your help. I'll see if I can negotiate your freedom from the bishop."

"I'm sure you will, Sandun. I have faith."

Two days later, Sandun met with his Holiness, the Bishop of Sirosfeld. Sandun was accompanied by Maklin, who acted as scribe. The bishop was attended by one other priest, who sat silently beside a stack of heavy tomes, also taking notes.

Sandun, quoting from the Straight Law of the Temple, asked for Kagne's release with a penance of exile, under his supervision. He explained that his mission was of some importance, and that King Pandion had commanded the enterprise and had requested all appropriate aid be given in furtherance of the Archives Expedition.

The bishop, curiously young for such a high rank, was not from Kelten. Judging by his accent, he was from Jibur although, like most senior prelates, he had changed his name upon his appointment to his new rank of the temple: "Tempered Spear of Innocent Justice." A ridiculous name, thought Sandun, but fortunately a name that civilians did not have to use when addressing him.

The bishop's words were arcane, his grammar hard to follow, and he talked of divine laws of holy estate and juxtaposed anathemas. After what seemed like an hour, with his head swimming in a maze of words and poorly understood concepts, Sandun requested a recess.

Outside the vestibule, Sandun asked Maklin for his thoughts.

"Master," said Maklin, "I think he is asking for money."

Sandun restrained himself from the oath that immediately came to mind; it was best to avoid profanity anywhere near the temple. "So, all this talk of rites and rulings from the Council of Kalcheldon is really just a shakedown by the bishop?"

"I believe so, Master. Several years ago, I spent more time than I would have liked on the task of harmonizing the records of the king's appointments to clerical positions. Part of the records included temple objections to some candidates and the subsequent responses. The temple used similar language to what the bishop was saying inside. The old annotations from the king's scribes were usually just this: the temple is asking for more money."

Sandun was familiar with that branch of the Archives. Every scribe had to spend at least a year with one of the least interesting areas of the records. The more promising the scribe, the more challenging the records. The "Clerical Appointments" section was infamous for its complexity and the bizarre cross-referencing of documents of previous controversies, some of which were hundreds of years older than the dispute in question. Sandun had spent his "Year Underground" working on the ancient rights of water and mining, an equally nightmarish subject where some claims could be traced all the way to the foundation of the Kingdom of Kelten, more than seven hundred years in the past.

"I'm reluctant to offer him money. Sho'Ash knows we have little enough now, and prices here are higher than even we anticipated."

Maklin replied, "From the documents I read, I believe such a gift is formally called an Electrum Testament of Faith."

"Electrum? Ha-ha! You must be joking! No one uses that currency any-more." Sandun knew from old land deeds that electrum, a mixture of gold and silver, was once minted in small ingots and used to purchase rare tracts of land, such as abandoned temples or ruined castles.

"The temple still uses electrum," replied Maklin. "King Kranus gave a gift of electrum when he wished to appoint his nephew as Bishop of Thalapolis, against objection from the Central Synod of Pella."

That the Kings of Kelten went to great lengths to get their blood rela-tions appointed to senior positions with the temple hierarchy was common knowledge. Even so, Sandun was impressed that Maklin was able to retrieve this fact from his warehouse of a memory.

"I see," said Sandun thoughtfully. "Perhaps the Mark of Sirosfeld will help defray our costs. In any event, why don't you talk to the bishop's scribe and see if the two scribes can negotiate a price? I'll hazard a guess that it is unseemly for a bishop to haggle over money like common fishmonger. Best let the juniors handle such things?"

"I'll do my best, Master."

When they reconvened, Sandun changed the conversation to the orga-nization of the Diocese of Erimasran. The bishop was only too happy to oblige. Then Sandun asked to see the temple's maps, and at a gesture from the bishop, the silent priest left the room. Maklin followed him.

Sandun explained the ostensible reason for his expedition: namely, that they were looking for a long-lost library that was reported to exist in the ruins of Rasilimni.

"Indeed?" said the bishop. "I have never heard that name before." They waited a minute, then two, in silence, drinking a fine red wine. Finally, Maklin and the priest returned with several large parchment sheets, and together they spread them out on the table. Using the oldest map, Sandun pointed to a faded mark, some 150 miles east of Sirosfeld.

The bishop said, "This is a mountainous area with some few villages, but I see that it was once a much larger community. Here is the notation for 'Komitia' or 'Province.' Strange, there is no indication of a major temple at Rasilimni, but it may have been an administrative center even without a notable temple. Well, there are many ruins from the Pellian Empire, even here, at the end of the earth."

Maklin caught Sandun's eye and nodded his head. Sandun expressed his gratitude for the bishop's time and promised to return with good news soon. The bishop was puzzled by Sandun's farewell but blessed their enterprise as they left.

Outside the temple, Sandun asked Maklin for a number.

"The bishop's aide said that a donation of ten pounds of electrum would be sufficient."

"By Hurin's hairy feet! How many pounds of gold would that be? Five? Six?"

"The most recent document I recall set the ratio of gold to silver at 40 percent. That was twenty-five years past."

"Four pounds of gold! Six pounds of silver? Absurd. When did the temple become so hungry for money? Perhaps out here on the frontier, the temple thinks it is safe to extort a knight's ransom for an ordinary man on a trumped-up charge of heresy."

"I could not say, Master, but…" Maklin paused to dredge up numbers from his memory. "Over the last one hundred years, the average cost to the king for getting his choice appointed to a bishopric has gone up substantially—by more than 50 percent."

At this point, the mark's page appeared in front of them and bowed. "Master Sandun, Scribe Maklin, the seneschal wishes to meet with you at your earliest convenience."

They followed the page up the hill to the mark's castle. Inside the cold stone halls, they met with the seneschal in his private room near the mark's audience chamber. Sandun described his meeting and the bishop's aide's proposed price for Kagne.

Even the seneschal seemed surprised. "At half that price, it would still be excessive. There is more going on here than meets the eye. What is your impression of the bishop?" he asked Sandun.

"Honestly, he fits every stereotype of foreign priests who are sent here by command of the temple's offices in Pella. He exudes contempt for Erimasran, and I do not doubt that he expects to be transferred to a better bishopric in a year or two, taking a goodly supply of gold with him for his travel expenses."

The seneschal was taken aback at Sandun's anger. "Master, please, it is not wise to speak of the bishop in this fashion, even among friends, as I hope you consider me to be. Doubtless, opinions and ideas are freer in Seopolis than they are here. In Erimasran, men are loyal to the office of the bishop, no matter who currently occupies it. The old bishop was revered, nearly as a saint."

"Well, the old bishop may have been a saint, but this one does not impress me. In any event, I can pay only a quarter of what the bishop's man suggested. And that would leave the expedition without reserves."

"Master Sandun, my lord the mark has given me to understand that, in exchange for a favorable report from you to the king, he would donate a reasonable fee to have this matter resolved. If Kagne Areka is agreeable to you as a guide and if he goes with you and remains out of Sirosfeld for some time, then you can offer the bishop six pounds of electrum, for which we will reimburse you. That should satisfy all parties."

Sandun was both surprised and relieved at the seneschal's generous offer. "I am most grateful, Master Seneschal. And I have the highest regard for the Mark of Erimasran. You can be assured I will report favorably to the king. But as the old expression goes: 'Words fly away, while gold stays where you place it.' May I ask why you are going to such lengths?"

The seneschal chose his words carefully. "My lord, the mark, is aware of Kagne's popularity in the north. Further, Kagne has been helpful on several occasions in organizing the northern clans' defenses against raiders from Issedon. Finally, and I say this without any disrespect for the temple's edicts, my lord is sympathetic toward his people's desires to sell valuable crops and therefore make a living in a difficult land. Still and all, my lord is unwilling to oppose the bishop in this matter. My lord hopes that the next bishop will be chosen from within the Kelten priesthood, as is traditional. Thus, the sooner the current bishop moves on to a new position, the happier everyone concerned will be. Your arrival and your need for Kagne's services help my lord resolve what had seemed to be an intractable situation."

"I think I understand. As the temple says, 'A gentle rain benefits both farmer and fisherman alike.' You have my deepest thanks. Can I make this offer to the bishop tomorrow?"

The seneschal said they could and that the money would be ready as soon as an agreement was reached.

The next day, Sandun and the bishop matched wits in a battle of erudite speculation on the causes of the fall of the Pellian Empire. Meanwhile, Maklin and the bishop's aide talked together in whispers. Eventually, Maklin signaled that an agreement had been reached. After a fine meal made with some unusual and expensive ingredients, along with fresh fish brought from Lake Tricon, the bishop said that he was willing to pronounce a sentence on Kagne Areka of exile from Sirosfeld under the surety of Sandun for a period of not less than a year.

"I believe you have a gift for the temple? To help with our charitable works here in Erimasran?"

"I do, Your Holiness." The barbed but subtle inflections in Sandun's use of the honorific were either missed or ignored by the bishop.

"That is well," replied the bishop smoothly. "We all must do our part to see that the holy words of Sho'Ash and his temple are followed throughout the Archipelago, here in Erimasran no less than in Pella."

Later that day, a small detachment of the mark's guards came to the inn where the Archives Expedition was staying. In Sandun's room, the head guard took off his thick belt, which cunningly folded open, revealing six pounds in gold and silver coins, all mixed together. The coins were transferred to a chainmail-covered leather wallet, which had been emptied due to spending on the trip. Sandun and the entire Archives Expedition then walked to the temple; at the door to the annex, he handed the pouch over to the bishop's aide.

A minute later, the aide returned with a document stating the terms of Kagne's release; Kagne stood behind him, blinking in the afternoon sunlight.

Sandun introduced Kagne to the men of the expedition.

"Men of the Archives Expedition! I present to you, Kagne Areka. He is to be our guide as we travel into the outer wilderness of Erimasran."

Kagne stepped forward and smiled broadly. He bowed, sweeping an imaginary hat off his head. "Gentlemen, together we will find that which is lost, we shall right that which is wrong, and we will have a great time doing it!"

A window above the annex door opened, and a young lady was briefly seen as she dropped a small embroidered scarf down to Kagne. He took the scarf from the air and then grandly saluted the woman. "Farewell, Liris," he said to her. She closed the window and drew the curtains, but it seemed she was still standing watch behind them.

As they walked back to the inn, Sandun could not help but ask Kagne, "Who was that?"

"That was Liris, the daughter of the bishop. A very lovely girl with a sweet disposition."

"And you know her?" Sandun said, rapidly spinning possibilities in his mind. Pieces of a puzzle seemed to be clicking into place.

"Well, yes. But let's not talk about her. Thank you for getting me out of there. I can't say I was pleased to read the paper I signed. Banned from travel to Sirosfeld for the next year? How can I negotiate for the villages of Tokivanu if I can't come within fifty miles of the center of government?"

"That is actually the least of your troubles, old friend. You are coming with me on a very long and dangerous trip. If we survive, your troubles here will vanish like the fog under the midday sun."

Kagne looked at Sandun and then nodded. "Oh? Where are you going?"

"You are coming with me, yes?"

"Yes, yes. Since I am exiled from here for a year, you have one year from me. Where are we going?"

"You swear it?"

Kagne got down on his knees and looked around. "This is just like my vision. I was kneeling, in a dusty street. The sun was behind your head, and I couldn't see your face, but you were wreathed in light. And I said, I said...I, Kagne Areka, will follow you for a year and a day, going where you command. Bearing any burden. By the Spear of Sho'Ash, I swear it."

Chills ran up and down Sandun's spine. He had never heard anyone swear an oath like that, not to him. *Is this what nobles feel*, he thought, *when a knight swears his oath of fealty to his lord?*

Sandun tried to reply; his words seemed clumsy in his mouth. "I accept your oath. I shall repay loyalty with honor. I shall repay oath breaking with hatred. By the sword of Saint Hurin, I swear it."

Kagne got to his feet and brushed his knees off. The other men of the expedition looked at him with new eyes. His act was unexpected, almost out of the old stories about the Lost King and his Shining Knights, but there was a ring of truth in his words. "So, where are we going?"

Sandun leaned over and whispered in his ear: "Serica."

That evening, Kagne disappeared for a couple of hours. When he returned, he seemed much happier. Sandun could hazard guesses as to why, several of which were not mutually exclusive.

"I was going to stay with a woman tonight, but I could not rest without hearing your plan. Tell me everything." Kagne smiled his most ingratiating smile and sat next to Sandun in the room he shared with Basil. While Basil quietly worked on additions to his travel map, Sandun explained the reasons for the expedition and recounted their journey so far.

Kagne then talked about what he knew of the land. "I grew up knowing that Serica is on the other side of Tirala Mountains, but it's like a fairy tale to us. The Tiralas are impassible—at least that is what the wise men of Tokivanu all say. When I look at this map, I have a rough idea of where the trail discovered by 'Jon of Stenston' starts. But there are many canyons that wind their way up between peaks, most lead to unscalable cliffs, or you end up on the highland wilderness, and beyond that there are mountains of such height as to make the Alps look puny by comparison. In my life, I have gone twice into the highlands. It was cold, dry, and with very little game. I know the people near Seopolis think Erimasran is more desert than not, but for us, the highlands of the Tiralas are the true desert."

Kagne looked carefully at the map. "I suggest that we seek the starting point of this path and then follow it as best we can. While we could head into the highlands and try to find the remains of the path there, I think it would be unwise. It is very dangerous in the highlands, mostly due to the weather and a sickness that strikes many people down. Much safer it would be to search for the trail down in Nukivanu, where there are food, water, and people."

"Safer?" Sandun smiled without any mirth. "Did I mention that spies from Issedon may know of our expedition?"

"Why, no, you did not. Did you broadcast the news in the streets of Seopolis? Did you nail a recruiting poster on the gateway of the great pier?"

Sandun explained the efforts made at deception and their failure.

"Ha! I thought I taught you better tradecraft than that. Though, in fairness, I admit to some boasting of my deeds to a few comely lasses—when I was younger, of course."

"Perhaps you still do? It's not every day that a bishop's daughter drops a scarf down to a man on the street."

Kagne flushed. "That's...well, it's different, I had to convince her of the truth of my mission."

"I can guess some of reasons why you were locked up by the temple. And heresy is not at the top of the list."

Basil chuckled at this; Kagne refused to talk about it further.

The next day, the expedition set out from Sirosfeld, heading east on a road as though they were journeying to Rasilimni. On the third day, unobserved, they left the road and went north, heading for their true destination of Nukivanu.

They saw farms in the distance as they traveled. Usually a farm house was near a lakeshore. The expedition wended its way through great fields of grass and sometimes met flocks of sheep or herds of cows. Sandun thought that the vegetation looked much like what he had seen north of the Evgos River in Kelten. Erimasran had a reputation for great heat in the summer and vast tracts where nothing could grow, but this land—at least in early spring—did not look like what he had imagined.

He asked Kagne about the land and what the summer heat would bring.

"As the tadpoles say, spring is heaven, summer's not. Summer's sun dries up most streams and turns the fields yellow. But every year the lakes seem fuller. All farmers complain about the weather: too hot or too cold, too dry or too wet. Only one year in twenty is good. But it seems to me that we have been getting good years more often than that. For a farmer, there is always more to complain about. Perhaps one day the king will create a new town or two, settle some of the landless tenant farmers who barely eke out a living in the Torobeus valley or Hippoliada. This land can feed many more people."

During the day rests, Sandun helped Basil with his maps. Although Erimasran was much less watered than in the west of Kelten, there were small streams that cut across the plains. Most water flowed down from the Kelten Alps, heading east, while some larger streams tended southwest. The lakes fed by these streams were scattered across the vast plains, like the footprints of titans who had walked the earth when it was still young and soft.

No great river flowed from the north to the south except for the mighty Monnes Corant at the southern border of Erimasran next to Potomopolis. The Monnes Corant flowed out of the Tiralas, but its current was violent and the passages the river had carved through the land were like that of a knife that sliced through a wedge of soft cheese.

When they made camp, Basil would go hunt with his dog, while Sandun wrote the expedition log entries and made rough sketches of the terrain. Kagne offered to hunt with Basil, who politely begged off. Kagne had hunted in the land but was just as happy not to. Sandun knew Kagne usually smoked dream weed in the evening; the scent was familiar to him. Sir Ako and his scouts never smoked; it was forbidden in every Kelten military force and as a rule, the professional soldiers felt dream weed made a man weak. The scouts held to wine, which was part of their daily rations.

Over the first week, Kagne taught them about traveling and camping unseen. He knew many tricks: which rocks were porous and which plants gave off lingering scents when bruised. He taught them about taking paths that would not be followed and, perhaps most importantly, how to make nearly smokeless fires that could not be seen unless the watchers were looking down on them from high above.

Following the techniques Kagne taught took an extra hour at the start and end of each day. But the results were indisputable: when Sandun walked away from the camp in the middle of the night to experiment, he found from a quarter of a mile away there was no hint of a campfire and no odor of smoke—at least nothing for his nose. The one problem Kagne could not solve was the sound of the mules. Mules will bray occasionally throughout each day, rain or shine, happy mules, sad mules—it does not matter.

"If I could breed a pack animal with a mule's strength and agility but one as silent as a raccoon, I'd be a rich man," Kagne said after the mules started braying, one after the other. "If we camp in narrow valleys, their sound can be muffled, but on the trail, the only way to keep them quiet is to kill them."

Scribe Maklin didn't like the sound of that; he had grown fond of the beasts, and they liked him in return. "These are good animals; don't you talk of hurting them!"

Kagne replied, "In the northland, we don't use mules. We don't need their surefooted skills, and oxen are plenty strong enough to pull our wagons. Our horses and hunting dogs are trained to stay silent. But I understand why you have them, and I don't know of a better animal when we go into the mountains. All that aside, noisy animals and careless men draw unwanted attention."

In the evening, the scouts played cards and told stories beside the fire. As usual, Sandun and Basil were not invited to join. Kagne sat beside Sandun, and they talked about the past. They reminisced about the days they spent pushing a cart up and down the streets of Seopolis.

"So you are a master in the Royal Archives now?" Kagne asked. "How did you end up there?"

"After the night when the temple guards kicked down our door, I headed south," Sandun answered. "Some money I buried ten miles outside of Seopolis; I dug it up, and then I just kept going. The farther from Seopolis the better, that's what I thought. There was little chance those fat rule-keepers were going to catch you, and there was nothing I could do to help you if they had."

"You're right about that," said Kagne. "I jumped in the bay and swam north to the pier. Made it to my contact's warehouse, but I caught a chill. They sent me upriver in one of their boats while I shivered sick for a week."

"Well, I ended up in southern Kelten, a valley called Sun House," Sandun continued. "By chance, at the pub I learned from his manservant that Baron Segwaris needed a man who knew his letters but was not part of the temple. The baron was an older lord, and worn down by the wars and the deaths of his two sons."

Sandun paused and looked at the fire. "To take a long tale and cut it down to size, a year passes and I hear that Pandion's army of rebellion has crossed the border and there is talk in the pub about joining. Baron Segwaris tells us that while he won't take a side between Pandion and King Oniktes, he won't think ill of any man that sides with Pandion. Even in Sun House, we heard tell of the cruel fate of the White Princess, and some of us were moved to risk all.

"Three of us, we left in the night and headed south. No sooner do I arrive at Pandion's camp when I see they have wrapped the cords wrong on a ballista they have just finished building. I remembered the trick of such things from watching my father at his work."

"Your father built cranes, if I remember aright," Kagne said.

"Cranes and other engines for the Earl of Hepedion."

At this Basil started and looked sharply at Sandun.

"The *former* Earl of Hepedion. Basil here, well, he showed up the next day. Since I knew something about them, I was put in charge of several ballistas, and Basil became my spotter. He has a knack for reading the wind and distance from miles off. When our ballistas fired, they didn't miss."

"And the Royal Archives?" queried Kagne.

"After the battle of Agnefeld, Pandion's army goes north so he can be crowned king." Sandun smiled as he thought back on those heady days. "I don't mind telling you that a very fine time was had by those of us who joined *before* the battle. Anyway, a month after his coronation, King Pandion asked me if I would like to take a vacancy in the Archives. I knew a little of them thanks to some letters I wrote on behalf of Baron Segwaris, so I said yes. I've been there ever since."

Kagne whistled. "You took quite a risk, joining Pandion's army. Wasn't he outnumbered three to one? And to fight against King Oniktes, the victor of a dozen battles? I would have stayed far from that fight and called myself lucky."

Sandun shrugged. "I was young. And no one—and I mean no one—liked Oniktes. Well, that's all in the past. Sho'Ash willing, I'll not see such a battle again."

They continued northward, and small changes could be seen on the land: fewer trees beside the creeks, and the lakes they saw were, according to Kagne, so shallow that they often disappeared entirely from midsummer until the winter rains. A few of the lakes they passed were surrounded by an unusual gray clay in which nothing could grow. These lakes seemed like mirages, tricks of the desert, unreal, set amid miles of desolate cracked mud flats.

One day, Kagne brought them to a campsite where hot water bubbled out of the ground and then drained into large pools of bath-temperature water. The large pools seemed natural, but Kagne said they had been dug by men a great while ago. All of the men, except the those on guard duty, took off their clothes and waded into the pools after the evening meal. Sandun found it pleasant to rest in the warm but odd-smelling water.

He looked up at the sky and remembered one year when his family traveled north to the famous hot springs of Lemateka, a day's journey from their home in Hepedion. It was fall, and King Pandion II had arrived with his court when the autumn grape harvest festival had started. By royal decree, the hot pools were opened to everyone. Too young to drink wine, Sandun had jumped into the water and surfaced next to a pretty girl with long, wet, black hair, her linen shift clinging tightly to her body. That was the first time he noticed a girl as a girl: desirable. He chased her, she laughed at him, he splashed her, and she told him her name. The next day, he looked for her at the hot pool and in the festival booths, but he never saw her again. More than twenty years gone, he still remembered her name, Pelema, though her face was now just a blur.

When the guards changed shifts and the two who had been on watch came into the water, Sandun realized for the first time that one of the scouts, Olef, was a woman. As she took off her clothing and slipped into the water, there was simply no question as to her sex. No one else in the pool made any comment, though Kagne stared at her. Apparently, everyone else knew that Olef was a she and not a he. She looked up at Basil and then looked down at the water.

There was nothing that forbade women from joining the army, but while camp followers were plentiful, women warriors were exceedingly rare. Most soldiers considered it bad luck when a woman tried to accompany a military unit if she was armed with anything more than a knife. However, many times he had seen women go to town with the soldiers who were buying or requisitioning supplies. And of course, women followed their men on the march. Most knights had a woman for their tent; earls usually had two.

The day of the battle started like the other days.

The expedition had reached the land called Nukivanu. It was at the far edge of Kelten, an isolated place with little sign of human habitation.

According to the old map, they had reached the start of trail east to Serica. But five days spent searching had yielded no results; no sign of any trail had been found. They rode into canyons that ended in steep slopes or rocky walls.

Wild animals were in abundance: lizards scuttled away in the dust, and vultures circled silently over ridgelines. Basil hunted every morning, bringing back deer or small antelopes for them to eat.

At dawn on the sixth day, the air was chill, the skies clear. As the sun warmed the land, clouds slowly built up over the towering mountains to the east.

Before the scouts set forth on their daily search, Kagne returned to the camp from his morning lookout. His countenance spoke unmistakably: worry, fear. "In the night, my sleep was broken and uneasy," Kagne said. "I have been looking north since dawn. There is a haze growing at the horizon and a sound in the air, like a herd of antelope far off. I fear the worst: riders from Issedon coming south. We should lie low and prepare to fight."

The scouts looked at Sir Ako. Silently, he looked at Kagne, who stared back at him defiantly. Then Sir Ako nodded. Everyone changed their preparations from scouting to battle. Bows were strung, tested, and then unstrung. All the arrows were brought out and divided among the men. Sir Ako, with Sergeant Torn's help, put on his armor: lightweight, strong pieces of curved metal that covered his upper body. Sergeant Torn wore a thick brigandine coat that covered his arms and hung down to his thighs. The others put on sleeveless jacks and light helms over their leather.

Kagne lay down on a rocky outcropping above the campsite looking west, scanning the plains below. Sandun went to his side and passed him the farseer glass. The only sound Sandun could hear was the buzzing from grasshoppers and the rare bird call.

On previous days as they'd headed north, Kagne had detailed the typical Issedonian raid: half a dozen groups of twenty-five to fifty men each, mostly mounted, always sending pairs of men between each group throughout the day to exchange information.

"They don't gallop and rarely trot. Instead, they canter steadily, saving their strength, and keep to hard, rocky land to minimize dust," Kagne explained. "They concentrate with speed once a target is found. At first, there are a few men; within an hour, one hundred; and within four hours, their whole force. It's like they appear out of the ground. Flight is unwise— they pick off stragglers with arrows from afar. They mostly scout all around a village before making an attack, and they leave scouts posted throughout the battle to warn of any approaching Kelten forces. Our best hope is concealment. If we spend the effort to hide by sun and by moon, they may go past us, unknowing. That is, if they aren't looking for us."

When questioned about what they should do if spotted, he recommended defending and not running into the hills. "Never run into land you do not know. Better to fight on ground of your own choosing." The other scouts nodded their heads in agreement.

Kagne continued, "Running up the hills tires you out more than you expect, and the air is curiously thin in Erimasran. Also, running uphill—it leaves you exposed to accurate, long-range shots. A man going uphill moves slowly and predictably. It's the same as hunting deer. A deer in the bush is cloaked with leaves and branches; the deer that runs up the ridgeline is an easy mark.

"Lastly, running increases your fear and lifts your enemy's spirits. We have stories in my village of settlements where the men broke and ran, seeking to escape, and most were killed by the raiders, even when the village warriors outnumbered the raiders. We have other tales of when villages held firm, and it was the Issedonians who gave up, sometimes at the mere rumor of the Kelten cavalry riding north. When they turn north, the Issedonians retreat in haste, and those who cannot ride or cannot run are left behind. Slow raiders never return to their homeland."

No one questioned Kagne's warning. In the days since he had joined them, it had become obvious that he knew the land as well as any of the scouts knew the border of Fiodroch. So the men cautiously walked about the valley where they were camped, seeking to fix the layout of the land in their minds: the rocks and ravines, trees and bushes. The mules were led into the riverbed and firmly tethered to the strongest trees that grew near the water. Hidden from view, they munched happily on tender leaves. As before, Maklin guarded them, axe in hand, a shield on his left arm.

The plan, if they were discovered, was for Sir Ako and Sergeant Torn to draw attention in the middle of the clearing. Everyone else was to hide in two groups, one on either side of the valley. They hoped the raiders would attack immediately and not wait for the whole force to gather, thinking a lone knight and his squire would be easy prey. The archers would shoot first the horses and then the raiders. With luck, none would escape to warn the other groups.

By noon, with the sun beating down, the heat made it difficult to see far, but a strange, faint rumbling sound could be heard by all. It was not thunder, but Sandun could not have guessed what made the noise.

"They are coming," Kagne said simply.

Everyone took their places. The scouts followed their own practice and covered their faces with mud. They stuck twigs into their belts and baldrics. Sandun, Basil, and four scouts were on the south side of the camp; Kagne and the other scouts could not be seen amid the rocks and hard shadows on the northern slope.

Again, the waiting. Sandun's mind filled with thoughts and inner debates. Was it coincidence that the Issedonian raiders had come? Was this just a raid to steal livestock, or were they looking for the expedition? If two hundred or more Issedonian raiders found them, death was all but certain.

Sir Ako and Sergeant Torn were both sitting in the shade, sharpening all the weapons they carried: swords, daggers, hatchets, even the mace spikes were touched up. No one said anything. Sandun thought about burying his notes under a rock. *Too late for that now. Must concentrate.* He practiced archery in his mind, thinking about the lessons Basil had been giving him.

Now Sandun could see dust and hear the sound of trotting horses. A small group of men, more than twenty and less than thirty, came up into the valley. This was the first time Sandun had seen the savage eastern Issedonians. They were all bearded, and they were covered in dirt, perhaps deliberately. Their clothing appeared to be a mix of cow leather and deerskin. Most had short bows, though he saw two with very long bows.

Almost immediately, they spotted the camp. Their leader rode forward; he had a tall helmet decorated with two long, curling ram's horns.

Sir Ako put on his helm and took up his sword and shield. Sergeant Torn, similarly armed, took position just a little behind him.

The Issedonian leader spoke. Sandun had heard the language before; many ships from Issedon sailed down the coast to trade at Seopolis. With difficulty, he could understand what the man was saying.

"A knight in armor, at the edge of the Tirala Mountains. Explain yourself."

Sir Ako raised his visor and responded with the foulest oaths Sandun had ever heard; a growing fury was in his voice as he slapped his sword against his shield. Insulted and enraged, the Issedonian drew his sword, lifting it up to the sky. And then he let out a great cry of pain as an arrow pierced under his upraised arm and into his chest. He toppled from his horse and fell to the stony ground with a thud like a slab of meat dropped onto a kitchen floor.

All the other hidden archers fired their bows, and nearly every arrow found its mark. Horses reared and cried in pain and terror as arrows struck their bodies. Sir Ako and Sergeant Torn yelled, "For Kelten!" and charged into the suddenly chaotic mess. The surprise was total.

"No quarter!" bellowed Sir Ako as he hewed down men who had fallen off their horses and were struggling to switch from bows to their shortswords or daggers. Two horsemen at the rear suddenly turned and galloped away. An arrow hit one horse in the haunch, but it kept going. Sergeant Torn, with savage efficiency, slammed raiders to the ground with his shield and then bashed their heads in with his mace, which was soon covered in blood and gore.

Abruptly, the fighting was over. A few moaning Issedonians were quickly silenced with expert dagger thrusts into their eyes, and that was all. Two horses remained unharmed, most were dead, and a few had galloped off—riderless—into the plains. The ground with covered with blood and offal.

The men all gathered together at the scene of the fighting. No one was injured. "More will come," Kagne said grimly. The mules, smelling blood, were braying and pulling at their traces. Sergeant Torn had some men drag the bodies off into a pile beside a large boulder north of the camp. Everyone drank water and gathered unbroken arrows. They threw most of the Issedonian weapons and the few pieces of armor into the stream bed.

Sir Ako gathered Kagne and Torn to plot the next fight. "What will the next group be like?"

"They don't know our numbers," Kagne replied. "The two cowards that fled will spend hours seeking more of their allies. They will tell a tale of how they were defeated by a sudden attack of thirty or more archers hiding in the rocks." He smiled grimly at the other scouts. "If they are searching for the Archive Expedition, then they may gather a hundred men before coming back. I doubt that all will gather to attack us, for fear they are missing the real expedition as opposed to an unknown diversion." Kagne continued, "When they come, I think they will spread out, form a line, try to drive us off the hillsides and down into the valley, which will then become a killing field."

"We could go into these hills, defend that hilltop for example." Sir Ako pointed to a rounded hill about two miles northeast with a commanding view over the plains below.

"I don't like that. The hilltops here are mostly barren, without trees or bushes. Even the rocks are small up top. With no protection, we could be showered with arrows while the Issedonians are hidden behind good cover from below. After several hours, with all of us injured and some killed, they would charge, and the end would be certain."

"What if we keep going in the mountains?"

"If we move fast, we leave tracks clear enough to be followed. If we move slowly, we don't have enough of a head start to lose them. We cannot go faster than the raiders. They catch up when we are tired, lost, and on ground that none of us knows. Again, the ending is certain." Kagne's words painted a picture the others could easily see in their minds.

"So, we are dead men?"

"Maybe not. If the raiders are looking for us, that means they are not attacking the villages. My people will not sit idly while Issedonian raiders head south. Swift messages will be sent to Sirosfeld, and likely they were sent days ago when the raiders first crossed the border. So we can expect the Kelten cavalry to arrive sometime. Further, the villages will send out hunting parties of their own to find out what the raiders are doing and where they are going. The land may seem empty of friends, but they are out there, and in numbers."

Sir Ako came to a decision. "Another surprise, then. We shift north, hiding our supplies among the rocks here. We leave the noisy mules where they are. We concentrate, hidden in the next valley. If the raiders haven't found us by nightfall, we move into the plains west. With Sho'Ash guiding us, we attack them from the rear." Sir Ako outlined his plan with broad sweeps of his arms. Everyone gathered around him and muttered agreement.

"A bold plan, Sir Ako." Kagne pulled at his mustache, considering the idea. "I would not expect it. They will not expect it."

"After the fight, if any of us are alive, return here to the camp," Sir Ako commanded.

Four hours later, as the sun was gleaming red against the horizon, a large line of riders appeared in the plains heading toward them. The expedition was two miles north of the camp that morning, strung out along another ridge, hidden amid the manzanita and deer brush. Thunder had been booming faintly in the afternoon, and the barest hint of rain was in the air, a few drops blown far from the taller hills. Riders were approaching from the southwest, heading for the battle site.

Basil, using his farseeing glass, counted seventy mounted men and at least two more at the nearest edge who were on foot.

"They will not find us before the night falls. Look, they are stopping. Here come some scouts." In the next few hours, as the sun set, the raiders sent scouts into the valley; they came out again and conferred with a small cluster of men near the center of the line.

A low horn sounded, and gradually the line of men moved forward into the darkness. It was getting very hard to see, but it appeared that many of the raiders had dismounted and were walking ahead of their horses.

Kagne whispered to the others, "The moon will not rise for another three hours."

Sir Ako told everyone, "Soon we move out. Stay low, stick together. We attack them from the north. A pure night fight. Their numbers will count for nothing!" There was a light in his eyes that Sandun had seen before, in the faces of some of the knights before the great battle of Agnefeld.

Basil said to Sandun, "I hate hunting at night. Can't aim properly."

One of the oldest scouts, Padan, replied, "We train for night fighting, sword and shield, shield and sword." The scouts were armed with shortswords and small shields in addition to their preferred bows.

Damar, the cowherd from Sun House, said, "At least we can tell who is who in the dark. These dog-loving Issedonians stink to high heaven, not like the soldiers of Fiodroch." He fingered his sword

While Kagne kept watch on the advancing raiders, Sir Ako gathered his men around him. "Men, hear now the last words of Sho'Ash."

One of the men raised his hand. "Yes, Kinot?" asked Sir Ako.

Kinot said, "Sir, I have something to confess."

"Go on. It does us well to hear the words with a clean heart."

"The last night in Sirosfeld, I cheated at cards. I, ah, humbly beg your forgiveness. If I live, I'll make amends, I promise, especially you, Farrel," he said, turning to another scout. "I didn't spend it all on that black-haired lady, but she was worth it."

"Not luck after all," Farrel grumbled. The red-haired man lifted his bow and sighted towards the horizon. "You can repay me by acting as my shield while I shoot the bastards this night."

Sir Ako continued, "Before Sho'Ash took the spear and strode into the throne room of the Black Terror, he gathered the faithful around him, and he said to them, 'Although I go to face that which no man can face, I believe.'"

Here all the men joined him: "I believe good will triumph. With faith, I will defeat evil. With courage, my spirit will live forever. And I will join the shining company of heroes. So it was, so it is, so it shall be."

With that said, the group headed silently west out into the dark plain, circling around the end of the line of the enemy, which was advancing slowly east into the hills that they had abandoned.

Soon, they guessed they had passed the line of Issedonian raiders. Sir Ako called a halt. He whispered urgently, fiercely: "Now, we hit them from the rear. We will drive them before us like wolves drive sheep. In the night, one man seems like a score. We will panic them, and they will fly from our wrath. Do you believe it? Do you believe it! For Kelten!"

A night fight was one of the most dangerous military engagements. Most commanders would rather face three-to-one odds in the day than risk a night battle. In the dark, men panicked easily. A man was just as likely to kill a friend as he was to attack a foe. But they were in a compact group, and the enemy were spread apart. For a while, surprise would be on their side; however, unless the Issedonians broke and ran, their numbers were too great. They would surround the Archive Expedition, and it would die.

Still, Sir Ako's confidence was infectious. He seemed completely convinced that they would defeat the raiders. Sandun thought Sir Ako must harbor doubts, but if he did, he did not show them, did not acknowledge them. He sounded supremely confident. Sandun wondered: perhaps Sho'Ash felt the same way before the end, fearing defeat but not wanting to show his fears to the faithful. But that was ridiculous—Sho'Ash was a god.

The first raider went down without a sound. He was on foot and not paying any attention to what was behind him. Kagne crept up on him like a mountain lion and then covered his mouth and cut his throat at the same moment.

The next man in the line was riding slowly, his body clearly silhouetted by the faint light lingering at the horizon. Three scouts used their bows, and all three arrows struck the raider at the same time; he fell, making little noise. The Issedonians paid no attention and kept moving. The man's horse, seemingly used to men falling from its saddle, simply stopped. Ten more raiders were killed in similar fashion before the enemy captains figured out what was happening.

Now would be a good time for them to panic, Sandun thought, but if some fled in the night, he could not see it.

The raiders lit torches, but their light gave Basil and Farrel targets to shoot at. Four more raiders were hit with arrows before they abandoned the torches. The Archives group heard shouted commands, and it was clear the enemy were organizing, trying to pin down and surround the Kelten warriors.

"Time to attack," Sir Ako said. "For Kelten!" He charged into the darkness; Sergeant Torn and the others followed him, swords in their hands glinting in the night. They all yelled as loudly as they could, hoping to intimidate the enemy, trying to make darkness and fear their ally.

The rest of the fight was hard to piece together even after it was over. Sandun stayed close to Basil, stabbing any raider who came in range. Basil shot arrow after arrow into the melee. Sandun saw Maklin charge into the fray with his axe swinging, but his strong swings, useful for chopping wood, left him exposed to counterthrusts, and he went down after a minute. Kagne appeared once next to Sandun and Basil, his hands gripping oddly shaped daggers, his arms dark with blood. He said something that made no sense and then vanished into the night. He looked wild, almost feral.

Sir Ako and Sergeant Torn fought as well as Sandun had seen any pair of warriors fight. Sir Ako seemed to sense blows before they were made, his metal shield deflected cuts and thrusts, and he beat down men with his sword, then his axe, then his mace. Sergeant Torn stayed by Sir Ako's side, defending him from the rear and dispatching the men Sir Ako had knocked down. Their years of training together allowed Torn to guess when Sir Ako was going forward to attack and when he was pulling back to lure the enemy into a deadly riposte. Sergeant Torn was remarkably skilled at tripping attackers with blows to their legs and feet, and his attacks were nearly impossible avoid in the darkness. Sandun killed at least three men who had been knocked to the ground by Torn's sneak attacks.

Then Sergeant Torn was down; Sandun didn't see what happened to him. Sir Ako fought on alone; the rest of the scouts kept out of the range of his powerful swings, but they were fighting with him. Sir Ako seemed unstoppable, a lion in the night, smashing faces, breaking spears, cursing his enemies with a stream of foul oaths.

Then a new group of men appeared, shouting, "Kelten! Kelten!" Sandun guessed these men must be from the Tokivanu villages—one of the hunting parties Kagne had mentioned earlier. Now all the men of the Archives Expedition again started yelling, "Kelten! Kelten!"

Another minute of confusion and screams, and suddenly the Issedonians were running away. The village warriors who had joined the fight followed them into the darkness. Surrounded by crying men and moans, Sandun found Sir Ako kneeling on the ground beside Sergeant Torn. The sergeant's sword arm was nearly severed from his body, there was blood all around his waist and legs, and he was motionless. Sandun felt Torn's neck and found no pulse. Already his skin felt cold. Sir Ako kept repeating his name, over and over. There was nothing to be done.

Sandun went to find Maklin. The young man was alive, but he seemed unaware of the world; he didn't respond to his name. By starlight Sandun could see the scribe had been stabbed by a spear or javelin through his thigh, near the knee. Sandun took some clean cloth he had brought with him and tightly wrapped it above the wound as a tourniquet.

Out of the night, the other members of the expedition appeared by twos and threes. All were injured: Norris had lost several fingers on his right hand. Eki, supported by two of his comrades, had a dagger in his back. He cried out in pain as Sandun removed the blade and jammed clean linen into the gaping wound.

Looking around, Sandun realized the fighting had taken them close to the entrance of the small valley where they had camped that morning. Without saying much, they carried Torn's corpse and Maklin's unresponsive body back.

Kagne appeared, his hair a mess of blood and grass. More blood dripped down the side of his face. At first, he spoke to them in a language none could understand. Seeing their incomprehension, he shook himself and sat down.

"The warriors of the northern villages are hunting down the remnants of the…of the…" He slapped his face with his bloody hand. "They tell me the cavalry from Sirosfeld is fighting with another large group south—on the other side of those hills." He pointed. "We can't see it. Anyway, the mark's soldiers will win. The word will go through the north, spread like wildfire, and more men will come out hunting. None of those filthy…none of them. Not one of them will live to see Issedon again." He stood up and howled like a wolf.

Sandun thought the people who lived here in spite of the raids from Issedon had to be as fierce as the raiders.

Sir Ako told Kagne, "Torn is dead. Maklin, Norris, and Eki are wounded." Then he stood up and in a loud voice said, "We won. Outnumbered seven to one, we beat them. They broke and ran from us like the whoresons they truly are. And why? Because we are best warriors in Kelten!" Everyone cheered. "Bring out the wine, all of it. Tonight we honor our dead and celebrate our victory."

As they bound their wounds with strips of linen, some of the men went to the hidden packs and pulled out all the bottles and skins filled with Zeres wine and brought them back to the fire pit. Others gathered up the scattered firewood and soon built up a massive blaze. And they drank.

Sandun felt half-drunk already, giddy, torn between powerful emotions: relief, joy, fear, and sorrow all mixed up. But they all drank for hours deep into the night, toasting their success, yelling out challenges to the night sky. After midnight, Basil was puking the wine back out, and Kagne lay on the ground, staring up and muttering words in his northern language. The other scouts were sprawled about the camp, wrapped in stained blankets or slumped against stones.

Only Sandun and Sir Ako were still talking, singing snatches of songs, draining the last bottles.

In his drunken haze, Sandun finally asked the question that had been lurking in the back of his mind ever since Sir Ako had first ridden up to the door of the Archives. "Tell me…tell me what it's like. Yes, tell me what it's like to be married to that golden-haired goddess."

Sir Ako nodded as if he fielded that question all the time. "It's great. What a beauty. What a figure on that woman."

Sandun thought he detected a lie. Maybe he was drunk—actually, he *was* drunk—but Sir Ako's words rang false.

"Don't believe you. I don't believe what you are saying. That is a lie. Tell me the truth. Didn't we face death together? I demand the truth! What is it like to be married to the most beautiful woman in Kelten?"

Sir Ako wiped his mouth with his injured hand and grimaced. "Oh. You demand the truth, do you? Brothers in arms we are, and you demand the truth? Well, I'll tell you the fucking truth!" He stood up and peered down at Sandun with bloodshot eyes. "She treats me like a fishmonger! She treats me like I'm not worthy to touch so much as the hem of her dress. She looks around our small manor with our three house servants and she thinks—'Why did I marry this pauper knight!'

"Never, never marry a beautiful woman. Oh, wait. No, you can marry a beautiful woman, if you are the fucking king! Or my brother. His wife can't match my Lilly's looks, but she's fine. And she worships the ground he walks on. It's always, 'Yes, my lord' and 'As you wish, my lord,' and she means it. Yes, she means it. Maybe, just maybe, she means it because one day, my father, His Lordship, will die from a stroke or break his neck hunting, and then she will be a great lady, the Earless of Agnefeld.

"But my Lilly, she thinks she has nothing more to hope for. Ah, there's a dim chance I'll advance. I might be elevated to the smallest, most minor barony in some desolate county, perhaps here in glorious Erimasran! But only if there's a war, and I'm a bleeding hero in it, and I don't get skewered by some shit-eating peasant. No, odds are I'll never be more than I am, and she hates it, she hates not getting a new dress every month, she hates living in Agnefeld instead of living in a blasted mansion in Seopolis. And she hates me—because she thinks she could have married better."

He spat on the ground and then sat down. He was breathing hard. Sandun offered him the last of the wine. Sir Ako drained it and threw the bottle off into the night. It smashed against some rocks.

"And who is she? No better than I, lower even. Her father was a knight, a lesser knight. But two years as the queen's fucking handmaiden spoiled her rotten. With half the men of Seopolis come to see her every day. Men like you, eh, Master Sandun? Great lords praising her long honey hair. Queen Joaris showering her with dresses and gifts. By Saint Pererline's tits, the way she carries on now, you'd think she was the daughter of a bloody earl, with a vast estate as her dowry. As Sho'Ash is my god, I wish she'd married someone else. Then I could have found a woman who actually wanted to be my wife."

Sandun had nothing to say.

"I volunteered for this command," Sir Ako said quietly. "Told her it would bring me fame, bring me the notice of the king." He paused. "I did it to get away from her." Sir Ako struggled to stand up but failed and slumped onto his side. "Why am I still awake? Is there any more wine?"

"Go to sleep, Sir Ako," said Sandun. "Go to sleep, you great bloody hero."

Sandun rose unsteadily to his feet and, although his mind felt clear, he found it hard to walk. He checked on the other men. Maklin's wounded leg was covered in dried blood, but the tightly wrapped bandage seemed to have halted further bleeding. His breathing was shallow but even, so Sandun thought he would survive. Everyone else was asleep.

Lastly, he came to the body of Sergeant Torn. They had arranged his body and covered all but his head with shields and broken weapons to keep off any scavengers in the night. Sandun stood looking up at the black sky dotted with stars as a cold wind blew down from the high mountains to the east. He wondered about Sergeant Torn. Did he have a wife? Children? His spirit was gone, and what had he left behind in this world? A body, soon to be nothing more than dry bones buried at the edge of civilization. Sandun shivered.

He thought to himself: *Who will mourn me when I am dead? No wife, no children. A sister whom I rarely see. My parents are dead. If I die, as seems likely in the coming months, I will have accomplished nothing of note. Even in the Archives, my name will be remembered for a perhaps decade, no more.*

He walked back to the camp and wrapped himself up in blanket. *I will succeed*, he vowed. *I will find the path to Serica. I will return and marry and raise my children.*

But a coldly logical part of his mind replied, *And what if you fail?*

He said aloud, "Then I will die in the attempt. Sho'Ash will know I did my best."

PART THREE

The Tiralas

Ten days later, unambiguous evidence of the path was discovered by a pair of young men from one of the traveling villages. After the battle, about fifteen young warriors from the villages had stayed behind and taken up the search for the path while the Archives Expedition recovered. A promised reward of thirty crowns proved ample incentive. What these two men from Tokivanu had found was unmistakably an ancient path and very close to where the map indicated the path would start.

The most convincing evidence was found in a rock pile: the second stone from the top had a mark on it, the sign of Jon of Stenston, the mapmaker. No one, other than Sandun and Basil, had seen that mark before.

Looking at the stone in his hand, standing in the dry valley, surrounded by the silent men of the expedition, Sandun felt as though ghosts were calling his name. Against the odds, the path was real. And so the journey would continue. Into the Tiralas. Into the unknown.

The promised reward was paid out by Sandun from his depleted funds, and the two northmen went away very happy, each holding fifteen crowns, a small fortune here in the far reaches of Erimasran.

The next day, Maklin and the two most seriously injured scouts, Eki and Norris, left the camp and headed south with the few remaining cavalry that had stayed in the area, hunting down the scattered Issedon raiders. The mark's cavalry were going back to Sirosfeld, victorious and with a few prisoners. At first, Scribe Maklin protested with some heat that he should stay with the expedition. "This is my duty, Master Sandun. I swore to find the path and travel to Serica with you and with Basil. I'll heal soon. I will walk again."

"No, good scribe," said Sandun. "You were a hero in the battle; you go back with valuable news and maps. You will be a master in your own right before the year is out, if I guess true. This journey that we take into the Tiralas will test us all to our limits."

Maklin tried to argue, but Sandun held his hand.

"I know somewhat of medicine, Maklin. I deem your wound will keep you halt for at least half a year, and mayhap much longer. Although you can ride, you would have to turn back with the horses when we reach the jagged slopes which are surely in our path. As you can no longer fight, someone will need to return with you. I bid you be content with your fate. Against our guess and despite the bloody-handed Issedonians, the mission has succeeded. Tell the king we go into the unknown, at his command."

Maklin could not dispute his injury. In truth, even gentle riding pained him, though he tried his best to conceal it from the others. So he took the journal pages that Sandun had written and copies of their maps and rode away with Norris, and Eki, and the cavalry from Sirosfeld.

Several young men, all from Kagne's village, volunteered to go with the expedition, but Sandun, after discussion with Sir Ako and Basil and Kagne, turned them down. As far as anyone knew, the mountains were empty of human life; ghosts and other monsters of legend were, it was hoped, exceptionally rare. The expedition would not succeed in reaching Serica by force of arms. Instead, more people meant more mouths to feed.

Sandun strongly considered sending all the scouts and Sir Ako back, releasing them from their service to the Archives, but he hesitated to make that decision for several reasons: if the path were lost, they might need to explore multiple routes, and they might need to cut down trees to make a temporary shelter. Twelve men going into the Tiralas seemed safer than three. The true reason—that he had grown fond of Sir Ako and the scouts—he held in his heart. After the battle, they had become a band of brothers.

Basil was anxious to start heading up the path as soon as it was discovered. He counted the days till winter, when the Tiralas would become death's hunting ground. By his reckoning, they still had enough time to make the passage, but every day was precious. And so, packed and with somber hearts, they headed up into the Tirala Mountains.

The Tiralas were feared in Kelten. In stories and legends, they were haunted mountains, the end of civilization, a desolate wasteland of high, wind-blasted plateaus surrounded by ever-taller peaks covered in snows that did not melt and occupied by monsters the likes of which were not to be found anywhere else in the world. Now that they had reached the Tiralas, the mountains inspired dread in Sandun, and during his brave talk with Maklin, his words rang hollow to his ears. He felt an air of unreality as he and Maklin argued. In his heart, he wanted to go back to Tebispoli instead of going up and east, and he suspected that Maklin felt the same.

As they rode slowly up the long canyon, Sandun thought about the nature of his feelings for the scouts. He did not know them well, not like he knew Basil or Kagne, but they had risked their lives when they could have run. They were alive because all of them had fought together, faced their fears and outrageous odds, and come out on the other side. It was, he concluded, a unique bond among men. As he searched his feelings, he realized that now he would risk his life for them, and he felt they would risk their lives for him, though he could not explain why.

The scouts treated him differently—not like one of them exactly, but almost. Now they joked with him and beat him at cards. In their unofficial hierarchy, he now ranked just behind Sir Ako, taking the place of Sergeant Torn.

Basil and Olef became close in the days after the battle. Basil didn't talk about it, but sometimes Basil's dog came over and sat beside Sandun for an hour when Basil and Olef were not to be seen.

While they played cards, the other scouts made subtle comments about her affair with Basil to Olef, using hunting analogies that were unfamiliar to Sandun. Olef responded in equally arcane language, apparently telling them that she was going to do what she was going to do. All this was said while talking about deer and antelopes and wolves. As it didn't seem like anyone was going to resort to knives, Sandun stopped worrying about the matter.

Likely as a result of Sergeant Torn's death, Sir Ako became much more open about his life to Sandun. He was by rank and by birth far above everyone else on the expedition. Military tradition and custom placed a strong barrier between officers and their men. It was necessary, explained Sir Ako, because sometimes you had to order them to die. However, Sandun was not under his command and, as the king's agent, Sandun was somewhat outside the normal social ranking as well. Sir Ako began to treat Sandun like a confidant and advisor. And as a teacher as well—Sandun had a great deal of knowledge about history and the acts of the noble families. The history of the last hundred years in Kelten was very complicated, what with the civil war and the nearly successful conquest of Fiodroch, and while Sir Ako knew the broad outlines, he was eager to learn more.

As the third son of an earl, with both older brothers of sound mind and body, Sir Ako was not expected to inherit the earldom, and so his education of "high politics" was half that of his brothers. He could have gone into the priesthood, but he had always been big for his age, and the life of a warrior had appealed to him. His life story, such as it was, was interesting to Sandun, as men like him rarely entered the histories. It was odd that, although Sir Ako, being a knight, was highly ranked in Kelten society, however among the people he knew well, his status was low, and he felt this keenly. In the company of his father or older brother, he was insignificant, little better than a servant. Among the great lords, his opinion counted for nothing. He was just a knight, and there were at least fifteen thousand of them in Kelten. By contrast, there were just a shade less than a hundred earls and only five marks and but four dukes, each one of whom commanded the respect of the king. Sandun sensed that Sir Ako wasn't escaping just his wife's disdain.

For Sandun, life over the last decade had been very comfortable. Among the people he spent his time with, he held a high status: a Master at the Archives was a fine position. His mother had lived to see his elevation to that rank, and she'd been so happy she cried through much of the ceremony.

It was curious to see how different Sir Ako's perception of his own life was compared to Sandun's impression of what his life should have been like. Sandun thought Sir Ako was like a man who was surrounded by rare and wonderful books that his friends and relations could read but which were forbidden to him.

Sandun wondered if Sir Ako had ever had any real friends except for Sergeant Torn. Being the son of an earl, he ranked above all the other knights of his age. As a military commander, his men had to be kept at a distance. As for the nobility, Sandun thought only one other earl or duke had a third legitimate son around Sir Ako's age, and he lived in the north near Thalapolis. For his part, Sandun liked Sir Ako.

Basil looked at the world with the eyes of a hawk, though he said little. His observations were profound, but his speculations beyond the natural world were rare. And Kagne had become so sensitive to the land that he talked about it as though it was alive, as though it talked back to him. Sandun admired the man Kagne had become, but he did not understand him. By contrast, though Sir Ako did not have a great mind, he had a determined one, and he had a thirst for learning, especially for the history of wars and battles.

Kagne was the obvious person to handle the mules now that Maklin had departed. Kagne had long experience leading pack trains and skill with animals. For their part, the mules seemed to take special pleasure in coming up behind Kagne and braying at him. All told, it was a very different group that rode up into the Tirala Mountains on that late spring day, compared to the group that set out from Tebispoli three months earlier.

Trail markers like the one that they found at the start of the path were rare, likely due to the passage of hundreds of years. Only one more pile was discovered as they wended their way up through a canyon filled with dry bushes.

When Archives Expedition finally reached the top of the pass, a frozen wind blew snow in their faces, and Sandun could see little of the land ahead, only tall peaks rising high above the clouds in the distance. With his cloak wrapped around his face to keep the ice from biting, he kept his head down. Using the pale sun as their guide, they headed due east and hoped.

By the late afternoon, the sun had warmed up the land enough to force the cold winds above their heads. The snow was not more than a few inches deep, and countless tufts of dry grass could be seen covering the undulating path. Every mile or so they passed a large boulder and on the western side, sheltered from the wind, there were usually several thorn bushes. Where the snow had blown clear, antelope scat could be found. Occasional animal skulls peered at them with empty eyes.

They camped beside these large rocks and burned grasses and dried bushes for their fire. Basil returned from his hunt with one fat white-haired rabbit. "Little game," he said, "but unwary." After sunset, the wind died away. Walking away from the camp to gather dry grass, Sandun felt the stars' presence more keenly than ever before. Away from the fire, the stars were bright and seemed to fill the sky like a growing host.

In the past, Pellian legends said the sky was like a flat plate held up by two giant trees that grew from the tops of the tallest mountains at either end of the earth. But for more than a century, it had been known that the earth was a perfect sphere. In the college of astronomy in Tebispoli, Sandun had seen the latest models of the stars marked out on hemispheres of clear glass. The astronomers now claimed that the stars were fixed to a number of vast spheres that completely surrounded the earth and each other.

The invention of the farseer glass some fifteen years ago rattled the astronomers. Before Sandun left, there was talk in the The Frog on Rock—the Tebispoli tavern he frequented—about stupendous discoveries made with the very newest and largest farseers. Master Obis, a casual friend of Sandun, had told him late one evening, a year before, that he had observed faint dots of light orbiting around Dyus, the second-brightest planet. The man had clearly drunk too many glasses of beer, and Sandun dismissed his talk as confused rambling. But now he wondered, as he stood in the freezing wind and looked into the vast black sky, how many stars were there? Were there more stars that man could see? And if so, why?

Over the next five days, the expedition traveled east, as the highest peaks of the Tiralas rose in front of them. Were it not for the map, Sandun would have given up the journey and turned back. The mountains they faced were so tall and so steep, so covered with thick masses of ice and snow at their base, that to look at them caused a dizzy fear, as if one's mind rebelled against the sight. No man could climb over such high, sheer mountains.

But the map urged them on, and as they advanced closer, what appeared from a distance to be a solid wall of colossal rocks was revealed to be several overlapping ranges, one in front of the other. And strangely, there was a somewhat flat valley that snaked its way between these ridges. They rode into this valley, staring up from side to side as the cliffs mounted higher and higher above them, yet the way forward was easy, laughably easy.

It was like seeing a terrifying shape, say a dragon, that loomed out of the darkness and yet, as you forced yourself to draw closer, it suddenly became clear that it was just an old tree and some shadows behind it. Sandun began to laugh in relief, and hope sang in his heart. Some of the other scouts laughed as well, but only for a little while. The mountains loomed above them and occasionally, as the afternoon sun warmed the upper snow fields, avalanches would careen down the mountain slopes. All of them were afraid of avalanches, but walking in the middle of the valley was scant comfort; giant boulders, which had certainly rolled down from the rocky ridges, were strewn across the valley floor.

In the evening, a freezing wind blew down the valley, carrying bits of snow with it. They had to build a windbreak out of broken stones before they could attempt a fire. Fortunately, a great quantity of bone-white dry wood lay along the edges of the valley, close beside small, icy streams.

"I can't believe this valley," Sandun said to Kagne as they were riding the next morning. Everyone was bundled up, as they were in deep shadow even though the sun shone on the horns of sheer rock far above them.

"I mistrust it as well. It seems more like a dried-out riverbed than a true mountain valley. Where are the bushes, the mountain junipers? This is sand and rock and quick-growing grass. I fear what may come down on us. A flood? An avalanche of boulders?" Kagne was unusually dour this morning. None of them had slept well the previous night with the wind whipping the fire about as they huddled as close as they could for warmth.

Basil pointed to a pile of stones at the edge of a thick grove of tall pine trees. "Another trail mark. We are still on the path."

Sandun was cheered by the stone marker. If a trail mark could survive nearly three hundred years, it was also true that whatever floods had carved this channel had not returned.

All that day, the valley gradually narrowed and climbed more steeply upward. The rocks were harder to avoid, and often the horses had to be led by hand up and over large outcroppings of man-sized boulders.

Again in the evening, the freezing wind blew down on them. The noise it made as it rushed past the huge rocks was eerie, like great water organs playing tuneless songs in the lonely night.

"It sounds like the march of the dead," said Olef. Everyone looked at her as she huddled against Basil, wrapped in a patched woolen blanket. "In my village, once or twice a year a strong wind would blow from the south, and a low moaning sound would be heard, different from the wind. The old folks would shake their heads and say, 'The dead are marching, coming to claim one of their own.' And we would all go inside and bar the doors and wait out the night, tending the fire."

Sandun wanted to ask if more people died when the south wind blew, but he kept his words to himself. People always died; if the village was large enough, someone would die every fortnight. In Seopolis, there were burials every single day. In any event, with the wind sounding like demons on the loose and their fire streaming sparks into the darkness, it was hard not to believe that on some nights the dead really did march.

The next day, clouds wreathed the summits of the hills. Judging from the clouds' gray, faded look, it was likely snowing higher up.

The horses were hungry, as there was very little grass for them to eat. And even the mules were having trouble getting over the rocks. The mountain slopes were not as steep as they had been, but that was small comfort as the snows pushed down into the valley. It seemed that soon they would be blocked by thick snows or impassible rock ridges, or both.

Sandun wondered if they had set out too early. If they became blocked by deep snows, could they afford to wait for the snows to melt? When he mentioned this to Basil, the hunter shook his head.

"We have no time. We made just sixteen miles the previous day, and only a bit more the day before. Already this is the end of Pentamon; midsummer is less than thirty days off."

After midday, the valley turned, and now they found themselves at the bottom of a bowl. All around them, except the way they had come, was a ring of great snowy fields set between tall black spires of stone. The bowl was shrouded with gray clouds, and snow drifted down around them. There were no signs of any stone piles and no obvious path to take, and though some snow fields reached up to nearly vertical ridgelines, they seemed impossibly steep to climb.

Sandun called a halt. If they were going to get through this, scouting would be required.

The rest of the day, they chopped down two dozen small trees and made a primitive lean-to shelter. The snow where they camped was not deep and under it, the horses found grass from last summer. They ate it, but it was not very nourishing. In the late afternoon, the clouds broke up, and the sun shone down on the valley.

"This place is fine in the sunlight. On a bright day, it would likely be dazzling with the light reflecting off the fields from side to side," said Sir Ako.

Looking back the way they'd come, they could see that they were already higher than some of the mountains west of them. Very distant in the clear air, there were hints of white far, far to the west.

"Look, are those the Kelten Alps?" said Wiyat, whose long brown hair was being blown around his face by the swirling winds.

None could say for certain; perhaps the white was just clouds or perhaps that was the last view of Kelten that they would have for many months.

Sandun took out his farseer glass and examined the slopes around the camp. Basil and Sir Ako did the same with their devices. They compared notes after dinner, as the light faded from the skies.

The bowl due east of them looked less steep than the others, but Basil thought that there was a sharp ridge directly behind it and therefore a steep chasm between. The bowl to the north rose higher, but no one could see any indication of a mountain or anything beyond it. Going south was clearly impossible unless they could fly. The three of them stared at the map, but it was no help. North was the only reasonable choice.

The next day, Sandun, Basil, and Kagne tied ropes to each other and, using branches cut down for walking sticks, they struggled up the north slope. The day was again cloudy, but the snowfall was just a dusting of flakes. The snow on the ground was very deep in places, and when they got too close to the pine trees, they sometimes fell into pits that were difficult to escape from.

They returned exhausted around noon, and Sir Ako, Padan, and Jon followed up the path and then broke new ground through the snow, heading up the bowl toward the ridge.

They came back in the late afternoon, frozen from melting snow, their clothing soaked when it wasn't stiff with ice. A blazing fire helped to revive them, but two of Padan's fingers refused to warm up, and Basil thought it might be frostbite. He had Padan soak his hand in lukewarm water—a trick he had learned from an old hunter in the Modrokora.

The next morning, three more scouts went out; they returned at noon, defeated by the steep slope. Sandun, Basil, and Kagne again went out, carefully wrapped, with new sticks carved with shovel-like blades at one end. When they reached the farthest point in the beaten path, Sandun was amazed at how far they had come. It seemed like just a hundred feet was all that remained till they reached the top.

Those last hundred feet were much more difficult than any of them had imagined. Every ten feet it seemed a gap opened up in the snow underneath them, as the snow was draped like a sheet over an irregular rock field. More icy crusts fell down on top of them, and always the swirling winds blew fresh flakes into their faces. The three men changed places throughout the afternoon with Sandun in the lead first, then Basil, then Kagne, and then Sandun once more.

Sandun, his heart pounding and sweat running down his face, pushed his way through an overhang of snow and found that he was looking out over the other side of the ridge.

He gave a great shout and then was dragged back by Basil, who assumed Sandun was in grave danger.

"We are through! Let me go! Let me see the other side."

"Sandun! We are underneath a cornice of overhanging snow! If it breaks off, it will bury us alive. Quiet!"

"You and Kagne stay back then. I must see."

His hands wrapped in now-frozen socks, Sandun carefully tunneled his way. He ignored the snow shelf overhead and looked out into a new valley with hints of green no more than a couple of miles away.

To his surprise, the slope on the other side of the ridge was completely different from their side of the mountain. It was a northeast-facing slope, and while there was some snow on it, boulders and smaller rocks poked their way through. From where Sandun was lying, it looked like a very gentle slope heading downhill—nothing like what they had spent the last two days laboriously climbing up. Perhaps three miles away, there was green grass beside a small pond, and a copse of pines stood to one side.

Looking farther, he could see for many miles, but in each direction, distant mountains covered in white rose into the sky like clouds.

Sandun went back to his friends; each in turn went up gingerly to the hole in the snow and looked out. Without saying much, they went back down to the camp to talk things over.

While they warmed up by the fire, Sandun described the view from the top of the ridge.

Sir Ako pointed at the ridge. "We cannot take the horses up." They all nodded. Perhaps if the snow melted, the ridge could be ridden over, but how long would that take? And there was much farther to go. They had nearly two thousand miles to travel and five months—at best—before winter. "If we do not eat the horses, then we must either set them loose or send them back with some men."

None of them wanted to kill the horses. There was no discussion of that.

"We can nay set the horses loose. Poor beasties would starve or be food for wolves," said Olef.

"I agree. And one man alone cannot handle all the horses. So it must be two who will return to Sirosfeld," Sir Ako said "Who wants to go back?"

None of the scouts said anything.

"Since you leave this up to me, I am sending Jon and Kinot back with the horses. The rest of us will continue so long as we are able."

In the evening, as the setting sun turned the high peaks the color of roses, Sandun lay beside the fire. His mind felt untethered to the ground, and his arms and hands trembled when he didn't force them to stay quiet. Sir Ako sat beside him, and they had a whispered conversation.

"Sir Ako, you do not have to go over the snow ridge with us."

"You are right; we don't have to. Yet I must go, and I'm sure my soldiers feel the same. I cannot leave you and Basil and Kagne in the trackless wastes of the Tirala Mountains and retain even a shred of honor. We are brothers now. Honor forbids me from abandoning you, and so my men and I will follow, till our strength gives out. We are the Archives Expedition."

Sandun was absurdly grateful but found no words to say. Overcome with emotion, he covered his face with his hands and wiped away tears. Sir Ako clumsily patted him on the shoulder and then walked back to the fire.

In the morning, the scouts redistributed food and supplies between the horses and the pack mules. Sandun and Basil both felt dizzy and had no appetite. Kagne examined them and said that they were suffering from mountain sickness. Several of the scouts, including both Kinto and Jon, now admitted they felt poorly as well. Sir Ako had perhaps guessed that they were suffering ill effects from the mountains and had chosen them for that reason.

"It's like a curse. The only way to make it go away is to leave the high hills," said Kagne. Sandun didn't feel like laughing, but they were not going to be leaving the high hills for months to come.

Kagne took care of Basil and Sandun, the others spent the day working on the path, stamping it down and making it more suitable for the mules. By the afternoon, thanks to a combination of rest and the herb tea Kagne fed them all morning, Sandun felt somewhat recovered, and so he put his new notes and sketch maps together for delivery to Sirosfeld. Basil made hasty copies of the route onto a second map—"In case we get lost on the way back," he explained.

That night, the mood around the campfire was somber. The following day, if the mules could make it up the snowy path, the group would split and perhaps never see each other again. This was different from the departure of the two scouts and Maklin after the battle, because then there had been no real choice. Jon and Kinot could continue, yet they were turning back. Since Sir Ako had given the order, there was no shame in doing what they were told, and all agreed that they could not simply abandon the horses. And yet, it felt like leaving comrades in the face of terrible danger.

They sang the song of farewell. It was a sea song, but it fit the occasion.

> *In the high summer, after the fling,*
>
> *I sailed abroad to serve my king.*
>
> *And my dearest dear, I left behind*
>
> *So oft she swore her heart was mine.*

And all the time I sailed the seas,

I could not find an hour's ease.

Thinking on my sweetling girl,

Though never a word of her I did hear.

At last I sailed into Seopolis town.

I searched the streets up and down,

Inquiring for my sweetling girl.

Nary a word of her could I hear.

To Stenston and her father's hall

I went at last, and I did call.

My daughter is married now, she's a rich man's wife.

She's wed to another far better for life."

Oh curse your gold and your silver too,

And curse the girl that won't prove true.

When all her former vows did break,

Went with another for riches' sake.

Since the girl is married that I adore,

I'm sure I'll stay on land no more.

I'll sail the seas till the day I die.

Break through waves rolling mountain high.

The next day, the horses were left tethered together, and everyone helped in getting the mules up the snowy bowl. The two men who were going back pushed themselves harder than the rest, but no one commented on this. The mules proved their worth despite much braying, and they followed the trail and crossed over the ridgeline and stood in a small group amid the half-buried rocks on the northeast slope.

For several minutes, the group stood around and stared into the distance. Finally, Sir Ako said it was time to go, and he waved to the two men who were heading home. They turned and, without a backward glance, walked up the hill and disappeared over the snowy ridge.

The remaining party, now down to ten, clambered down the slope, drawn irresistibly to the pond and the green grass, though the pond was covered over with ice, and the grass was just a half inch of new growth. As they looked around, more inviting campsites beckoned farther down the slope. So they continued till they reached an unfrozen lake with a large stand of pines. Here they camped and dried out.

"Seems so quiet without Kinot telling one of his ribald stories," Farrel said. "Even if he did cheat at cards."

"And Jon, always with a cheery word," Padan said to Olef, who nodded her head.

"He always did fancy you," Wiyat said, as he was building up the fire.

"That's not so! He's a good friend, naught else." Olef said this with her eyes wide.

"By the Spear, he told me himself not six months past."

"Wiyat!" Sir Ako exclaimed, giving the young man a stern look.

That was the end of that conversation.

Sandun and Basil were ill with splitting headaches, so after the meal, Kagne and Sir Ako scrambled up a rocky outcropping to the east to survey the land. As near as they could make out, the valley they were in was a long oval, tending north by northeast. After their report back at the camp, Sandun stared at the map in frustration; it was unclear if they were following the path or not. They should be heading east, so north was wrong, but crossing over the newly revealed east ridge, which looked like exposed fangs for ten miles or more, was unthinkable.

The next day, beside a lower lake, they discovered another trail marker. No other marker could be seen in any direction and at this point, it did not matter whether they had taken the correct route or not. They kept descending, and everyone's hearts lifted as they walked on damp soil from which snow had recently retreated. Little pink ice flowers poked their way up through the layers of pine needles that covered the ground. Spring had come to this high valley, and birds were calling while squirrels chattered at the travelers below them.

No sign of human habitation could be seen, and Basil found deer easy to bring down in the evening. At night, they heard wolves howling, calling out to the moon or warning the humans away. Once, Kagne spotted a line of at least seven wolves traveling through a grassy meadow a mile or two south, heading up the valley. They made sure the fire burned strong all night and kept the mules close at hand.

Whenever they came to a clearing, incredibly tall mountains could be seen in all directions. Gradually the valley leveled out as it bent eastward, and on the fourth day a large mass of reeds with a lake beyond them came into view. It was certain that the land was a marsh all around the lake, so the expedition stayed high on the south slope. The lake was large—not as big as Lake Tricon, but they spent two days wending their way past its muddy shores. Great flocks of white birds could be seen near the middle of the water, nesting on tiny islands and feeding on whatever small creatures lived in the waters.

At the eastern end, the lake turned into a vast expanse of shimmering mud, and tall, long-legged fishing birds stalked about the flats, poking their sharp bills down every minute or so and then tilting their heads up to the sky, at whiles calling out to each other with a three-note trill. They passed several large nests in old ruined trees, and Wiyat dexterously climbed up to one nest and then lowered down a clutch of large eggs, which the expedition ate with gusto in the evening.

Now they could see the mountains that blocked the east end of the valley, and one great hill stood out. It was a beautifully symmetrical cone-shaped peak, very like Mount Shioni in the far north of Kelten, completely covered in snow and ice all the way to its summit. It towered over the other peaks on its flanks, and while it looked like a gentle slope to the top, Sandun did not doubt that this was a dangerous illusion. Few men could boast of having climbed Mount Shioni, and that only in midsummer when the snows were least.

Here the map had a curious spiral-shaped mark. Sandun and Master Eulogo had studied it with their most powerful magnifying glass back at the Archives, but the mark's meaning remained a mystery. Now, as they approached the wall of rocks and cliffs that barred their way, Sandun was again dismayed at the apparent lack of a route leading out of the valley.

Near the mountainous wall, freezing air seemed to pour down onto them from above, like an invisible wave of cold water. The trees were few and stunted, and high above them great eagles wheeled and gave voice, their harsh cries echoing off the rocky slopes. The next day, one more trail marker was discovered, but looking up into the hills, the expedition could see no path.

The week spent in what they now called "Bent Blade Valley" had refreshed them.

"There is a way through," Farrel said to the group. "One thing I learned from delivering the king's messages: there is always a way through. We just need to find it."

The most notable feature in the land east of the marker was a jagged opening into the rock about one half mile up the slope. At first, all of them had scouted past the opening, as caves had an evil reputation in Kelten, being rare and often occupied by bears or mountain lions or perhaps even monsters. But as no path was found after two days of searching, Sandun and Basil ventured into the opening. Using ropes tied around rocks at the mouth, they climbed down and found utter darkness.

Sandun took out four of the glowing orbs that the king had given to him as his gift to the ruler of Serica. He gave two to Basil and kept two, sometimes holding both in one hand. As their eyes adjusted to the faint green light, Sandun and Basil discovered the cave was not at all like the caves in the Kelten Alps; instead, this cave was more like a tunnel, and after a short flat section, the tunnel began heading steeply uphill.

Basil examined the rock of the cave wall and shook his head in wonder. "I have never seen anything like this before. No man made this, yet the rock is hard and smooth."

"It looks like the wine cellars of the Arkoamplo estate in Nemiada. See how it curves overhead? But it is so damp, and the air is nearly freezing." Sandun shivered and jumped up and down to try and keep warm.

"Do you think it goes anywhere? Could this be the route?"

"We will need warmer clothing and the fur cloaks to keep the water off. Then we can find out."

The two men returned to the camp. The other scouts argued against further exploration of the cave. Some said it was unnatural; others said it was worse than unnatural—it was the creation of the Black Terror. In a bid to calm their fears, Sandun brought out some of the glowing orbs and passed them around. In the daylight they were not impressive, but they clearly were glowing, and this magic seemed like it might offer some protection from any ghosts or terrors that lurked in the cave.

Basil and Sandun returned to the cave after lunch and made their way into and up the mysterious tunnel. The floor was very slippery at places, and in several dips there were shallow pools of ice-cold water that they could pass only with agile climbing around the edge of the tunnel. But up and up the cave went. In a few places, thin spires of rock were broken and lying on the cave floor. With only the faint green light of the orbs to see by, neither man could say for certain if the stone spikes had been broken deliberately.

Sandun felt a rising excitement the farther they went. They had gone at least a mile and climbed hundreds of feet upward. What could it be other than the path? Although at times the roof came close to the floor, it never closed off completely. Still, the cave was narrowing and now, three or four hours in, his hands were numb from the cold, and he had slipped and fallen and bruised his knees and elbows many times. Twice he was on the verge of telling Basil it was time to go back, but something drove him on.

Basil said, "The air smells different."

Hiding the glowing orbs in his sleeves, Sandun looked up into the darkness. He saw nothing, but he felt the air move. Up until now, the air had been frozen and stagnant. Going forward, they came to a pile of massive rocks that filled the tunnel up to the ceiling. And there was light!

Unmistakable light came down from a broken hole in the tunnel's roof. Scrambling around cracked boulders that dripped with slushy snow, Sandun managed to climb out of the broken tube and stood blinking in the evening air as the last sunlight faded from snowy fields around him. He turned about, shaking his head like a dog just out of a lake, and suddenly the thunderbolt of vision was granted him. He was looking east at a path to a high saddle between the great conical mountain (which they had named Mount Pandion at Sir Ako's suggestion) and a lesser hill to its north. There was a path to the east!

Basil joined him and then put his hands to his mouth and yelled out a great hoot. He grinned at Sandun and then started to laugh.

"All this time, I didn't believe it. All this time. But it's true. Jon of Stenston really made the trip to Serica and back. And we are following in his footsteps, traveling a route that no man has taken for nearly three hundred years. I didn't believe it." Shaking his head in amazement, Basil picked his way closer to the edge of the cliff that overlooked Bent Blade Valley below. Sandun followed him. From the top of the cliff, they could see the pinprick of firelight from the camp several miles away.

"Halloo!" Basil shouted. If there was any response, it could not be heard. The chill air was rolling down the mountains at their backs, driving all sound before it. Taking out his farseer glass, Sandun saw one figure at the camp waving a piece of burning wood overhead. Basil shouted again and a couple of eagles, disturbed by the noise, flew out into the great space and circled in the empty air, adding their calls to his. Basil laughed and shouted like a lunatic for several minutes.

Happy but worried about the cliff edge, Sandun drew his friend back to a safer spot beside a great rock, protected from the wind blowing down on them. They ate the little food they had brought and took pleasure in sitting in the fresh air, watching as the long lake's still waters reflected the orange evening light, set down on the land like a fiery ruby lying between a maiden's breasts.

Rested, they came back to the tunnel entrance and lowered themselves down to the wet stone floor below. Hours of painful and toilsome effort waited for them, but they were both filled with excitement.

Bone weary and chilled by icy water and frozen air, they returned to the cave mouth around midnight. Sir Ako and Olef and most of the other scouts were waiting for them with food beside a small fire. Filled with excitement, Basil described the tunnel and the path at the top to his rapt audience. Sandun passed around the glowing orbs again: in the night, the orbs glowed brightly, as though lit by a green fire.

Together, they walked slowly back to camp. Sandun sat down beside the main camp fire; wrapped in his blanket, he contemplated the discovery. He was happy, but a part of him felt disconnected from any emotion. He was on a mission, and the mission would continue. He thought of Jon of Stenston, the mapmaker. Had he discovered the tunnel? Perhaps he had followed some earlier explorer? And how did the tunnel come to be? Questions filled his mind and then faded away as he crawled in the tent and fell asleep.

The mules were not going to go through the tunnel.

Getting the scouts to enter was a challenge enough, but the mules dug in their hooves and refused utterly to venture inside. Different mules, trained from birth to haul ore out of mines like the ones near Zanthos, would have gone in without complaint, but these were not such mules, and the expedition did not have the time or, in truth, the inclination to train them and get them accustomed to being underground.

After several hours of fruitless effort, Kagne flat out said that the mules would not go. This time there was no thought of sending men with the mules all the way back to Sirosfeld. Instead, the choice was between butchering the animals or setting them free. It was a choice like the one they'd made with the horses, but this time no one had any strong feelings one way or the other. The deciding factors were the time it would take to salt the meat and the fact that no one relished eating tough mule meat when they still had fresh venison to eat. So they set the mules free.

Now they had to choose what to keep and what to leave behind. Food and warm clothes were critical; extra weapons and armor were set aside. With great reluctance, the scouts put aside their shortswords and shields. Sir Ako put his mace and one of his daggers in the pile, saying ruefully to no one, "That is a month's pay there."

Two scouts, Damar and Wiyat, dug a deep hole and lined it with flat rocks taken from the shattered piles of stones near the cliffs. The weapons were carefully wrapped in the packs that the mules had been carrying. Everything was buried and a large stone set on top. They paced off the distance to a large tree and then scored the tree bark with the sign of Saint Hurin and the number of paces. Basil dutifully recorded the details on his personal map. Everyone acted as though they were coming back this same way.

The mules stood around the camp, puzzled by the preparations and the burying of their packs. The men waved good-bye to the animals and, one by one, climbed into the tunnel. The mules stood at the lip and brayed anxiously at them, their calls echoing in the darkness.

By the end of the day, everyone was outside again: cold, wet, bruised, and very happy to be through the pitch-black, freezing cave. Sandun collected all the glowing orbs from the men and locked them away in the armored pouch.

Four days of travel on the broken, rocky shoulders of these new mountains.

Four days of scrambling up and over strange rocks, some as light as wood chips and filled with small bubbles, others like vast snakes that had oozed out of the ground and then slithered down the slope only to freeze and remain motionless till the end of time.

On the morning of the second day, they came upon jets of steam that shot out of the ground with an eerie roar. Everyone hated the sound and smell. Downslope from the steam jets, scalding-hot, foul-smelling water trickled out of the ground and gathered into pools that steamed in the chilly morning air. They gave a wide berth to this cursed land, except Basil and Sandun. Both of them remembered the hot springs of their youth, and this seemed similar. Walking up closer to the hot pools, Sandun found strangely colored rocks. Inside a large pool were all the colors of a rainbow: red, orange, green, and blue. The vivid colors were so unexpected and Sandun and Basil were so excited that Sir Ako came over, and then all the other scouts overcame their fears and came up to the pool. Soon they were like young children, excited at seeing a sailboat for the first time, calling out and pointing at different spots of the pool. Then Padan stepped on a fragile piece of white stone that broke under his weight, and he fell forward with a cry. He put his hands into the steaming water to save his face; fortunately, the water at the edge of the pool turned out to be the temperature of soup, and he was not badly hurt.

"The rocks here are more like sandstone or dried seaweed," said Sir Ako. "Best to keep a distance, despite the unearthly beauty to be found in the waters."

They continued east. On the fourth day, a thunderstorm hit them. The sound of the thunder grew and grew till it seemed like a titanic drum as big as a mountain valley was being beaten by a gang of demented giants. Lightning split the afternoon sky, searing the eye with an image of crazy white lines. Soon the clouds lowered, and they were in a thick fog as the rain came down in fat drops. They huddled beside a large rock that offered no real shelter. Suddenly Sandun felt his skin crawl, a sensation like coming out of a bath when a stiff breeze blows open the window and fills the room with cold, dry air. A bolt of lightning came down not fifty feet away, blinding and deafening the expedition. All of them got down on their knees and prayed to Sho'Ash to save them. Fear was in everyone's voice, and even Sir Ako stumbled over the prayers.

Sandun thought back on the words of the Mark of Sirosfeld: "The Tiralas will kill you with supreme indifference."

He shouted out wildly, "We are on his journey! Sho'Ash protects the wanderer who travels through empty lands. Our mission serves his will!" Sandun didn't know if he believed all of what he said, but as the lightning moved away and the thunder grew fainter, everyone else, in turn, took Sandun's right hand and pressed it to their forehead, just like they did in the temple, as though he were the high priest.

The next day, after the sun had dried all the previous rain off the stones, the clouds that had followed them ever since they climbed out of the tunnel vanished, seeming to prefer the company of the great mountains behind them. The air became unusually hot and after lunch, some men took off their shirts. Kagne had to warn them against letting the sun shine for long on their pale chests and backs. "All men know of sunburn, but we tell stories about the sun in Tirala Mountains. It is not like the sunlight in Seopolis or Torobeus. It is stronger even if it is not as warm."

Despite the warning, two of the men had angry red backs by the evening, and they slept poorly that night. After that, everyone tried to keep the sun off everything but their hands and arms.

The sixth day from the cave, the path they had been following bent northward and then took them into a steep canyon. The air was curiously hazy, but the cause of the haze was unclear. Coming out of the canyon, they found themselves in a large valley, about the same size as the Bent Blade Valley but with steep cliffs to the east and north. At the edge of sight, west of them, there looked to be a large lake.

Sandun first noticed nothing more than an odd line of hills running in the middle of the valley from the eastern cliffs toward the lake. But as he stared at them through his farseer glass, the hills became more and more curious. First, he noticed that they seemed spaced evenly across the valley. Next, he realized they were in a straight line. Lastly, and this was very hard to see in the haze, the hills seemed to be shaped like statues. Like giants.

Sandun went up to Basil and Sir Ako and quietly suggested they look at the hills in the middle of the valley. "A bit odd, don't you know." The two men took out their farseers, and they soon saw what Sandun had seen. There was no movement. The valley looked empty, but the line of giants was disturbing, or even frightening.

Sandun held a brief meeting with Sir Ako and Basil while Kagne used Sandun's farseer glass.

"They don't seem to move," Sir Ako said.

"The line seems to extend into the lake," Sandun offered.

"I believe there is something between each 'giant,' connecting them in some fashion," said Basil, who had the best vision.

"We have to tell the men," said Sir Ako. So they did, and they passed around the farseers.

For hours, the expedition silently watched the valley. Several streams, like the one beside them, flowed partway out into the valley but then turned and headed toward the lake. The valley floor was covered with small shrubs, and green rushes grew in the parts of the streambeds that they could see. Birds flew back and forth. Other than bird calls, it was utterly silent, but there was no sense of menace. Two of the other scouts also said they could see something connecting the "giants," but as the light changed in the afternoon, the line of giants faded into the haze.

With no sound and no movement, the expedition members talked about going across the valley the next day to explore the closest "giant." Going east did not seem possible, as the rock face of the canyon was tall and appeared nearly vertical. Damar suggested they could head west toward the lake and see if the line of giants existed on the western end of the lake. No one else thought that was a good idea.

As the sun set, Sandun stared at where he guessed the line of giants reached the eastern end of the valley. The reddish light illuminated the far cliffs. Then, for at least a minute it seemed like a glint of light was shining, reflecting off some glass-like surface. As the sun sank below the hills, the valley turned dark, and throughout the night there was no sound or light.

The next day, the expedition members all walked from their camp where the canyon trail reached the valley floor and toward the closest giant. The statue, which it clearly now was, had been carved in the shape of a man, about fifty feet tall, pulling with both arms on what looked like a rope that left his hands and formed a straight line to the next statue ahead. The figure was braced against a large pyramid with elaborate but abstract designs on it. Each statue they could see was facing the same way, toward the lake.

The statue was awe inspiring. It was larger than any that Sandun had seen, and to find it here, in the middle of the Tirala Mountains, was shocking—it was so drastically out of place. A hundred questions bubbled in his mind, most importantly: Who made them and why?

They all slowed as they approached the giant, instinctively keeping a healthy distance in case it started to move. From their stopping point, Sandun could tell that the rope the giant was holding was not a real rope but something metallic. It was a dull orange-red color, perhaps rusted iron, but other than the color, there was no sign of corruption, no staining of the giant's hands.

The artistry was as impressive as its size, with bold sweeps in the simulated fabric of its chiton and a well-defined face. In shape, the giant was like a man with a flattened nose, mouth curved up in a smile, muscles tensed but not straining hard. The chiton it wore was like a long robe that went from its neck to its feet, which were covered in boots.

Sandun turned and headed east, away from the lake, to the next giant in line. Everyone followed.

"I've never seen anything like this before," Farrel said quietly.

The next giant was not identical to the first. The face was similar but with a different look and a different expression: less pleased, more tension in the mouth. Each statue was about a quarter of a mile apart. Sandun and Sir Ako veered from the line and walked closer to the rope that hung about twenty-five feet above the ground. The ground directly under the metal rope was eroded. Snow might have settled on the great rope above and then melted over years, decades, perhaps centuries.

"How old are these?" Sandun asked Sir Ako as they walked back to the others.

"I know something of old stone walls, at least the walls of my father's castle outside Agnefeld. These are newer than the oldest walls. I'd guess two hundred years."

"Excluding the makers, might we be the first men to have seen them?"

"Aye. But this work must have required the labor of thousands, unless those who did the work were close in size to the figures we see."

"You speak the truth, though my mind has spun in circles trying to imagine a reason for all this." Sandun had thought of several possible explanations, but all were deficient in some way.

The next giant they passed was clearly a woman but otherwise more alike the other statues than different, except the figure portrayed in rock was bald. The dome of the figure's head was odd, somewhat out of proportion to its body.

"Think you can climb this one, Padan?" Farrel said. "You always talk of your days as a youngster climbing the hills around Lefkoati."

Padan looked carefully at the stonework, shading his eyes from the sun with his hand. "I could, but I don't want to," Padan replied.

As he approached the next statue, Sandun decided this one's head also seemed a bit odd, though in truth it was very hard to tell as he was standing on the ground looking up at a face many body lengths above him.

By lunch, they were hot and thirsty. Although several streams came down from the hills on the south side of the valley, none of the streams approached the stone giants, possibly an accident but equally likely a product of engineering by the giants' builders. They had almost reached the eastern cliff face, and they ate a lunch of dried fruits and nuts and salted ham while taking turns staring through the farseers at the wall where the final giant stood.

This last figure was different from the others in several respects. First, the face was carved in a great grin of mirth, as though the model for the statue had been close to laughter the whole time he was being sketched. Second, his chiton was different, with a high collar around his neck. Finally, hanging down from a carved necklace was a medallion, with some sort of figure in the middle. The farseer glass was no help in making it out as it was covered in shadow. The stone medallion was the first piece of jewelry they had seen on any of the statues.

"If that isn't the ruler of the people who made these, then I am a toad," Kagne announced to them all. It seemed a fair assumption to Sandun, but he kept turning over in his mind the question of who and why.

The last giant was braced against a cliff face that looked natural and yet seemed somehow cleaner than the other cliffs they had passed. Also, there was very little rubble at the foot of the cliffs on either side of the laughing statue. He thought about the light he had seen the previous sunset; he scanned the cliff face intently for more than half an hour, but he saw no sign of anything reflective.

The silence was oppressive near the rock wall. Even the birds seemed to shun the area. No streams or rivulets came down from the eastern cliffs. After consultation, Sir Ako and Sandun chose to walk up to the final statue and yell out a greeting.

"Why don't we just leave this place?" said Farrel. "I'm not afraid of Issedonians, but I am afraid of giants."

"No one has ever found giants," Sandun said in his most reassuring voice. "To be sure, the Sogands are all thought to be more than six and a half feet tall, but they aren't giants. If the stories from the latter days of the empire are to be believed, then no giants have ever been found in the world. Anyway, there is no sign of any life here, no paths, no doors, no farms."

"Nothing but these giants, and someone built them."

"You've seen the faces. Whoever built these statues at least had a sense of humor."

Farrel grumbled, but no one had any other objections.

The two men strode toward the giants. Sandun felt much less confident than he hoped he looked. As they walked, Sir Ako said quietly, "You are sure about there being no giants?"

"Yes."

"What about dragons?"

"One thing at a time, Sir Ako. Praise Sho'Ash we never see a dragon."

Coming up to the cliff face, Sandun felt more certain that it was unnatural, but nothing leapt out. There was just a sense of symmetry to the rocks and steep stone faces. There were several grooves in the rock near the base of the cliff, as if heavy blocks of stone had been moved over the ground and then the marks had been imperfectly smoothed over. By his guess, they were standing in front of a nearly perfectly concealed gate.

Sir Ako put his mouth to his hands and yelled out at the wall, "We are travelers from the Kingdom of Kelten. We come in peace." His voice echoed off the hard, sun-baked rocks, but there was no answer.

Sandun looked all around the last statue for clues. Like the others, it also had its back to a large pyramid of rock. But the pyramid continued all the way to the cliff face without any sign of obvious joins, and the shaped stone just merged smoothly into the "natural" rock. He saw that the great metal rope being held by the statue went straight back into the rock wall, as though a giant had pushed a stiff rod into a soft clay.

The two men rejoined the others, and they all walked over to the nearest stream coming down out of the western hills, where they made camp.

Before the sun set, Sandun went west toward the second-to-last statue. His goal was to line up in roughly the same angle to the sun as he had been the previous evening, in the hope that whatever had lit up in the evening would do so again.

He sat down beside a lone manzanita bush, its red, smooth bark contrasting with the dark-green oval leaves. He stared intently at the cliff face. Basil joined him a few minutes later, with his dog by his side.

"Here is the big mystery to me," Basil announced. "No animal droppings. There are water, plants, shelter in the canyons. Why is there nothing on four feet here in this valley? No deer, no rabbits, no ground squirrels. It's uncanny."

"Perhaps the giant builders don't allow burrowing animals to approach their precious statues."

"Well, we cannot stay here for long. I've never seen hunting this poor. What are you looking for, anyway?"

Sandun replied, "I saw sunlight reflecting off something shiny last evening. I hope to see it again and investigate it."

"You think there are people behind this rock face?"

"I do."

Later, when the sun was at the horizon, a square of reflected sunlight again appeared about two-thirds of the way up the cliff face.

"Ha! I have you," Sandun exclaimed. Basil was ready with his sketch paper, and he rapidly filled in the significant features of the cliff face around the presumed window. The sun set, the cliff turned gray, and the reflection vanished.

When they returned to the camp, Kagne proudly showed off some edible roots he had collected from very ordinary-looking green shoots that grew beside the creek. Basil just grunted. A bit of a rivalry had developed between Kagne and Basil. Kagne's knowledge of plants and herbs was remarkable, and two of the scouts, Gloval and Wiyat, had begun to follow him and learn his plant lore. Olef and Padan instead looked to Basil and copied his hunting techniques when he let them accompany him.

Sandun was happy to have both men working on finding food, and the roots Kagne found were a welcome change from the animals they had been eating as they traveled over the high hills beyond Mount Pandion. He himself was more of a fisherman; there was nothing quite so relaxing as setting a line by a lakeshore, under a tree, with a good book to read.

As they ate Kagne's boiled roots, Sandun talked about the reflection he had seen up on the cliff face. The early stars were in the deep-blue sky as they looked over the eastern cliff, and they talked about whether it was possible to climb to that spot.

Basil and Padan debated feasible climbing routes. Padan was skilled at scrambling up and over rocks. Basil had spent many days hunting for wild mountain goats across the scree slopes of the Modrokora Mountains in the north; he had learned early that he could make wonderfully far shots when he was shooting downhill.

After some time, the two men had agreed upon a route for the next morning. Olef announced she was going with them. "I've spent more time climbing on thatched rooftops than rocks, but I'm light and small."

Sandun wondered about Olef's career before she had joined the scouts, but he held his tongue. Basil and Padan agreed, saying that three climbers were better than two.

All the ropes were taken out of the packs. Sandun thought the ropes were looking a bit dry, so he soaked them for an hour before coiling them up and setting them out on a flat rock. Two products the Kelten traders were justly proud of were ropes and sails. Melnehlanian shipwrights made the best sailboats, and the best war galleys were still made in Akia, but Kelten craftsmen made the best ropes and sails in the Archipelago.

The next morning, even before the sun rose above the eastern hills, Basil, Padan, and Olef set out. The rest of the group moved down to the second giant, which they called "The Grump" as the face on this giant was, if not unhappy, then at best resigned to holding his great metal rope. They stood in the shade as the sun climbed higher and watched as the other three made their ascent.

Basil and the other climbers went up the far left, although the "window" was closer to the right side of the cliff. About a hundred feet up, there was a shelf that went horizontally across the face of the cliff. From below, the route looked possible. But once there, Basil found the ledge to be incredibly narrow with sections that were little more than a hand's width. Below, the drop was nearly straight down. After safely crossing the ledge, Padan took the lead, and then Olef went first. The other two would try to brace themselves in case the leader fell, but in many locations, there was nothing to brace on.

After several hours, they were nearly underneath the "window" but still about seventy-five feet below its presumed location.

Basil was again in the lead when suddenly he was attacked—an eagle came at him. Shouts from Olef and Padan below him gave a second of warning, and then the bird had sunk its talons into his outstretched arm and tried to pull him off the wall.

Basil had seen eagles pull young mountain goats to their deaths, and so he clung to the rock like an oak with one hand, while he grabbed for his hunting knife, which he had pushed behind his back. The other two climbers could do nothing to help Basil; they tried to prepare as best they could if he should fall, and they shouted curses at the eagle. The raptor pecked at Basil's face, trying to put out an eye, but Basil fended off the attack…and nearly lost his balance in the attempt. He swayed away from the wall and then desperately pushed up with his legs to reach a new and stronger handhold.

The eagle flew off briefly to try and strike again, to sink its killing talons deep into Basil's flesh. With his free hand, he yanked at his belt and managed to bring his hunting knife within reach. Pulling it out, he slashed at the deadly bird as it came with its talons out, aiming for his head. Basil's strike was poorly aimed, but he did graze the creature, and it screeched in pain and dismay. He slashed it again, and this time he cut into its body, near the left wing.

With a despairing call, the eagle spun away from Basil and fell through the air to land in a heap several hundred feet away from the cliff's face. Shaking with rage and fear, Basil pulled himself up again and found himself staring at a nest of sticks and dried branches, feathers, and bird droppings.

Two large eggs were in the nest. Basil pulled all the of the branches away and threw them down the cliff. With no place to put the eggs where they wouldn't be smashed, he threw them off the cliff as well.

He sat in the remains of the eagle's nest while the other two climbed up and joined him. Olef cleaned away the blood on his face with a bit of the water she was carrying and used some linen to bind up the deep cuts on his arm.

"It's strange that we saw no sign of the eagle during the day," she said.

"Perhaps it hunted at night, or perhaps it didn't hunt in this valley," replied Basil.

Padan took the lead going up the rest of the way to where the window ought to be. They came to another rock shelf, this one wider than the one below. While Padan rested, Basil edged along to the left while Olef went right.

After fifteen feet, Basil became aware that he was looking at a suspiciously smooth and almost glassy-looking rock face. He was just about to say, "I think I've found it," when the rock face opened into the mountain and strong hands pulled him inside. It seemed pitch dark inside to his sun-dazzled eyes. He heard the sound of his rope being cut, followed immediately by that of a stone door grinding shut.

It took some time for Basil's eyes to adjust to the dim light inside the cliff, so at first, he could see almost nothing. Hard, calloused hands gripped his arms as he was led into the mountain. He was not roughly treated, but his captors were insistent. The corridor they took went steadily up, with occasional landings where other passages joined. Every hundred paces it became very bright; looking up, Basil could make out shafts filled with light. He assumed the shafts reached the surface.

Looking at the men around him, he was not surprised to find that they looked like the stone giants outside; what was surprising was that all of them were quite short, none taller than five feet, the shortest he guessed at four feet nine inches. They were armed with what seemed to be small swords reminiscent of the old Imperial design: single-edged falchions.

The corridor went on, they made several turns. Gradually the excitement in his blood vanished, and he found that he was very tired and increasingly out of breath. He finally stumbled and sat down, deliberately, to see what they would do. His guards spoke in their own language, which sounded a bit like birds chirping, and then one gave him some water from a flask he carried on his belt. Another guard offered him a piece of salted, dried meat. The soldiers relaxed their grip on his arms. Perhaps they thought he could not make his way back through the maze of passages they had taken, which was certainly true.

Basil considered staying where he was and demanding to be released, but there were many, and as they had not harmed him yet, his curiosity won out. So he let them guide him onward. After another hour, they reached an area where people lived. First, he smelled burning wood and cooking. Later, the sounds of people walking and talking were audible. His stomach rumbled, and a different guard fished out a tuber from a bag at his belt and offered it to Basil.

Basil took it. The tuber smelled a bit like a potato, so he tried a bite. It tasted like a radish, with a sharp, sudden flavor. He ate the whole thing and thanked the man.

The corridor entered a large and low-ceilinged room, its far wall blazing with light. Basil's eyes soon adjusted to the light, and he saw that the far wall looked out over a snow field that rapidly sloped away and out of view. Miles off were more snowy mountains.

He was conducted up a wide stairway. Other people came into view and when they noticed him, they stopped and stood silently. A few seemed to be female, and they were all bald. His guards now carried themselves differently; Basil suspected that their superior officers, maybe even their ruler, were up ahead.

At the top of the stairs he was shown into a washroom with a basin of chilly water. The basin could easily be filled with more water by a faucet with an elegant lever. Such water systems were becoming common in Seopolis, at least for the lesser nobility. Basil washed away the bits of dried blood on his face and arms and then rejoined his escort.

The room they now entered was smaller than the first room he'd seen, but the ceiling was taller, and the windows looking out over the high mountains were of astonishing clarity and great size, with pieces of glass that were much larger and clearer than any Basil had ever seen before. His escort showed him to one of the chairs, which was made of carved wood, the seat covered in white wool. Then they waited. Basil looked at the peaks and valleys outside the glass wall. He knew from the direction of the late afternoon sun that the room looked west, and looming over the lesser hills he saw the giant cone of Mount Pandion, some hundred miles away.

A new group of richly dressed men and women came up the stairs. One man, wearing a medallion like the one on the final statue, sat on a large chair that was on a dais two steps above the floor. The others took chairs along the wall.

An old man to the left of the "king" spoke, and then one of the guards spoke, and then there was a general discussion. Basil was feeling very tired and lightheaded, and he stopped paying attention after ten minutes.

Why couldn't they have collected Sandun? he thought to himself. *I am no diplomat. Sir Ako or even Kagne would be better suited for this task. And how am I even going to communicate with these Piksies?*

For surely that was what these people were. Like all natives of Kelten, Basil had been raised on stories of the little people who lived in the land when the first explorers came over the deep sea from the Archipelago. In the stories, the Piksies were mischievous, small, and very knowledgeable about the land. A few places, such as Lake Tricon, had names that supposedly were given by the little people. They had vanished from Kelten soon after the settlers arrived, more than a thousand years ago, long before the Kingdom of Kelten was founded.

Basil did not doubt that these little people sitting and talking in front of him were related to the same Piksies from the children's stories. He smiled and shook his head; it was a wonder to be in the presence of creatures of fable.

At a signal from the "king," an older man with thinning hair stood up and approached Basil. He had a tablet and chalk, and he wrote out, "What name?" He held the tablet and the chalk to Basil.

This came as a relief to Basil; he instantly felt a warm rush of affection for the old man. To think that after all this time there was still someone who had bothered to learn Kelten writing!

He wrote, "Basil Vono" on the black slate and then said it aloud.

"Why here?" wrote the man.

Basil wrote as simply as he could: "Seek road to Serica."

The man consulted an old book and found a word; he said what sounded like, *Sah-rice.* "Where from?" wrote the man.

Basil wrote, "Kelten." He said it out loud, looking around the room, wondering if they would recognize the name.

At the name *Kelten*, all the Piksies stirred and looked at him with a strange expression on their faces.

The translator smiled at him, but after some comments from the "king," he wrote, "Draw map Kelten?"

Basil was happy to oblige, and he quickly drew out the coast and the rivers and lakes. His drawing was then passed around to everyone in the room. By this point, the sun was setting, and the room was filled with reddish light. Servants appeared, bearing ornate silver goblets filled with a yellow drink. A glass was offered to Basil, and he accepted it. It tasted like mead, which was now rarely made in Kelten. Platters covered with tiny disks of seared meat were brought around to everyone. It was young goat, Basil thought, and delicious. The mead went right to his head, and he felt as though he had drunk four glasses of wine in a row.

Somehow the guards had his farseer glass in their hands. The old man wrote, "Look?" on the tablet. Basil waved his hand in agreement and ate more of the roasted goat.

All of the Piksies were fascinated by the farseer glass. The technology had been invented in Melnehlan about fifteen years ago, but the knowledge spread through the Archipelago with astonishing speed. Basil first saw one in King Pandion's rebel army. Now they were commonly used by ship captains, scouts, and hunters like himself, though good ones remained expensive.

It penetrated his befogged mind that the Piksies had never seen a farseer before. And, if they weren't going to just take it from him outright, they might be willing to trade for one. He thought of the story of Rik Witingdon and how the young cabin boy had made his fortune by giving his cat to the King of Ridanos. *If I were a proper diplomat, that is exactly what I would do,* Basil thought. *I would go over and present my glass to their king.*

To his surprise, he found himself doing just that. He walked over to a young Piksie woman who was looking through the glass, and he held his hand out. She, somewhat uncertainly, handed the glass back to him. Then he walked a bit unsteadily to their king and got down on both knees, holding the glass up to their leader.

The king took the glass from Basil and said something to his advisors. There were chuckles from several. The king, a middle-aged Piksie who was looking a bit fat, stood up and smiled at Basil and shook his hand. Basil now was able to see the design on the king's medallion: it was a mountain goat, with curled horns, rearing up on its two back legs.

At a command, Basil was escorted from the chamber and down the stairs to a room off the large hall. The old Piksie with his chalkboard came along half an hour later and inquired, using chalk, if Basil wanted sleep or if he wanted more food and wine. Basil circled the word "sleep," but they brought him corn cakes and water and as well as a bed. Basil fell asleep within seconds.

The next morning, Basil woke with a headache that would not go away. He suspected mountain sickness as he was near the peak of a tall mountain and the air was exceedingly thin. After a breakfast made of yesterday's goat mixed with millet, the old Piksie translator brought him to a nearby room with a window that looked out over a field dotted with white goats browsing on new grass.

They spent the morning in a struggle of half communication, half flailing around words and concepts. Basil was convinced that almost anyone was better suited for this role than he, and he made an attempt to tell the linguist that he wanted to go back to his friends.

By now he had discovered the translator's name: Ruthal of Gate Town. The people called themselves the Dinmos, a name that seemed oddly suggestive of something, but Basil could not put his finger on what it reminded him of. Their king was called Ekmon, but whether it was a title or his name was unclear.

After lunch, Basil slept for an hour, and then he was awakened by the same group of soldiers. Their armor, which he now paid more attention to, seemed like the armor he had seen on the statue of Saint Hurin in the great temple of Seopolis. He was nearly certain that no one had worn armor like that for a thousand years.

He returned to the hall of the Ekmon. Different Piksies, even a few children, were gathered. The Ekmon summoned Basil to stand before him and then, after a short speech, he signaled Ruthal to come and translate. Ruthal wrote, "Gift accept," and then, "Gift give."

Now, a strange Piksie came forward. With a thrill of fear, Basil felt his hair on his arms prickle. The Piksie looked as though he did not see what everyone else saw. He jerked his head at odd intervals, and he often stared at the floor. As he got close, Basil could hear him humming or perhaps growling. He held a sword and a dagger on a belt and at the Ekmon's command, he put the belt around Basil's waist.

Basil had learned the word for thanks in the Piksie language, and feeling very embarrassed, he tried it out: "A-Shosh-ee."

In turn, Ruthal tried out some Kelten: "Ank-oo."

More untranslated words were said, and then Basil was escorted out of the room. He followed his guards downhill, and they walked for hours, likely following a similar route to the one he had taken the previous day. Ruthal accompanied Basil, and following behind were several porters carrying large packs. From the smell, Basil was confident that the bags contained food.

They did not hurry and stopped to rest at several landings where water was collected in stone, trickling down from above and draining out from a hidden tube at the rear before it overflowed the basin.

With no warning, they reached a vast hall, a cavern that wound its way far back into the depths of the mountain. Only faint illumination came from shafts cut into the high ceiling. Somehow Basil knew the cave had not been used for lifetimes of men. He wondered what purpose this great empty cave served. Was it for marshalling an army? Was it a quarry? Perhaps the cave was natural? But no, the walls had been carved out.

The Piksies paid no attention to the vast empty space. They walked up to the wall, which apparently could be opened. Two groups of soldiers went to large wheels on either side of the cavern door. The sound of metal bars clacking against each other echoed through the cavern, and then they began to turn the wheels. At first there was no sign of movement, and the only sound was of a metal cable rubbing against metal rollers above the cave door, nearly hidden in the gloom.

Then a line as bright as white-hot metal appeared in the center of the door. Gradually the door opened wider and wider. When it was just large enough for the porters with their packs to squeeze through, the soldiers stopped turning the wheels. At a gesture, Basil stepped forward to make his way out of the opening. As he did, he heard faint sounds of surprise and command coming from his friends.

Basil, with a huge grin on his face and joy in his heart, pushed his way through the open gate and waved and shouted at his companions. Sandun and Olef came running up to greet him. His dog ran up and barked twice and then nuzzled his legs. Sir Ako and the rest of the expedition stood around their camp, waiting and ready for a fight.

"Basil Vono, my old friend, I have never been happier to see anyone in my entire life." Sandun shook his hand. Olef came and kissed him on his cheek. "But what is this? Who are these?" Sandun asked as the Piksies came out of the revealed door. The Piksie soldiers stood with their weapons drawn, protecting the porters, who dropped the bags one by one in a line by the cliff face. After bowing to Basil, most returned inside. Lastly, Ruthal came out, blinking in the sunlight and holding his tablet and chalk and his old dictionary.

Although four of the guards stayed outside, the great door began to shut. Slowly the crack closed and then vanished.

Everyone crowded around Basil as he told the whole history of his journey through the city of the Piksies. When Ruthal heard their repeated use of the word *Piksie*, he frowned and said, "Dinmos. Dinmos!"

Basil tried to use the word, but *Piksie* kept slipping out as he described what he had seen.

When he got to the Ekmon's gifts, he drew the knife out. They all looked at it, remarking over its workmanship and testing its edge.

Ruthal wrote emphatically on his slate board: "stone cut."

He then gently took the knife from Basil's hand and went over to a rock lying half buried in the ground. He pressed the knife blade firmly against the rock and slowly, the knife blade moved down and cut the rock into two pieces.

Everyone stood and stared with their mouths hanging open. Ruthal looked around at them and started to laugh. He laughed till tears streamed down his face, and soon everyone had to join in.

Basil used the knife to cut at the rock. He thought it was like cutting a piece of hard cheese. You applied a firm pressure, and the rock just parted. There seemed to be an odd sparking coming from the blade in the cut. He passed the knife to the others.

When Damar tried to wiggle the knife back and forth, Ruthal animatedly objected. Shaking his head, he wrote, "Only down," and circled it twice.

"Perhaps it is brittle and only has strength in one direction," Sir Ako proposed. "Swordsmiths can make wonder stone into a blade that holds an edge fine enough to cut hair, but if you strike the flat of the blade on an anvil, it shatters like glass."

Now Basil drew out the sword; it was a medium-length blade, similar to the swords of the Piksie guards, straight but sharpened only on one edge. It had an odd notch near the tip.

Ruthal wrote, "copper cut." He pointed to the dagger in Olef's belt. She drew her dagger and Basil tried shaving a piece of the pommel off. Again, the strange sparking, an odd hum, and the Piksie sword cut through the metal pommel like peeling an apple.

Realizing the value of what he had been given, Basil felt very uncomfortable with the two Piksie gifts. Taking the sheath off the belt, he put the Piksie sword into it and handed it to Sandun, saying, "I don't ever use swords, and as leader of the expedition, I want you to have this. I'll keep the knife, though I imagine it's useless for skinning."

Sandun tried to refuse, but Basil would not budge. Sandun protested that Basil had given away his farseer glass and that the Piksie king had given him the gifts. Basil stood firm.

"I'm giving it to you, Sandun," Basil said. "It was given to me and I'm giving it to you."

Basil took Sandun's farseer in exchange, but all of them knew that the "copper cutter" could be sold at the Seopolis market for the price of a small town, if they ever returned to Seopolis with the blade intact.

Relieved at the return of his friend and thrilled at the gift of the Piksie sword, Sandun formally drew the sword out. Holding it aloft, he said "I name this sword 'Skathris,' which comes from the ancient language of Pella."

Sir Ako nodded. "That's an odd weapon you have. I'll have to train you so you can use it properly."

Basil introduced Ruthal to Sandun and explained that he had difficulty in communications. Sandun and Ruthal sat down together in a shadow close to the cliff-door. Soon they were engaged in a dialog as the chalk dust blew about them. Basil and Kagne sat close by, watching intently and offering suggestions. The others went to inspect the packs, which indeed contained food.

Sandun asked about the sword and dagger, "How made?"

Ruthal wrote, "stone singer." Seeing Sandun's incomprehension, he continued and wrote, "piksie magic." Then he laughed at his own joke and erased the words.

Sandun next asked about the stone giants. Ruthal looked up at the first giant, pointed at its face, and wrote, "old ekmon." Then he wrote, "stone singer" followed by, "40 years." Then he pointed at the sun in the sky and wrote, "187 years."

Sandun wrote, "Why?"

But Ruthal could not explain; he spent fifteen minutes poring through his dictionary and finally came up with the words: "lake temple."

The sun was dipping behind the western hills, and one of the Piksie soldiers came up and said something to Ruthal, who then nodded his head.

Using the chalk and some halting words, Ruthal explained that if they returned from Serica, they should stop by this place and that he would like to join them on their road back to Kelten. Sandun agreed at once but then wrote, "Why?"

"Kelten, ancient home – many songs – beautiful sea – beautiful river." Ruthal then wrote, "see before die"

He looked at Sandun with such an expression of longing that Sandun himself felt the stirring of homesickness in his soul. It was as though Sandun was sitting in Ruthal's clothing, gazing at a man who came from the mythical land of the blue ocean with its mighty surf and the quiet rivers that flowed peacefully through the great valley, only to return to his own shoes and realize that he was that man. His home was like a dream to other people, just as Serica was a dreamland for the people of Kelten.

"We will come back this way. Look for us next summer or the summer after."

With that, Ruthal got up. They shook hands, and everyone came to bid the old Piksie farewell. Basil picked Ruthal up off the ground and hugged him. "A-Shosh-ee, Ruthal," he said. "Till we meet again, with Sho'Ash's blessing."

The Piksie guards somehow got the attention of the others on the inside, and the gate opened again, very slowly.

Ruthal was about to go inside the stone door when a look of panic crossed his face. He hurriedly got down on his hands and knees and wrote, "dead city ghosts danger" on his tablet.

He showed this to Basil and Sandun and pointed east. With this ominous warning, he vanished inside the door, which then closed shut, leaving them alone before the gate.

The next morning, while they were rearranging their packs with the new food they had been given, they heard the sound of cow bells, as though they were back at Lake Tricon. Soon, five wooly goats appeared with empty packs slung across their backs. One Piksie, leading the rams, bowed to them and then vanished up the canyon from whence he had come.

Basil and Sandun did not doubt that this was the doing of Ruthal, and everyone was filled with gratitude toward the Piksies.

"I can die happy, now that I have lived long enough to see a Piksie giving me gifts," Kagne said.

Everyone knew what he meant. In the children's stories that the Keltens told, the Piksies usually took things and then disappeared into the wilderness, waving the items over their heads, chortling with laughter.

They loaded all the food onto the goats, who proved to be very docile creatures. No one in Kelten had used goats as beasts of burden for many years. Goats could not carry as much as mules, and their wool made them unsuited for the warm summer months in the great valley. However, within a few days, everyone had come to appreciate the woolly animals' gentle nature.

Sandun thought that since the goats were always following the expedition and not going out of sight to graze for days at a time, he would take off their bells. Also, it was impossible to imagine they were traveling secretly with a band of musical mountain goats following along behind. But when he took off their bells, the goats stood there with such mournful expressions in their eyes that he relented and put them back on. They brightened up immediately, and after a day Sandun simply didn't hear the tonking sound of the bells.

The expedition now set out north and west, hugging the northern side of the valley, looking for the path that would take them up and out of the valley of the giants. As they expected, the line of stone giants reached into the lake in the middle of the valley. Three giants were partially submerged and a fourth was almost completely underwater. They had been keeping count of the giants and had reached thirty-nine.

"I bet there are forty of these," said Kagne. "The old man said forty."

"He wrote that and then wrote 187 years," Sandun corrected him.

"Maybe they built one every year for forty years? If you had several oversized stone cutters like Basil's Piksie knife, I wager you could make a new giant every year."

"That sounds reasonable," Sandun replied.

Kagne smiled; it wasn't often that he came up with a theory that Sandun hadn't already thought of.

"And what do you suppose 187 years means?"

"I don't know. Maybe it's been that long since the start of the giant project or perhaps its end." Kagne offered this suggestion, but further speculation was useless.

They found the trail out of the valley and followed it up to the high meadows. The snows had all melted, as it was now the middle of summer. When he wrote the log that evening, Sandun was surprised to discover that the expedition had been on the road for five months. Snow would start falling in another four months or perhaps sooner. How far had they come? Basil and Kagne were the best judges of distance traveled; they would argue over half-mile estimates at the end of most days. The expedition seemed to be inching its way along the map, but progress was steady.

The trail was becoming easier to follow. Farrel claimed this part of the trail had been used as recently as fifty years ago. Damar disagreed and put it closer to a century. Still, every time they found another trail marker, it lifted their spirits. They weren't lost in the vast Tiralas; they were following a trail heading east, to Serica.

For several days, the trail took them up and down over some ridges that ran north to south. Finally, the route headed due south up a steep-sided canyon with a swift-rushing stream in the middle. When they reached the top, they found they were on gently rolling land with thick forests and curiously regular grassy fields between the bands of trees.

Then they discovered tree stumps in some of the fields. Unmistakable evidence of human activity, but from long ago.

At this point, Sandun did take the bells off the rams, and it was a silent and watchful group that traveled along the edge of the fields.

The sky, which had started clear in the morning, was now overcast and threatening rain. The only sound was the wind through the needles of the pine trees. When they halted for lunch, Sandun took out Jon of Stenston's map and noted that they were likely near another of the curious marks.

"I hope it is not the city of the dead that Ruthal warned us against," Basil said as he looked over Sandun's shoulder at the map.

"Long-abandoned fields, no sight or smell of people living; whatever made you think we might be coming near to a dead city?"

"I can read the signs as well as any man, and I say no one has lived here for a hundred years."

They were following the remains of an old road through another stand of trees. The road straightened out, and now they could see a gray lake ahead. Exiting the forest, they found the lake to be quite large; the road bent southward, staying close to the shore.

They passed to the right of several ruined houses partially concealed in some trees. As they reached the top of a low hill, they could see the length of the lake and, close to the foot of the hill, the remains of a ruined city.

They all sank low to the ground, and the scouts looked in all directions. Basil handed the farseer glass to Sandun after he had used it for several minutes. "Nothing human lives down there," he said.

The town's wooden buildings had all been destroyed by fire, leaving only remains. The larger stone structures were surrounded by piles of rubble. Sandun could barely make out traces of soot on some of the stone walls that were still standing.

Sandun had seen burned castles before, and fire had laid waste to the eastern half of Huripolis three years past, but the magnitude of this destruction left him feeling depressed. So much effort undone. So many lives and stories cut short. A few cities had reportedly been destroyed in the lands of the Archipelago over recorded history, usually the work of earthquakes or floods, but the temple did its best to keep the destruction of war to a minimum. Kelten, Issedon, and Fiodroch had captured each other's towns and even cities upon occasion, but rarely had any towns been leveled.

He did not doubt that something terrible had happened here; this was no natural disaster. Most likely the town had been destroyed and all the inhabitants either killed or carried away as slaves. They all felt the same: no one wanted to go near the ruins. So they skirted wide around the town, staying close to the forest edge. In one field they saw human skulls protruding from the soil. Perhaps a group of townsfolk had been gathered here by the unknown assailants and executed. None of the expedition wanted to find out more.

By the evening, they were a mile south of the last buildings of the ruined town. Little was said by the fire that night save for speculation as to the identity of the attackers and the people who'd once lived here.

After midnight, Sandun woke to the howling of a dog. Basil's dog never howled and yet now it was howling, a low, mournful wail, a long call into the silent night. The fire had gone out, but to the north, a faint glow came from the ruined city. Sir Ako was up and looking through his glass at the town. A wave of fear swept over Sandun. "What do you see? What do you see?"

Sir Ako's voice was choked and strained. "The dead walk. Ghosts are coming out from the ruined city."

Hundreds of pale, faintly blue translucent shapes were bearing down on them. The land before them seemed to glow as they passed over it.

"Get the fire going, for the love of Sho'Ash," Sandun spoke in a daze. But as he watched the ghosts advance upon them, there was nothing but grunting and curses behind him. The coals were as cold as stone, and no spark would catch on the tinder. Now the ghosts were halfway across the empty field. Each was in the shape of a person, some short, some tall. Although they moved, they seemed to be drifting like wisps of glowing fog.

"We must flee!" cried Wiyat.

"No," Sandun said in what seemed to him a quavering voice. "No ghost in Kelten ever harmed a person who stood their ground."

"So certain, are you?" Sir Ako said. "We aren't in Kelten anymore."

"I'm certain."

Ever since Ruthal's hasty parting words, Sandun had been thinking about what they should do if they did encounter the city of the dead. There were a number of haunted houses in Kelten, and people in Seopolis commonly reported seeing a ghost wandering the execution grounds south of the city. But while the ghosts had often been terrifying, people had only been injured when they panicked and ran away in blind fear.

Now that he was staring with his own eyes at an army of ghosts, fear and panic threatened to rise over his mind and send him screaming away into the black forest behind them. But the coldly rational part of his mind refused to surrender. He put down his fear and walked out from the camp to meet the dead head on. Kagne joined him. Sandun looked at him; his face was lit by the pale-blue light.

"I don't believe in ghosts," Kagne said.

Sandun was too anxious to respond. Instead he found himself repeating under his breath the credo of the Archive: "The greatest minds have passed away. The greatest kings are buried in tombs. We preserve the memory of the past so that their efforts shall not be wasted."

Now the ghosts were almost upon them. He could see they were in pain, some screaming soundlessly, others twisting and jerking as if they were suffering their death agonies over and over. Some had no heads. Many seemed to be burning.

Behind Sandun, Basil was comforting his dog, and Sir Ako was going from scout to scout, telling them to be brave.

The first ghost came right to Sandun. It stared right through him with no recognition, no hint of comprehension in its eyes.

Although he could have stepped aside, he put his hands out and quietly said, "Begone."

The sensation of touching the ghost was unlike any Sandun had ever felt before. His hands felt as if they were touching something and then nothing, and so fast was the transition it was almost beyond his ability to understand. And the ghost vanished.

Kagne put his hands out to ward off a ghost, and it vanished as well.

Seeing this drastic result, Sir Ako and Basil came over and stood beside them. One by one, the others stood up and came over, standing shoulder to shoulder, holding out their right hands, silently rebuking the unquiet spirits.

Sandun couldn't say how long they stood there. He didn't feel tired, no one talked, and the ghosts came on and on by the thousand only to vanish without sound on the hands of the living.

At the end, there were simply no more ghosts on the field. The night was old, but no sign of the sun was on the eastern horizon.

Sandun stumbled back to his blanket and fell into a deep sleep. He did not wake until the sun was high in the sky. When he woke, one of the rams had pulled its tether stake out of the ground and was licking Sandun's face.

"Let us leave this accursed place," Sir Ako said. On that, no one disagreed. They pushed hard that day and were twenty-five miles south and east of the ruined city when they finally halted for the night.

That evening, Sir Ako led them all in the simple service of prayers. Everyone gathered in a circle, heads bowed, as Sir Ako read the prayers and they repeated after him. Sandun found it hard to retain his composure, but he mastered his emotions and thanked Sir Ako afterward.

In later years, the expedition members would sometimes gather and reminisce about their adventures, but they almost never talked about the city of the dead. Other travelers doubtless returned to the lakeshore, following the old route, but if they met with an army of ghosts, no rumor of it came to Kelten.

Four weeks passed as the expedition made its way across and between more snowcapped peaks. Unlike the clearly defined ridges of the Kelten Alps or the first range of the Tiralas, the peaks in this area were usually isolated, independent from each other. The trail lazily curved around the peaks, going up a bit and then going back down again, offering less challenge than crossing the hills east of Tebispoli.

The lack of physical challenge did not prevent the group from fraying and bickering over ever-more-insignificant issues. Basil and his hunters barely spoke to Kagne and his group of plant finders. Kagne had introduced his team to his seemingly endless supply of dream weed. This made for tense hours during the daily march when he and the "Rooters" would be laughing at the most trifling things while the others most definitely did not share the joke.

By now, Sir Ako and Sandun were coleaders, with Basil as the unquestioned master of meat and Kagne the master of vegetables. All things considered, the expedition was working well, but the strain of daily travel had forced Sandun to call for a day's rest every five days instead of the usual rest on every seventh day that they had maintained for months until the city of the dead. Part of the reason, in addition to the wear on bone and feet, mind and soul, was that the land was less suited for human travel.

The land was dryer than the area around the dead city. The trees were shorter and more sparse. Less cover meant fewer deer or mountain goats. Streams were less frequently found and naturally, plants that humans could eat were harder to find beside the waters.

And still the land remained empty of humans. When they did find the occasional building, it was in ruins from age or burning. Whoever had cleared this land of its former inhabitants had done so with ruthless and determined efficiency.

Once in the hills far south of the trail they saw smoke, but it was most likely the remains of a recent forest fire. As the summer heat wrapped its arms around the earth, forest fires started easily. Lightning blasts a dead tree one time out of a hundred, starting a blaze that sets a mountain afire. Everyone in Kelten, even in Seopolis at the sea's edge, knew the sight and smell of it. All towns were surrounded by fields and cleared acres. The towns that failed to keep the practice paid a dear price.

Another time, far to the north, they spied a cloud of dust, without doubt made by riders moving with some haste. The team halted and deployed as for battle, but soon Basil reported the riders were heading due north.

"What could you see?" Sandun asked.

Basil was thoughtful and slow to answer. "I deem that a creature like a shaggy bull was being ridden. But I've not heard of such a thing before."

Sir Ako replied, "I have. Part of the training when command of a hundred was given me. A day with the minister of war and his staff at the armory in Huripolis. At least some of the Sogand tribes ride an animal called a buffalo, which looks very like a shaggy bull." He paused. "We need to be more careful. I made out that group as near fifty strong based on the dust they stirred. I do not like our chances against fifty mounted Sogand warriors."

No one thought his fears unfounded. Although Sogands had never crossed Kelten's borders, their raids had destroyed many towns of eastern Issedon. Thessagon, farther north, had been reduced to a third of its size from the time of the empire's height; some ambassadors reported that Thessagon had lost all lands fifty miles east of the sea. What remained was a string of grimly defended walled cities. The losses had not improved their people's dispositions toward Kelten, though, for reasons that remained as cloudy as the forest-cloaked coast of Thessagon.

In the reign of King Maklinos, the Kelten army had gone north to fight the Sogands in Issedon, led by the murderous Ors Divar. Kelten arms had, of course, carried the day. Kelten archers outranged anything the Sogands carried. Sogand efforts to trick the Kelten army by feigning retreat were ignored. Finally, a massed charge met with bloody defeat as the screaming Sogand horsemen ran into wooden stakes and unbreakable Kelten knights standing shoulder to shoulder in front of the archers.

Maklinos the Great went on from that victory to conquer most of Fiodroch—a glorious time in Kelten's history, but long years gone.

Here, in the middle of the empty lands, their band would be poor sport for fifty mounted Sogands, even if the buffalo were not as agile as horses. For the next week, they traveled slowly and with more care to leave no trace of their passage.

The Piksie goats continued to rise in everyone's estimation. Their hoofmarks and the scat they dropped were native to the land, and they were as quiet as mice when their bells were taken off them. They seemed to have learned something about their new owners; this time there were no sad looks from the animals as Sandun and Kagne packed their bells away.

One evening, after his sword practice with Sir Ako, Sandun broached the idea of trading weapons.

"You are much better with a sword and shield than I will ever be. You should use Skathris until we return to Kelten." Sandun made the offer with Skathris's blade wrapped in a long rag.

Sir Ako waved his wooden practice blade in the air and smiled. "A kind offer, but no. My fine blade is a beautiful weapon, but it's just a weapon. I'll tell you a secret I learned many years ago when I was a squire."

He came and sat down on a fallen tree. They were camped inside a forest that was thick for this part of the Tiralas, half a mile off the trail. "Sir Killis—the bastard, I called him, though only in my mind. He trained me from when I was ten till I earned my knight's sword at seventeen. Looking back on it with the passage of years, I still hate him for his cruel buffets, his mean remarks. Here I was, an earl's son, being treated in such a fashion. Oh, I burned, Sandun. Every night for years I seethed with hatred.

"Anyway, he taught me this: the true knight fights and wins with whatever he has. Whatever he has! A knight wins with a blow to the face with a mailed fist. Or with a swift kick to his enemy's groin. Or by tripping, or throwing sand in his eyes. A knight wins by using a dagger through the armpit, or a mace to the back of a helm, or an axe splitting the enemy's shield. Or with a bowshot from atop a castle wall. And yes, a knight wins when—dressed in full plate armor—he charges out into the night with a sword in one hand and a shield in the other. All of this and more. A knight trains body and soul for battle every day of his life, until he is too old to swing a sword for two hours solid, and then he can train a squire of his own."

Sir Ako leaned back and looked up into the sky. A few clouds were fading into darkness; Ares and Zeus were already visible in the heavens.

"I won the melee held in Agnefeld when I was nineteen. Already two years a knight. Quite young for a champion, I thought. My father comes up, slaps me on the shoulder, and then goes over to old Sir Killis and he tries to take his hand and shouts for all the world to hear, 'You did it! You trained him well, you old bastard!' And Sir Killis stands there, very uncomfortable, and then finally takes my father's hand, and then he walks away."

At this, Sir Ako stated to laugh, and he kept on laughing till tears ran down his face. Everyone but the guards on duty came over, but Sir Ako simply continued the story.

"So, that evening, I learn from Baron Barstown, one of father's oldest friends, that my father and Sir Killis have held a grudge for years. Years! Tree-cutting property dispute, some such. However, ten years ago, my father asked a few of his barons who might be the best man to train a knight, meaning me. Barstown, and perhaps others, 'suggested' Killis. And that is why I spent seven years with that cold, dour man and his unsmiling, penny-pinching wife and his children. And yet withal, a master of the art of polemarchy."

Everyone waited in silence to see if Sir Ako would continue. As a rule, commoners in Kelten knew nothing about being a squire; it was not talked about. They knew the legend of Sir Garris, who spent years as a kitchen scullion but was so strong he defeated a knight using just a stick and so saved Queen Wen the Fair. But that was just a fairy tale from the age of the Lake King.

Ordinary people saw squires at tournaments and at court: silent, anonymous, wearing their master's coat of arms. Knights never talked about the time before they were knights. Instead, they seemed to spring full grown out of green grass, tall young men, striding up before a packed crowd, now kneeling, now being dubbed a knight and then given a ceremonial shield with a new coat of arms.

All we see, thought Sandun, *is the glory, the lines of men in burnished armor, their flags flying behind them as they wait for the opening day of the yearly grand tournament in Huripolis. The bravest and finest warriors in the whole of the*

Archipelago, defenders of the realm. We never see the years of struggle, of loneliness, of pain and humiliation. Perhaps not seeing family more than once a year for High Holy Week? The method of training a future knight seemed strange to Sandun, but it worked and had done so for centuries.

Sandun asked, "Did you ever get any satisfaction against Sir Killis?"

"I beat him once: single duel, blunted two-handed swords, first to yield. Three years gone. He stood up, bowed briefly, and said, 'Well fought, Sir Knight,' and then limped off the field. I'll tell one last thing, and then I'm for bed. A knight lives by the Philosopher's Golden Mean in anger, as in other things."

Sir Ako then quoted the famous maxim: "*All virtue lies between evil extremes.*" He continued, "Anger is a virtue. We hone it like a blade; we build it up and keep it burning throughout a fight. A fighter without anger hits weakly, moves slowly, thinks instead of acts. A warrior blinded by rage leaves openings in his attacks for deadly ripostes, or he strikes too hard and leaves his weapon wedged in the other man's shield. Or, worst of all, he charges too deep into enemy lines and is stabbed in the back by some serf with a sharp stick."

Sir Ako concluded, "A true knight teaches his squires the virtue of anger and how to wield it." He looked at them all with an unreadable expression. "Now, go to sleep."

PART FOUR

Gipu

baligmon, the ninth month, was waning, and they were still several hundred miles from the border of Serica. Summer was pulling up stakes from the Tiralas, and the nights were chilly. Food was holding up well enough, though salt was beginning to be a worry. No doubt when people had lived in this land, they had located salt outcrops and were happy to trade salt to travelers in exchange for a few coins. But the expedition had no time to search for salt, and unless they blindly stumbled upon a salt lick, they were just going to have to make do with their dwindling supplies.

For several days they had been approaching a great range of mountains directly east of them, across another high valley filled with bunch grass and deer brush. The far range of hills seemed unusually green and then, in the still, early morning air, Basil said he could see smoke rising from several different locations.

This occasioned lots of speculation and opinion. Sandun got out the map and again, there was an indication of something at roughly the location Basil indicated. "The fact that there are multiple smoke fires indicates that whoever they are, they aren't afraid of raiders."

Everyone wanted to see someone new. They were all profoundly lonely, though Sandun would have denied it at the time.

So with hope held aloft by threads as thin as gossamer, they pushed on.

Marks on the trail and on hills gave further proof of human habitation. Fenced pasture fields, stones placed in streams to make them easy to cross, lean-to wooden shelters—all of these and more gave proof of active human life. Their spirits rose throughout the day.

"We are being watched," said Basil that afternoon. He pointed toward some trees to the north.

Olef agreed. "And to the south," she said. "They are keeping their distance, but they act like they don't care if we know that they know."

"How big is the town?" Sandun asked Sir Ako, who was studying the air and the hills.

"Big. The haze reminds me of Tricon. I'd say at least ten thousand. Is this not Serica?"

"No," Sandun replied. "Serica is reported to end at the east edge of a great range of mountains, just as Erimasran ends at the western slopes of the Tiralas."

"The Tiralas must be horrific in the winter. All the endless miles of land we have walked, but in wintertime, shrouded with a blanket of snow." Sir Ako put away his farseer glass. "To speak plainly, Sandun, we need rest. We have been going at an incredible pace for months. We need at least a month to recover, and that puts us into Dyusmon. If the people here are friendly, we should consider staying through the winter."

Sandun thought about that idea for the rest of day, playing out different times and routes in his mind. He had hoped to get out of the Tiralas before winter. But really, what time pressure was on them? They weren't expected back for three years. Sho'Ash knew they could all use rest. Though Sandun refused to complain, his feet pained him more and more each day. Kagne had twisted an ankle on a slippery rock while crossing a stream and had been manfully limping along ever since. Everyone was nursing some ailment, though so far, nothing had been serious enough to halt them for more than two days. But how much longer would their luck hold out?

That evening, Basil said they would reach the mountain town by the afternoon of the next day.

In the morning, they cleaned up more than usual. Sandun had to admit that they all looked more like savages from Issedon than soldiers of Kelten. Still, without knowing more about the inhabitants of the city, it made little sense to dress their best, especially if they were just going to try and kill you.

Sir Ako put out a line of scouts: Padan and Olef to the left side of the trail, Farrel and Damar to the right, and the rest walked along the path in single file. Sir Ako led the way with Gloval taking up the rear. The track was lined on both sides with tall pine trees, and it meandered between stony outcroppings and empty pastures.

By three in the afternoon, they could see the city. It had encircling walls, at least twenty feet tall, with high and, to their eyes, unusual square towers spanning the walls every quarter of a mile.

People were coming out of the gates and lining the road, apparently to greet them. Small boys ran up toward them and then turned and ran back down the road. There were lots of bright colors, and a large flag flew from the gate tower. Basil said it was a blue turtle; Sir Ako thought it was a black raven on a field of blue. Then he ordered the scouts in, and so the expedition walked the final mile as a tight group, gazing in wonder at the strange people who had come to see them.

The people of the town were unlike any collection of people Sandun had seen before, mostly dark haired, many short with round faces. Others were very tall and looked somewhat like the largest clansmen of Thessagon. He noticed that brown hair was uncommon and that the true yellow hair was even more rare than in Kelten. A few men, especially older men, wore beards. Many, but not all, had the distinctive ears of the Serice, pointed at the top.

Two groups of soldiers were seen, one to the north and the other to the south of the road. They were armed with tall spears and clad in thick-look-ing armor—padded leather perhaps. The soldiers didn't seem to be worried or nervous, and this made the Kelten expedition more relaxed.

As they approached the gate, the crowd following along, they found themselves in a huge circle of people facing those who were apparently the city leaders: an assembly of some twenty men and two women dressed in very colorful garb, with lots of blues and pinks and some red accents—fine clothing, well fitted.

The man who was most important, judging by his bearing and the elaborate decorations on his robe, stood forth and loudly proclaimed some-thing. He then said what might have been the same thing but in a different language. Sandun stepped forward when there was a slight pause in the lan-guages and said, loudly and clearly, "We are from Kelten. Kelten." He turned and pointed due west. Then he saluted in the traditional Kelten fashion by slapping his left shoulder and holding his right hand toward them, palm out.

As he'd hoped, the word "Kelten" was known to at least some of the people in the group. An older man with a yellow hat was brought forward from behind the dignitaries, and he held his hands out, trying to quiet the crowd. When he had some semblance of quiet, he said, "Hello. Greetings, Kelten men." His accent was peculiar, with words that were strangely length-ened, but for that, it was intelligible.

Sandun's relief was so vast that he staggered, but Kagne put an arm under his elbow, and he regained his composure.

"Greetings, sir. My name is Master Sandun Eiger. Is this Serica?"

The older man translated Sandun's words to the other people and then replied, "This city name Gipu. To ask. Saying long years since Kelten men come to Gipu. Asking: Why come?"

Sandun loudly said what he hoped would be crowd-pleasing words: "We have come to reopen trade between Kelten and Serica. When we return home, many more traders will follow us." He made great big gestures, trying to act and sound like the important merchants he had heard many times in Seopolis.

The man with the yellow hat translated, and the words had an electric effect on the people around him. Everyone was talking louder and louder; it was like the announcement of the new year or the naming of the champion of the grand melee to the crowd outside the stadium of Seopolis. Words were repeated over and over, people smiled, and then a hidden orchestra of horns and pieces of ringing metal began playing. The man wearing the richest robe came up to Sandun and shook his hand with both of his hands. He was introduced as "Itor." The older man with the yellow hat introduced himself as "Gushi."

Quickly, it was a party. Strong drink was poured into silver cups and passed around to all the members of the expedition. Small dumplings coated with nuts and honey were presented to them on silver platters. Joining a party of ten thousand people after being alone in the hills for six months was such an overwhelming experience that the rest of that day remained a blur of color and movement and sound and taste.

Later, Sandun vividly remembered a small woman, very pretty, hardly dressed in some gauzy red dress, laughing; unexpectedly, she was kissing him, and she tasted like a wine that he had never drunk before, and she felt soft and warm and so wonderfully alive that he thought in one blinding flash, *I have never kissed a woman until now*—which was certainly not true, and yet the memory remained and, in some sense, it *was* true.

After at least an hour in front of the city gates, they were conducted through the narrow streets of Gipu, with children and women hanging out of upstairs windows, waving at them and shaking strips of cloth and laughing. The street opened onto a plaza, also filled with people; everyone was drinking, and the noise was loud. After their months alone in the Tiralas, the sheer noise humans were capable of making in small, crowded streets nearly overwhelmed Sandun. In front of one large building, servants poured out glass after glass of a dark drink to anyone who held a cup or mug to them. The expedition was then led to a large building on the far side of the jammed plaza.

They entered, the doors to the building closed, the roar of the crowd abated, and all at once Sandun could think again. Their translator stood on a chair in the entrance hall and managed to convey the news that they would stay here in the "house of guests." A big feast was being prepared, and they would be going across the street to the "house of rulers" in the evening for a banquet. They were welcome to go back outside and join the "cogmash," which would continue for the rest of the day.

Three of the scouts and Kagne volunteered to go back outside and mingle with the people of Gipu. The rest went to explore the rooms and wash up before the banquet. Upstairs, Sandun and Sir Ako and Basil had a rapid conversation about the city and their situation.

"The walls are well maintained. The guards looked capable," Sir Ako offered.

"The city, from what I could see, is quite dense, more so even than Thalapolis. More than fifteen thousand people, I think." Basil seemed surprised at the density of the housing.

"They appear pleased to see us," Sandun said. "The fact that they have a linguist who has kept some small knowledge of Kelten language after all this time…well, it suggests they live by trade. I can imagine they would like to see the ancient west road revived. If we avoid committing capital offenses, I think we should be fine. I'll try and learn something from their translator, Gushi, before dinner."

Sandun went back down and found Gushi in animated conversation with two other men, Itor and a little man who waved his arms around in circles like a windmill. With patience, Sandun learned Itor's full name: Lord Itor da Laska. The way the people acted toward Lord Itor suggested that he was not the ruler of the town but something equivalent to the Lord Mayor of Seopolis.

Gushi reintroduced himself as "Gushi da Etchana" and the arm-waving man's name as "Ortzi da Gokoet." As to the dispute, Sandun had no clear idea what it was about, and his efforts to learn more were limited to the following words of wisdom: Gipu—city of trade.

The evening's banquet featured music, as well as dancing by eight very attractive young women. The food was small cubes of meat roasted on skewers and dipped in different sauces, some green and spicy, others milk based. The Keltens were encouraged to drink copious amounts of the dark liquor, which Sandun learned was a fortified wine made from pears and tiny apples.

After the meats and steamed vegetables had been eaten, more young women came out and sat beside the members of the expedition. They all said, "Hello," and their names; apparently, they had been coached within the last hour. They smiled and laughed at the men, feeding them more balls of crushed nuts mixed with honey and plying them with drinks.

Olef fended off the girl that was trying to feed Basil, and when the girl realized Olef had a claim on Basil, she got up and went over to Padan's side, shooing away the girl that had been fawning over Padan. There was clearly some sort of pecking order among the women.

Sandun immediately recognized the woman who sat by his side; she was the same small woman who had kissed him in the street earlier that day. Now, in a halting fashion and with many foreign words mixed in, she told him that her name was Ashala, that she was the daughter of Gushi, and she had learned a little Kelten along with other languages from her father.

Sandun was happy. He asked her if she knew the language of Serica. Ashala nodded and spoke several sentences in a different language that Sandun assumed was that of Serica.

A few minutes after Sandun and Ashala retired to his room at the house of guests, a soft tap at the door was followed by a short conversation with a servant outside the room. Ashala brought in a beaten-metal ewer filled with hot water and then a wooden bucket with cool water. She mixed these into a wood tub and invited Sandun to the bath. Sandun lost no time in getting in; opportunities for cleaning on the trip had been few. To Sandun's surprise, Ashala took off all her clothes and washed Sandun from head to foot, getting covered in water and soap as she did so. Her warm, wet body touching his own coupled with the months of isolation from a woman, and it wasn't long before they were in bed together.

The next morning, she was still lying next to him contentedly, like a warm cat. Part of Sandun was quite willing to leave things as they were for a long time, but he worried about the possible reactions of the men of Gipu—especially her father, from whom he hoped to learn as much as possible in the coming days.

"Don't you have to leave?" he asked her.

Ashala thought about this with half-closed eyes and then pulled herself closer to him. "No," she said. "We two, together now. You stay."

Sandun had read about some odd marriage customs in other lands such as Thessagon, where women picked their husbands, but this seemed an unlikely turn of events.

"We are going to Serica. I am going to Serica, not staying in Gipu."

"Hmmm, yes, later. But now you stay, and now I your wife. I...learn Kelten speak, you learn Gipu and Serica speak. All happy. Is our...way? Path?" She held her arms out as though she was holding the city between her splayed fingers.

"Do I have a choice? Suppose I like a different woman?" Sandun was teasing her but curious to see what she would say.

Ashala sat up; her long black hair tumbled down in a wave reaching her bare breasts. "I best woman. Know Kelten better all others. I choose you, you choose me. You like another woman better, you sad." Then she smiled at him and said, "We two, good two. No lie."

That much, thought Sandun, was undeniable.

Nothing outside of bed was done that day. As the sun set, the expedition gathered for their evening meal in the large common room on the ground floor. Sandun was not surprised to see that each man had a young woman sitting next to him, serving him tea and food—except for Basil. Olef seemed unusually solicitous toward Basil; the competition was forcing her to play a different role, for a while at least.

The dramatic arrival in the town the previous day and the sudden addition of the young women had changed the relationships between the expedition members. The conversation was just small talk and overeager praise for the food and drink. They tried to sing one of their after-dinner songs as they always had on the trip, but it seemed awkward with the women there, so they stopped after the first verse.

Sandun also observed the way the women behaved. They seemed quite comfortable with the situation, and Sandun soon concluded that for many of them, this was normal. He resolved to ask about the city and other traders later.

Ashala said little, but it was clear she was listening intently. Sandun subtly drew attention to Ashala's language skills, so the others were made aware that at least some of what they said was not a secret.

Sir Ako was unusually curt and ill tempered for the next several days; he complained about the smell of the city and dust in the air, all of which was very out of character as he rarely complained about anything. Later in the week, Sir Ako, Kagne, and all the scouts save Wiyat and Olef came down with colds. Sandun was blessed with an iron constitution, and he almost never fell ill. The airs of Gipu held no powers of sickness over him.

Seeing that men were taken care of by their women, Sandun spent happy days wandering the city with Ashala, relaxing in this unexpected haven at the edge of the Tiralas. Indeed, he was very blithe. Gipu was strange, interesting, unexpected, and seemingly not very threatening. Ashala gave every indication of being happy to be with him and to act as a guide, teacher, student, and lover.

Occasionally, Basil and Olef joined them when Sandun and Ashala went out into the city. Olef had let her hair grow longer since midsummer, and in Gipu she started wearing colorful blouses, which she bought at the market near their lodgings. She and Basil stayed in the same room, and their relationship seemed to blossom now that they could have some privacy.

Sir Ako had a new woman by the end of the first week; her name was Eria. She was taller and prettier than the first woman who had picked Sir Ako on the night they arrived. Eria wore her hair somewhat like Sir Ako's wife used to do when she was living at the palace in Seopolis.

What went on behind closed doors with regard to the young women of Gipu who were now sleeping with the men of the Kelten expedition was just not talked about—by anyone. Set against the moral standards of Kelten, what they were doing was, to a degree, sinful. Simply paying a whore for "a bit o' fun" was not a crime in most Kelten cities, but living with a woman without marrying her was a sin, and the temple would force couples who started living together to marry. Sir Ako, married to a noble's daughter, was deeper in sin than the others. It was much the easiest solution for all of them to pretend that what was happening was not actually happening.

In any event, Sir Ako's new woman was very agreeable to him, and he was soon back to his old self, practicing fighting exercises in the courtyard every day for hours at a time while Eria gossiped with the other women or did needlework. All the women, except Ashala, sewed, decorating hats and gloves and shirt sleeves with small glass beads and tiny disks of copper.

After three weeks of delightful fall weather, the snow fell, sweeping across the land and making travel even inside the city rather treacherous. Training was the only thing left, and soon all the scouts took up the military exercises, joined usually by Basil, Kagne, and Sandun. At Sir Ako's request,

Sandun found space for an indoor archery range that doubled as a training hall. Every day, Sir Ako would lead the expedition members through the city to the hall. This attracted the notice of some men from Gipu's guard. A few of the bravest Gipu soldiers came and joined them in mock combat with wooden weapons. But their fundamental assumptions about hand-to-hand combat were so very different from Kelten military style that it was hard to manage even solo bouts.

Sandun spent a few days trying to learn about Gipu. He learned that Gipu was one of three trading cities that existed in the Tirala Mountains, roughly on a north–south line. The trading cities survived because merchants in caravans routinely traveled from Serica to the trade cities and onward, both north and south and even southwest to a city of the "little people" known as the Orenik. In addition to goods that they created and sold to the merchants, the people of Gipu found gold in mountain streams, and copper was mined in the hills around the city.

Regarding the history of Gipu, Sandun learned little, as both Ashala and Gushi would turn most questions about the city into a diatribe about how one clan or another had been working to subvert the efforts of "the good people." Sandun wondered if the town's history was really nothing more than internecine rivalries between different families. It seemed so, and lacking any interest in how clan Ordoke had outmaneuvered clan Gokoet thirty years ago, Sandun gave up.

Instead, Sandun shifted his efforts to a more pressing matter: namely, what was happening in Serica. Here also he was disappointed with the fragmentary knowledge possessed by both Ashala and her father. This much was known: eighty-five years ago, a fierce tribe of "warriors from the north" called the Kitran defeated the last King of Serica. Their leader was called Tolu Tem, and after his conquest of Serica, he was called Emperor Tolu of the Kitran Empire.

"All cities acknowledged Emperor Tolu," Ashala told Sandun. "Fantu'veri, Hotan, even Gipu paid him great treasure to end siege and destruction. After Tolu's death, sixty or seventy years past, life in Serica has turned from bad to very bad. Floods, famines, and plagues. Happily, Gipu left alone. Stopped paying tribute and ignored." She smiled at him.

"And what about now, in Serica?" Sandun asked.

Ashala stood up. They were in one of the unoccupied rooms on the third floor, which they had started using as a school room. She stretched her arms up and spun around in a circle. She looked over at him, a sly smile on her face.

"Do not know," she said. "Very confusing. Merchants from north province Zelkat say 'fighting and revolution.' Merchants from central province of Kunhalvar say, 'peaceful and good weather.' Then other merchants from southern province of Vasvar tell stories about many kings in Serica appear like lightning and Kitran soldiers all gone. If Kitran gone, is good, yes? Back to old days of peace, maybe?"

Sandun nodded. Sir Ako and Basil agreed that the Kitran must be one of the Sogand tribes. That the Sogands were divided internally into great tribes the size of nations was well known in the Archipelago. The Keltens didn't care what their names were, as it was believed that they were all equally followers of the Black Terror and thus accursed.

The next day, Sandun and Ashala went to visit her father, who lived just a few streets west of the guest house. Gushi had a bit more knowledge to add. He unrolled his map of Serica and pointed out locations.

"Zelkat, under the control of the Red Swords. They had a king; he died fighting the Kitran, but his young son still rules." Gushi tapped the paper with his finger and then shrugged his shoulders. "So we hear."

He pointed at the center of the map. "Kunhalvar, perhaps under control of Red Swords. Unclear. Not ruled by king but a governor, called the Lord of Tokolas."

Then Gushi pointed to the province with the large lake beside a river, closer to the bottom of the map. "Vasvar: ruled by a king for several years. Claims allegiance with Red Sword of Zelkat, but merchants tell us those words are empty."

Gushi sat back down in his chair. Ashala came over and put her hands on his shoulders. He smiled at her and then looked at Sandun. "Of the other provinces, we know little. Buuk? Kisvar?" He shook his head. "Only Dombovar, the last province of Serica to resist the Kitran, that is controlled by the Iron King. Five or six years now, he has ruled. But Dombovar is three thousand *tik* from Gipu. Not as far as Kelten, but a long journey."

Sandun, Sir Ako, Basil, and Kagne all met in the evening to discuss the news.

"King Pandion directed you to meet with the king of Serica," Sir Ako stated. "Yet there seems to be no king of Serica, or maybe there are ten petty kings like the thirty princes of Melnehlan. I know not how to proceed."

"At least the Sogands or the Kitran no longer appear to rule," Sandun replied. "That would be terrible news to have to bring back to King Pandion."

"By the Spear, our journey would end here if that were so." Sir Ako spoke the plain truth. The Sogands traded with no nation of the Archipelago.

Merchants who tried to cross their lands were brutally murdered, their goods stolen. The temple held that trade with the Sogands was proscribed.

"Melnehlan has a king, as I recall," Basil said slowly. "The princes are powerful, yes, but the king is more than a figurehead. Perhaps one ruler is more significant than the rest? Wouldn't the man who rules the last province of Serica be the most important?"

"We are here to trade," Kagne stated. "Does it matter who we trade with? If we can exchange glowing orbs for Serica-glass and return home, I count that as a success. What really matters is finding a ruler who respects traders, one who deals honestly. If there is no single king, doesn't that give us the freedom to choose?"

One day, when Ashala was out with her younger sister, Mashia, Sandun came to visit Gushi. He was sitting in a leather chair in his study, which was lined with old books and papers faded with the passage of years. Sandun thought he recognized one ancient book at the top of a shelf, covered in a thick layer of dust. At a wave from Gushi, Sandun took it down. It was handwritten by scribes in Pella, a now-obscure work covering the life story of Sister Demostheia, the successor to Saint Pellar in Akia. The vellum pages were cracked, and the book was four hundred years old if it was a day.

Feeling a bit embarrassed, Sandun asked Gushi about the young women who had attached themselves to the men of the expedition. He didn't mention Ashala by name.

Gushi nodded sympathetically and tried to explain: "Gipu city lives off trade. Happy traders return to Gipu instead of Hotan or Fantu'veri. Some have family here; this is very good for Gipu. Some children stay, others become traders. Serica very rich but not peaceful. Gipu not rich, farming difficult. With peaceful trade, Gipu a thousand years old."

Gushi looked at Sandun and smiled. "This very old tradition of city. Hotan, richer, better land. Fantu'veri, they have gold and mine precious stones. Gipu? Friendly city, beautiful women. Ashala, she likes you. Keltens, all very brave, very strong. This is good. Trade with Kelten would be very good for Gipu."

It bothered Sandun that they were not actually traders. The leaders of Gipu were going to some lengths to feed and house the Archives Expedition, yet they had arrived in Gipu with very little to offer in exchange. One thing the expedition could offer the Lord Itor was an accurate map. Basil, with help from Sandun and Sir Ako, created a large, highly detailed map and then had a copy made for the Lord Itor. The map occasioned great excitement; soon, copies of Basil's map were being made and sold by Lord Itor's scribes. To Sandun's surprise, cheap imitations were on sale a week later.

At first, it amused Sandun, as he walked through the market with Ashala, to see low-quality maps being sold in stalls. One urchin had the gall to run up to him and try and sell him one of these fraudulent maps.

But thinking on it later that day, he became concerned that the low-quality maps might well drive out the expensive, accurate maps, and so merchant caravans might fail to reach Erimasran because they followed a bad map.

He took one of the bad maps to Lord Itor and tried to convince him that the fake maps should be destroyed. This resulted in a frustrating conversation in which neither party was able to communicate his true thoughts to the other. Sandun resolved to work harder on learning the language of Serica, which he hoped would allow better communications with the leaders of Gipu.

He also spent an hour each market-day, if the weather wasn't too foul, signing his name on good maps to Kelten and expressing his disapproval of bad maps. He tried speaking Serice to the locals; some knew it well enough to talk with him, the rest shrugged their shoulders or responded in their own language, which Sandun could make little of.

Kagne spent his time exploring Gipu. His woman, Amete, was rather shy, and it seemed they found little common ground. So Kagne went off by himself. Sometimes he brought back interesting plants from the market, and Amete would smile before taking them into the kitchen and cooking them. Kagne also visited the local temples; when he discovered a good one, he would take Sandun over to see it.

Both men found it odd that the worship of Sho'Ash was not to be found in Gipu. Sho'Ash was so well established throughout the lands of the Archipelago that it was hard to conceive of a city of men that lacked a temple or two. Yet in Gipu, there was no temple for Sho'Ash.

Instead, Kagne found several temples filled with small statues, all seeming the same, and each with a flame burning in front of it. The priests at the temples, rather impassive men in white robes, waved at the statues and said, "Janko'aran," but what "Janko'aran" did or meant to the people who came into the temple was unclear. The language of religion and philosophy was far beyond Sandun's skills after his few months of learning.

Other, larger temples were found by Kagne outside the city walls. Why the temples were outside the city was mysterious, as it flew in the face of all experience in Kelten. One of these temples was wooden, open to the air on three sides, with a roof covering a large human figure. Ashala explained this figure as "Gipu God." However, the next temple they visited a week later had a different figure, seated and not standing, and Ashala also called it the "Gipu God."

"Perhaps the people of Gipu worship a pantheon of gods, like the ancient religion of Akia?" Kagne offered. It seemed as good an explanation as any.

Ashala was with Sandun most of the time, except one day a week when she disappeared and did not talk about where she had been. Otherwise, she took her role as translator very seriously, and her knowledge of Kelten speech improved almost as fast as Sandun's knowledge of Serice. He found her company enjoyable, and although she was not the Kelten ideal of a tall, thin blonde, she became—over the months—very pleasing to his eye.

Sandun had never lived with a woman before, and in other circumstances he might well have thrown her out after six weeks just so he could be alone again. But right now, Ashala was absolutely vital to his mission. He needed to know the language of Serica as fast and as thoroughly as possible.

He had worried about the language problem as soon as they'd begun planning the expedition eleven months ago. Diplomatic communication in the Archipelago was simple, thanks to the old empire and the work of the temple. In the Archipelago, every educated person could understand every other educated person. The Pellian Empire was dead and gone these last seven hundred years, but its language lived on and could be heard in temples from Erimasran in the east all the way to Maspan in the far western seas.

However, Serica had no common language with Kelten. Traders in olden days had somehow managed to get by, so Sandun was reasonably confident that something would work out, but really it had been pure hope as opposed to a plan. Discovering Gipu with its dim memory of Kelten was great good fortune, and Sandun intended to take the fullest advantage of it.

The language of Gipu remained difficult for Sandun, and so he ended up spending all his time learning Serice from Ashala. The people of Gipu seemed comfortable with the fact that none but they knew their own language. Outside of the Gipu women and Gushi, the Keltens made few friends in Gipu except one: Nagor.

Nagor was the captain of the north gate guards, and he developed a friendship with Sir Ako. Eria could translate a few words between the two men, and sometimes Ashala helped. But as leaders of warriors and skilled fighters, they shared a common outlook and camaraderie that transcended the language barrier. On several occasions, Nagor had dinner with the Kelten expedition. He was tall and quite agile, and he talked about leading scouting expeditions all around the borders of Gipu.

Nagor's weapons and armor were of great interest to the Kelten soldiers, and the scouts discussed the fine points of the blades and armor of the Gipu warriors long past the point where Sandun cared.

One thing Sandun noticed in the deep winter nights was that his Piksie sword, Skathris, had a faint glow to it. He had been practicing with the sword under Sir Ako's instruction ever since Basil gave it to him. But up until now, it hadn't *looked* like anything more than a good blade of steel. Perhaps it was due to their schedule when they were traveling in the Tiralas: always up at dawn and in bed within an hour of night. Whatever the reason, the sword had a faint glow to it, most noticeably along the cutting edge. The color was a bit like fire, though more yellow than red.

Sandun asked Basil about his Piksie knife. Basil hardly touched it since it was not designed for skinning animals. When he took it out, it looked the same as any other steel knife. Inside Basil's room, one evening, the two men experimented with the Piksie blades on various objects. They learned that Basil's knife could cut metal as easily as stone, but Sandun's sword had no special properties against stone. Neither blade had any special ability against wood or leather.

"It's magic, for certain. No rhyme or reason to it," Basil said with a shrug.

Sandun had to agree.

Once, in the middle of winter, just before the High Holy Week, Nagor invited the Keltens to dinner at his house. He lived in a modest dwelling near the wall, and it was filled to bursting with all the Kelten expedition, as well as his family and relatives and friends. Nagor was married to a woman only a bit shorter than himself, and he had three children. The two boys were like their father: unafraid of the strangers from across the mountains. His daughter, still very small, slept in a cradle carved from an aromatic wood; she smiled readily at the women who came over to see her but frowned at every man except her father.

Food came in a steady stream from houses next door. The party spilled out into the street, and Padan and Damar, who both had consumed several mugs of the local *agardoa*, took off their shirts and wrestled in the snowy street for a quarter of an hour. Padan, bigger and stronger, had the early advantage, but Damar, with years of experience roping cattle, finally got him in a hold from which he could not escape.

Back inside Nagor's house, musical instruments were brought out, and the Gipu men sang strange songs while three young women danced and spun around in the middle of the room.

The next week, the Kelten expedition held its own celebrations for High Holy Week; however, the celebrations were muted. High Holy Week meant a great deal to all of them. Every year, families tried to visit relatives, and on the day of renewal everyone gathered at the biggest temples to watch the story of Sho'Ash reenacted. Lacking family, friends, and a temple, they made do with what they had. The Gipu women helped to prepare food, but only Ashala and Eria stayed to watch the Keltens read selections from the book of prayers that Sir Ako carried with him.

After the readings and the feast, an early night settled over Gipu city. Sandun put on his heaviest cloak and walked the snow-clogged streets, thinking about life back home in Tebispoli. Time was marching along; this day was the dividing line between one year and the next. The image of a crow perched on a pine branch was often used to represent this division: one eye on the past, the other looking to the future.

He wondered about his sister and her family. She had married a modest brewer of beer and lived still in Hepedion with their four children, though the youngest was very ill when Sandun had left. He thought about his uncle and his family, who grew apples in the hills outside of town. Barring illness, Scribe Maklin should have returned to the Archives and sent word to Sandun's relatives about his continued journey into the Tiralas, unless King Pandion thought the expedition should remain a secret.

I expect they have given me up for dead, Sandun thought to himself. The winter weather, the short days, the freezing nights, left him melancholy. He now chafed at the winter's delay. On the maps he had seen in Gushi's library, Serica looked so close! But the passes were closed. Gipu was a world unto itself, locked away while the snows held fast, until green-fingered spring put forth her power and melted the ice.

The longer they stayed in Gipu, the more mysterious the people became to Sandun, in some sense. There seemed to be something missing from the city, though Sandun couldn't say what exactly. Gipu was welcoming on the surface yet insular. There were subtle rivalries between people born out of long-past slights, and he felt that he was floating on the surface while larger fish swam deep in the waters. To be sure, there were ancient enmities between the noble houses in Kelten, but the size of Kelten made it easy for enemies to avoid each other except at rare state occasions when all the nobles were expected to visit Seopolis and pay homage to the king. But here in Gipu, there was no escape from the internal conflicts and political games.

Sandun, somewhat by accident, learned from Ashala that each of the Gipu women was from a different clan and that the clans each expected "their man" would become their ally in the subterranean Gipu disputes. Due to the language barrier, the Keltens remained oblivious to this dimension of the relationship. This disappointed almost all of the Gipu clans except one: Lord Itor's clan, Laska. By accident, when Sir Ako had rejected his first woman, her replacement, Eria, came from the Laska clan. Two months later, when she became pregnant, Lord Itor was positively jubilant and became much more friendly to Sir Ako and to Sandun, who could converse with him using Serice.

At least two of the other clans felt that the Keltens, having reached Gipu, should now turn back to Kelten and begin the process of guiding trade caravans across the Tiralas. Sandun, Sir Ako, and the rest of the expedition had no intention of returning home yet. They were here to see the fabled land of Serica, and nothing was going to stop them. Sandun's response, that the merchants of Gipu could send their own expedition west across the Tiralas to Sirosfeld, elicited wary looks and the hand gestures used by the people of Gipu to ward off evil. Clearly, the path west was too dangerous for the men of Gipu.

As to the city of ghosts, Sandun had, reluctantly, made inquiries. He learned little more than a name: Karmo. It had been destroyed more than one hundred years ago, presumably by the Sogands, though what tribe had done the deed and why were unknown. The only survivor had been a teenage boy who stumbled into Gipu in the early spring, frostbitten and starving. He had raved on his sickbed for a week or more about fire and evil spirits, but when he finally recovered, he claimed to have no memory of how he had gotten to Gipu or what had happened to Karmo. One expedition, led by two brothers who had been born in Karmo, set out soon after, but it never returned. After that, Karmo was written off the trade routes and never talked about.

About one month after the Kelten new year, the people of Gipu held their own celebration, marking the coming end of winter. By now, Padan's woman and Damar's woman were both pregnant, making their clans happy; Wiyat's woman had been replaced with a girl even younger than he was, and they appeared to be getting along very well. Perhaps most importantly to the expedition, Olef was pregnant, though that was not announced and, naturally, none of the Gipu clans cared.

At the conclusion of the new year's festivities, Lord Itor invited the Kelten expedition to a great feast in the town's main building. The highlight of the event was the music, which lasted for nearly two hours after the dinner.

Sandun was particularly struck by one song. It started out with an instrument much like a lute, though with fewer strings; the singer was a middle-aged man who stood, holding a walking stick in his hand. As he sang, a woman began tapping on small tubes of hollowed-out wood. The tapping sound spread insistently through the music, like the marching of feet or the clacking of gears inside a water mill. The singer was serious, almost biting off the words, and then the drummer joined in, hitting his drumskins with sharp blows like a pine branch cracking apart in a hot fire. The climax was reached when three men blew on horns, rapidly drowning out the singer as the horns called out a melody that was both triumphant and oddly sad.

Sandun saw a few of the older men and women in the audience brushing away tears at the end of the song. He asked Ashala what the song meant.

"Many years past, a terrible winter was," she told him. "Lasted long and long. Food gone, many sick in Gipu. Dead and dying. Atuko, young and brave, caravan leader, he left town, going east to Serica. To bring back food and medicine. Returning, the snow tried to stop him, but he pushed on, through the storm, making a path for the others to follow. He died just when he saw the walls of Gipu. A great hero to us. Lord Itor is related by blood, through five generations. I have heard the song many times, we all have. I don't know why the old ones cry when they hear the song."

Five days later, a merchant caravan arrived in town.

The weather had been good for the previous seven days, cold but clear. The merchants' arrival was not entirely unexpected as, according to Ashala, in many years a caravan would arrive during the winter.

The merchants, with shaggy cows as beasts of burden, were thickly bundled, looking more like walking heaps of leather and fur than men. Once inside the gates, they headed for the house of guests, which the expedition had been comfortably occupying for the last five months. Several of the merchants left the group and went off with women and children that they knew from previous trips. The others stayed in the large house and warmed themselves by the fire. Sandun was able to converse with them; the merchants were all from Serica, and they were heading back there soon. They expected to do just a little trading in Gipu, but they had been south in Hotan all winter and were now eager to return to their homeland and sell their goods.

The leader of the merchants was a tough, stocky man with graying hair, about forty-five years of age; he gave his name as Rogge. His brother was with him on the trip, but he was off spending time with a woman in Gipu. So Rogge sat, warming his feet beside the fire in the guest house, and talked to Sandun.

After describing something of the trip across the Tiralas, Sandun asked Rogge about the news that had sent them north to Gipu.

It was bad news that had come to them—bad news from southern Serica. Refugees from the province of Vasvar had arrived in Hotan about one month past. They said that a senior general, a man called "Two-Swords Tuno," had seized control over the government and had put to death the previous king and his family. The refugees were certain war was coming, as rumors of press-gangs combing the smaller towns for men swirled into the city. Some families, those willing to brave the snowy path and with connections in Hotan, fled Vasvar with what they could carry and counted themselves lucky when they arrived.

The merchants did not wish to run the risk of their goods being seized by soldiers preparing for war. It was an easy decision for them to head north to Gipu and then take the trail east out of the mountains. Rogge said their new destination was Tokolas.

"When do you expect to leave here?" Sandun asked.

"About a week's rest here, then we go east," Rogge replied.

"Will the passes be open? The men of Gipu say the passes are closed for at least another month." Sandun was surprised at Rogge's lack of concern.

"The men of Gipu…" Rogge waved his hands in the air as though brushing away cobwebs. "The trail east to the Tea Hills; its not that hard. Early, yes, but we are heading home. We have handled it several times before. This time will be no different."

Sandun brought this information to Sir Ako. At the training hall, away from the Gipu women, they talked over the news.

Everyone in the Archives Expedition was eager to take the trail to Serica. They had waited out the long winter months with resignation, as the Gipu locals had assured them that the road east was too risky until the snows melted. The Serice merchants' confidence was just the spark that the men of the expedition needed.

Over the previous year, the difficulties of the journey made the members of the expedition all the more determined to reach Serica. Reaching Serica would give meaning to their trip, and the significance of the goal justified every step. Sandun felt that death was the only alternative to reaching Serica, and they were not there yet. One final chain of mountains separated them from the great rivers and cities of Serica.

"Find out more about this city they are heading to," Sir Ako said. "What is good about Tokolas?"

The next day, Sandun found Rogge out with the oxen. He talked about Tokolas while checking on the harness and the hooves of the big pack animals. Sandun helped as best he could.

"Tokolas not the biggest city, but centrally located, and the government is honest," Rogge explained. "Merchants are taxed, yes, but the taxes are fair. Once you get within their borders, it is safe—or as safe as anywhere these days." Rogge sighed. "Times were bad before but now, with ten different rulers and marauding gangs of warriors and former soldiers, it's hard for a merchant to make an honest living. Some lords are better than others, and with the death of King Borsos in Vasvar, the Lord of Tokolas is the best one left. A modest man, that's certain. Seems like half the other lords have declared themselves king or even emperor, but not him. For several years, he has been just the Lord of Tokolas. Perhaps now he is called Lord of Kunhalvar? I don't know."

"Is he the most powerful ruler of the ten?" asked Sandun.

Rogge pulled at his short, neatly trimmed beard. "No, I would not say so. The Iron King must have the largest army. But everyone has been building their strength, ready to fight off the Kitran horde. No one knows where the Kitran Empire's army has gone. Years and years ago, when the revolts started, people expected the great horde to ride down from the north and crush everything. But they didn't. Why? Lots of rumors, lots of wild stories about dragons and witches and dark sorcery—nothing I would credit."

Sandun followed Rogge back inside. They drank tea together beside the fire. Sandun looked at Rogge's hands: they were veined and calloused from long years of pulling on ropes and leading pack animals.

Rogge looked back at him with a steady gaze. "Been four hundred years since there was trade to Kelten. The merchant guild still has old books about it. Twice I've heard proposals from young traders wanting to make the trip. Never went beyond talk. Back in the days of the Gold Kingdom, the trade was pretty much one direction: Serica-glass and fine silk went west, gold and silver returned." Rogge said this with a note of disapproval in his voice.

"Was that a problem?" Sandun said, with curiosity.

"Too much gold and silver is a problem for any merchant. Better to trade goods in both directions. The Kitran don't care about Serica-glass, nor silk. Trash and vanity they call it. But gold and silver? That they will kill for. I don't mind turning a profit, if I can sell goods for three times what I paid for them, I'll take your silver. But I don't want to carry ingots of metal when I could be carrying goods. Less danger, you understand."

Rogge lowered his voice, "You traded with the little people of the mountains. That sword you wear—made by them, I wager. Such weapons are sought after among collectors in Serica. The knives, those are really special—some strange stories about them. Some are…well, for lack of a better word: magic. The sort of thing that ends up in the treasury of a true king. If you have one, and I'm not saying you do, my advice is: keep it hidden."

That evening, the Archives Expedition gathered for dinner. Sandun recounted Rogge's comments. He spread out a map that he had copied from one in Gushi's library. "The merchants are going to Tokolas, capital of the province called Kunhalvar. It is not the closest major city, but it is well run, and its leader is, by their thinking, good to merchants. Further, it is centrally located in Serica, and we can go elsewhere if Tokolas is not to our liking."

"All of us remember the civil war of Kelten," Sir Ako said firmly. "We can trust that Sho'Ash will ensure that the best man will win."

It was decided. They would leave with the merchants and head east, on the last stage of the journey to Serica.

PART FIVE

bazeny

The day of departure was stormy. The Gipu women very theatrically wailed and cried copious tears. Their fathers, come to collect their daughters, looked on with unreadable expressions. Lord Itor explained to Sandun that this was their custom and not to think anything of it. And that the expedition would be welcomed back with open arms when they returned before next winter.

"You have blessed our town with what, I am sure, will be strong and healthy children. Come back in a year and see them!"

The biggest argument took place between Basil and Olef.

"No, you cannot go. You must stay for at least the next year." Basil was quietly emphatic.

"And I must go with you. I can still yet ride. And draw a bow. There is hardly a bump!" Olef pointed to her midriff.

However, despite her words, Olef was noticeably pregnant; she had put on some weight, but then they all had in Gipu after the months of hard travel on the road and eating tough deer or scrawny rabbits and Kagne's bland boiled roots.

"Fine, you haven't gained more than eight pounds, and you can still ride. What about next month? And the month after that? And the month after that?"

"'Tis no matter. We will arrive at this big city, Tokalas or whatever it's called, in two months' time. I've seen the maps, heard the talk. By Sho'Ash, I know what you've been thinking these last weeks, and I'm not staying."

Basil retorted, "If you knew my thoughts, why did you say nothing?"

"Because I'll have none of it. Remain here, surrounded by strangers? Nay. I'll not lie awake nights wondering where my man is and if he'll ever return or if he's dead in a ditch due to some Sogand's arrow that's laid him low." Olef angrily tossed her hair. "I'm not some noble's daughter, them that's taken to bed for months afore the baby's due. My mum went north, near 150 miles, carrying me, so she said. In search of the Kelten soldier as put the child in her. I can do the same."

Basil looked at Sandun and Sir Ako in mute appeal. Sir Ako just shook his head and turned to checking supplies on the rams.

Sandun had to agree with Olef. "I think it's better if she comes with us. The merchants from Serica seem convinced that Tokolas is as safe and well run as any city can be. We should make it in two months, assuming no floods, hostile armies, sieges, and so on."

"But the risk, if the child is born early…" Basil said with concern in his voice.

"Then blame yourself, blame her, and yes, blame me if you want. It's well known that the Great Commander's army traveled across the Archipelago with a woman for every man and nearly as many children as there were soldiers by the end of his wars. You didn't have to 'hunt the doe'—as you well know."

"Aye, as I know."

So it was settled: Olef was riding with them. So also was Ashala. She sat on the saddle of a small horse, looking very pleased. Gushi stood beside her horse, examining the harness. After the decision to head east was made, Sandun had gone to talk to Gushi at his home.

"You are leaving soon, I hear." Gushi was in his study, while several younger women were writing translations in a room next door. "We will miss you. Our knowledge of Kelten has progressed much since you have come. My daughter is nearly fluent now, I think?"

"Yes, she has a great talent for languages. So much so that I'd like to have her accompany us to Serica, with your permission."

Gushi stood up and looked out the narrow window. A cold draft came through a small opening, though he, like the other residents of Gipu, seemed heedless of the winter air. He sighed.

"I have talked with her; she wants to go with you. See Serica! I wish times were less troubled. If she were expecting a child, it would be out of the question, but as I gather she is not…well, yes, Ashala can accompany you to Tokolas." Gushi turned away from the window and looked searchingly at Sandun. "Children are important in Gipu. Important to Gipu's future. An expert translator of Kelten may be important later. It is uncommon for

Gipu women to leave. I expect her to return, and I expect you to bring her back home. Since my wife's death, Ashala and her sister Mashia have been a comfort to me. Still, you Keltens have more than kept your side balanced. Five, perhaps six women with child. I do wonder why Ashala is not among them. You enjoy her in bed, yes?"

Sandun felt his face flush, and his mouth went dry. "I do, sir. We…we are in bed often. I daresay no woman can ask for more."

"Well, we can hope for better results in the future."

"We can get married, Ashala and I." Sandun said this out of a sense of desperation as a mass of conflicting emotions roiled in his mind.

Gushi waved his hand dismissively. "Marriage in Gipu is more complicated than you imagine. It is not like Serica, or Shila, or Rakeved, or anywhere. By our customs, you already are married, or *konta*. However, the fixed relationship, *askonta*, that is only found between a Gipu man and a Gipu woman, and it includes an alliance between clans. You are not from Gipu; you have no clan. *Askonta* would not be proper. Ashala may go with you to Serica, but be careful with her!"

And now, with the farewells all said, the expedition headed out of Gipu, accompanied by their faithful Piksie rams and Basil's dog, following the Serice merchants. Nagor and his guards escorted them beyond the city walls. As they walked, Nagor pointed out some landmarks that they could use to help them find their way back to Gipu.

The trail they followed went south for two days. Then, beside a stone watchtower manned by Gipu soldiers, the trail divided. One path continued south toward Hotan, and the other turned east, heading toward a small gap in the great mountains. Here Nagor bade them farewell. He and Sir Ako embraced, and then Nagor gave his final words, which Ashala translated.

"Nagor says: Be careful, my friends. Serica is at war. Be on your guard. Return soon to Gipu." They all shared a final mug of *agardoa*, and then they parted ways. The flag of Gipu, a dark crow flying in a blue sky, fluttered in the cold wind from the tower.

Soon the trail followed a rushing river that collected waters from the highlands. After half a day's travel, they were amid the mountains, and the river was below them as it carved its way deep into the earth. The canyon became steeper and narrower, the trail twisting and turning along the side of the valley like a snake.

Snow flurries drifted down from lowering clouds. The merchants showed no concern about the weather, though the men from Kelten were nervous.

Sandun took the opportunity to have further conversations with Rogge. Ashala rode just behind, translating the occasional word or phrase. The merchant leader talked about the troubles of the last two decades, mostly the plague that had crossed the land from east to west, killing young and old indiscriminately. "Sometimes, we'd ride up to a village and everyone, *everyone* would be dead or *hao*."

Sandun looked at Ashala questioningly. She said, "Run away."

Rogge said that in previous years the caravans would travel a regular route from Sasuvi, west and over the mountains to Gipu, then north to Fantu'veri, south back through Gipu to Hotan, and then east, through the mountains to Virloges. From Virloges they went upriver, past Lakava, and returned to Sasuvi. Now with all the fighting between the Red Swords and the Sogands, Sasuvi was not safe for merchants. "One set of city guards will steal everything; another will steal half but keep all the mules. Last year, a trader I knew was executed for 'profiteering.' Profiteering? Blame merchants because prices are high? Like blaming the Mur River for not holding to its banks when the rains come. No merchant will go to Sasuvi now. May they enjoy the mountain-high prices of Dumbovar apple wine for the next few years."

On the road, in public, Ashala set her face in an expression of disinterest in her surroundings, as though living outside of Gipu was a decidedly inferior change in circumstances. But in their tent, she was all smiles. Despite the hard ground, she was especially enthusiastic for love, as was Sandun. On the road, being away from Gipu, the journey became an adventure for the two of them. Travel brought new things to talk about and deepened their feelings for each other. Away from the safety of Gipu, Ashala was more dependent on Sandun, and he felt in turn a greater responsibility for her.

At lunch on the second day, Sandun brought up the question of tactics with Sir Ako and the others. The merchants described the land ahead as uninhabited. But once they left the mountains, they would be in the flatlands of western Serica.

Sandun said, "The merchants are hopeful about the road to Tokolas, but we should proceed expecting trouble. Law and order have broken down such that even city guards are no better than highwaymen. What should we do?"

This prompted an hour of debate from everyone. That the merchants would not fight was agreed upon by all. "Scatter to the four winds; every man for himself, I predict," said Kagne with the consensus view.

"The robbers will try to attack out of ambush, knowing the road, and with advance warning of our coming," Sir Ako said, speaking from long knowledge of bandit attacks.

"We could stay off the main roads?" offered Padan.

"Even if we do, we must needs plan for an attack," said Sandun. The words of Gushi, that he needed to keep Ashala safe, echoed in his head.

"We shall have two scouts ahead and two behind, in visual contact with the main party. Rotating twice a day, all but Olef. Those in the main train at the time of the attack, pull packs off the animals and form a breastwork. The scouts will work back toward the main group, picking off bandits at range. No heroics. The merchants are not with us and are not a priority. That said, the more bandits that die, the less likely we are to be attacked in the future."

By this point, everyone had trained long enough under Sir Ako to understand what he wanted. Kagne and Sandun had become adept with bows and could reliably hit targets at range, and all of them were comfortable with close combat: with weapons and without.

At Gipu, they had purchased swords and other gear of war, replacing the things they had left buried before they climbed the lightless tunnel beside Mount Pandion.

Two days in, the mountains soared high above them. Water came rushing down from above. The path they followed crossed stream after stream, along bridges of ancient stone and more recent ones made of wood. Without past centuries of labor that had been undertaken to make these bridges, to travel ten miles would have taken a week or longer instead of a day.

The air was warming and only rarely did snow fields extend down across the trail. Temperate breezes from the east warred with the chill air flowing down from the Tiralas to the west. The plants were changing; pines gave way to broad-leafed trees, bare rocks to grassy meadows.

Finally, the trail took them over a small knoll and there, looking down a wide and expanding valley, they could at last see the vast plain of Serica laid out before them. Even the merchants, who had seen the view many times before, took a break and sat beside small fires, sipping tea and toasting to their future good fortune.

The Archives Expedition gathered together and gave thanks to Sho'Ash for his blessings. Then they all shook hands and said three cheers for King Pandion. One of their last Zeres wineskins was opened, and they all shared a mouthful of the sweet Nemiadan wine. Sandun told them that the expedition had left Tebispoli one year ago. That was a sobering thought; they had been gone now for a year.

The Serice merchants, having finished their tea, were anxious to depart. So on they went, down the hill to a shelter in the valley. That night the air was fragrant with the unfamiliar smells of tea plants and night flowers unknown to the lands of Kelten.

The next day and every day thereafter they came across farmers, who looked much like the short people of Gipu, with very round faces, and all of them had the pointed Serice ears. When they smiled, which was often, they revealed teeth stained dark brown. Some of the older women had teeth that seemed nearly black, a look Sandun found both unnatural and ugly.

At a small village just off the path, the villagers invited the caravan to stay and join them for tea and trade. Small disks wrapped in dry leaves were brought out and passed from the farmers to the merchants. Eventually, as Sandun watched with an eagle eye, he was rewarded as one of the cakes was unwrapped. Inside was a dark mass of dried, shredded tea leaves.

Even here, in the high hills at the edge of Serica, indications of war could be seen. Few young men were visible, and those that came into view were armed with spears like those of the Gipu guards: tall and made of a dark wood. Young women all had small children about their feet or on their backs. Unmarried young women either did not exist or were kept hidden from view. The marketplace was not much more than a clearing with a single empty building on the side for rainy days.

The tea was good, and in the evening a large fire was built and the tea farmers came down from their hidden houses and sang songs while beating complicated rhythms with sticks that they threw from hand to hand.

Sandun could not understand more than one word in ten. Ashala told him that the tea farmers spoke a language more similar to the language of Gipu than that of Serica.

"How many languages are spoken in Serica?" Sandun asked with a sinking feeling.

"Oh, well…" She rattled off the names of fifteen languages. "Each province has its own way of talking. In Gipu, we rarely see merchants from the coastal provinces of Aonnihad or Monoarvar, but they sound so funny; it's hard not to laugh when they speak, though that would be rude."

Sandun felt his heart drop. To be sure there were many different argots and dialects spoken in the Archipelago: Kelten, Melnehlanian, the Imperial tongue of Akia, the provincialisms of Falsten and Sastras. But he had been taught that everyone in Serica spoke the same tongue. "Does anyone speak the Serice the way you taught me?"

"Silly man-goose, of course. I was taught the right way to speak." Ashala seemed certain, but Sandun harbored doubts.

Another two days brought them out of the tea hills and onto the great rolling plains of Serica. The change was remarkably abrupt: the hills just ended and to the east, there was nothing to be seen but the sky and low hills on the horizon. Great white clouds floated high above the land.

Nowhere in Kelten could you stand and not see hills. As the expedition left the Tiralas and walked onto the vast and unfamiliar plains of Serica, a nervous fear took hold in Sandun's mind. They were a small band of foreigners traveling into a great land filled with unknown dangers and an uncertain political situation. The temptation to turn back and head for home was strong. But curiosity and a deep desire to actually see Serica's great cities were stronger.

Now that they were in Serica proper, the threat of bandits was real. In response, the merchants tried to force the Keltens to go first. Sir Ako refused, instead insisting the scouts not out patrolling stay in the center of the pack train. Then the merchants argued over who would be first; no one wanted to be at the head of the column, but then again, no one wanted to be at the rear either. Eventually, the merchants agreed that they would switch positions on a daily basis. Rogge and his brother managed the negotiations, though Sandun observed that either Rogge or his brother was usually somewhere near the front every day.

Although they avoided the main road, crossing over farm fields was nearly impossible for the merchants with their heavily laden ponies and mules. The scouts were usually able to pick their way following small paths, but often they had to come back to the main road, so there were breaks in their knowledge of the land ahead.

Along the way, they met people, mostly farmers or travelers going from one small village to another. When they saw the Kelten men in the main group, most people expressed surprise. Despite their hats and their cloaks, the Keltens' faces were unusual for Serica, with larger noses and narrower faces, and whenever they talked together, it was obvious that they were strangers from a very distant land.

In turn, the people of Serica that the expedition met wore a distinctive style of dress, more like a robe than the usual shirt and pants. The clothing was usually brown or gray, much less colorful than the robes worn by the people of Gipu. Sometimes in the small villages, a few women would be seen wearing bright colors such as orange or yellow. White robes, common attire in Kelten for men and women affiliated with the temple, were conspicuous in their absence from the dress of the Serice.

As the days passed, the peaks of the Tiralas gradually sank toward the horizon until finally they disappeared entirely. It was spring here in Serica, and the fields were freshly plowed or covered with tiny shoots of green crops, mostly wheat or some other grain. The air felt thick and rich, dense with dust and moisture. Ashala complained about the air, but everyone else in the expedition enjoyed the change from the thin dry air of the mountains.

Another week of travel, and now the wagon track they followed was complemented by a small but happy river that grew as other streams joined in. Ranch houses could be seen on the tops of the gently rolling hills where the soil was not as good. The Keltens saw shaggy cows and goats, and occasionally sheep grazing in the pastures.

"I've come to realize that farms are the same no matter where you go," Sir Ako said one afternoon. It was hot, not much breeze. The farm they were walking past was being worked by a large group of men, women, and children, pulling weeds and turning earth. Part of one field was covered with water, with young green stalks of rice already waving in the air.

"This does look very like the farmland around Opomos. To think we came all this way, just to end up in Kelten's great valley," Sandun replied.

"More trees," said Basil, "and fewer large animals. Not the same as Kelten."

The merchants called out their goods for sale: "Copper pots! Fine rugs! Woolen cloaks!" The farmers waved them off and kept working, though a few curious children had to be corralled by their older siblings. Digging out weeds was a job Sandun knew something of, from the vegetable garden in the backyard of his parents' house. He was happy to let other people plant crops; it was a common enough occupation, and there was plenty of work for everyone who wanted it.

The next village they arrived at was protected with freshly cut wooden poles buried partway in the ground. Ten armed men stood guard at the gate, while in the distance there was the sound of construction: hammers echoed in the midday air. This was the town of Hazeny, the largest they had seen thus far in Serica. The guards talked to Rogge for some time before allowing them in. There was suspicion in the way the guards held their spears, in their narrowed eyes, in their tight mouths. Inside the town was a hum of activity with women carrying covered baskets of food and men and younger children digging pits beside the houses. No one talked to the merchants, no one asked them what they had for sale. Sandun thought these were the preparations for war.

At the center of the town was a tea house. Here the merchants were able to stable their animals, and then they went inside for food and drink. The tea house, a large, two-story building was next to a temple and another building surrounded by walls six feet high. Two big men in armor stood beside an open gate. Next to the door wardens, Sandun saw a large metal fish hanging between two posts. It looked comical with its gaping mouth and faintly surprised expression. At first he had no idea what purpose the fish served, but then he noticed a wooden mallet dangling from a rope beside it. He guessed it was a sort of bell.

In the tea house, the people talked in hushed voices. The merchants were in a group and, unlike in the other villages they had passed, no one came over to talk to them or sought to buy something.

Sandun asked Ashala to see what she could learn. She took some dirty clothes and disappeared for an hour. When she returned and hung up the clothes to dry in the back of the tea house, she told him that there was fighting to the east.

"The women say that a village called Wheat Town, about ten miles away, was captured and ravaged. Some say the men of Hazeny should have gone to help, others that the town should keep to its own. The men all go out armed every day, and fields farther out have been left unplowed. Also, building the wall, which we saw on the way here."

"Do they know who attacked the village?" Sandun asked.

"Those who lived fled when they saw the attackers in the distance. Some said they were Sogands, others said they were Red Swords from the south."

After dinner, Sandun was sipping hot tea, a drink that was gradually becoming more palatable to him. As he logged the expenses of the day, a Serice gentleman came up. With his rounded face, he looked somewhat like the tea farmers of the hills, but his eyes were bright, and there was a palpable sense of being in the presence of a man who was used to command.

His clothing was simple to the point of being devoid of interest. Unusually, he had both a beard and a mustache, which marked him as one of the educated elite. Standing behind him was a much younger man who said very little but smiled frequently.

"This humble person begs leave to introduce himself. I am Valo Peli, a traveler. This man hears from the merchants over at the other table that you are emissaries from distant Kelten?"

"We are. We have traveled more than a year to reach Serica, and we have farther to go," Sandun replied.

"This man asks, where you are going?"

Sandun eyed the man; he seemed guileless, but Sandun detected a subtle mind. "We are traveling to Tokolas with those merchants."

"And this man asks, are you not going farther? There are several capital cities where ambassadors such as yourself could visit, though which one represents the true government is difficult to say."

Sandun was uncomfortable with this line of questioning. "Who are you?"

Valo Peli paused and then motioned toward a table where he had a pot of tea. Sandun followed him, and they sat down together.

"This man seeks also to travel to Tokolas, and the road ahead seems quite dangerous for the two of us." Valo Peli waved at his companion, who came over and sat down at the table.

Sandun told him, "We have not seen many travelers on the road so far. You might be the first. I'd like to know why you wish to go to Tokolas? You aren't a merchant. Do you have family there?"

"No, my family is to the west of here. My clan has grown tea in the hills for many generations, but I do not." Valo Peli put his hands together as though indicating that picking tea leaves was not his role in life.

Sandun tried a different tack. "Does your friend speak? Does he have family in Tokolas?"

"My *oblas* can speak, but he is not from Tokolas either."

"I don't understand that word you used. *Oblas?*"

"Ah. *Oblas*—one who follows as I teach—you know the word 'student'?" Sandun nodded.

"Your knowledge of Serice is very good, though judging from your accent, you learned it from one of the mountain towns in the high hills."

"We stayed the winter in Gipu."

"Just so. You will consider my request? Though it may seem unlikely, I have some ability in archery. And my, ah, student, is not completely devoid of talent."

At this, the young man smiled broadly. Valo Peli glanced at him, and the young man bowed and withdrew.

Sandun excused himself and went to find the others.

"What did he want?" Sir Ako asked.

"He said he wants to join us on our trip to Tokolas. But he would not say why he wanted to go, only that he was a traveler. Clearly he is concealing something, but I have no idea what."

"Well, we can hardly block the road. If he wishes to follow us, I don't think we can stop him." Basil pointed out the simple truth.

"He did say that he was good with a bow. As for the younger man, there is something in how he moves," Sandun replied, somehow justifying in his mind the idea of taking Valo Peli up on his offer.

Sir Ako said, "I can't see any reason not to trust him. Who are we? We don't represent a threat to anyone here. Even in the middle of the civil war, Kelten always treated ambassadors from other nations in the Archipelago with courtesy."

Kagne, sounding reluctant, said, "I don't mean to be the voice of gloom, but speaking as a man who has run into complex situations that resulted in imprisonment—my imprisonment, to be specific—we don't know what we are walking into. Perhaps there are reasons why one group in Serica would regard us as a threat."

"I can have Ashala ask around. She seems to be good at ferreting out local gossip. When are we leaving?" Sandun put this question to all of them.

Sir Ako pulled at his new beard which he had started growing around the start of the new year. "This talk about a recently destroyed village up the road worries me. The people here look like they are preparing for a battle. I don't relish the idea of staying just to be caught in the middle of a siege, nor do I like the idea of running into a military formation of unknown size on the road. On balance, I think we should go soon. Tomorrow or the next day. Trust that Sho'Ash will see us through."

Sandun went to talk to the merchants. With no one in the town interested in their wares, they were eager to leave. So the decision was made to leave around noon the next day. That night, Sandun explained to Ashala the strange offer Valo Peli had made. She said she would ask about him the next morning.

"I am very useful to you, yes?" Ashala snuggled up next to Sandun in their bed.

"Yes, my Ashala." Sandun stroked her long black hair.

The next day, Ashala went out early. She was back in an hour.

"I could not find much for you. Valo Peli is a stranger to this town. He walked into the inn about eight days ago. He does not talk much. But he did say when he first arrived that he was going east to Tokolas. Also, the women are convinced that he is a…" Here Ashala trailed off as she tried to think of a translation. "He is, or could be, a *demelzo*, a graduate of the best school. I didn't know there were any such men left alive. I thought the best school was destroyed when the Sogands captured Naduva years and years ago. But that is what they say. Serice women can tell these things."

Ashala had an expression that Sandun had seen before. If asked to explain, she would go off on a five-minute story that would reveal nothing he could understand. Now he knew better than to ask, so he thanked her and went to find Sir Ako and the others in the courtyard.

"I'm going to ask the Valo Peli fellow to join us," he told Sir Ako. "His story has been the same since when he arrived. He wants to go to Tokolas. Also, he may be a Serice scholar."

"I see. Well, his servant is over there. He has been watching us for the last half hour."

Valo Peli's student was standing at ease under the sloping tiled roof of the first-floor entrance. He seemed to be perfectly happy to be there, and he smiled when Sandun approached.

"I'd like to speak to your teacher, Valo Peli, if you know where he is?"

The young man answered, "Certainly. My master is having his morning tea. Please follow me."

Sandun was escorted up the stairs and into a small room where Valo Peli sat on a low stool, sipping from a tiny cup of tea whose aroma filled the room. Valo Peli finished the cup and stood up, facing Sandun. Sandun resisted the temptation to bow to him.

Valo Peli said, "Tea. There are many poems written about it. Every time I drink it, I am reminded of my childhood and smell of the tea cakes stacked inside my family's house, ready to be sold to the merchants going east to the great cities. We are heading east together, yes?"

Sandun said, "Yes. I accept your offer to join us on the trip to Tokolas. We intend to leave around noon. Can you be ready?"

Valo Peli nodded and then put out his hand to shake Sandun's, a gesture common in Kelten but unusual in Serica. "Thank you. I believe this will prove to be a *good* decision for all of us. Now I must make ready. I will see you at noon."

Sandun went back down the wooden stairs and told Basil and Kagne about his decision.

"Another scholar, Sandun? You may find yourself out of your depth. Aren't the scholars of Serica famous for their erudition? Hope he doesn't turn out to be just like your Master Eulogo." Basil said this with a smile on his face.

Kagne said, "A mysterious scholar who just happens to be waiting here for us to turn up so he can join our caravan to this Tokolas place. You can't make this up. Though I must say, his servant seems like a very handy fellow. Do you notice all the maids here eyeing him?"

Sandun hadn't noticed, but now that Kagne pointed it out, it was clear that Valo Peli's student did attract quite a few admiring looks from the women working at the tea house. Sandun resolved to find out the young man's name, so he went over to him. "I'm Sandun Eiger," he said, and he put out his hand.

The young man shook his hand as though he had long practiced the greeting. "This humble student is named Lathe, of the family Rupp. My homeland is west of here, near the town of Segvarket. I am grateful that you allow us to travel with you. My master was anxious to leave Hazeny."

Lathe continued, pointing at the packs loaded onto two mules that he had brought out from the stables. "We are bringing delicate objects with us. Please avoid rough handling of them."

"To be sure," Sandun told him. "We will let you handle your own goods."

About an hour after noon, they were ready to go. Everyone was standing around, eating fried balls of wheat stuffed with cooked pork. The tea house owner came out and passed around small cups of tea. He seemed unusually cheery—perhaps relieved that the guests were leaving.

Sandun attempted to settle the account for their stay, but the owner waved his money away. "Master Valo Peli has already paid your bill. Farewell. When times are more settled, please come again."

Valo Peli and Sandun exchanged looks. Sandun said nothing. Instead, the enlarged expedition headed out of Hazeny, east toward the great river and Tokolas beyond.

Sir Ako said they should head toward the destroyed village, as it would make no sense for whoever destroyed it to come back. So they headed down the road that the villagers pointed out to them, accompanying their directions with comments suggesting the expedition were foolish or insane for wanting to head to a place that had recently had such terrible luck.

They were approaching the destroyed village as the sun was going down. Shortly before they prepared to stop for the night, the main group came across the remains of a wagon partially off the road. The two scouts in front had been off to the south, making their way through a wheat field, and had not noticed it.

Kagne was at the front with Padan when he gave a shout of dismay. "There are bodies here. Two…no, three. No, four. All dead."

The rest of the main group approached gingerly. Sandun wrapped a scarf around his face, while Ashala stayed back with the Piksie rams. The bodies appeared to be the remains of a family fleeing from the village: a man, a woman, two small children. Sandun couldn't recall ever seeing children killed in war, though he had seen many dead children in Kelten, especially in the half year he and Kagne spent living under the docks of Seopolis. In the capital city of Kelten, children died of disease, starvation, and abuse. Hardly a week went by without a small body being found, stranded like bleached sea shells at the high tide line. Here though, the cruelty of the killings was obvious from the wounds. None of the Keltens were unaffected by the terrible sight.

Sandun ordered four of the merchants to start digging graves. They objected, saying this wasn't even in their home province, much less their home village. Angry and upset, Sandun cursed at them and took one of the new picks that the expedition had acquired in Gipu and began hacking at the earth. The other men of the expedition helped him, taking turns. Sir Ako and Padan moved the bodies one by one into the hole, and then they covered it.

Valo Peli now appeared with a flat piece of fresh wood. On the wood he had written some words in Serice. Sandun recognized only a few words: "four" and "family" and "murder." Valo Peli hammered the wooden stake into the fresh mound.

"What does it say?" Sandun asked him.

"I wrote, 'Here is a family of four, murdered fleeing the town.'"

No one wanted to camp near the broken wagon, so they turned around and went back half a mile and then made a somber camp.

The next day dawned with a thick layer of clouds blocking the sun. Sandun expected the clouds would vanish by midday, typical for this side of the Tiralas. There was some discussion about the wisdom of continuing on down the road; they feared what they would see. Sir Ako stuck to his plan. "Wherever the killers are, the least likely place is straight ahead."

Valo Peli was not convinced. As they made ready to depart, he said quietly to Sandun, "Whoever did this, terror was their purpose. Expect the worst."

The Kelten expedition was alert. Weapons were checked, arrows were pulled out of packs and made accessible. Sandun looked at Valo Peli's bow; it was very different from the Kelten bows—not as long, but made of layers. When used, it bent almost into a half circle and fired an arrow with great force. By contrast, Lathe carried only a long staff of polished wood and had two short sticks of the same wood in his sash. His usual smile was absent; he seemed to be matching his teacher's studied, neutral expression.

As they moved into the town, it was as bad as Sandun feared. Bodies were strewn across the street, and others could be glimpsed within the smashed houses. Some of the buildings had burned, but the town had not been deliberately set on fire. Sandun thought that Valo Peli was correct: the town had been left as a fearful warning to everyone nearby. But why? What message was being sent? And by whom?

As they reached the far edge of the town, Damar came running up. "Band of warriors approaching from the northeast, heading this way," he said. "More than ten, less than twenty. Mounted on shaggy cows."

"Sogands," Sir Ako said, and sent Gloval off to warn the southern scouts.

"Kitran warriors," Valo Peli said, with sadness. As the news spread, most of the merchants ran off back down the road. Only Rogge and his son and his brother stayed. Rogge pulled a short, heavy sword from one of his packs, and his brother did the same.

The remaining men advanced up the road to meet the Sogands. The plan was to copy the success of King Maklinos and rely on the very long range of the Kelten bows. Damar went back to Wiyat with orders to take up a hidden position to the north, within bowshot of the main group. When the two southern scouts, Farrel and Padan, came running up, they were sent back with orders to hide close by and pick off unwary enemies.

The main group pulled the packs from the rams and built their crude fortification, shaped as a semicircle in a bend in the road. It wasn't much to look at. Sir Ako swiftly put on his armor, with Olef's help. Basil's dog growled as the Sogands came into view.

The reputation of the Sogands was outsized; stories told of their great strength, their unnatural ability to shrug off terrible wounds, and their tactical skill. This was coupled with the temple's teaching, for hundreds of years, that the Sogands were in league with the Black Terror. According to the temple, the Sogands were agents of evil on this world, given superhuman ferocity by Naktam. But the only thing the Keltens said now was Kagne's jest: "We get to fight Sogands. If I live through this, I'll never have to pay for drinks at any pub in Kelten for the rest of my life."

The Sogands did not even shout a challenge; they just rode forward, holding spears up in the air, gathering speed as they got closer. The defenders fired early, at extreme range, to slow them down and make them wary. Remarkably, some shots that should have hit their marks were knocked out of the air by two of the riders using their spears. Sandun had never seen that done before.

The Sogands rode closer, and then two of the sixteen attackers went down, and two buffalo were killed. Now the Sogands were within seventy-five yards, but their commander broke off the attack. At a shouted command, they turned around and pulled back out of range. The Kelten expedition stood up on top of their packs and jeered at them.

During the fight, Sandun had noticed that Lathe had used an ancient weapon, a sling, to throw rounded rocks at the riders as they approached. Slings hadn't been used as weapons in Kelten since the days of the Pellian Empire. Slingers were famous in old stories about the Great Commander; his army had a group of slingers renowned for their uncanny accuracy and their use of specially shaped lead weights. Every now and again, a lead "sling stone" would show up at the market in Seopolis—supposedly from the days of the Great Commander, though who could say if it was true.

Valo Peli said, "They will circle us." Sandun translated for the others.

Sir Ako replied, "If we had more supplies, our burg could be better. As it is, retreat is impossible." Left unmentioned was the ignominious flight by most of the merchants. Sir Ako blew his short whistle, which signaled the outlying scouts to rejoin the main group.

Basil, using his farseer, noticed that one of the Sogands had broken away and was heading north. Valo Peli was noticeably interested in the farseer, which suggested to Sandun that the technology hadn't yet reached Serica.

"We can see farther than they can," Sandun told Sir Ako.

"Not sure that is helpful to us," the knight replied.

As Valo Peli had predicted, the Sogands begin circling around the Kelten burg, one after the other. They were only eleven now, so they had large gaps between them.

"Concentrate fire on one rider at a time. No one can block two arrows at once," Sir Ako said.

The Sogands took out their short horse bows and rode closer. At Sir Ako's command, the Kelten archers all took aim at a single rider and fired. He tried to turn and gallop away, but his effort was useless. He went down, and the Kelten expedition cheered. Again they stood and fired toward another rider, but this time the other Sogands let loose their own arrows. More accurately than any of the Keltens predicted, several Sogand arrows struck home. One hit Rogge in his back, and he grunted with surprise and fell to the earth. Another went through Olef's arm as she was preparing to fire her own arrow. She dropped her bow and sat down without a word, clutching at the arrow in her arm, blood streaming between her fingers.

Sir Ako expertly broke the arrow in Olef's arm in half and then, lifting her arm up, he drew the rest of the arrow through her flesh. Olef gritted her teeth but remained silent as Sir Ako wrapped up her arm in a clean strip of linen that had been made ready for such use.

Basil was filled with a cold fury; he shouted to his dog, who ran off toward the circling Sogands and momentarily distracted one buffalo with his snarling and biting. Basil shot that rider dead with an arrow into his neck. Heedless of the Sogand arrows that flew past him, he shot two more out of their saddles. The six remaining Sogands now broke off their circling and retreated toward a small hill topped by a lone building surrounded by a fence.

"We need to go after them. Finish them off before more come!" Kagne shouted. At the same time, Valo Peli had cut away Rogge's shirt and was examining the wound. The arrow had gone deep, and blood was coming out steadily.

"I should have run off like the others," Rogge said weakly.

"You may live. I'll have to cut the arrow out to stop the blood. Bite on this." Valo Peli handed Rogge an unbloodied part of his shirt. "Hold him firmly," Valo Peli said to Rogge's son and brother. Valo Peli took out a small, sharp knife from a pouch of tools and, after washing the wound with some strong liquor, he expertly made an incision up the man's back and swiftly cut out the barbed arrow. "This needs to be sewed up, but we don't have the time right now. Lie here and don't move," he said as he stuffed gauze into the wound and then wrapped Rogge's chest tightly with a long strip of cloth.

Then Valo Peli stood up and said, "More Sogands will be coming from that direction." He pointed northwest. "They will be trying to sneak up from behind us. It is what the Sogands on the hill are waiting for."

Ashala, who had been curled up into a tiny ball beside the packs, translated Valo Peli's words into Kelten while Sandun and Basil examined Olef's injury.

Sir Ako was skeptical. "If more were coming, they would come directly to the site of the battle."

Valo Peli could tell from Sir Ako's expression that the knight was not convinced. "It is their way. They have great confidence."

"I'm not going to leave those bastards up on that hill and go off on a wild goose chase. We are going to deal with these bloody-handed murderers now." Sir Ako pointed emphatically toward the hill with his sword.

Valo Peli said, "I will head back east a short way. I will signal you with smoke when I see the Sogands approaching. Any aid you can offer then would be welcome." He and Lathe carried two bags with them as they left. Sandun was torn but in matters of battle, he trusted Sir Ako.

Leaving the caravan leader, his son, and Olef behind in the burg, the rest of the expedition advanced toward the small hill. Kagne made sure each of the felled Sogands really was dead. "That one is dead now," he said, wiping his knife on some grass.

"These Sogands are, without a doubt, the same that slaughtered the villagers of this town. They showed no mercy then and attacked us without even the offer of parley; they will get no mercy from us." Sir Ako was grim.

"Rather surprising to see them return to the ruined town, isn't it?" Sandun asked Sir Ako quietly as they neared the hill.

"Yes. I don't understand it. That Valo Peli fellow seems damned certain that more will come from the northwest, which also makes no sense to me. But I will not second-guess myself in battle. Time enough for that after the fighting is over."

Going uphill as the skilled Sogand archers shot at them was more difficult than Sandun had imagined. Each Sogand warrior stayed behind cover and ducked out to fire an arrow and then hid back behind a wall or an overturned water tub or pile of wooden fence posts. With the expedition down to just eight, progress was slow. Sir Ako was in the lead, and he took two solid shots: one to his chest and one to his sword arm. Both glanced off his armor. His shield also protected him from two more arrows.

Sir Ako then divided the men into two groups: one would advance, while the others stayed ready to shoot at anyone who showed his face at the top of the hill. With this tactic, at least two more Sogands were disabled, if not killed. The Kelten men were getting ready to set fire to the piles of wood, using wadded-up balls of dry grass, when Basil shouted that smoke was coming from the center of town.

"Damn it all to the Black Terror! What is going on today?" Sir Ako was angry at himself and at the world in general. "This lot here will have to wait." Sir Ako left three scouts with Basil to keep watch over the Sogands on the hill. Then, leading the remainder, he headed toward the column of smoke now rising into a patchy blue sky.

Ten minutes later, they heard the sound of men fighting. There was a loud sound, a bit like thunder, and then a large ball of smoke rose into the air.

"What was that?" Padan said.

"I have no idea," replied Sir Ako.

In another minute, the fight came into view. Valo Peli could not be seen, but every ten or twenty seconds, an arrow would suddenly strike one of the Sogands, and he would go down and not get up. Valo Peli was apparently inside one of the buildings, perhaps on the second floor. What prevented the Sogands from rushing into the building was the student, Lathe, who was defending the doorway.

Lathe was fighting in a manner that was completely foreign to the Kelten men. It was such an astonishing display of combat that they all stopped for a spell and watched. He moved with incredible speed, using two sticks, one in each hand, to block attacks and then shift to make blows of own to his enemy's face or hands. He constantly moved, shifting his target, keeping the Sogands confused as to who was under attack and when he was exposed to an attack from the rear. But as remarkable as the fighting was, he could not keep it up for long.

There was a strange smell in the air, somewhat like the acrid, smoky odor of wet leather left too close to a fire. Already several bodies were on the ground, Sandun guessed that around ten Sogands were attacking. Sir Ako sent Padan and two other scouts off to the side to shoot at the Sogands from the rear while he advanced down the street with Sandun and Kagne by his side.

Sandun had the strange Piksie sword in his hand. He was used to the weight and feel of the weapon now, after months of practice. But this was the first time he had used it in battle. He wondered what it would do. It didn't cut metal when wrapped in cloth or leather, but now? While Sir Ako bellowed out his challenge, stoking his anger, Sandun tried yelling a few curses of his own, feeling a rush of hatred set fire to his blood. The Sogands and the Kelten men came at each other like two rams butting heads. Seeking to try out his blade, Sandun actually aimed a blow at a large Sogand's sword; the man blocked his attack with a look of disdain that changed to shock as the Piksie sword cut the weapon into two pieces, making a high-pitched whine as it did so. Sandun rapidly shifted his blow and cut into the Sogand's face, turning the warrior's head to an open wound. The Sogand fell with a gurgling cry.

Sandun found a new enemy and tried his attack again. Like the first man, this warrior casually blocked Sandun's blow only to see his weapon inexplicably sheared off as though it were made of a willow stick and not iron. He too died with a look of disbelief on his face. Several arrows now struck the remaining Sogands in their backs; Padan and his men hit them with well-aimed arrows that cut through armor or struck exposed vitals.

Only one Sogand was left. Lathe was almost dancing around the big warrior, hitting him with a rain of blows to his head and his limbs. But the Sogand took the abuse and kept on swinging. Blood dripped down his face from a blow to his forehead and one leg was lame, but he bellowed abuse at his tormentor and swung a large axe through the air with great sweeps, any one of which would have cut Lathe in half. Sir Ako ended the fight by expertly stabbing the axe man in his side as he swung again at Lathe, who just managed to duck under the blow. The big Sogand tried to stab Sir Ako with a dagger he pulled from his belt, but Sir Ako was ready for that and simply heaved the man off his feet by putting his shoulder into the Sogandian warrior and toppling him over like an overburdened wheelbarrow. He landed in the blood and muck in the street, and Kagne jumped on him and slit his throat. With that, the fighting was over.

As he looked at the bodies of the dead Sogands lying in the street, Sandun realized that the Sogands didn't look normal. There was something about their arms and their body proportions that made him wonder if the old stories about Sogands being not human might actually be true. He had seen Piksies up close, and they definitely did not look human. Now, as he observed the Sogand warriors with their heavy faces and long arms, he felt a strange mix of emotions. Should he care that he had killed several of these… creatures? They had murdered hundreds of human villagers; perhaps they themselves did not care when they did so? Perhaps they killed humans and thought it was like butchering cattle? He resolved to ask Valo Peli about the recent Sogand rule over Serica, when he had the chance.

Valo Peli came out of the house with his bow in his hand. "This man thanks you for your speedy arrival. My vantage point was not ideal, and the Kitran soldiers were close when I first observed them." He bowed and then continued: "I regret to say that I fear a third force is heading our way. I believe they are following a common Kitran tactic and have therefore split their force into three divisions. We have met the 'lure.' This was the 'hook.' Last will be the 'shark.' The last group will be the largest, and it will come in a line formation, heading to the sound of fighting, looking to kill anyone fleeing the battle."

Sir Ako said nothing. He was winded, having taken some hard blows during the last fight.

Sandun said, "Do you have a plan for dealing with the shark?"

"This one has a plan. I want the shark to bunch together. I want them to come down this road and then stop here. Then, my student and I will destroy them with *lopor*. To accomplish this, I want two of you to pretend to fight, here, in the middle of the street. Make as much noise as possible. Others can help with the noise. The Kitran will be confused and curious, a powerful combination, thus drawing them together. The pretend fighters will then run into a nearby house, and then the shark will die." Valo Peli stood there with faint smile on his face.

When Sandun translated the plan, Sir Ako shook his head in disbelief, but he was no longer willing to argue with the man. Instead, he asked, "How long do we have before the shark shows up?"

Valo Peli said, "Not long. Soon, I believe. We must make ready."

Damar ran back to tell the others the news. Sandun suggested that he and Kagne stage the pretend fight. "Kagne and I worked something like this once, in a pub, to get out of paying for some rather expensive wine. I think we can do it again," Sandun told Sir Ako.

"As you wish. The rest of us will be close, inside these houses, when the demons of the Black Terror show up. What is this *lopor* Valo Peli talked about?"

"I don't know," replied Sandun.

Sandun and Kagne discussed their fight and practiced some moves. "We will just use daggers and throw punches, like that previous time," Kagne said as he demonstrated a few moves. "No cutting." As Kagne was the more skilled dagger fighter, Sandun would be the "faller"—the one who would take the fake blows from Kagne.

Meanwhile, Valo Peli and Lathe were taking large round balls from their pack and preparing them for use. Then they went swiftly down the road, each carrying a sack full of the strange things.

As Valo Peli had predicted, about twenty minutes later a group of Sogands on buffalo came into view at the western edge of the town. Sandun and Kagne went through the motions of brawl, while the others, hidden inside houses, shouted abuse and random threats.

Sandun spent a fair bit of time on the ground, having been knocked off his feet by some clever moves of Kagne. He was able to see the Sogands that were slowly approaching. "There are more of them than before," said Sandun

"If Valo Peli's balls of *lopor* don't work, we are in for a tough fight. Six against twenty?" Kagne pretended to drive a blow into Sandun's face that missed him by an inch.

Sandun stood up and then spun around and fell down. Kagne's punch hurt even though he had not put his weight behind the blow. As Sandun stood up again, he could see the Sogands clearly; they were still about fifty feet away and looking in all directions.

Sir Ako shouted: "Go! Go!"

Sandun ran in the direction of the house that Valo Peli had been occupying earlier, with Kagne pretending to chase him, shouting furiously at him.

Inside, Sandun grabbed his sword and his bow and continued up to the second floor. Peering out from the door of a ruined balcony, Sandun saw several round things, trailing smoke behind them, being thrown into the group of Sogands. To his utter astonishment and delight, the balls exploded into smoke and fire and a huge noise. It was unlike anything he had ever seen before in his life. If a bolt of lightning had suddenly come down from the sky and blasted the ground in the midst of the Sogand warriors, the devastation would have been no less. Sandun could only gape in stunned wonder as two more explosions occurred in quick succession.

He covered his ears and then picked up his bow and fitted an arrow in case some of the Sogands came out of the smoke toward them. But none did. As the smoke cleared, the street revealed a scene of riderless, bellowing buffalo running down the road the way they had come. Lathe was stepping between sprawled bodies and delivering sharp blows to the heads of those who were beginning to recover from the explosions.

The Kelten men came out from the houses and shouted and laughed at the wonder of it all.

"The Spear of Sho'Ash come down in righteous thunder could not have done more!" shouted Sir Ako.

Kagne was jumping up and down. "This is the greatest thing! The greatest thing!"

Sandun found Valo Peli coming out of a building and embraced him. The man was smiling faintly; all around him was the strange smell, apparently of burnt *lopor*.

The Sogand commander, wearing metal armor and with a plume of horsehair on his helmet, struggled to his knees and pointed at Valo Peli. Sandun could barely understand his words, but he seemed to be saying, "Lord Boethy, why do you attack us? Who are you fighting for?" The expression on the Sogand's face was clearly that of a man who had been bitterly disappointed—or even betrayed.

In apparent sudden fury, Valo Peli picked up a Sogand sword and struck the man in the face with the flat of the blade. The Sogand's helmet flew off and rolled into a puddle of blood. Valo Peli struck the man again, knocking the Sogand back onto the ground.

Valo Peli shouted, "I see you. I see what you have become. You murder without reason, you kill farmers and villagers to instill terror. You rape the women, kill children, and leave the bodies to rot! And you dare to question me? Arno Boethy does not live any longer. He does not know you; he is dead of shame. My name is Valo Peli!"

With that, he gave a terrible cry and, using both hands, swept his sword through the Sogand commander's neck. Blood spewed forth, covering the bottom of his robe with gore. Valo Peli, with a tightly controlled voice, told Lathe to put the head into a sack. "That head may be worth a few coins in Tokolas."

The Archives Expedition left Wheat Town and followed the road back the way they had come to Hazeny. They arrived around nightfall, all of them too weary to do more than put one foot in front of the other.

The guards at the gate had already been spooked by rumors from the cowardly merchants who had fled at first sight of the Sogands, and they were suspicious of the bloody and exhausted foreigners. However, Rogge's brother shouted and cursed at them and swore they had won a great victory. Lathe was persuaded to pull out the head of the Sogand leader from the bag.

The sight of this bloody trophy changed the mood in Hazeny dramatically. Frowns turned to smiles. Women and children came out from their houses. Soon cooking fires sent smoke into the air. The Keltens were washing beside the central well of Hazeny when the women started bringing them tea and dumplings and more—not very subtly either.

The town surgeon sewed up Rogge and was optimistic about his chances. Olef was cared for as well. As long as no infection set in, her arm would fully recover in a month or two.

News of their deeds spread rapidly, mostly due to tales told by Rogge's brother, who had done the least in the battle. But then, as Sandun reflected, it was often those who had done the least who boasted the most. An expression from Torobeus was apt: "The empty barrel makes the most noise."

That evening at the inn, Sandun slept the sleep of the dead, and he didn't go down to the common room till the next afternoon. Ashala was extremely affectionate that morning. Later, he learned that a group of the village guards went out to the site of the battle early in the morning. They returned shortly after sunset with several carts full of weapons and armor looted from the battlefield. The spoils of war were piled in a heap in the center of the village and offered to the Keltens.

Basil took a fancy dagger. "To match the Piksie knife," he said.

Sir Ako was toying with the Sogand leader's helm with the horsehair plume. "Too foreign," he finally said.

"Go ahead and take it," Sandun urged him. He suspected Sir Ako wanted it. It would need to be fitted to Sir Ako's narrower face by a blacksmith, but it suited him. Sir Ako relented and took the helm.

Kagne choose one of the Sogand bows. Ruefully he said, "I need to shoot better. I was bloody useless in the battle." The other scouts choose daggers, finely worked belts, and other oddments, and the rest was left for the villagers.

The headman of the village came out of his compound and solemnly praised them, saying, "In these times of upheaval and uncertainty, your brave deeds will long be remembered. You will always be welcome in Hazeny." He then gave an order, and a line of ponies was led out from the compound. "These are but a token of our appreciation. Ride to the great river, and think of us."

The next day, the merchants who'd fled approached the Kelten expedition as they were sitting in the tea house, drinking tea. The merchants all went down to their knees and begged leave to stay with the expedition on the journey to Tokolas.

Sir Ako frowned and shook his head. Sandun stood and said to them, "In our land, we do not take back men who have proven faithless in the hour of need." He pointed to the doorway. "Get out, and don't bother us again."

Ashen-faced and trembling with shame, the merchants left the tea house and did not return while the Kelten expedition remained.

Later, Sandun went to visit Rogge in his room upstairs. He looked weak and spoke in a whisper. Sandun told him the expedition was leaving in two days and that he was welcome to join them. Rogge thanked him for the offer but whispered that he was staying here for some weeks.

"Is there anything we can do to help?" Sandun asked.

"No, Master Sandun. My boy tells me that he has made good trades with the people here in Hazeny, what with the change of mood since the battle. I'll stay here till I'm recovered. I hope to see you again in Tokolas in a few months' time."

The subject of the Piksie rams came up the next day. Damar said the rams needed shearing, as the weather was too warm here in Serica for their coats. Everyone glanced around the table, but no one had the desire to do the job.

Gloval said "I was a cowherd, not a shepherd." Damar nodded in agreement.

Finally Kagne said, "Oh, all right, I'll do it. After all, every highlander from Erimasran knows how to shear a sheep."

Sandun told him, "I'll help you."

Ashala was able to borrow several large scissors from the leather currier. Eventually, the whole team joined in the effort, with Olef watching from the side and making jokes about their chances for future employment. The goats' patience and good temper were put to the test, and there was much bleating and some cuts to each of the animals by the end of the afternoon. Afterward it was pretty funny, and they all drank several bottles of the extremely potent liquor of Hazeny, which was the only strong drink they had found in Serica thus far.

Ashala, with the aid of Rogge's son, was able to sell the sheared wool for a good amount of money. Whether it was really valuable wool or whether the buyer was just being generous was unclear. Sandun was happy to get some more funds; as they traveled into more settled lands, food and lodging were going to cost money, and their Kelten coins were of interest only to the occasional collector. He had made some exchange of Kelten coins in Gipu to a few hopeful traders, but it was not nearly enough to last them for months. Sandun had given one of the glowing orbs to Lord Itor in a private meeting. Considering the long months and the warm hospitality they had received, it seemed a paltry gift, but Lord Itor had been very appreciative and had given them a generous gift of his own in the form of Serice coins.

"For your expenses on the road," Lord Itor had said. "Remember, come back to Gipu!"

Valo Peli and Lathe had stayed hidden out of view ever since their return to Hazeny. Sandun suspected the reason for this, but he said nothing, nor did he ask about Valo Peli's final impassioned words to the Sogand leader. He did quietly suggest to the team that they not talk much about Valo Peli's role in the battle.

Sandun told Ashala the whole story of the battle. She had heard of "thundering powder" and had once seen it in the form of a large decorated "drum," which was exploded with a great noise and sparks in the middle of Gipu on the first day of the Year's Celebration. Its nature and means of manufacturing were a complete mystery.

"The Water Kingdom used it against the Sogands in the last years of their long defeat. The Sogands say it is a weapon unworthy of them, and they rarely use it. That is all we know about it," Ashala told him.

As to the name "Lord Boethy," which the Sogand had called Valo Peli, this was unknown to her. Sandun ordered her not to repeat it to anyone.

Ashala agreed and then coyly said, "They are calling you *Sword Breaker*."

"Why me? How could anyone know what I did?"

"The people here are not stupid. They may look like ignorant farmers, but they know a bird and flour makes honey. They found two broken blades of the Sogands, and they know you have a Piksie sword that everyone thinks must be magic. It is, isn't it? Magic? Just like in the legends?" Ashala waved her hand at the sword that, like the bag of glowing orbs, Sandun kept by his side at all times.

"The Sogand blades were poor quality. Anyone could have broken them," Sandun replied without much conviction.

Ashala laughed. "Said the mouse to the cat. Everyone knows that the Sogands have the best weapons money can buy. Vicious and brutal they are, but they know tools of war. Ever since they took control of Serica, their warriors have the best the Serice craftsmen can make."

Two days later, the Archives Expedition said farewell for the second time to the town of Hazeny. This time, their leaving was completely different. Kagne had apparently gained the affection of two young women, and they comically glared at one another while each held one of his hands. He grinned when Sandun commented, "It's a good thing we are leaving now, or there would be trouble in few days."

"Hah. Sogandians may kill us tomorrow. I see no harm in living today."

Padan was teased by Damar, and everyone laughed when he admitted that one of the serving girls had sneaked into his bed the previous night.

"And what was I supposed to do? Kick her out?" The girl ran up to Padan and pressed a small carved stone into his hand, and she then ran off into the tea house just as the expedition was about to ride off.

Sir Ako had held himself aloof from all the frolicking. He had been ill tempered ever since the day of the battle. Sandun resolved to include him in his future discussions with Valo Peli. Personally, he agreed with all of Sir Ako's decisions before and during the battle. That they had been mistaken was no shame. Serica was a strange land with a different way of conducting war. Assumptions that held true in the Kelten or the Archipelago might easily prove wrong here in Serica.

This time, they took a different route, going south a whole day before heading east. Now that they were mounted and had no collection of merchants slowing them down, they were able to make better speed, though the Piksie rams could not be coaxed to go much faster than a walking pace.

Sandun made it a point to talk to Valo Peli whenever the opportunity presented itself. He made sure that Ashala translated for Sir Ako. At first, it was hard to get Valo Peli to say anything substantial, but when Sandun asked about the history of Serica, that opened a floodgate of information.

Sir Ako enjoyed history and so for days, Valo Peli held forth on the long and complex history of Serica while Sandun, Sir Ako, and Ashala listened. Some of the old history was known to the scholars of Kelten, but the more recent events of the last three hundred years were all new.

At the evening campfire, Sandun and Sir Ako would retell some of the best war stories they learned to the rest of the scouts. Valo Peli listened intently and even asked Ashala to translate some words for him. By the end of the second week, Valo Peli had learned some Kelten language.

As Valo Peli talked about the past, Sandun recognized a man after his own heart, a scholar and a fine intellect. He also was remarkably modest, talking about himself only occasionally and as a minor figure in larger events.

Valo Peli said about the Sogand conquest of Serica:

"For centuries, four tribes of Sogands lived in the far northern plains, always at war with one another but often raiding across the borders into Serica. A hundred years ago, the Water Kingdom was weak, and strong kingdoms ruled what had been Serica's northern lands. The Water Kingdom, ruling from what they called the 'temporary capital' of Naduva, contented itself with waiting out the barbarians, paying tribute to keep peace, waiting for the barbarians' inevitable collapse.

"It did not work out as the wise men of the Water Kingdom expected. It is true that the northern kingdoms, the Palahey and Minak, did collapse, but their fall was due to sustained attack from the Kitran.

"Never before had the Kitran been the most powerful of the Sogand tribes. But under the leadership of their 'heavenly' war leader, Beeshe Tem, they subdued the other tribes of the north and attacked in all directions. They attacked Serica, Minak, Shila, and most of all, they attacked Palahey.

"Alas, for the wise men of Serica and Shila, their study of history played them false. None regarded the Kitran as a real threat. Each kingdom was more concerned with the war *after* the Kitran than the current war with the Kitran. So the individual northern kingdoms all weakened slowly, year after year, and never made an alliance against their common enemy. Until it was too late. Until they no longer had the strength and, like ripe fruit, they each fell under the domination of the Kitran. This took twenty-five years, and all that time the rulers of the Water Kingdom rubbed their hands with glee but otherwise did nothing.

"Yes, the Water Kingdom stopped paying tribute to Palahey, but did they use the wealth to build up their armies? Not really. Did they help Shila when the Kitran attacked? To their great shame, they did not. When the Kitran sent raiding parties down the Mur River, did they help the southern provinces? To their even greater shame, they did not.

"Every year, the Water Kingdom advisors told their king that the Kitran domination over the other Sogand tribes, the Gokiran and the Turan, would end, just as similar alliances had done in the past, and when it did so, the Water Kingdom would be ready to pick up the pieces and remake the glorious Gold Kingdom. So the Water Kingdom's armies sat behind their walls and waited. And every year, the Kitran gained strength.

"When Beeshe Tem, warlord of the Kitran, was assassinated by a Minak princess just before her kingdom was burned to the ground, the wise men of the Water Kingdom were certain—certain—that the Kitran alliance would fall apart, just as they had been predicting for years.

"But it did not happen. Instead Beeshe's youngest brother, Isti, gained the allegiance of all the tribal leaders. He continued the wars started by Beeshe, and after some years, Palahey was conquered, and their last kings both died on the same day. The Kitran under Isti raided in all directions, taking Serice farmers as slaves, leaving death and ruin in their wake. Isti died after nearly ten years of rule, and again hopes were high in Serica that the Sogand alliance would collapse this time, as many rivals claimed their right to rule over all the Sogands.

"In truth, the wise men of the Water Kingdom were partially correct. There was a split that turned into open war. Each of the great Sogand tribes are composed of clans, and there are blood feuds between the clans. Most of the Turan clans supported one grandson of Beeshe Tem, while the Kitran and Gokiran supported another grandson named Tolu Tem. The war ended rapidly, too rapidly for the Water Kingdom to take advantage of. The Turan clans—defeated—fled to the far west, vowing revenge but without the strength to match their words.

"The winner, Tolu Tem, now had an army of unsurpassed power, filled with conscripted soldiers from every land under his control: most of the Sogand tribes, the remaining warriors of Palahey, an allied army from Shila, and even soldiers conscripted from of the western provinces of Sakhat and Zelkat. With this massive force, he laid siege to the cities of the Water Kingdom, one after the other.

"Too late, the Water Kingdom realized its folly. Too late, the wise men woke to their danger. In its final death throes, the Water Kingdom fought with no little courage, and they introduced new, powerful weapons, including *lopor* or 'thunder powder,' which I used at Wheat Town.

"But Tolu Tem was perhaps the greatest of the Sogand leaders, at least in his early years. Unusually for a Kitran, he gathered men of talent to him, from all of his subject peoples. When the Water Kingdom developed *lopor* as a weapon, it was only a few years before Tolu's armies were using that same weapon against the Water Kingdom.

"No walls built by man are able to stand against massed barrels of *lopor* set against them. So the Water Kingdom was, in the end, betrayed by its own invention. The capital of the Water Kingdom, Naduva, was taken after a terrible siege. With that victory, Tolu Tem was now the undisputed ruler over all of Serica, and much more besides. He styled himself *Emperor Tolu Tem, Ruler of the World*.

"Many men of Serica now joined Emperor Tolu, thinking that he was wise enough to rule, that he would be the first of many kings who would rule as the kings of Serica had ruled before him. They were wrong."

Here Valo Peli stopped, and it was clear from the pained expression on his face that he had no wish to continue the story. That evening, with Ashala's assistance, Sandun related Valo Peli's tale to the Keltens.

Several days passed before Sandun could persuade Valo Peli to continue the history, bringing them up to the present.

The expedition was now very close to the great river called the Mur. The land was marshy, with many small lakes. They had joined a main road, and news of their victory over the Sogands had gone ahead of them. How this had happened was unknown to Sandun, but at every town they arrived in, people greeted them with open arms, or at least with respect. Some people recognized Sandun's description, and he was called Sword Breaker, which made him feel quite odd.

"You must tell us your part in all this, since you clearly played a role," Sandun said for third time to Valo Peli as they were riding through a dense forest, the trees tall on either side of the road and forming a vault of green above their heads.

"All right, all right, this one will tell you. Since you must know these things, and despite the shame the telling brings."

And so Valo Peli told Sandun his own story:

"My family is from the tea hills, which you traveled through on your way from Gipu. This one was selected at an early age to study at a good school down in the flatlands. Having mastered the basic learning, this one moved to a better school in Sasuvi. Again, this one mastered the material and passed their tests. Eventually, I was sponsored to Daka by the master of Sasuvi academy. Daka was and is the capital city that the Kitran had seized from Palahey and made their own. Emperor Tolu was dead many years before I arrived, but there were still traces of his ideas to be found amid the rot, the decadence, the wanton cruelty, and yes, the splendor of the city. That was thirty years ago."

He sighed. His eyes were lost in a vision of past.

"I kept out of trouble. I did the tasks that were assigned to me. I read reports. I forwarded recommendations to my superiors. In those days, the administration still limped along—perhaps on a broken leg and without shoes, but it moved. I was sent to run a small district near the capital. Looking back on it, a plum assignment, though I took no pleasure in being close to the capital. Year after year, I saw it change for the worse, more desperate men willing to do anything for food: steal, rob, even murder. And women, young, poor, willing to sleep with any Kitran for a chance to birth a Kitran child and be given official status and a small stipend. But with so many women flooding into the city, most just ended up in brothels or begging on the streets.

"Years passed. I moved up in the ranks. I developed an unusual interest in *lopor*—what was once key to Tolu Tem's victory was now frowned upon, considered sorcerer's art by the new Kitran emperor and his advisors, the Council of Eagles as they call themselves. *Lopor* was viewed as a product of 'decayed' Serice thinkers. I believed it could be used for more than war: to clear boulders out of roads, perhaps even to build dams made not of trees and dirt but of rock. But *lopor* was only used for war. Only used for destruction. I was given command of a small group of men, and I trained them to use the powder in the form of large 'bombs.' It was effective. Rebel strongholds fell to us in days, where before Sogand forces had sat fruitlessly outside the walls for months.

"I was given more men, more money. It seemed I was the only man the rulers in Daka trusted to use *lopor*. I made it better, put it in smaller containers that still had the power to knock a man down or kill him.

"Ten years passed, and great revolts broke out all across the country. Everywhere, people were painting their swords red or tying red cloth to their weapons. I don't know how it started, and no one in the government knew. So many people were arrested, tortured, but no one knew. It just seemed to appear out of nowhere."

Sandun dared to ask a question "Why 'red swords' or 'red cloth'? You told us there once was a Fire Kingdom—was it related to that?"

Valo Peli nodded. "A very perceptive guess, Master Sandun. It was related, but in an odd way. We believe in cycles. We are taught that everything around us is in a state of flux and change. I'm sure you know this also. By convention, we start with fire, and it produces ash or earth. Earth generates metal, and the prime metal is, naturally, gold. Metal produces water, which generates trees. Trees burn and create fire. As so the cycle continues.

"One hundred years ago, Serica was ruled by the Water Kingdom, which is associated with the color blue. The next element in the cycle is wood, associated with the color green, but Emperor Tolu choose to break the cycle. Instead he called his empire the 'First Empire'—ignoring the previous millennia of Serice history. Outside of Daka, everyone calls it the Kitran Empire. Many Serice now say the days of the Kitran Empire are ending and the next kingdom will soon take its place. After wood comes fire, which is represented by the color red. So the Red Swords are saying they are supporters of the next kingdom, the successor to the Kitran Empire's undeclared Green Kingdom.

"To continue my tale of regrets: for seven years, this one was assigned to military duties, fighting against the Red Swords. Suppressing bandits in the name of the emperor in Daka. In those days, my name was Arno Boethy. But this one—I became sick of my deeds. The government I had once served had vanished like a dragon into a cloud. All that was left was hate, and killing, and evil. There is no one good left in Daka. Not one! All the good men I knew have been executed. All the corrupt but harmless men are dead as well, their wealth confiscated and their women enslaved. The only people left in Daka are the most ruthless, most brutal, most depraved. How many emperors have there been in the last five years? Three? Four? Who can keep track any longer?

"Filled with bitterness, consumed by sorrow, I quit three years ago and retired to my home village. I should have resigned ten years ago. In fact, it would be better for Serica if I had been drowned at birth! No! It's true. No less than the truth now. I have served evil for nearly thirty years, and I only hope to make some amends and serve good with what little time remains to me. That is why I am going to Tokolas. All that I have heard tells me that the ruler of that city is the best man ruling any part of Serica today. If the stories are true, I will offer my head to him, and perhaps he will take me up on my offer."

Here Lathe could restrain himself no longer. "Master, you served the government with honor. You were called 'incorruptible.' You were respected even by your enemies. I've seen your home; you have no great wealth. Everyone in your village venerates you."

Lathe's voice dropped as he said, "Your children love you."

Valo Peli straightened his shoulders and mastered his emotions. "That is but little consolation. My last hope now in this life is that the Lord of Tokolas will see past the evil men that this one served and will consider my reputation for honesty and my veneration for the Great Teacher. If not, then not."

Sandun asked Valo Peli what he knew of Serica today.

"This servant, a native of Serica, was never part of the grand strategy meetings in Daka. This one was but an instrument, not the architect. You know that Serica is now split apart. Many provinces are independent, while others pretend loyalty to the government in Daka but send no taxes and never have soldiers to spare for fighting beyond their borders.

"The Red Swords have taken much of central Serica. Up and down the great river Mur, the Red Swords hold sway, but they are divided among themselves. The largest territory is called the Red Lake Kingdom, comprising the province of Zelkat and some of Sakhat. The Lord of Tokolas controls the ancient province of Kunhalvar. He used to be an ally of the Red Lake King, but he now runs his province in accord with the old ways.

"Beyond Daka, the greatest power is found in the province of Dombovar, with its capital of Naduva, where the Iron King sits on his golden throne.

Naduva was the last capital of the Water Kingdom, and the province of Dombovar is still the richest in Serica. Ten years past, the Iron King gathered together an army of common laborers from the hill towns around his home. With his army, he drove the Kitran out of Dombovar. He crowned himself king and has ruled for several years from his rebuilt palace. Although his court is said to be magnificent, he is a man of little learning, and the great wealth of his territory seems to have corrupted his spirit. He seems to have no connection to the Red Swords, but whether that is a good thing or bad is unclear to me. What does he believe in other than himself?

"The Red Lake Kingdom is unappealing. I don't believe in their Radiant Prince or their prophet and his vision of the goddess coming to cleanse the land of evil. I would swallow my misgivings and offer my services to the Iron King of Dombovar, but why not see if the Lord of Tokolas lives up to his reputation? It is most likely that I will be reviled no matter where I go. I have little hope for the future, but I must make the attempt."

After hearing his story, Sandun found he had a great deal of sympathy for Valo Peli. He knew many people in Tebispoli who had worked for the evil King Oniktes. Some few, like Master Eulogo, had just done their jobs quietly, harming no one. "Keeping the wheels of government spinning," as Master Eulogo put it dryly. But others—shire reeves, bailiffs, tax collectors—had followed King Oniktes's orders, and upon his death and King Pandion's accession to the throne, they had lost everything. Most had lost their positions, some had been hounded from office by mobs of angry peasants, a few had even been killed.

Perhaps it had been unwise to accept Valo Peli's offer to accompany them. But that was water under the bridge. He was one of them now. In Sandun's experience, you didn't often pick the men you fought beside, but loyalty proved by battle was treated like a sworn oath in Kelten. Sometimes, this loyalty was given to a bad man, as King Oniktes undoubtedly had been. But it was their tradition.

PART SIX

Kunhalvar

Around midday, at the Kunhalvar border, the Archives Expedition caught up to a line of carts. At the end of the line was a gate and soldiers. Without doubt, this was a border crossing.

To the north, several large tents were set up in a clearing. About thirty men were practicing for war in the field. Sandun had seen this before outside of towns and cities in Kelten: men with spears, running forward and then pulling together and stepping backward while keeping in formation. Hoisting the spears into the air and turning to face the opposite direction and then bringing the spears down again. All done to the cadence of shouted orders from a barrel-chested, red-faced man—the universal sergeant who is always in charge of training young men for war in every land under the sun. Other men were doing chores: chopping wood, sawing, carrying water. The soldiers went through their exercises with vigor, punctuated with loud shouts; the officers moved about the camp with speed.

The road at this frontier outpost was surrounded by tall willow trees, and sitting in the shade was pleasant. However, after fifteen minutes' rest, Sandun walked up to the head of the line to observe. An officer, about Sandun's age and wearing leather armor, was asking questions of a young farmer standing beside a loaded cart. Sandun heard him ask where the farmer was going. The farmer said that he was looking for a place to settle where it would be safe. His wife stayed on the cart; two small children next to her were silent.

"If you don't want to go far, there is good land south of here. Several men like you have chosen to go there this week already. If you want to be on the other side of the river, then you may go down to the ferry, and it can take you across the river. An official there can give you further directions." The officer had certainly said the same thing to lots of people, but he seemed to care.

"How much will it cost? We are very poor."

"Nothing. The Lord of Kunhalvar has unoccupied land and wishes for it to be farmed. All he asks is that you pay your taxes at the next harvest and that you obey the laws. Simple, yes?"

The farmer's relief was palpable; a big smile broke over his face, and he got down on his knees and pressed his hands together in front of the officer. The soldier had clearly seen this reaction before and gently lifted the man back to his feet.

By now, some of the other soldiers had noticed Sandun and the Kelten expedition. One came over to the officer, said something, and then went over to the biggest tent, nearly running.

Half an hour later, about twenty soldiers came across the clearing, escorting an older man who wore a colorful green robe with a modest-sized animal embroidered above his heart. As the man came closer, Sandun realized the animal depicted was a raccoon, looking to its left.

Sandun stepped forward, with Basil at his side, and at a command from Sir Ako, the rest of expedition came and stood in a line behind them. The officer waited till the man in the green robe arrived, and then he said, "Who are you, and what do you seek in the province of Kunhalvar?"

Sandun replied, "I am Sandun Eiger, and we are an embassy from King Pandion the Third of Kelten, to the Lord of Kunhalvar. Our king desires both friendship and trade."

At this reply, the old man in the green robe advanced toward them and said, "News of emissaries from distant Kelten has reached this outpost. And it takes no great insight to see that you and your companions are not from this land. Yet, should we let you go on to our capital of Tokolas simply based on your words? Do you bring some proof that you are who you say you are?" The green-robed man spoke like Valo Peli, though he sometimes used words that Sandun had never heard before.

Fortunately, two weeks on the road listening to Valo Peli's history of Serica had given Sandun a fighting chance at understanding this official. "I have a document from my king." Sandun went to his pack and took out everything before finding the tube with the rolled-up parchment at the bottom of the bag. He carefully unrolled it and showed it to the green-robed official.

The old man looked at the document and then said, "I can tell you have been carrying this a long time. Though I cannot read it, this seems sufficient proof to me. Allow me to send my report with an aide on your journey to the capital. The next boat that sails directly to Tokolas will not arrive for two days. If you do not wish to wait, you could cross the river and ride the rest of the way. Will you allow me to offer you some tea while you consider?"

"We are anxious to reach the end of our journey, and we have ridden long enough to think sixty miles more is but a child's distance. However, we will gladly share some tea with you before we continue," replied Sandun.

Valo Peli and Lathe elicited no comment from the official; they said little and gave every impression of being little more than servants or guides found on the road.

The official in the green robe introduced himself as Scribe Jelesik and showed them back to his tent. There they drank tea for an hour while he made small talk. "Rumors of a group of strangers from Kelten reached us yesterday. These were intermixed with stories about a battle at Wheat Town, where a company of Sogand raiders was utterly destroyed. I gave little credence to the two stories but looking at you now, I can see you are mighty warriors with striking bows. I would have thought they were fighting sticks until I observed the notches at the end and the long arrows that all of your men carry."

"We did have a role to play in the battle of Wheat Town," Sandun replied. "But doubtless the rumors exaggerate the numbers we faced. We fought a small force. Our victory was fortunate." Sandun had learned from Valo Peli's style of conversation that modesty was prized as a virtue in Serica.

Jelesik's assistant produced a document, which his master signed using an elaborate design; it took at least a minute for Jelesik to create the intricate mark at the end of the document. He handed it to Sandun.

"This letter of safe conduct relates to your expedition's journey to Tokolas. In these troubled times, one can hardly say any place is safe, but I urge you to be slow in resorting to your weapons. The army of Kunhalvar patrols the roads and does its best to keep the bandits and lawless subdued. I doubt you would be mistaken as bandits by our soldiers, but I urge caution."

Sandun gave the letter to Ashala to read. She read it and then nodded, and Sandun thanked Master Jelesik for his hospitality and his letter.

They rode away from the post, joining the stream of people that had passed through the border crossing and now were heading down to the river.

This was their first night inside Kunhalvar territory, and they stopped in the late afternoon at a bustling little village. The local tea house was doing good business with men sitting around the small tables drinking tea or the grain spirit called *zloty*. Most of the men looked like tradesmen of the town, there to drink, exchange the day's news, and flirt with the young women serving the tables. Despite the crowd, there were a few rooms available for the Keltens.

The differences between Hazeny and this village were noticeable. People were busy, but there was less fear. The guards at the gate were like the guards at the border outpost: disciplined and, if Sandun was any judge, determined.

There was a difference also in the way the people went about their tasks. For some time, Sandun could not put his finger on it, but eventually he concluded these were a people at war. He had seen something of this during the year of King Pandion's rebellion: not much laughter, and many people moving with purpose.

The expedition attracted some notice, but most of the townsfolk had better things to do then gawk at the strangers at the back of the inn.

As they were heading to their rooms, Valo Peli had a quiet word with Sandun. "A man came in after us. I recognized him from the border post camp. He is dressed as a common laborer. You can guess that his purpose is to watch you." Valo Peli said this in a very even tone, with no surprise and no dismay.

Sandun thanked him and informed the others. The rest of the Keltens chewed over this news in their own way. Some were resigned; Kagne and Padan were upset.

"This place worries me," Kagne complained. "No one seems to be having any fun. And now we are being watched? The sooner we leave, the happier I'll be."

Padan was contemptuous. "The first embassy from Kelten in more than three hundred years, and they are worried we are spies? It is to laugh."

Sandun was not concerned. In several discussions among the senior archivists, the topic of the king's confidential reports had come up. It was known that King Pandion employed spies and received written reports from some of them, but these reports were never delivered to the Archives. One well-connected archivist let slip that the reports on the doings of the

Fiodroch ambassador were never written down, despite or because of the noble women he had seduced over the last five years. Given that the Lord of Kunhalvar was surrounded by enemies, it made sense to Sandun that he would have many spies and that they would pay special attention to strangers from distant lands.

A low, wet fog greeted them the next morning as they prepared to set out. The day's journey was through a thick forest of river trees. The road twisted this way and that as it wove a path between small lakes.

When Sandun asked about the lakes, Valo Peli said, "The great river Mur makes these lakes. I have seen old maps that show the river as quite different from how it runs today. No one understands why, but there is no stopping her. One must build towns some miles back or on top of hills to avoid the Mur. Floods were partially responsible for the destruction of Serica's first capital, Soltvarkas, which is not far north of here. The great earthquakes also played a role."

"Earthquakes?" asked Sandun. "They are commonplace in Kelten and in many islands of the Archipelago. But none of our books talk about earthquakes in Serica."

"Earthquakes are regarded by most as a sign of heaven's displeasure. Few would talk about such things, as they reflect badly on everyone. Do you regard them lightly in Kelten?"

"Earthquakes destroy farmhouses and fences far more often than they destroy cities." Sandun replied. "It is hard to think of any great crimes done by simple ploughmen. Our temples teach that the quaking earth represents the ongoing struggle between Sho'Ash and the enemy. It has little to do with the acts of mankind. Or so we believe."

Shortly after noon, they reached the port. The buildings all looked ramshackle, and the soil was soft and muddy. But as they reached the last house at the end of the road, the great river was spread before them, and it took their breath away.

The Mur looked more like a lake than a river, yet the water was moving, rushing, hurrying from north to south. No river in Kelten could compare to the great river Mur. It was vast, and the far shore, though thickly forested, was distant and hard to see. The Mur wasn't noisy, but it seemed alive, its surface constantly changing. Large waves came downstream and then passed, leaving the waterway a bit shallower, till another large wave came down, almost as though it was breathing. The water was dark but not inky. Sandun tasted the water; it tasted of earth.

A small group of people were already waiting to cross. Most were farmers with their few possessions lying beside them, wrapped in rough cloth and coarse ropes. A few soldiers and two merchants were waiting with bulging sacks on mules.

As they watched, a boat approached from the eastern shore. It was long but rode fairly high out of the water. At first it was hard to see how the boat was moving, but as it got closer, they could see the men on board pushing it along with great poles. The boat did not head for the ferry point; instead, it ended up some half a mile downriver, and then the men poled the boat upriver close to the shore, where the current was weaker.

The men pushing on the poles were tall and wiry thin. Their effortless balance on the boat as it swayed from side to side reflected a lifetime of experience on the water. The people waiting in line ahead of them boarded the boat, and then it shoved off with a cheery wave from the captain at the tiller.

Sir Ako haltingly asked Valo Peli about fishing on the river.

"Many great fish live in the Mur. But not good fishing," Valo Peli told him. "The current is too strong. Better fishing in the lakes and smaller streams that come into the river from either side."

An hour later, the ferryboat was back. Sandun showed the captain the paper that Scribe Jelesik had given him the day before. Sandun expected the ferryboat captain to ask for a translation, but instead he slowly read the document, calling one of the younger men over to help him with one of the words.

"On official business, are you? No charge to you. On you go. Warning to you: riverside gets tricky in the afternoon, hard to see things in the water." The captain's speech was hard to understand. Some words he used were unfamiliar to Sandun, who looked at Ashala; she shrugged. Riverboat language was not part of normal Serice language education.

The boat, seen up close, was long and wide enough for four men to stand abreast. The boatmen were a cheerful lot, with lots of jokes and laughter as the expedition moved their horses, the Piksie rams, and their packs on board. The horses were blindfolded and tethered firmly to the central timber of the boat. The Piksie rams were tethered but not blindfolded. The passengers were strongly told to keep to the center, as the boatmen needed at times to run from one side of the boat to the other.

Crossing the rivers of Kelten was never a cause for concern; as a result, the expedition was carefree as they sat amid the packs and ropes in the center.

But Sandun saw that Valo Peli was visibly nervous, and Lathe seemed even more concerned as he scanned the water.

"Are there monsters in the river?" Sandun jokingly asked Valo Peli.

"Yes, though rarely do they come this far north. It is the spring flooding that has begun, and many are the hidden dangers crossing the Mur. Still, it looks safe enough today. I have seen it when a storm whipped up waves taller than a horse…that was not a good time for crossing." Valo Peli shook his head at the memory. Sandun nervously wondered how deep the river was and how big the river monsters were.

When all was ready, the boatmen pushed off and poled their way through the shallows near the shore. Sandun knew enough about boats to tell that this ferry had a shallow keel, and it swayed back and forth while eddies in the current pushed it first in one direction, then another. The captain was at the tiller in the rear, while an equally sun-beaten man was at the bow, staring intently at the water ahead of them and yelling unfamiliar words back to the captain.

The water became choppy, and huge upwellings of water appeared and disappeared all around them. Many tree branches and pieces of broken bark rushed past on the surface of the water. They were now out in the main current of the river, and the poles could no longer be used to push the boat; instead, the river boatmen used their poles to fend off oncoming flotsam. Although the boat was being carried by the current, it was traveling at an angle, and sticks and broken treetops banged into the upstream side of the boat. Some of the pieces of flotsam were quite large, and the whole boat shook when squarely struck.

Basil's dog, who at first had been happy to look around at the water, was now lying unhappily between his master's feet. "I've never been on a river like this," Basil said loudly. "It beats out every river in Kelten put together. We are only halfway across. By Hurin's Beard, this is inspiring!"

Sandun was about to respond when yelling broke out from three of the pole handlers on the upstream side. They were pointing at a large shape that had emerged from the water. The captain stood up and looked intently at the shape upstream and the water between them, and then he yelled strident orders as he pushed at the tiller. He was trying to turn the boat to head directly south with the current. At the same time, more of the pole men came over from the other side of the boat.

The boat turned slowly, and the distance between them and the dark shape narrowed. Now Sandun could see that it was a great tree trunk, with several broken branches still hanging off the trunk. It was almost completely submerged, perhaps waterlogged or made of some dense wood that barely floated.

The boat was nearly parallel to the distant shore, but the great tree trunk was upon them. The pole men moved around the stern of the boat, shouting at one another, poking at the water. Even in its broken and decayed condition, the tree trunk was a monster, and the current was carrying it right toward them.

The captain strained at the tiller, the boat began to veer again, and the pole men, legs braced against the deck boards, pushed at the trunk with all their might. To try and balance the load, the Keltens moved toward the front of the boat while staying low and holding tightly to the gunnels.

The trunk slipped past the boat, making great scraping noises. Branches dragged across the underside of the boat, pulling at the keel like claws. Suddenly, the tiller twisted out of the captain's hand, and he was thrown to the deck with a cry. Something had caught the boat, and the ferry began tipping over.

The lookout ran from the front of the boat to the rear and wrestled with the tiller as water surged dark green over the side. Several poles snapped. One young pole man had an elongated saw blade on the end of his pole, and he attacked the tree beneath the water with a frantic energy, sawing up and down while the boat twisted and groaned.

Padan was praying loudly to Sho'Ash. Ashala clutched a piece of broken pole, her eyes wide with fear. Olef was looking about in all directions, like a cat about to jump off a ledge, while Basil had his arm around her.

With a shout, the man with the saw cut through the underwater tree branch, and the boat slowly righted itself again with more groaning and scraping noises. Two of the pole men found buckets and started bailing out the water at the bottom of the boat. The captain sat up, but he was in evident pain, using one arm to hold the other tightly against his body. The lookout replaced him at the tiller, guiding the boat away from the trunk and toward the eastern shore.

With the danger over for the moment, Sandun tried to suppress the urge to laugh but found he couldn't fight it. Kagne looked at him quizzically and said, "You always did have an odd sense of humor, Sandun."

"No, it's just...too ironic. For us to have crossed the deadly Tirala Mountains only to be drowned crossing the Mur. What a joke that would be!"

"The stars told me that we would make it back to Erimasran. We were in no danger." Kagne seemed to be unafraid of the river. Likewise, Sir Ako had shown no sign of fear.

The rest of the trip was uneventful. They reached the eastern shore and slowly poled their way north to the east ferry, crossing through shallow waters. Once they were evidently safe, everyone became quite talkative, and Padan led them all in a song of praise to Sho'Ash, the song usually sung on the last day of High Holy Week.

After singing, Sandun asked Sir Ako why he had been so unconcerned about the crossing.

"I liked my chances on this river. With my older brothers, I've been down two of the swift rivers that flow from the Alps and join the Saperchios near Agnefeld. If the boat tips over, I learned you stay with the boat and wait for it to run aground or for other boats to rescue you. This water's not too cold; we could last for an hour, maybe two. Ah, I should have mentioned that once we got on board."

Sandun did not reply; traveling down rushing streams in small boats was beyond his knowledge of the world. Even fishing in the ocean was a thing that few men did unless they made their living at it because of the danger.

They disembarked, their packs and shoes wet. Sandun went to the captain and offered him a dozen coins for his trouble.

The captain shook his head in refusal. His shoulder was sprained, but no bones were broken.

"I thank you for the offer, but I cannot accept it. We should have avoided the *abalta* and given you a smooth crossing. It's my fault, and I hope you will not hold it against me when you speak to the lord. I'm sure he will understand as he's one of us."

"Truly, I had not heard that." Sandun was nearly certain the captain was exaggerating the Lord of Kunhalvar's relationship to riverboatmen.

"Aye, our lord comes from riverboat stock. His father and grandfather before him poled boats on the river. The family fell on hard times, lost their boat, and then died of the plague, but he's from riverboat folk as sure as the sun is hot. He knows what our life is like."

This news was deeply shocking to Sandun, and he mulled it over all the rest of the day and after dinner. For nearly the entirety of the nine hundred years of Pellian Empire, the emperor had claimed descent from either the Great Commander or one of his relatives. And for the last six hundred years of Kelten's history, the king could trace his line back to King Agiden the Founder. The idea that a commoner might become a ruler? It was profoundly unsettling. Who would follow such a man? How would he know he was chosen to be the king?

Sandun did not include the captain's claim in his daily log entry, but he resolved that he would—carefully—ask Valo Peli about it when the opportunity arose. Not for the first time, Sandun questioned his decision to lead the expedition to Tokolas instead of one of the other great cities of Serica.

The next day, as they rode on the main road to Tokolas, Sandun quietly asked Valo Peli about the Lord of Kunhalvar.

"Yesterday, the captain of the ferry said that the Lord of Kunhalvar comes from a family of riverboatmen. I doubt not that I mistook what he said to me."

Valo Peli looked at him with surprise. "Not at all. You understood him correctly. Didn't I mention this? He was born to a very poor family, and he spent most of his life penniless."

Sandun tried without success to hide his dismay. "How can he rule a province? How can he hope to become King of Serica? He is just a commoner."

Valo said, very matter-of-factly, "That is of no matter. The founder of the Green Kingdom came from a humble background. He was the best man, and heaven approved of his character. He became king and founded the Green Kingdom. When a kingdom falls, as the Water Kingdom most definitely fell, then the founder of the next kingdom can be almost any man. The Iron King, who rules a very large territory farther east, is a former iron miner, and his family mined iron in the hills for many generations. His background is not important. What matters is his character."

Valo Peli paused and looked at Sandun with interest. "How is the king of Kelten selected when one kingdom falls?"

Sandun replied, "In general, the kings of Kelten are always drawn from the same family. The current king, Pandion III, traces his descent from a line of kings dating back some six hundred years. The idea of a commoner becoming king, that is…hard to imagine."

"But what happens when a kingdom comes to an end?" Valo pressed the issue. "How is the new king selected?"

"I suppose one of the great lords would become king. Likely someone closely or even distantly related to the previous king."

"That is not our way. In Serica, a man may rise very high, even becoming a chief minister. And yet his children, while they can enjoy wealth and some measure of respect due to their father's great position, unless they study hard and are diligent in their duties, they are likely to have only minor positions, or none at all. We say, 'A minister's son is rich but lazy, and his son in turn will become a townsman with a fancy scroll on the wall.' That is often how it works out."

Sandun was not convinced by Valo Peli's assertion. Perhaps in a time of civil war, such turnover might occur, he thought. But surely, once the war had ended and a new king was in power, the great lords would gain title to vast estates and would pass them on to their children and so on, for hundreds of years, just like it was in Kelten, Fiodroch, Jibur, Melnehlan, Akia, and the rest of the Archipelago.

The remainder of their journey to Tokolas was free of trouble. The road was well maintained and frequently patrolled by mounted soldiers. The towns they rode through were busy but orderly. The lands on either side were rich, well taken care of. In all directions, farmers were out working in the fields. The expedition's "safe conduct" pass was frequently inspected by guards at town gates and occasionally by mounted patrols, and they were always treated with polite respect. On both nights, they were put up at the finest tea houses at no charge.

Sandun's misgivings about the humble origins of the Lord of Kunhalvar gradually faded into the background, as it was clear to everyone that this area was at least as well run as the lands around the great estuary in the center of Kelten. Whoever the Lord of Kunhalvar was, judging from the towns and roads they traveled, his reputation for good government was justified.

Finally, they reached Tokolas itself. The road was filled with carts and people of all descriptions going both to and from the city. A special escort of foot soldiers met them, and again their pass was inspected, but this was merely a formality. Word had gone ahead, and the ambassadors from Kelten were expected. They were escorted through the streets of the city with speed.

The journey into the heart of the city was a blur of sights and sounds. A sea of faces looked at them as they traveled along a major thoroughfare toward the center of town. This was a mighty city with a huge population, that much was obvious. In other respects—architecture, street layout, and even markets—the city was different from every Kelten city Sandun had seen.

He saw more wood than bricks and more walls than fences. They passed through a market that was a great square filled with tents and carts, instead of the wide streets that doubled as markets in Kelten. Most signs he saw were words, not pictures.

The one thing that struck Sandun above all else was that very few houses were two-story buildings, and almost no building was any taller. Even past the market square, shops lined the thoroughfare. As he looked at the shops, noting the products they offered for sale, Sandun was amazed to see not one or two but at least fifteen booksellers, and one block contained five bookshops next to each other. In the whole of Seopolis, there were just two shops that sold books: one next to the Great Temple and the other near the Guild Hall.

In Gipu, Sandun had been impressed by the large collection of books Ashala's father had, but now he realized that he'd had no conception of how widespread books were in Serica. How many people knew how to read and write, he wondered. Most men in Kelten could barely write their own names. The priests, rich merchants, and many of the great lords all had their letters but beyond that, literate men were few.

What would it mean to live in a country where literate men were common? He knew himself well enough to know that he took great pride in his ability to read and write. It was a rare talent in Kelten, but perhaps not rare at all in Serica. When had this change occurred? No reports of old told of any great numbers of books or learned men in Serica. Something had happened in the last three hundred years…but what?

Lost his own thoughts, Sandun suddenly realized they had turned off the main street to one lined not with shops but with tall walls and large gates. Behind the walls, large and decorated rooftops could be seen. The noise of the city faded away. Big men with short spears stood beside some of the gates. Sandun was reminded of Dromo Thalas, where the houses of the great lords lined up along the way to Sita Elaf, the king's palace. A few minutes later, they came to a tall gate. They dismounted and walked through to a courtyard, where they were greeted by a young man in a blue robe, clearly an official of the Tokolas government.

The man introduced himself Scribe Renieth. He explained that the Lord of Kunhalvar was honored to have the embassy from Kelten come to his capital and that he hoped to meet with as soon as they had rested from their "journey of ten thousand tik." Renieth said that this building had been set aside for their use as long as they stayed in Tokolas and that they could ask for anything and it would be provided. A cook and housekeeper were on staff, and they should not hesitate to make a request, as it would assuredly be speedily granted.

Sandun expressed his thanks and appreciation for this generous hospitality. He said that they looked forward to meeting with the Lord of Kunhalvar at his earliest convenience. Sir Ako tried out his Serice, which he had been working on even in Gipu, and expressed his thanks as well. Valo Peli and Lathe stayed quietly in the background.

Renieth showed them around the building. It was two stories tall, with numerous small but comfortable sleeping quarters on the second floor and a dining room, library, and kitchen on the first floor. All in all, more than enough space for the expedition. Sandun detected a musty air to some of the upstairs rooms, as though they had not been occupied for some months or years, and brick-lined rooms below the ground floor were still being cleaned as they toured the building. In the back, there was a stable with room for their Piksie rams and several horses. Finally, there was a small plot of land adjacent to the building, freshly hoed, a large pile of weeds lying to one side.

That evening, at dinner, Sandun shared out the very last skin of Zeres wine that he had bought in Sirosfeld. He thanked each of the expedition members, praising each one individually.

"Thanks to your heroic efforts, we have reached our destination. We have traveled more than three thousand miles from Seopolis to this great city of Tokolas. The divine blessing of Sho'Ash and his saints have protected us as we crossed the Tiralas, for which we are unworthy, but for which we give thanks. We have accomplished a feat that will live forever in the Annals of the Kingdom of Kelten. With the continued favor of Sho'Ash, the journey back will be shorter and safer. But let's not worry about returning home just yet. For now, we can relax and enjoy a month or more of peace and rest."

In his lifetime, Sandun rarely made a prediction that was more mistaken.

PART SEVEN

Tokolas

Sir Ako Bous Rosen, third son of the Earl of Agnefeld, knight of the realm of Kelten, commander of a company of Lord Arris's light horse, was a free man. He walked down the main street of Tokolas just before noon, and no one needed him, and he had absolutely nothing to do. For more than a year, he had shepherded the Archives Expedition from Tebispoli all the way to this great city in Serica, which was apparently their final destination. Every day he had worried about the next day's march, and the assignments, and the men, and the food, and the morale, and the threats, and on and on.

But now he was a free man. For the moment, there were no orders to give. The guards outside the luxurious house assigned to them were big, capable men who kept a sharp eye on any suspicious people that approached. They were drawn from the household guards of the Lord of Kunhalvar—Ako had checked.

Sandun was closeted with the Serice scholar, Valo Peli, going over protocol and the fine points of meeting a very high-level official without making a fool of oneself. Doubtless Ako would be required to attend the meeting, but he was confident that by staying silent and copying Sandun, all would go well. If there was something important he needed to know, he was sure Sandun would not hesitate to tell him. No one knew when they would actually meet with the Lord of Kunhalvar. The official who saw to their housing and food, Scribe Renieth, had assured them that his master "very much wanted to meet them," but whether he would have time later this week was unknown.

Sir Ako's scouts were tired from the trip and more than a little overwhelmed by the size and crowds of the city. All of his men were from the countryside, most from the southern part of Kelten, and only a few had even visited Seopolis. Yet the capital of Kelten was smaller and much less imposing than Tokolas. Sir Ako had visited Seopolis often in his life; it was a normal city to him. Tokolas—big and busy as it was—still was just another city.

But the crowds were intense. People by the thousands, or the tens of thousands, were out on the streets, going places, doing things, fixing the cobblestone roads, putting up new buildings, tearing down old ones, pulling small carts loaded with bags, or carrying great loads on their backs. In every direction, smoke from burning coal drifted up to the sky. The main street was lined with shops selling food, and the sellers often had people whose job was to cry out that they had food for sale. The cacophony of vendors yelling their wares and the general hubbub of people talking as they met on the street joined with the occasional shouts by guards. A few blocks in Seopolis could rival this for an hour or two around noon, but Tokolas was much the same all the way to the city gates.

Ako had little difficulty in making his way through the crowd. He was taller than most of the people on the street—indeed, one of the largest men out walking, though he saw a few near giants working at a couple of the construction sites. He finally reached the city gates and stood there for a time, examining the state of the defenses and the soldiers while chewing on some spicy roasted meat he'd bought from a street vendor.

The walls were old, but he could see many signs of recent repair work. The sounds of stone being hammered told him that more repair work was going on nearby. The guards were busy checking the flood of people coming into the city from outside. Farmers with carts loaded with food came in with just a wave, as did the day laborers with tools in their hands or sacks on their backs.

His professional curiosity at least partially satisfied, Ako turned around and headed back up the street. The midday heat, the dust and smoke, and the unrelenting bombardment of noise had created in Ako a powerful urge to find a quiet tea house like the one they'd stayed at in Hazeny. However, the ones he saw were right by the street and seemed to offer little more than a streetside location. So he went on.

Close to the central government buildings, he saw a quiet street with some trees growing along the margin of the road. Trees were a welcome sight, and as he walked along the road he noticed that the people weren't yelling. The few street vendors stood quietly beside their carts, which had

Serice words painted on the wooden sides. A large gateway opened up on his left; beyond was a haven of grass and large trees with a collection of old buildings constructed in a different style from what he had seen thus far.

This is either a temple grounds or a school, Ako thought to himself. So he walked in, and immediately the noise of the city trailed off like a flock of crows that were flying fast away; within seconds, the raucous cawing was replaced by the sound of water falling into pools. The people on the grounds were either writing on large pieces of paper or were walking in small groups, talking quietly.

Following a path, he came to a circular pool of water set amid carved stones. Around the pool were marble benches with carved animals supporting the seat. On one bench was a woman—a young lady. He looked at her and found he could not look away. She was captivatingly beautiful with an oval face, unblemished skin, and long black hair that seemed to shimmer in the light. She was reading a book, and her posture, the way she held her hand, was like a painting. She looked up at him and smiled with a happy, open expression.

Ako felt his heart pounding in his chest, and his face grew hot. The young woman shyly looked away and then looked back at him. *So this is what it is like to be bewitched,* he thought as he found himself walking closer to the woman. She wore an unusual dress that was different from the Serice dresses he had seen; it was made of white silk and hugged her body.

He stood near her, feeling a bit foolish and hesitant to try his poor Serice. Instead, he bowed as though she was a noble; when he straightened up, she smiled again and then hid her face with her hands.

"Are you one of the *opmi* from Kelten?" Her voice was music to his ears. It was low but precise. "A little bird told me there were *opmi* from Kelten nearby. And I thought to myself, how wonderful, I should like to meet one. And so I have waited hours, and now, here you are!" She smiled again at him, a smile that lit up her face. Ako thought that having this woman smile at him was one of the best things he could imagine. He felt a little dizzy, as though all the blood had left his head.

Perceptively, she said, "You must be very tired. You have come such a long way, thousands of tik. I remember when I first came here from my home in Rakeved, I was so tired, I could hardly gather the strength to eat, and that is very unusual—my family used to say I never missed an opportunity to eat."

After saying this, her face fell, and she looked sad. Ako felt the sun had gone behind a cloud.

"I am a bit tired, but I have been walking up and down the main road today. I went down the west gate and then returned. This spot is very… good," he assured her.

The woman smiled again. "That is not the right word to use, oh no. You would call this place *gopash*. The word you used would apply to a horse or a sword." She looked at his sword. "Are you an *opmi*? I've always wanted to meet an *opmi* from Kelten."

Ako didn't know what an *opmi* was. "I'm a knight of Kelten." He drew his sword. "This was given to me by the king of Kelten."

The woman clapped her hands with delight. "Knight? That sounds like an *opmi* to me. And to think, all I had to do was sit here. Everyone comes to Tokolas, that's what people say nowadays. But do they ever leave?" At this her smile faded away, and she was silent briefly.

Although Ako missed quite a number of the words she used, he found her presence captivating. In more lucid moments he thought to himself: *I'm flirting with this woman, and I'm married.* But of course, he had lived with Eria, that pretty girl in Gipu, for months, and she was likely carrying his child. And his real wife was three thousand miles away and despised him. After an hour, he stopped worrying about it. He was happy, and she was a delight, smiling and holding her hand up to her mouth and laughing. She was everything he found desirable in a woman: beautiful, elegant in her dress and her manner, shy and yet open about her likes.

For the rest of the afternoon, they sat together and walked about what he learned was the School of the Great Teacher. Ako also learned that her name was Russu Tuomi and that she had accompanied her father on a long trip from her home in Rakeved to Kunhalvar. Shortly after they arrived, her father had died quite unexpectedly. Since then she had been in mourning, living with a wealthy Rakeved merchant close by, an uncle named Atos Vepsailin. She had been in Tokolas for one year.

"Since then, I've been waiting for a delegation or merchant caravan to come and take me home, but there has been no word. And it's springtime, and I feel I can't stay inside any longer. I want to go and explore and see the city. But I can't, not on my own. And Uncle Atos's servants are so dull, the Rakeved ones are scared of shadows, and the Serice ones are both *holumzaty* and *pulbums*."

Ako's expression betrayed his lack of understanding.

Russu took his hand and said in a conspiratorial voice, "They despise us. Oh, I shouldn't say it, but it's true. The Serice think of us as uneducated barbarians. We used to be part of the Gold Kingdom, but that was years and years in the past. We still study the same books, use the same words for writing. We haven't changed…well, not much. But to the Serice, we are like…oh, I don't know. Different, lesser."

She paused and looked at him seriously. "Those Serice men, they would never dream of talking to me like you do, as though I was a real person. No, they'd be standing there thinking, 'There goes that barbarian princess, prattling nonsense.'"

"You are a princess?"

"Oh, not an important one. My *touroushi* father was king long ago. There are more than 150 women of my rank back home. The Tuomi family is very large."

This revelation simultaneously made Russu less approachable and more desirable.

She noticed his reaction but seemed to misinterpret it. "Don't worry. Rakeved is a small kingdom. I'm sure you are a much more important person in Kelten than I am in Rakeved."

Ako said nothing but nodded his head. *I will be, when I return,* he thought to himself.

Finally, Russu said that she had to return to her uncle's house, or he would worry and send out searchers. Ako offered to escort her back. She bit at her lower lip and then nodded. Walking close but a little behind him, Russu guided him to a large house just one block east of the school. Guards were at the gate; they looked different from the Serice soldiers—not as large, with darker skin, and with round ears, unlike Russu. They were visibly relieved when she walked up.

"I'll see you tomorrow? We can explore the city together?" Ako said hopefully.

"Yes, if it doesn't rain. You can protect me from the shadows my uncle is worried about."

I can do that, thought Ako. *I can definitely do that.* With Russu at his side, he felt confident of his chances against a dozen men.

Ako floated back home, not seeing anything around him. The image of Russu in her white silk dress occupied all his mind. He arrived late for the meal the expedition shared together. He was oblivious to the looks Basil and Sandun exchanged.

After dinner, Sandun attempted to explain some of the fine points of Serice etiquette, but Ako could not force himself to pay attention. "Look, I'll just stand there and do what you do unless you signal otherwise."

Sandun gave a heavy sigh but did not press the issue.

The next day, Ako practiced combat in the morning with special effort. He had tossed and turned all night but was full of energy nonetheless.

Around noon, clean and wearing his best clothes, Ako stood at the gate where Russu had left him the previous evening. Moments later, the young woman slipped out through the gate and stood facing him. Her hair was pinned up, although two strands hung down to her shoulders. She wore a yellow silk dress with a green sash. "I am ready. What shall we see?"

Ako had a limited grasp of the city geography but said, "The east gate market."

Russu smiled. "The horses are sold in the east market. Let's go! I like horses."

One of the guards said something to Russu with a concerned look, but she waved him off.

Ako held his left arm out to her; she looked at him quizzically and then lightly touched it with her right hand, and so they walked down the street together. Ako had to control his emotions; no knight walked around a city with a stupid grin on his face.

Russu pointed out a few of the buildings they passed, but the words she used to describe them meant nothing to Ako. The farther they walked, the smaller the walls and houses became. Gates become just doors in low walls. Then shops appeared on either side of the street, and the noise increased. Dust in the air mixed with smoke from dozens of fires cooking food for the midday meals. The street opened up into a plaza: this was the east gate market, bigger than any market Ako had ever seen.

Although he couldn't see any horses, he could smell them; the unmistakable scent of horse manure was coming from near the big tower, doubtless the east gate. When they reached it, Ako was unimpressed. The horses for sale were of poor quality. Some were quite old and in Kelten would not be suitable for a day's rent in Seopolis. However, Russu was pleased to see them, though she did comment on how unhappy some of the horses appeared. Ako asked one of the horse merchants where the good horses were sold.

The horse seller, his face weathered and his hands stained from years of leather polish, held his hand out and turned it palm up and then palm down several times. "It's the war," the man said. "All the good ones are with the cavalry. Hard to keep even bad horses in stock. If I had any good ones, I'd have to sell them quiet. If I had any."

Ako knew what the man meant. Horses got sick just like men, and keeping the scouts supplied with fresh horses was a constant struggle for the Kelten army, even in peacetime.

The other animals for sale—pigs, cows, goats, chickens—all looked good. Healthy, well bred. In fact, he thought the pigs were bigger than any he had seen back home. Everyone knew that Kelten just wasn't good pig country, not compared to Melnehlan.

Russu eventually lost interest in the animals, and so they turned back, heading toward the carts filled with vegetables.

Ako wasn't aware of any danger, yet without really knowing why, he drew his sword just as a pair of short men brandished long, curved daggers and tried to stab Russu. Using his sword as a shield, he blocked one overhand stroke and then shoved the man violently back into the crowd. With his left hand, he punched the other man in the face, sending him sprawling to the hard ground.

Russu produced a long needle from her hair and stabbed at the first attacker as he rushed toward her, but her aim was poor, and he jumped past her thrust. Two more men who looked a little like the guards outside her uncle's house joined in the attack on Russu.

There was shouting and a surge of shoppers away from the fight. Ako paid no attention to the civilians. His rage and anger had risen like a great wave on a hitherto calm sea, and with a fury he slashed at every man who approached. One fool fell for a simple feint to the face while Ako dropped his point and stabbed him hard in the upper thigh. Another would-be assassin thought he could block Ako's sword slash with his curved dagger. Ako laughed as he fought through the block and forced his blade deep into the man's neck; blood spurted out of the wound, and the man fell. Ako lowered his head and yelled as he charged toward the first attacker, but it was a ruse; he veered to the right and suddenly ran his sword all the way through the second attacker's midriff. The man's surprised expression lasted just a second till blood ran out of his mouth.

Ako jerked his sword out of the man and faced their first attacker. His rage was burning like a living fire, hotter than any he could remember; he barely managed to hold himself in check, waiting for the assassin to make a move. The man, with a dirty blue cloth wrapped around his head, his simple shirt torn, his eyes wide, glanced about the ground at the bodies of his compatriots. There was no help there. He yelled some strange words at Russu and then turned and ran. Ako gave chase briefly, but the assassin was like a snake, darting through the crowd, slipping between market stalls. Ako realized that he was not going to catch him, and there might be still more assassins waiting to attack the Rakeved princess.

He returned to find Russu standing, shaking but defiant, holding her long steel needle in one hand and one of the assassins' daggers in the other, a ring of gawking shoppers around her.

"Do you want to talk to the city guards about this?" Ako asked her.

"I…I don't know."

"Then let us leave this place. I'm sure people know where to find me."

Ako grabbed Russu's hand, and they walked away from the bodies on the street. Several people shouted at him, urging him to stop and explain, but Ako ignored them and pushed on into the market. Blood was dripping down his left arm, and he had a cut on his right hand. As often happened after a battle, he had no idea how either wound had occurred.

Russu, seeing him bleeding, stopped for a moment. Using the dagger, she cut a strip of fabric from her yellow dress and wrapped it around his hand. She wrapped another strip around his upper arm. It slowed the bleeding.

They continued on and took a side street back to the expedition's house. Russu said nothing. Finally, Ako asked, "What did that man say to you?"

Russu replied slowly, reluctantly. "He said my family should not have come here, and that the Soinine were with Iron."

"What does 'the Soinine are with Iron' mean?"

"I don't know. He spoke in the language of eastern Rakeved. The Soinine are a strong faction within the royal family. To be with Iron? Perhaps it means the Soinine support relations with the Iron King. But this is too much to believe. Would the Soinine murder a member of the royal family, here, in Serica? Over a political dispute? It's too much. I can't believe it. If news of this returned to the capital, it would be…but then maybe this news will never reach Hemina. Oh…"

Russu stopped dead in the street and swayed from side to side. Ako reached over and pulled her next to him. They stood there together for a few moments, and then Russu drew some deep breaths and pulled away.

"How strange. I felt so odd. You saved my life. Those men were going to kill me. My own countrymen." She paused and then, rather solemnly, she said, "In my country, if a man saves a woman's life, the man can ask any one thing from the woman. It's called a 'life gift.'" Russu looked up at Ako with a wan smile. "It's in all the old stories. I never expected I should ever actually have to say this. Oh, how does it go?"

She got down on her knees, keeping her face cast downward, and said, "Russu Ti Tuomi swears that she owes *osetia loken* to Ako of Kelten." She looked up at him and said, "What do you wish of me?"

Ako resisted the obvious and just said, "Do I have to make my choice immediately? Here and now?"

Russu got up and smiled, covering her mouth. "Oh no. You can wait for years and years. At least that's how it is in the stories. But don't wait too long. The longer the man waits, the worse it becomes for everyone. I must say, you did very well back there. In Rakeved, we have many good warriors. We prize war skills highly in my country, not like the Serice. And I have seen some duels fought before our king. You're good, just like in the stories we have about Kelten *opmi*. I was terrible, but in my country, women don't fight any longer; it's not proper for a princess. We mostly use these hairpins to kill ourselves if a man is threatening to rape us."

Ako was just walking along, letting Russu talk as he mulled over the idea of having a "life gift" from this stunning young woman. It was both intoxicating and disturbing in equal measure. He decided to say nothing about it for the moment. Instead, he said, "We are going back to the Kelten embassy for now. It's safer. Several of the men who attacked you looked a great deal like the men guarding your uncle's residence. Till we know more, you need to stay with us."

Russu was silent for a while and then said, "I agree. Though I do not understand how that could be true."

Once inside the courtyard, Ako explained to Sandun and the others what had happened. Valo Peli just shook his head and said, "You people seem to have a talent for finding trouble."

A small, empty room was set aside for Russu. She went to lie down, and the housekeeper later reported that the girl was fast asleep.

Before sunset, a middle-aged man of average height but with a serious demeanor appeared at their gate; he carried a large leather bag over his shoulder. "I am Dr. Haz, and I am here to examine the *opmi* named Ako." The man looked like a doctor, and they let him in.

Sandun asked him why he was here, as no one had sent for a doctor.

"The Lord of Kunhalvar commanded me to be of assistance, and I do my lord's bidding."

The doctor looked at Ako's wounds with the barest hint of emotion. "Your hand will be fine. I see you are no stranger to such injuries. I will stitch up your arm. Give your arm some rest for a few weeks, and it should heal well." He picked up the dagger Russu had carried back and smelled it.

"I see no sign of poison, and the weapon seems clean. The Rakeved are known to use poison in their native land. Fortunately, it seems they did not bring it with them when they came here." The doctor poured some reddish liquid from a small vial onto Ako's wound; then, with deft fingers, he sewed up the deep gash with silken thread. "If it swells up and oozes fluid, have Scribe Renieth send for me. I should like to check on the Rakeved girl now."

Dr. Haz came back down shortly and told them the girl's breathing sounded normal and that she was doubtless exhausted from the shock of the attack. Sandun offered the man some of their coins, but he gravely refused them. "No need, gentlemen. We Serice know how to treat our guests from distant lands, even if the Rakeved do not." With that, he left them.

After dinner, Ako was detailing how he'd fought off the killers for his rapt audience, when a new party showed up at their gate.

"A Rakeved merchant claiming to be the young lady's uncle is here," said their door warden.

Ako, feeling a strong sense of irritation and other emotions, stepped out of the gate and onto the street. Sandun and Ashala followed him.

Russu's uncle was a short man. He wore an embroidered cloth wrapped around his head, and his robe appeared to glitter in the evening light. He had two armed men behind him, but they were not the gate guards that Ako had seen earlier. All were Rakeved, shorter and darker than was typical in Tokolas. "Is Russu Ti Tuomi here?"

"Yes, she is. Sleeping."

"She needs to return to my house. Please bring her out."

"No." Ako said this in his most commanding voice, the tone he used when he rebuked one of his men for breaking some rule.

"Perhaps you don't know who I am. I am Atos Vepsailin. I am her guardian. She must be returned to me."

"No. Russu leaves when she wishes. I know who tried to kill her today. Go away, little man."

Atos looked up at Sir Ako with a twist of hate to his mouth. "Kelten *opmi* you may be, but you are a stranger in this land. I will not bargain with you out here on the street."

"Then there is nothing more to say." Ako turned back and entered the courtyard. The gate was closed behind him.

Sandun sat beside Ako in the hall beside the fireplace. "Do you really think that man was behind the attempt on the girl's life?"

"Sandun, I was raised in the household of an earl. If someone is trying to kill you, it's a crown to a copper that the person behind the attempt is a relative. I don't know why he is trying to kill Russu, and I don't care. But I know this: if she goes back with him, she will be killed."

In the middle of the night, Ako was woken by a faint noise. It was repeated: a tapping at his door, faint, like the sound of woodpecker far off in the forest. His heart was beating in his chest as he walked to the door and silently opened it.

Standing small and shapeless in the gloom was Russu, wrapped in a blanket. Ako stood aside; Russu, with a hesitant step, came inside his room. He shut the door behind her.

She sat on the corner of his bed. She started speaking in a low voice, barely a whisper. Ako stood beside the door, listening. He caught some of her words, but he had to guess at part of what she was saying.

He heard her say "sleep" and "knives" and "dream." Then she started speaking more clearly.

"What have I done? They were going to kill me…for what? Who can I trust? I am alone." She began to make little choked sobbing sounds.

Ako knew some men who could listen to a woman cry without it clouding their judgment, but he was not one of them. He went over to the young woman and pulled her close, and then he kissed her. Her cheeks were wet with tears. She kissed him back, clumsily but urgently. In the back of his mind he was thinking, *This is trouble I don't need*, but as his hands explored the girl's body, all rational considerations were submerged in the oceanic swells of animal attraction. What little clothing Russu was wearing was soon off her, and she spent the rest of the night in his bed.

Two days after Sir Ako brought the Rakeved princess to stay with them "till it was safe," Scribe Renieth showed up in an agitated state and asked Sandun to follow him.

Curious, Sandun asked Ashala to come along. She put on her best shawl and then followed him out of the house and down the street. They did not go far before they were at the large open gate leading to one of the temples. Sandun had visited the temple closest to their house a day before, but while he wandered around the grounds for an hour, his mind was unsettled, and he took no comfort from the place.

Today, he followed Scribe Renieth into the temple grounds with an air of expectancy. Something was up—he just had no idea what. This temple was like a sparse forest, with ranks of younger trees and an inner core of old twisted trees of unknown age. Renieth gestured to him to go on while he waited at the edge of the ring of old trees.

Inside the ring of old, twisted trees, there was a small stream some six feet below the ground level. A stone bridge crossed the stream. Along the sloped banks were a group of carved stone turtles, all staring down at the water. Sitting on one of the turtles was a man about Sandun's age, his gaze fixed on the rippling water, like the turtles around him. The man wore a white silk tunic with black pants, and there was a jeweled ring on his left hand.

He turned at Sandun's approach and said, "Come and sit on one of these turtles. Supposedly they are 'keeping the realm in harmony' by balancing stone against water. Don't worry, they won't bite." The man had a striking face, with large dark eyes and prominent cheekbones. Sandun could tell the man had lived a hard life; his face was creased and the scar of an old cut ran down from his left ear to his jaw. More old, white scars could be seen on his forearms.

Was this the Lord of Kunhalvar? Sandun said nothing but took a seat on a turtle.

"You came all the way from Kelten, across the mountains, traveling for more than a year. An astonishing journey. How did you do it? Was there a road? Did you lose many men along the way? Why did you come? I admit that I wished to make the journey from here to Kelten when I was young. It is wonderful that you came to my city."

So this was the Lord of Kunhalvar. His enthusiasm was plain to see. Though Sandun did not doubt that the man had hidden chambers to his mind, this much was genuine.

Sandun smiled and responded, "So many questions. Where shall I begin? First, we had an old map to guide us. Also, in many places, we found the remnants of trails to follow. Third, one man died, three were badly injured and stayed behind, two were sent back with our horses when we reached a pass that the horses could not cross. Why did we come? We hope to establish friendly relations between Kelten and Serica, including trade."

"I see your mind is as good my advisors reported," the Lord of Kunhalvar replied. "Do you know there are rumors and more than rumors about you? They say you have a magic sword, one made by the secretive *Junithoy*. We know only this much about the *Junithoy*." He put his hands palm to palm, not quite touching. "And my advisors are completely divided on the issue. You don't look like a man with a magic sword; in fact, you look like a scholar."

Sandun had to laugh at this; it was exactly what he told himself every day. "You are right about that. I am a scholar. In Kelten, I help run our government's library." Sandun held up his hands. "These ink stains are the product of a decade of work. I will tell you this: as a gesture of goodwill, we did meet with a group of very unusual people. We call them 'Piksies.' I've never hear the word *Junithoy* before. In Gipu, they call Piksies the *Orenik*."

"As you no doubt have guessed, my name is Jori Vaina, known around the city as the Lord of Tokolas or the Ruler of Kunhalvar. My enemies call me the Beggar Duke, which is not really fair." Here Sandun saw a flicker of old pain cross Lord Vaina's face; it was replaced by a serious expression almost instantly. "I don't like to talk about those years, but I will say this. I had no money, and I traveled widely. Once I had a pair of cheap grass sandals, but when they wore out, it was back to bare feet."

Lord Vaina took off his finely worked leather shoe and showed off his right foot to Sandun's startled view. "They should call me 'Iron Foot Duke.' But then that would confuse men. No doubt some would say, 'But the Iron King, he must have iron feet as well?' We can't have that. My soldiers might think they should be fighting for the other side. Ha!

"Ten thousand tik is a long way to travel for trade. And over the Tiralas as well! Still, there was trade in the past. Why not again? What do you think of our land? My city? The great river is truly a wonder, isn't it? Nearly all the waters of Serica find their way to the river Mur, not to mention mud and trees and other things."

Sandun told him honestly that the great river of Serica was a wonder and that surely no river in the world could compare to it. "It takes courage to cross a river like that every day."

The Lord of Tokolas smiled at Sandun's remark. "Yes. My father and grandfather were tough. I remember going out on their longboat, early in the morning when the fog mutes the sounds and the sun is just a pale coin."

They talked for a few minutes, as Sandun tried to fit the story of his travels into the hail of questions Lord Vaina kept asking.

An official appeared at the edge of the line of trees. He did nothing but stand in the sunlight with his hands clasped together just above his heart.

Lord Vaina noticed the man instantly, and he stood up.

"I'm a busy man, as my advisors keep telling me. You would not believe how the hours fly past when almost every waking moment is devoted to running Kunhalvar. They even tried to allocate my time in bed with my women, but there the Iron Foot Duke put his foot down. Ha!"

At this, Sandun attempted to keep a straight face, but Lord Vaina looked at him and started laughing so hard that Sandun was forced to join in.

"I've got four women in the palace, and two of them are pregnant. My advisors say I should add two more, but they won't give me any time to actually *siswi* them. You traveled here with this *balish* woman." Vaina waved at Ashala, who had stayed up by the stone bridge. "We don't see women from Gipu in Kunhalvar, but the stories they tell…woo-wee! You know, I studied to be a priest of Eston for four years. No woman for four long years. Nearly killed me. After the temple was destroyed, I realized the Sogands had done me a favor by burning the place down. Though my hatred for them was not lessened by so much as a minnow."

At this point, the man at the edge of the trees theatrically coughed.

Lord Vaina said, "I really must go. We are setting up a fancy dinner in your honor. Did you know that you are the first embassy from a foreign nation to visit? When I am ruler over all of Serica, I will not forget. The official dinner is taking time to organize: a scholar is researching correct protocol. Lots of people are invited. Our allies in Sasuvi have been asked to come, but they might not attend. A bit angry that you came here instead of to their city, perhaps?"

Sandun was made breathless just listening to Lord Vaina thinking out loud.

"I'm heading back to the palace now. I come here every other day just to think by myself for half an hour. It wouldn't be a good idea to break that habit. I'll see about whether you can attend an informal dinner before the official dinner. We can talk more."

As the lord was walking away, he turned and he said in a very loud voice, "We know the details of your *opmi's* fight in the market two days ago. I did intend to meet with the Rakeved princess when she ended her time of mourning. Someday I'll need to know what is happening in her country. Perhaps her father counts as a foreign ambassador? But then, I never met him. If you stay away from assassins, we will meet again."

Sandun bowed formally to the Lord of Kunhalvar as he walked away. A group of eight previously hidden guards appeared from behind the trees and formed a protective screen around the lord as he left the temple grounds.

Ashala came up and stood beside Sandun.

"He is so young," Sandun said to her. "About my age, if I'm not mistaken. And he doesn't talk like the other officials. Hard to understand at times. What did he call you? *Balish*? And *siswi*?"

Ashala looked away. "I would not teach you such language."

"*Balish*, good? Or bad?"

Ashala sniffed and tossed her hair. "When the Lord of Kunhalvar says I am *balish*, it means he wants me in his bed. He already has enough women, I think."

"You didn't say anything to him. You didn't even get with fifteen feet of him."

"That man, Lord of Kunhalvar, he has, we say *echivarr*. Force, command. It's hard to explain. A few men have it, fewer women. It's like magic. A man with *echivarr*, you do what he wants. You be careful!" Ashala held Sandun's arm and looked up at him intently.

"I found him charming and remarkably good company. But I work for my lord, King Pandion of Kelten. I'm in no danger of changing my allegiance."

Ashala shrugged, and together they walked back to the house.

The next day, at noon, Scribe Renieth delivered an invitation for Sandun, Ashala, Sir Ako, and Russu Tuomi to come to the palace for an informal dinner with the Lord of Kunhalvar.

Sandun and Sir Ako went to Valo Peli and asked him about the invitation.

"An informal dinner with a ruler is not at all like the formal dinner we have talked about this last week," Valo Peli explained. "Instead, you are not to draw attention to the lord's position or to matters of state. All the guests must pretend that this is a simple dinner of friends. The lord may bring up serious issues, in which case you should discuss them seriously. But equally, he may just sing songs and drink *sogu*. I suspect, knowing Lord Vaina's reputation, that less drinking and more serious conversation will take place, but perhaps he will spend the time asking about your amazing journey."

The reactions of the two women were opposite. Ashala was thrown into a near panic. "No. I can't go. I'm sick. I have nothing to wear! What if he asks me questions about Gipu? No, it's impossible." Eventually she calmed down and allowed Sandun to convince her that she had to go and that she would be fine. As a translator for the Kelten ambassador, she was reasonably safe under the long-established customs of the Serice court.

"Yes, safe. That's true. Safe. Ah, now I know what to wear." Ashala disappeared and then half an hour later, she reappeared wearing a low-cut blouse and gauzy, nearly transparent pantaloons with a necklace that dropped a bright jewel between her breasts.

Now it was Sandun's turn to be shocked. "You can't wear that!"

"Ha-ha. Yes, I can. This is traditional Gipu clothing. A Gipu woman can live up to her reputation, yes? No man will ask me anything; they will be too busy staring."

By contrast, Russu was completely unperturbed. The terrors that drove her to sleep in Sir Ako's bed were not visible during the day. She expressed no concerns about the prospect of dinner with the Lord of Kunhalvar.

"I'm glad to finally get the chance to meet the man. I'm sure he doesn't care two oranges about Rakeved. I'll just sit there and listen to you men sing drinking songs, and I'll smile. I think I'll wear a green dress, so even if I don't say anything, it will remind everyone where I'm from."

Sir Ako looked at her quizzically. She clarified by saying, "The Serice like to call my country the Green Land. They are right about that much at least."

As the appointed time approached, they all gathered in the courtyard. Basil, Kagne, and the scouts all came to see them off. Ashala's costume provoked some admiring comments. The expedition had left Gipu months ago and, looking back on it, Sandun thought their time in Gipu had been well spent. While there, he had been too anxious about reaching Serica to appreciate it. In retrospect, Sandun had felt welcomed in Gipu, and not just by Ashala's warm embrace. He and the other Keltens had been the center of attention and were greeted with friendly hellos whenever they walked about. By contrast, Tokolas was so vast and so busy that even the Lord of Kunhalvar could apparently ride from the palace to the Tree Temple without provoking much reaction from the citizens. The Keltens in Tokolas were little noted.

No one said anything about Russu, but Sandun thought she looked like a princess. She stood at ease, poised and confident, her green dress like a bright emerald. He could tell that Sir Ako was head over heels in love with the young woman. Over the last few days, Sandun had noticed that Russu stayed close to the knight without seeming to make any such effort. The fact that they were sleeping together was common knowledge but not commented on by anyone yet.

A small group of cavalry rode up, and the four of them got on horses and rode with the soldiers to the palace. Russu could ride very well. Sir Ako complimented her on her riding.

"Thank you," she said in Kelten. Then she switched to Serice. "I know five languages. I'm sure I can learn another."

They approached the palace and then turned to the left and entered from the western gate. The palace grounds were surrounded by a large wall, and inside there were several houses, most single story, some two stories tall. They went into a large single-story building and were directed to seats at a table covered with dishes, glasses, and silverware. Within a minute, Lord Jori Vaina joined them, accompanied by two men, also his age, and two young and very pretty women. Lord Vaina introduced his companions as Generals Pojo Erdis and Esko Kun, along with their wives.

Any tension quickly evaporated, as General Erdis and General Kun were warriors and old friends of Lord Vaina. They joked and poked fun at each other. Sandun couldn't follow all of what they said because they spoke quickly and used words he had never heard before, but the food was excellent and the tea was heavenly.

Sandun had to ask, "Lord Vaina, we traveled through the tea hills to get here, and yet this is the best tea we have had. Where does it come from?"

"I know the answer to that," Lord Vaina said proudly. "The farmers in the tea hills carefully select the best tea and store that in special tea boxes, and it is sold for the highest price. Average tea is dried and sold in the round tea cakes, which I'm sure you have seen. The worst tea leaves, moldy and chewed by bugs, they save for themselves. If they keep any of the best tea, they don't share it with strangers. So if you want the best tea, you must come here to Tokolas and be prepared to pay a fortune for it!"

General Erdis said, "You worked in the tea hills after you left home, didn't you?"

Lord Vaina nodded but changed the conversation to talk about Sir Ako.

"Sir Ako, you killed three assassins in the market a week ago, saving the life of Princess Tuomi here. I salute you." Lord Vaina raised his teacup above his head and then drank it all down. The others did likewise. "The surviving assassin has fled Tokolas, or so my officials have reported. Perhaps General Erdis or General Kun could have killed all four, but perhaps not. I hear you are an *opmi* of Kelten?"

Sir Ako replied slowly, "The word *opmi* is not used in Kelten. I am a knight."

"Tell me, what does a knight do? How did you become a knight?"

Sir Ako had a whispered conversation with Ashala and then gave up and asked Sandun to answer the questions.

"Allow me to answer the questions you have posed. A knight is one of the best warriors of Kelten. Knights defend the country from attack, and they lead the armies when the king goes to war against his enemies. Sir Ako is the third son of a great lord of Kelten. His older brother is going to succeed to his father's land. His second brother is going to advise the older brother. Sir Ako chose to become a knight at around six years of age. He has won several contests of skill against other knights and is famous."

This provoked confusion and disbelief from Lord Vaina and his two generals.

"Six years old? Impossible. What could he have done wrong at such a young age?" Lord Vaina said this with some heat.

In turn, Sandun was taken aback. "Done wrong? Sir Ako is a knight. He has never done wrong. He was knighted by the king himself when he was seventeen years old."

"You are telling me that men choose to become warriors at a young age. And the King of Kelten himself *honors* such men?" General Erdis asked with disbelief in his voice.

"Yes. Exactly right."

The three Serice men looked at each other. The two Serice women sat next to their husbands with their heads down, not saying anything.

After sipping some fresh tea in silence, Lord Vaina asked, "How many knights does Kelten have?"

Sir Ako answered this: "There are more than sixteen thousand knights in Kelten."

This also was met with a curious silence.

Sandun asked what he thought might be a dangerous question. "Is there a problem with becoming a warrior in Serica?"

"Yes. Yes, there is. In this land—and I say this among friends—a soldier, a warrior, this a very low job, fit only for the stupid and the brutish."

At this General Kun said, "I'll drink to that. Bring out the strong drink. It's time for the brutes to drink hard liquor."

Sandun pressed the issue. "How do you defend your nation without a group of trained warriors or knights to lead the soldiers?"

"We have an army. Serica has always had an army. There are always poor men without land who join. They stay in the army till they can no longer carry spears. The older men teach the younger men how to fight. But for a man of talent, intelligence, a son of a great lord, for such a man to become a warrior? It is unthinkable!"

Lord Vaina continued: "I myself had almost no training as a warrior. But I was strong, and I could read, and I had a gift for inspiring men to follow me. I was put in charge of ten men when I first joined the Red Swords. I made simple plans with one trick or two, and they worked. I was put in charge of a hundred men. I made other simple plans that usually worked, and men followed me. I made a few mistakes, but I learned from them. Then I recruited these fellows and others from my hometown. They were better warriors than I, but men followed me. Men went where I pointed. And now, I'm here."

Lord Vaina continued, reminiscing. "My uncle was a soldier in the last years of the Water Kingdom. He told me stories about the *opmi* of Kelten. Men who trained their whole lives to be the best fighters in the world. It seemed like a fairy tale to me. Yet, here you are. And the stories are true. I am amazed and happy to see such days. Perhaps we can see you demonstrate your skills. I hear you practice every day?"

Sandun replied, "Why don't you have dinner with us? You can meet the men and women who traveled three thousand miles. The men would be happy to show off their skills."

"I like that. Yes, I like that. My advisors will complain that such an act would not be proper, but I'm not one of the rulers of the past. I'm going to change Serica, if I get the chance. It will be an informal dinner at the Kelten embassy, say next week?"

An older man, an official of some rank, came in through the door and came up to Lord Vaina's chair. He wore an elaborate silk robe with a black crow embroidered on his left shoulder.

Lord Vaina stood up. "This is Chief Minister Udek." The man merely nodded his head at the Keltens. "I must take my leave now. This has been a most interesting discussion. But duty calls. Which woman must I do my duty with tonight?" He said this with a wink to the others at the table.

"It is a surprise, my lord," said Minister Udek, with a dry voice.

"Perhaps it's a new woman, eh?"

"My lord has not picked a new woman yet, despite our humble requests that you do so."

"Well, maybe it will be a surprise for my concubine."

"No, my lord. She has been preparing for your visit all afternoon."

Lord Vaina said to the others, "You stay and eat as long as you wish. My duty to Kunhalvar calls me to some woman's bed."

With that, he left the room. It felt like three people had left, not just the one man. After a short time, it felt awkward to stay, so everyone stood up and said farewell, but they all left by the same gate. On the way back Russu said, "Well, at least he knew my name."

✤

When they returned to the embassy, Russu felt free to offer her critique of the Serice attitude toward soldiers.

"It is so funny. The Serice have forgotten their own history, they who pride themselves on never forgetting the lessons of the past. Did they conquer my country with big armies filled with criminals and led by brutish generals? No. Not at all. Their king of war himself came with his company of heroes, and they beat our best warriors through artful strategy and by duels with our champions. And so we surrendered."

Valo Peli rolled his eyes at this but remained silent.

"Seven hundred years ago, the Gold Kingdom's military power was unrivaled," Russu continued. "The glorious Golden King rode into battle at the head of his armored cavalry and defeated all who opposed him. The Gold Kingdom ruled from the Tiralas to the ocean. My people submitted to him without a fight, as they knew he could not be beaten in battle. All the world knew of his might.

"This attitude that all soldiers are brutes, scum of the soil, it is all the fault of the Water Kingdom. Bureaucrats of the Water Kingdom executed their best general, the one who saved them from the Palahey invasion. It was the scribes and bookish men who declared that the military was no place for a talented man. Because of that, we beat the armies of the Water Kingdom every time they attacked us. And that is why Rakeved is independent today."

Here, Valo Peli spoke up. "Princess Tuomi is correct in part. For a 'southern barbarian,' you are very knowledgeable about Serice history."

Russu snorted at him, but Sandun could tell she was pleased by Valo Peli's praise.

"Let me put before you the argument that the great chief minister of the Water Kingdom, Tors Sakay, made to his king." Valo Peli put his hands flat on the table and closed his eyes, reciting from memory. "The wise minister Sakay said, 'If men of great talent join the military, what then? Like all men of great talent and ability, they will seek fame and the fullest exercise of their skills. They will fight well in wars that are ongoing, or, if none, they will seek out wars, instigate them so they can demonstrate their talents. But wars are bad. Wars result in great expenses when they are fought. Tens of thousands of men and women and children will die as a result of a war. Farms are destroyed, terrible crimes are inevitable. To avoid unnecessary wars is a worthy goal for the state. Even when wars are necessary, as when a peaceful state is attacked by neighbors, what of the successful general? He becomes idolized by his soldiers, he becomes a focus of the people's admiration; in short, he becomes a threat to the king and to the stability of the nation. How to avoid these evils? By making the military a profession not suitable for the best and most talented of men. Instead, the best men are directed to the administration, where we, I mean they, use their talents and knowledge to improve the kingdom.'"

Sandun said nothing, trying to digest Valo Peli's argument. Ashala translated for Sir Ako and Basil and Kagne, who had joined them in the large dining room.

"Here are some additional facts for you, which you can judge." Valo Peli now buttressed his argument. "During the last hundred years of the Gold Kingdom, which Princess Tuomi praises, there were numerous civil wars and rebellions, and the first and most terrible of these wars was started by a rebellious general, a man of great talent and ability. By contrast, the Water Kingdom had not one civil war. No general ever took up arms against the king."

As Sir Ako understood Valo Peli's argument, he was moved to anger, but he held his emotions in check. He had learned to hold his tongue when listening to debates between his father and his older brothers. But inside, he seethed.

Valo Peli looked at them, these men from Kelten with such shock and anger in their faces, over ideas that were as basic in Serica as the fact that chicks, tiny balls of yellow fluff, turn into roosters or hens when they get older.

Sandun slowly offered this response. "Valo Peli, you told us on the road that the Water Kingdom was unsuccessful in battle. That it failed in nearly all of its wars. That it alone, of the kingdoms of Serica, was conquered by a foreign nation, namely the Sogands."

Valo Peli replied, "Looking back on Water Kingdom history, it does appear that they paid a heavy price for their disdain for their own military. Yes, the Water Kingdom's record in war is not glorious. Men like me, who were taught by men who knew the last ministers of the Water Kingdom, we were taught to revere their wise and benevolent stewardship over the Water Kingdom. We all look back at those ministers and sigh with regret that such men are not to be found today. Perhaps we look past their failures too easily. Perhaps we forgive them too much."

Now the discussion shifted to Kelten as Sandun, Sir Ako, Basil, and Kagne debated the role of the military in their country. It was a strange thing to even talk about, to question. It was like challenging the idea that fishermen should not pull fish from the sea—absurd on its face.

Sir Ako was adamant. "Valo Peli is spouting philosophical nonsense. Kelten is surrounded by enemies: Issedon, Fiodroch, Jibur, even Melnehlan might send a fleet against us if they thought we were weak. Every nation has enemies, and if your best men are not defending your borders and commanding your soldiers, you will lose. You will lose land, you will lose people. Perhaps the whole land will be conquered, like Aremaspan was centuries ago. As you said, Sandun, the history of the Water Kingdom speaks for itself. They lost. They were utterly defeated. And by who? By Sogands, a warrior nation if ever there was one. How many people died because the Water Kingdom failed to defend itself? How many cities were burned, how many women and children murdered by Sogand invaders?"

Sandun replied, "I agree with you, Sir Ako, but who can honestly say that all the wars we fought in Kelten after the death of Maklinos the Great were justified? Count Tichnis, the servant of kings, is he not cursed in taverns throughout Opomos? Is he not just such a man as Valo Peli describes? A man who caused wars seemingly for his own amusement?"

"Tichnis, now that was a man whose overbearing ambition resulted in the deaths of many a good knight." Sir Ako nodded vigorously. "Everyone agrees about him."

"And the scholars of the Water Kingdom invented 'thunder dust,' so they must be given some credit," Sandun said.

Sir Ako stopped short. He understood what Sandun had left unsaid, that his own leadership would have gotten them all killed at the battle of Wheat Town. His anger cooled immediately, and he got up and bowed to Valo Peli. In Serice, he said, "I have not properly thanked you for what you did in the battle of Wheat Town. You saved us."

Valo Peli looked a bit embarrassed. "You give me too much credit. But you are most welcome." Changing the topic of conversation, Valo Peli then said, "You all should know that I have made up my mind. I will offer my services to the Ruler of Kunhalvar. I think I shall go to his palace tomorrow and present myself."

"Perhaps you should wait and see if Lord Vaina will come here for dinner. Things might go better if you reveal your identity on friendly ground," Sandun said.

Valo Peli considered that. "Perhaps you are right. I agree. We shall see if he comes. I shall write an invitation for you."

The invitation was sent to the palace early the next day. Valo Peli spent the rest of the day out in the city. "Looking up old history. Something the Lady Tuomi said provoked my memory," he told Sandun.

Russu's uncle came over to the embassy again. This time, the young princess came outside and talked with him. Sir Ako stood next to her, and Sandun and Kagne stood off to one side, watching. Although Russu and her uncle spoke in the language of Rakeved, he was clearly telling her to return to his house, and she was telling him no. After about twenty minutes, he lost his temper and grabbed her arm. She slapped him with her free hand; he let go, and then she turned around and stormed back into the Kelten embassy. He left, rubbing his face ruefully.

"She's a handful, that's for certain," said Kagne. "I'm glad she is staying with us. Brightens up the place."

Sir Ako smiled at Kagne and returned to his practicing.

After a quarter of an hour, Princess Tuomi came down from her room. She looked calm, as though she had been painting watercolors in the garden, but her eyes were red.

"That man, he had nerve to call you barbarians. I told him we were just as much barbarians in Serice eyes. Then he said I had to obey him since my father died, and I told him that he had been living too long in Serica. That may be how they do things here, but not in Rakeved. My father is dead, and now I'm a grown woman. I make my own decisions."

Sir Ako came over to her and kissed her. Then he picked up his sword and looked at her. Russu looked back at him, her eyes wide, the hint of a smile on her lips, and then she went upstairs.

Later, while they were drinking tea in the warm afternoon, Sir Ako spoke quietly to Sandun. "She came to me. I mean, to my room. What was I to do?"

Sandun said, "We all hear the songs, Sir Ako. Though I confess, I'm a little surprised to hear the fame of Kelten knights has reached as far Serica and Rakeved. I guess the stories we tell each other in pubs about young women and young knights have some truth to them?"

Sir Ako nodded. "Much truth. When I was a squire, I was invisible to everyone, especially the nobles' daughters, who I pined after with little result. But when I was knighted, things were so different. It was not uncommon for me to find a young lass in my bed when I was spending the night in a new town. And when I won the tournament in Seopolis…I don't think you have any conception of what women are willing to say, what they are willing to do to…ahem, be with a champion knight. Noble women of Kelten like to pretend their modesty and virtue are beyond reproach. My personal experience tells me that their reputation is…um…somewhat at odds with reality."

"But what I am to do about Russu?" Sir Ako said in an aggrieved tone. "If Russu leaves here, she will be killed. And when she is here, she wants to stay with me. Not that she isn't…well, you know…"

Sandun slowly said, "I'm no priest of the temple; I'm your friend. We were sent to reach Serica and establish trade relations. On our old maps, Rakeved is just a province of Serica. I suppose it is possible that by keeping Princess Russu here you are complicating our mission, but I don't think so. In any event, she is your responsibility now. I think she is better off here. Maybe she is supposed to be here?"

"Don't you get all 'hand of Sho'Ash' on me," Sir Ako said. "My men may believe it, but not me. A knight makes his own destiny, through strength and wisdom and skill at arms."

"Except when a beautiful princess, who is in mortal danger, falls at your feet?"

"Er. Yes. Except for something like that."

The next day, a letter arrived from the Lord of Kunhalvar. Scribe Renieth delivered it personally. Sandun passed it to Ashala, who read it and then said to everyone in Kelten: "The lord is coming in five days for a dinner."

In addition to the letter, there were several pieces of paper tied together with a piece of silk. Sandun untied the silk and looked at the papers. The papers were very similar to each other and rather elaborately decorated, but otherwise they meant nothing to him. At the bottom of the stack was a map to a location in the city with some writing next to it. Ashala looked at it and read out: "The Kelten expedition will find this place of great value."

"What are these papers?"

"Something to do with salt. Five hundred cats weight of salt." Ashala shrugged. Sandun knew a cat weight in Gipu and Serica was close to a pound and three quarters. Why this was called a cat weight was mysterious, since only a kitten weighed so little.

Renieth tried to explain: it was a form of money. Quite a lot of money. This provoked even more amazement on the part of the Keltens.

"Paper money?" Farrel laughed.

"Money is gold or silver or copper coins," said Gloval, who had a talent for saying what was well understood.

Sandun tried to learn more, since he didn't really understand the concept. Ashala had heard of such things, but they were never used or accepted in Gipu.

When Valo Peli returned, Sandun showed him the pieces of paper "money." He looked at them thoughtfully and then he talked.

"Let me tell you a story." Valo Peli often explained things this way. "Many years ago, the Water Kingdom had a string of forts along the northern border. Most of the forts were far from any cities, and the forts had little in them other than soldiers and weapons. No coins, so they were not targets for raids from northern enemies. During times of peace, the soldiers grew crops and kept chickens and had cattle ranches south of the fort. They had nearly everything except salt. But salt is necessary for food and health. For centuries, previous kingdoms had sought cheap methods for getting salt to the forts, with a distinct lack of success.

"But one clever official working for Minister Sakay had a brilliant idea. A merchant takes a cartload of salt to a fort, say two hundred cats weight. In exchange, the merchant is given a piece of paper that says 'Give this to the official in charge of salt in the city of Tokolas, and he will give to you three hundred cats weight of salt in exchange.' You can see the benefit to a merchant in doing this. And the benefit to the fort is, all they need is some pieces of paper and ink. No Sogands will raid a fort to steal paper!"

Sandun interrupted, "That's very nice. But what does this have to do with money?"

"I continue my story," Valo Peli said with a trace of irritation in his voice. "A man with one of these pieces of paper worth three hundred cats of salt in Tokolas finds he has pressing business in a different city, say Sasuvi. As it happens, he learns of a great trade chance in the city, but he has no money, just this piece of paper worth three hundred cats of salt in Tokolas. He finds a fellow merchant, one who regularly travels between Sasuvi and Tokolas, and he says, 'This paper is worth three hundred cats of salt in Tokolas.' The other merchant looks at the paper and agrees. The first man says, 'Three hundred cats of salt sells for 5,000 copper coins here, I've just checked the prices. How many coins will you give me for this piece of paper?' The second man thinks for a while and finally says 'I'll give you 4,500 copper coins for that piece of paper.' And so the deal is done."

"Then what happens?" asked Sandun.

"That piece of paper doesn't end up in Tokolas. Instead, it is used in Sasuvi as a substitute for three hundred cats worth of salt, in coins. Everyone is happy. The soldiers find their forts are regularly supplied with salt. The government finds that its salt supply in Tokolas is hardly depleted, and merchants find that carrying around pieces of paper worth 4,500 copper coins is much easier than actually carrying around 4,500 copper coins."

"Each one of these pieces of paper is worth 5,000 copper coins? That is a very generous gift!" Sandun whistled loudly.

"Unfortunately, this story does not have a happy ending." Valo Peli clearly enjoyed telling this story, though Sandun did not know why. "For reasons that may seem obvious to the wise, the Water Kingdom ended up creating far more salt notes than they actually had salt in storage! Once it became known that even with an official salt note in your hand at the Tokolas salt storage building, you could not get three hundred cats of salt... well, the value of those salt notes sank so low that eventually no one would accept them any longer. You could put them to better use filling cracks in your wall."

"Oh."

"Do not despair. The eight salt notes you now hold were created by the new government of Tokolas. It says so right here." Valo Peli pointed to the words near the top. "These salt notes are different from the previous, worthless notes. If tomorrow you go to the salt storage building, they will, give you five hundred cats weight of salt per note."

"And then I have to find someone who will buy a wagonload of salt?" Sandun wondered what merchant would buy so much salt? A butcher?

"There is a better alternative," said Valo Peli with a smile. "You can go to a merchant, one of several who specialize in buying and selling these new salt notes. He will take the notes and give you coins in exchange. I suspect a lot of coins. Tomorrow we can visit one, and you will see."

Sandun explained the story of the "salt notes" to Sir Ako, Basil, and Kagne. All of the men were quite skeptical of this paper money. Though they were willing to complain about carrying around heavy bags of coins, none of them wanted to see this invention spread to Kelten.

Kagne alone was willing to see some good in it. "If I could carry a piece of paper that was worth coins, at any town I came to, that would put most robbers out of business. I can't tell you how many nights I've spent in fear, when I was carrying coins from one place to another in the unsettled parts of Erimasran. These 'salt notes' are easy to conceal, no one would know I had one on me, say hidden in my boot. But it would be terrible to find the note was suddenly worth half what you thought when you first got it. By the stars, I would not be the first to take such a risk!"

The next day, the whole expedition, set out, with Valo Peli leading the way. Ashala and Russu came with them. Russu said this was the first time she had actually seen "salt notes," though her uncle had talked about them.

Sandun took four of the salt notes with him, as well as the map. Valo Peli directed them to the west market. They came to a house right on the border of the market square. The merchant seemed to be prosperous: his house was built like a fort, with thick beams of wood and a narrow door. Large guards stood in front, gazing with an air of bored menace at the people passing by. Sandun showed the guards the salt notes, and they let him and Valo Peli enter.

Inside, the merchant, a well-dressed and narrow-faced man with a black hat, looked at the notes very carefully. He held them up to the light and pulled at the paper. Apparently satisfied, he said, "I'll give you sixteen strings for these four notes. How do you want it?"

Valo Peli said, "Ten in silver, the rest in copper."

The merchant made a careful entry in his logbook and then opened a large metal box using an elaborate metal key that hung around his neck. He took out ten silver bars, each with a small raised peg on the top that matched a hole on the bottom of another so they could be neatly stacked. He also took out six long strings of copper coins; no one had any desire to count all the coins on the string, but there appeared to be a thousand of them on each string.

While they were waiting, two other men came in; Sandun over-heard them talking about buying salt notes for use in a city called Hutnin. Meanwhile, the salt note merchant used his large scales to weigh each silver bar, and then he used a larger weight, shaped like a sleeping cat, for the strings of copper coins. With the money all weighed, Valo Peli politely thanked the merchant, and they left.

The strings of copper coins were quite heavy, and they made a shimmering sound when they moved. Sandun gave half of the money to Sir Ako and put the rest into his reinforced bag.

From the west market, they went north, following the map, into the older part of Tokolas. Occasionally the road dipped down, and they could see beyond the city to the great river flowing through the valley below them. Tokolas was mostly built on a bluff overlooking the river, likely to avoid flooding. But part of the city went all the way down to the docks and a harbor that had been constructed beside the river. Following Lord Vaina's directions, they turned off onto a side street just before the road began its steep descent.

The street was narrow, the houses old and weathered. It seemed a quiet street with nothing but tiny houses jammed against one another. One house nearby had an awning a few feet into the street, and a couple there were selling bowls of soup to passersby. The owner of the house came out and looked at them curiously and then said something like, "Men from Kelten here to see the temple!" He repeated this loudly to his wife.

She came out and looked intently at the expedition, and then she smiled and waved her hands. "Come with me, this way."

Sandun and the others all exchanged glances but followed the woman down the street till she reached a house that looked even older and more decrepit than the others. She banged on the door and called out something. The language in this part of town was hard for Sandun to understand.

Soon the door opened, and an old, white-haired man peered out. "Men from Kelten have come," she yelled at him. He looked up, and suddenly he smiled a great, warm smile and pushed the door open.

"Come in, come in. Thank you for coming."

Sandun went inside the house. It was larger than it looked from the outside. A light from a window above was shining down on an old figure, carved from wood, of a man dressed in armor and carrying a spear.

A thrill of amazement went right through Sandun. He looked carefully all around the statue, while behind him the other men were murmuring exactly what he thought: "Sho'Ash."

The old man, who was clearly a priest, came inside. Another, younger man was busy lighting candles and setting out an ancient book and a small metal chime.

"Welcome to the temple of Sho'Ash," said the old man in the slightly too loud voice of the partially deaf. "Built more than four hundred years ago. My family has served as the priests and caretakers for many generations. This is my son, who will carry on when I'm gone." He gestured to the younger man, who was helping to set up. "We normally hold service here once a week, but today is a perfect day to hold a service. I think right now would be best."

The members of the expedition were so stunned to find a temple to Sho'Ash here in the middle of Serica that they said nothing. Valo Peli, Ashala, and Russu went in the back of the temple, where there were some old wooden chairs, and took their seats.

The priest continued: "I say the service in Kelten, as I was taught by my father. Once, we could read from the Holy Book, but no longer.

The knowledge of reading the book was lost long ago. But we remember the words."

The Keltens all knelt while the priest intoned the words of the service in a strange, half-singing fashion. At first it was hard to understand the old man's words, though they knew what he should have been saying. But after a few minutes, Sandun became used to the strange accent, and he was suddenly transported back to the temple in Hepedion where he grew up, as the old, familiar words washed over him. The same words he had heard year after year. Suddenly he began to cry, though he could not have explained why. He didn't look around to see if the others were equally affected. It was the most profoundly moving service Sandun had ever experienced.

At the end, the old man stood among them and held his hands out. Sir Ako took one hand, Padan took the other, and then they were all holding hands as the priest gave the farewell blessing.

"Go now with the blessing of Sho'Ash upon you. And remember this: when you are battling evil, Sho'Ash is watching you. Wherever you go, even to the ends of the earth, Sho'Ash has gone before you, and he lights your way."

After they had walked around the room and talked to the old priest for a bit, they filed out of the temple. Before he left, Sandun broke one of the coin strings and gave the priest a heaping handful of copper coins.

On the way back to the embassy, they all became very talkative.

"That sure hits you right in the heart, doesn't it?" said Padan.

Olef was concerned about the state of the temple. "It needs work. Repairs. Fixing up."

Farrel agreed. "I took a look at his Holy Book. It's in terrible shape, pages falling out, letters so faint as to be hardly seen any more."

Gloval said that the statue needed major repairs. "I know something of wood. The statue of Sho'Ash is cracking. And I say it's up to us to fix it."

Sandun, still deeply moved by the service at the temple, said to them, "I've still got four more of these salt notes. Today, I'm going to give each of you a silver bar. And I'm going to allocate two of these coin strings to help repair the temple." This announcement was greeted with smiles and thanks.

Inside the embassy courtyard, he handed out silver bars to each of the scouts and to Basil and Kagne. "Two for Sir Ako, and one for our translator, Ashala. And two for me. Spend it as you wish," said Sandun, "but remember, as the Count of Torobeus said to me, 'Small things from Serica fetch very high prices in the markets of Seopolis.' I have some suggestions if anyone is curious."

Shopping was on everyone's mind now. With money in hand, they found their hearts filled with excitement at the thought of treasures from Serica. Lathe, Wiyat, and Gloval went off together, laughing as they walked out of the courtyard. Sandun suspected they were not looking to buy goods to trade, but that was their business.

He asked Scribe Renieth where he would go to buy fine Serica-glass. Renieth looked puzzled until Ashala explained. Then he nodded his head slowly.

"You are looking for *Magerinken*, the finest cups and vases. Times past, they were made at the old capital of Kemeklos, but now the best is created at Lakava. I can take you to merchants who sell only the highest quality."

Neither Sir Ako nor Russu had much interest in shopping for Serica-glass, but everyone else followed Scribe Renieth to a small group of shops southwest of the palace. The cups, bowls, plates, and vases in these shops were magnificent. The shapes were graceful and clean; the colors were bright, including several shades that Sandun had never seen before in Serica-glass: a bright yellow and a deep blue. Any one of these would be worth a house or two in Hepedion. Padan, Farrel, and Damar happily spent their silver cats on small vases that looked strong enough to survive the journey back across the Tiralas.

But Scribe Renieth was dissatisfied. He picked the cups up and looked underneath them and then set them down with a frown. "This one hopes to find better," he said outside the biggest shop. "One of my colleagues in the Ministry grew up in Tokolas; he might know something."

Basil took Olef back to the embassy; she tired rapidly, as the baby was due soon, less than a month.

Ashala was so eager to see more choices, she practically begged Renieth to take her to more shops.

"Paper?" Renieth mused out loud, but not even Sandun wanted to see paper.

"Silk?" he offered up, and this was instantly approved.

The shops selling quality silk were close by, and soon enough they were shown bolts of fine silk in colors brighter and more varied than the flowers in the king's garden. Silk came to Kelten across the great ocean from Buden. It was rare, and only great lords and high priests of the temple wore it on special occasions. In the Archipelago, people said the finest silk was made in Buden, but as Sandun looked at the weave of Serice silk and felt it between his fingers, he wondered if that was true. Unlike vases and cups made of Serica-glass, silk traveled well; it would survive any accident short of being soaked in water.

Prices were good. If the Keltens had brought silver across the Tiralas, they would have been able to buy Serica-glass or silk worth ten or even twenty times the weight of the silver bars they might have carried. Getting the treasures back home to Kelten undamaged would be no easy feat, but if it could be accomplished, money would no longer be a concern for any man who made the trip.

The next evening, after dinner, Scribe Renieth showed up with a letter in hand.

"This scribe now knows where to go. If you want to see *Magerinken* worthy of the name, follow me."

Sandun, Ashala, Kagne, and Valo Peli accompanied Renieth out into the city. Just a few blocks away, he knocked at a gate set inside a high wall. The gate opened, and the scribe showed the doorkeeper the letter. The door-keeper looked at them curiously as they followed Renieth inside. In the evening light, the building was like an enchanted palace. Willows trailed long branches over pools of still water. The main house at the center of the landscape was intricately carved in wood. An old woman came out to greet them, and even though her hair was white, she moved with elegance that suggested many years past, she was once one of the great beauties of the land. She called herself Lady Tihani.

That night, with just an oil lamp for illumination, Lady Tihani showed Sandun and the others the true meaning of Serica art. The colors of her cups and vases were rich and deep: blue like the sea at noon, yellow like yolk of an egg, red like a bead of blood. The objects she showed them had such a clarity of form that it seemed they were ideas made real, not crafted by man but brought into existence by sheer thought. Each one was unique and utterly itself and perfect.

"Would you like to purchase one of these?" she said to them, her thin voice perfectly clear though hardly more than a whisper.

Sandun didn't think a chest full of silver would be enough to buy even the least of the art she had shown them. He looked at Renieth and then at Valo Peli.

Valo Peli said slowly, "This one wishes to inquire if the Lady Tihani was once the wife of Minister Irini?"

The woman smiled faintly and said "Second wife. Long ago." She sighed and continued, "I retired here after his death. All his family are gone, save for me. Now I sell what is left and offer what I can to the Temple of Eston. Soon I will depart to my next life and forget all of this." She waved her hand as though casting flower petals into the air.

Sandun put his two silver ingots onto the table. "This is all I have."

Lady Tihani looked at him thoughtfully and placed a small red vase shaped like a teardrop, the size of a dove, into his hand. She collected his two silver bars and put them in a velvet-lined box that closed with a faint sibilance, like a wave retreating across the sand.

The days leading up to the dinner were busy. Basil worked on an elaborate map, using the finest paper, to present to Lord Vaina. Sandun bought a very elaborate box, similar to what the Lady Tihani had used the previous night and suitable for holding the glowing orbs. He placed the largest of the orbs in the box flanked by two lesser orbs, keeping two more in reserve. *For a rainy day*, he thought.

Sir Ako drilled the scouts on some combat exercises that would best show off their skills—mostly archery but with some hand-to-hand fighting and a few dramatic leaps added for good measure.

Sandun consulted with Scribe Renieth over the dinner arrangements and the food. He convinced Farrel to cook some beef, a favorite Kelten dish, for them. Farrel had often done the cooking on their long trip and more than once had complained about the lack of good spices for the meat.

"Now is your chance," Sandun told him. "You can buy whatever spices you wish. Supervise the cooks and make sure they don't overcook a good set of steaks, that's all I ask." Farrel's sense of pride overcame his reluctance to cook for strangers, so he agreed.

Lastly, Sandun asked Renieth to get him some poor-quality local swords. He was certain that Lord Vaina would repeat his request to see the Piksie sword work its magic, and he thought that denying the request would be unfriendly. Scribe Renieth came back two days later with a soldier who placed three serviceable swords onto the dining room table.

Sandun brought one to his room; that evening, he told Ashala to hold the sword in two hands.

"You once asked if this was a magic sword," he said. "It is. The Piksies called it 'Copper Cutter,' but it cuts through just about any metal. Watch."

He aimed at the blade that Ashala held and cut through it with a stroke. The sheared-off section of the sword fell to the floor with a ringing clang. Ashala uttered a strangled yelp and hurriedly put the hilt of the sword on the ground as though it were going to shatter in her hands like a piece of broken glass.

"What's going on in there?" Basil shouted from outside the room.

"All is well. Just testing the Piksie sword before tomorrow's dinner."

Sandun woke up early; the first dim light of a new day was filtering through the cracks around the wooden shutters. Ashala was peaceful, sleeping next to him, warm, comfortable. He smiled and stilled his impulse to leave the bed, to begin the day's tasks. Instead, he lay quietly and enjoyed this pause in time, this brief lacuna. *Happy*—the word floated up to the surface of his thoughts. He was happy. Happy with the young woman beside him, happy in the well-made room he was living in, happy visiting the great city of Tokolas, in Serica.

Eighteen months before: a master at the archives, every day poring over old books and deeds, writing summaries of land sales. He hardly recognized that man. He had grown. To say his horizons had expanded understated the case. The realization came to him: he would never go back, not to that life. Yes, he would return to Kelten; obviously, there was no question on that. But return to the Archives? No, that life was over. He was free. Free to become something else, someone else.

The Philosopher wrote that everything had a telos, a purpose, a final goal. Since that time, the wise had debated: Did every man have a telos laid down on him at birth? Or did a man have the power to change his telos? Was man, unique among all other living things, free to choose his own goal? And did some men have a hidden telos, one that could only be discovered by doing many things, by investigating the boundaries of ability and desire? Opinion divided on this, and the temple, unhelpfully, taught that all three of these were true, depending on the man and the will of Sho'Ash.

Sandun believed that because Sho'Ash was opposed by a power nearly his equal, no destiny was assured and therefore, no telos set at birth was necessarily carried through to the end. He knew Kelten's history well enough to know that many good men with good intentions had failed utterly in their designs. He could also recall the names of several evil men who had gained riches and power and lived for many years before their crimes had come to light. To his mind, Sho'Ash did not control a man's destiny; therefore, no one did.

He tried to put thoughts aside and moved closer to the sleeping girl. He smelled her hair and listened to the faint sounds of the city waking up; cartwheels rumbled along the cobblestone street below. A line of white light appeared on the wall past Ashala's bare arm. The sun was up—time to get started. Today was going to be a busy day.

Shortly after midday, a parade of men from the palace came over to inspect the building, the food, and the household staff. Several dozen guards stayed in the embassy, as did three other men, one of whom did not look like an official. Sandun recalled seeing him at the palace; then he had assumed the man was a servant. Now, in the light of the afternoon, it was clear that he was not one. His style of dress was unusual, with his arms bare up to his elbows; only laborers wore shirts like that. He wore several rings on both hands—also unusual. There was something disconcerting about the way he looked around at the people and things in the Kelten embassy—not quite contemptuously but as though he found them lacking in some essential quality.

After a few minutes observing the man, Sandun walked up to him and asked him what he did for the Lord of Kunhalvar. The man turned and studied Sandun intently. Sandun stared back, noticing that the man had the facial features of a Sogand. After an uncomfortable silence, the man spoke in a low voice. "You are correct. I do work for the Lord of Kunhalvar. I am a *krasuth*."

"*Krasuth*?"

The man was about to answer and then seemed to change his mind. He put his hands close together, palms facing each other, and then drew them apart and rotated his palms to face out toward Sandun. Rapidly, a mist formed in front of the man, obscuring his face and body as if a fire had blown a thick smoke in front of him. As the man put his hand down, the mist cleared away into thin wisps that vanished in the warm afternoon air.

"*Krasuth*," said the man with a hint of satisfaction. "You have many questions, which I will not answer. I serve the Lord of Kunhalvar, but my fraternity does not give away information lightly. We are not like the scholars of Serica." With that, he walked off toward the dining room.

Apparently Sandun would get nothing more from the strange man. Figuring that Valo Peli was in his room contemplating his forthcoming offer to Lord Vaina, Sandun thought about not disturbing him but then decided that the scholar might welcome the interruption. Sandun knocked on his door. At a word, Sandun opened the door and found Valo Peli pacing in his room, visibly and uncharacteristically nervous.

Sandun closed the door behind him and said, "Did you know the Lord of Kunhalvar has a *krasuth* working for him?"

"No. No, I did not. If he has one, does he have two or three? They usually travel and work in groups. Rare to find just one."

"You know something about them?"

Valo Peli snorted. "Hardly anything at all. They are very secretive. But they can create mists or fog and make a breeze where none was before. They seem to come from the north, but not all of them are Sogands. One story I heard was that the most powerful of the *krasuth* was able to... how to put it? Push aside arrows fired at him. It seems incredible but then, it's all very mysterious. Tales about the *krasuth* go back hundreds of years, but I've only seen one—eight years ago, outside of Kemeklos. Very strange and unsettling experience that was. The Sogands treat them with great respect."

Sandun shivered. Everyone in Kelten knew about the witches of Alteran. The witches' mystical powers over fog and snow were just the sort of frightening stories that adults told children on winter nights before the great year-end festivals. He remembered hearing his father tell the story of brave King Labotas and his encounter with the White Witch of the North. That night, too scared to sleep, Sandun had stared at the nearly full moon through his tiny window and imagined the White Witch coming down from the moon on a stairway of ice with her great black dragons beside her.

As he got older, he learned that Alteran was far from Kelten, north even beyond Thessagon, and since the people were unfriendly, few merchants from the Archipelago were willing to risk the icebergs just to be turned away from the docks by the grim folk of that land. Many of the educated men in Kelten didn't believe the witches had any powers at all, while the temple claimed all witches were in league with the Black Terror.

Having seen the *krasuth* create mist out of the air, Sandun was now inclined to believe that the stories from Alteran might have had some truth in them after all. He wondered if the *krasuth* was a servant of the Black Terror. Somehow it didn't seem so. If he were, wouldn't he seem more evil?

With so many questions and no answers, Sandun put aside his worries and concentrated on preparations for the dinner.

In the late afternoon, as the sun was going down into an orange haze, Lord Vaina and his companions—General Erdis, General Kun, and a very pretty woman—arrived at their door on horseback. Lord Vaina introduced the woman, saying, "This is one of my wives. Her name is Eun. She is from Shila, so she doesn't mind being around foreigners."

Sandun knew next to nothing about Shila, and he had never met anyone from that land before. Looking at her, he saw that she was indeed very lovely but not very different from other beautiful women of Serica.

Before the dinner, Sir Ako had his scouts show off their martial skills with some very accurate shooting, at admittedly rather short range. Then they showed off some combat techniques with close fighting, using swords and shields. This attracted great attention from Lord Vaina and his two generals. The Keltens had been puzzled to learn that shields were rarely used by the Serice soldiers. Lord Vaina seemed to like what he saw and applauded with vigor after some good blows.

Sir Ako's armor also was cause for much comment; nothing that the Serice soldiers used matched his armor for toughness and weight. Sir Ako took off his armor after the demonstration, and the three Serice men examined the pieces, commenting on their light weight and resistance to cutting and slashing blows.

As Sandun expected, Lord Vaina asked again to see his Piksie sword. Sandun brought Skathris out and then had Sir Ako hold one of the Serice swords out. Standing so Lord Vaina could clearly see what happened, he brought Copper Cutter down on the outstretched sword and cut it in half. This provoked a cry of astonishment from General Kun. Lord Vaina thoughtfully rubbed his chin and then asked to see both swords.

"I have another sword from your arsenal that you can test yourself," said Sandun. "It's a shame to destroy weapons, but I asked Scribe Renieth for some old training blades."

Lord Vaina carefully inspected the cut sword, the Piksie sword, and the last of the test swords. Then he sat back and asked Sandun to do it once more. So again, Sir Ako held out the sword and again, Sandun's Piksie sword cut through it with that same strange noise, unearthly and disconcerting.

Lord Vaina stood up and smiled broadly. "To think I have lived to see such wonders as this! Oh, Uncle, you were right. Your stories came true. This gives me hope! Who is to say what is and is not possible?"

Then they all went to the dining room and sat at the table for dinner. Most of the dishes were Serice, but the beef steaks were delicious, at least to the Keltens, and they all praised Farrel's cooking, so he had to get up and bow, with a very red face. Lord Vaina and his generals ate the steaks with gusto, but Russu and Eun of Shila just ate a few bites for politeness' sake. Russu said quietly to Sir Ako in Kelten: "Too much blood."

He said, "I'm happy to eat your piece," which he did, to the amusement of the other men at the table.

After the steak, Sandun got up and made a speech thanking Lord Vaina for his generosity and goodwill toward the expedition. While Sandun paused to fetch the box of glowing orbs, Olef excused herself and left the room. Sandun then presented his box to Lord Vaina, saying, "This is a gift from King Pandion, in the hope that friendship and trade will grow as never before. The world is changing; roads that were impossible are now possible again."

Lord Vaina opened the box and took out several of the glowing orbs. At his command, the servants took away most of the candles, and the room became dim. The orbs glowed with their strange green light. Gingerly he passed around several of the orbs to his generals.

Sandun explained that these orbs had been made in Kelten and that these and other goods could be traded to Serica in exchange for quality goods of this land.

"Light without fire, though not as bright," Lord Vaina said thoughtfully. "And these keep glowing for years?"

Sandun nodded.

"I can think of several uses already. Do you have any idea how much my government spends on candles for the ceremonies? No, I'm sure you don't. And lights for underground, when fire makes the air go bad and kills the miners? Or lights for boats at night on the river, which water cannot put out? Yes, these are things we would gladly trade for."

After the candles were returned to the table, Lord Vaina continued, "I'd like to have a thousand *opmi*, or 'knights,' like Sir Ako here. With Kelten armor and weapons, all our enemies would bow down to us. Serica would never need fear invasion from anyone again."

As he was drinking a toast to the men of Kelten, a messenger came in, out of breath. Based on his clothing, he was a young official from the palace. "Yes, what is so urgent that you interrupt my dinner?"

The young man handed Lord Vaina a scroll and said, "My lord, the fleet from Vasvar has sailed past our southern defenses on the river Mur. It is a great fleet, my lord, and they burned the fort and have declared that they are here to take all this land. We are under attack!"

Lord Vaina, his face impassive, studied the scroll. "So it comes to this. General Tuno makes good on his threats. I thought an attack was possible when we learned the Thrice-Blessed King had been executed and Two-Swords Tuno had taken over the government."

He paused for a while in thought. Then he spoke to the Keltens: "You are not from this land, and no one would deny your right to stay out of this fight. But Two-Swords Tuno is coming here with his fleet, perhaps within a week. I have no claim on your aid in this, my time of need, but I do ask. And further, I am willing to offer each of you a very sizable reward for helping me, for helping Tokolas defend itself."

Lord Vaina's appeal was far more than just words; he put his whole personality behind it. His large eyes turned to each of them individually. His expression was that of a proud man who has broken his usual self-confidence to acknowledge his need for them personally to help him.

"As you know, Kunhalvar is a small province. I am trying my best to make this land peaceful and prosperous, but we are surrounded by enemies. What have we done to cause this attack by the army of Vasvar? Nothing! General Tuno could send his fleet north to attack the Kitran Empire, but he has instead chosen to attack us." Lord Vaina sighed and wiped his hand across his forehead. "Most of my army is defending our eastern border against the Iron King. I will need every soldier to help defend this city. You mighty warriors from Kelten, you have no reason to help us, no reason to help me, but will you?"

Sandun was convinced by Lord Vaina's appeal.

Sir Ako said, "I'm not one to flee a battle."

But the other men, who could not understand Lord Vaina's words, were not convinced.

Padan was dismissive. "He wants us to fight for him, but who is he to us? Some foreign prince."

Damar said, "I fight for my king, and I fight for my brothers." The other scouts all said aye to that.

Sandun now had a moment of clarity. He could convince them; he knew it. But should he? The expedition had accomplished its goal; they could leave Tokolas tomorrow and be back in Erimasran by midautumn. If they stayed and fought for Lord Vaina, some of them might be maimed, some might even die.

In that instant, he knew he was not ready to go back. He was now some-one who could make a difference. After a decade of reading old papers and writing reports, he was doing something important, and he was not going to give that up—not now, not yet.

He spoke to the men: "Did we not just see the temple to Sho'Ash here, in this city? The only temple in all of Serica? Are we going to abandon it? Padan? Damar? Farrel?"

The three men looked down at the table; Padan shook his head slowly. Sandun continued: "We have traveled three thousand miles to get here. Are we going to turn around and retrace the footsteps we planted on the ground not two weeks ago? Will it be said of us that Kelten soldiers ran away from a fight? Would King Pandion say to us that we did well in running away from Tokolas?"

He could see the men nodding. He had them. "I say we stay and fight. I say pride demands that we stay and show the people of Serica that Keltens do not back down from a battle."

Sandun now stood up and drew his sword and held it up in the air, it glowed faintly in the dim light of the room.

"The Lord of Kunhalvar has asked us to stay and fight for him. He has offered you money, but I say you shall receive more. Stay here and fight and you—each one of you—shall be knighted! Yes, when we come through this, we shall all be knights of Serica! When you go home, you will no longer simply be soldiers of Kelten; you will be knights. And should any man challenge you on it, he shall have to answer to me."

"And to me also," said Sir Ako. "I'll be proud to call each of you 'brother.'"

"A knighthood you say? Now that's worth fighting for," said Padan, and he stood up.

The rest of the scouts, Farrel, Damar, Gloval, and Wiyat, pushed back their chairs, and each of them stood and raised their hands in salute.

Lord Vaina and his two generals looked on with approval. Even without translation, it was clear to them that the Keltens had decided to help. Sandun explained to Lord Vaina, "You are going to make them knights, or *opmi* as you call them."

"When? Now?"

"No, but soon after the battle. It is an old tradition in Kelten that common soldiers can be made knights by a king if they act like heroes on the battlefield. This means a great deal to these men."

Lord Vaina slapped his forehead as though a blinding thought had suddenly struck him.

"I can do that. And I can make more than your men *opmi*. I can make some of my soldiers *opmi* as well."

General Erdis and General Kun looked at each other and then back at Lord Vaina.

"I said earlier I wished for a thousand knights, but I can make a thousand *opmi* out of my own soldiers. My city needs *opmi*: men who are proud of being warriors, men who think it is an honor to defend their country from invaders. My advisors will hate me for this, but I don't care. This is a new world. We are now surrounded on all sides by enemies. If we are going to unify Serica, I must have not only great administrators but also great warriors."

General Erdis said, "*Opmi*...it has a good sound to it. *Opmi* have come to Kunhalvar from Kelten, and now we can have *opmi* of our own. It's like the secret tradition of the *opmi* has been brought here, and now it can spread. This idea of yours, Jori, is so crazy it might work. But what is an *opmi*, though really? Is it a rank? A special league of soldiers? How is *Opmi* Ako different from me?"

"Details!" Lord Vaina said. "I'll figure it out later. Right now, we have an invasion to defeat." He stood up; his eyes were alight. He went to each of the Kelten men and shook their hands.

To Sandun he said, "This has been quite a day. I thank you, and I'll send word soon. Since your *opmi* are staying to fight, I'll need your advice on how best to use them. Till we meet again."

With that, the Lord of Kunhalvar and his followers and guards left the embassy.

PART EIGHT

The Burning Tower

Later that evening, Sir Ako invited Sandun to the library and shut the door.

"Very convincing speech you gave. What happens when we get home and we have to tell the king that he has eight more knights? I have not the authority to dub my men knights, nor do you."

Sandun had been thinking about that very question ever since Lord Vaina had enthusiastically agreed to his idea. "Riddle me this, Sir Ako. If Padan went south to Jibur and did something extraordinary, like saving King Alforsa's life in a battle, Alforsa might well knight him, yes?"

"Yes, he might." A thoughtful expression crossed Sir Ako's face. "Oh, I see where you are heading. My men wouldn't be knights of Kelten. They would be knights of Tokolas or Kunhalvar who happened to be Keltens."

"Just so, and to continue my little dream play, what happens if Padan comes back home to Agnefeld from his Jibur adventure? Is he still a knight? Would he be allowed to call himself a knight?"

"It's a little odd, but I think he would." Sir Ako dredged into his memory of knights. "I think he would be a Kelten man with the title *Knight of Jibur*. But he would not be a Kelten knight."

"Just so. If this works out, we all return as Knights of Serica." Sandun leaned toward the fire and warmed his hands. He mused, "If we come back to Kelten with a caravan of Serice goods and a Serice ambassador with us, I wager King Pandion will dub us all knights of Kelten, and you will be made a baron."

Sir Ako smiled. "That's a big *if* you have there, but I'll play along. If the king gives me a barony, I will perforce have enough land to support several knights. A baron with ten knights is not uncommon." Sir Ako grinned. "I can imagine it now. That area around Nukivanu will become important as a gateway to Serica. The land is presently unorganized, just the free peoples of Erimasran and their wandering villages. Suppose the king gives me that land as a new barony; I will need knights to help defend it. Yes, this could all work out. Are you sure you want to be a knight of Erimasran? It will be a very different life from the running the Archives, my friend."

Sandun said hurriedly, "I'll worry about that when the time comes, not now."

"We are riding the eagle, aren't we? We may fall to ruin on the rocks or reach the peak of Mount Shioni. Right now, the view is good, but there are thunderstorms up ahead. Good night, Sir Sandun."

The next morning, Sandun found Valo Peli sitting at the table, drinking some of the superb tea that the Lord of Kunhalvar had sent to them. He looked thoughtful and sad.

"You didn't make your offer to Lord Vaina yesterday," said Sandun.

"They already know who I am. Or rather, who I was." Valo Peli stopped and said nothing for moment.

"Go on."

"General Erdis and I were talking as your men were demonstrating their skills. Unexpectedly he said to me, 'You were in command at the battle of Batasek seven years ago?' I could not deny it, as I was prepared to admit all later, after dinner. He then continued, 'Know this. One of the Red Sword leaders who died in that battle was the father of Lord Vaina's first wife, the Lady Osmo. She has not forgotten her father's death, and you are not forgiven." Valo Peli finished his cup of tea and sighed. "I am not forgiven." His words were like a stone dropped into a deep well. He turned to face Sandun. "Since I cannot serve the Lord of Kunhalvar openly, I now offer you my services as an advisor until you wish to release me. By tradition, I should have stayed at home and waited for someone to come and ask me for my aid. But these are untraditional times."

Sandun replied, "Valo Peli, I welcome your offer for as long as you wish to remain with us. And I'm sorry about what happened."

"I did my duty as I saw it," Valo Peli said very quietly. "I had the surviving rebel leaders executed as traitors to the Kitran Empire. I don't know if Lady Osmo's father was among them or if he died earlier in the battle.

There were four of the leaders. Hard men, defiant to the end. One man said, 'I die now, but when the Red Kingdom comes, you will die in shame while I will be remembered as a hero.' I thought nothing of his words at the time but now, they bite at my heart like a snake."

Sandun went and told the others that Valo Peli had pledged to them and was now their advisor. Most of the scouts accepted the news with little comment. Wiyat was clearly pleased; he had become friends with Lathe, as they were nearly the same age and shared a youthful buoyancy in their personalities.

Ashala was impressed with the news. "In Gipu, such a man would be greatly honored. Imagine a *demelzo* allied to one of the houses of Gipu." She made a clicking sound with her tongue, a Gipu custom that indicated you were wishing for a very lucky event to take place.

The next day, there was a strong feeling of tension in the air, and everyone in the household staff was on edge. By now, the rumor of the invasion by the Vasvar fleet had spread throughout the city. Hushed conversations could be heard in the kitchen. Outside, the city was on edge.

The question that Sandun heard frequently was: Why? Why was Vasvar attacking? Weren't the Kitran the common enemy of Vasvar and Kunhalvar?

At the second bell after sunrise, Scribe Renieth arrived from the palace with a request that Sandun join the war council meeting scheduled for the fourth bell. Ashala read the note that Renieth gave to Sandun. "It says that *Opmi* Ako—I mean, Sir Ako—and Valo Peli are invited to attend if they find it convenient."

Sandun hurried over to find Sir Ako studying with Russu. Over the last week, he had been studying Serice intently while she learned Kelten from him.

"I'll come with you," Sir Ako said. "Probably won't understand one word in ten. You can explain it to me after."

Sandun then knocked on Valo Peli's door. He was inside, reading an old book that he put down immediately. "What can I do for you, Master Sandun?" Valo Peli was slowly adjusting to his new role as advisor to the Kelten delegation.

"Would you join Sir Ako and myself at a meeting of the Tokolas war council?"

Valo Peli snorted. "So that is how Lord Vaina is playing this game! Have I become so predictable in my old age?" He paused while he considered the invitation. Sandun waited as patiently as he could.

"Yes, I will come. Apparently, I must swallow what little pride I have left and attend their war meeting as a foreign advisor. Not much better than Basil's hunting dog!"

Sandun was surprised at the anger in Valo Peli's voice, but he said nothing; he simply folded his arms and leaned against the wooden door frame.

"I should explain myself," said Valo Peli, clearly mastering his emotions. "The Lord of Kunhalvar appears to want my advice, but he and his advisors don't want to pay any political cost for it. My name need never be mentioned in the records. Well, who do I have to blame but myself? I denied my name rather forcefully in Wheat Town, didn't I?" Valo Peli stood up. "I'm ready to go. As a 'barbarian advisor,' I'm allowed to wear the customary dress of the people I represent. Perhaps I should dress like you Keltens, and then no one will recognize me, least of all the Lady Osmo."

"If you wish, you can wear one of Kagne's shirts. He is about your size. I have a new leather jacket that you can have. It was made for me according to our style, as a gift from Lord Itor of Gipu. I prefer my old jacket, though. It fits me well, and the two of us have been down many a road together."

They set out on horseback for the palace. Valo Peli looked uncomfortable in his Kelten clothing and kept shrugging. "I suppose I, like the Lady Tuomi, shall have to learn more of your curious language. If only I were her age, such learning would be much easier."

Again they went in through the side gate. As they approached the entrance, a stream of messengers could be seen going in and coming out. Sandun wondered if Lord Vaina shouldn't set up his war office in the middle of town, like King Pandion had done in Agnefeld before the last battle against King Oniktes.

They were directed to a large, high-roofed building near the center of the palace complex. As they walked up the steps, Valo Peli whispered to the two men, "The Lord of Kunhalvar is using the Audience Hall for a war council. It is…unorthodox."

Inside, they found Lord Vaina dressed in a formal robe with a saber-toothed tiger embroidered on the front. He greeted each person by name and welcomed them to the council.

The men present were a mix of military and civilian officials, along with some men whose roles Sandun could not guess. Also, the strange *krasuth* was there, accompanied by another man very unlike him physically but with the same style of dress and the same expression of hauteur. He was a short man, with a dark face and a short black beard.

When the last man arrived, Lord Vaina introduced the Kelten delegation to the other council members.

"The men from the warrior nation of Kelten have agreed to lend us their aid in this unexpected assault. When the snow falls, they bring coal! This man"—Lord Vaina pointed to Sir Ako—"is a real *opmi* of Kelten. And yes, the stories of their skill are not exaggerated. He and nine others annihilated a Kitran *bastiuani* of fifty men, without losing a man."

Lord Vaina's statement provoked some murmurs from the military men.

"And now, we will hear the latest news from the river."

One of the men, who was dressed as neither a soldier in armor nor an official in robes, spoke.

"New counts reveal twenty-nine and not twenty-five large ships, but only two of the massive giants, not three. Roughly a hundred and ten smaller vessels. Total Vasvar forces at more than thirteen thousand but less than ten thousand are soldiers who will leave the boats and fight. A report arrived this morning: as of the afternoon two days gone by, both of the border river forts were attacked and taken. All of the large boats of Vasvar fired heavy spears, and these were extremely effective, able to make repeated shots against the same location. The gates were smashed rapidly."

"And we had no warning Vasvar was working on such a weapon?" General Kun asked, with some heat.

"Only rumors, and they were dismissed by most within the Group of Eight, mainly because such weapons would be of no use against the Imperial army."

Sandun guessed that this man was a spy. Perhaps the "Group of Eight" was a collection of spies?

The Lord of Kunhalvar stepped in to nip the recriminations in the bud. "Gentlemen, we have all been deceived. Everyone in the council thought that King Borsos still retained at least some power when Two-Swords Tuno denounced General Lasso and had him executed twenty months ago. Clearly we were wrong, and General Tuno was in control of the government soon after Lasso was executed. Despite all the sweet words coming from the South River Kingdom, given the size of their fleet they have been planning this attack for at least the last year, perhaps longer. I firmly believe they are coming for Tokolas, not Sasuvi. What is your recommendation, General Erdis?"

"Meet them on the river. Send our fleet down to attack them. Use fire ships and our superior knowledge of the currents and sand banks to destroy them before they reach Tokolas."

"Pojo, I know you and your riverboatmen are itching to fight on the river but really, we have…what? Thirty medium-sized boats and twenty ferries, along with some small fishing boats. I know the riverboatmen of Vasvar; they used to come up here often. They are not quite as tough and not quite as good at navigation as your men. But even so, with their numbers, they will win, and then all our boats will be sunk and you along with them. We need to build up our river forces before we can challenge this Vasvar fleet. If we win this fight, we will do that, later. Minister Udek, what is your advice?"

Sandun remembered Minister Udek from the informal dinner party the previous week. He bowed gravely to Lord Vaina before speaking.

"If the Vasvar fleet sails up and down the river, do we care so very much? They have invested what must be a great deal of time and labor building weapons that are useless more than a mile from the Mur. When they come to fight on shore, after a short distance, they will be out of range of these boat weapons and then, all their effort will have been for nothing. Thus I recommend we draw them away from the river and then destroy them in battle."

General Erdis's face was like a looming storm, but again Lord Vaina forestalled his attack by raising his hand. "I thank the minister for pointing out the weakness in the Vasvar army, but we cannot lose control over the river. What of our towns and villages on the west side of the river, or on the northern bank? Are we to abandon them while Two-Swords Tuno sails through the heart of our lands, flouting our rule? No. On this I must insist. Our plan must result in the rapid destruction or, if possible, the capture of the Vasvar fleet. Without control of the river, Tokolas will die.

"What news from our friends in Sasuvi? I see Forit is eager to tell us something."

The man Lord Vaina called upon said, "A messenger reached us this morning with news a week old. It is strange news, my lord: the Prophet announced the Red Swords will again march to reclaim Kemeklos; the vanguard was to march out by today with the main body to follow soon after."

Everyone could see this news surprised Lord Vaina, but he rapidly mastered his face while the man continued his report. Very little of it made sense to Sandun; there was something about a prophecy and dreams, and how the defeats of last year were all going to be put right by the return of the Radiant Prince.

"You think the Radiant Prince will go with the army?" asked Lord Vaina.

"I do, my lord. The Prophet said the Prince would come to his capital, and all his enemies would flee before his glory."

"Extraordinary. Why now? If General Tuno brings his fleet north up the Nava River, and the Red Swords army has left? Sasuvi would fall."

"Will not the Prophet turn back when he hears of the Vasvar fleet?" asked General Kun.

"I do not know. The Prophet has been—erratic—for several years. He might turn back, but I fear he is being led by another one of his visions, and I need not remind you what resulted last year from following his dreams. But now for the report from the east."

Another military officer, who Sandun had never seen before, gave a short update in clear and simple language.

"Minor skirmishes continue all along the front. Unreliable spies report the Iron Duke has been drilling his troops with more than normal vigor. Reliable reports state that horses are no longer for sale anywhere in the Iron Kingdom. This is four days old, received last night via regular courier boat."

Lord Vaina nodded. "No sign of any joint offensive by the Iron Kingdom and Vasvar? Good news, though I am not surprised. The South River Kingdom never recruited any diplomats of note. Two-Swords Tuno may be a competent general, but he has no appreciation for the other elements of statecraft. Lastly, news from the empire?"

Another military officer reported that the news was the same: various reports of Kitran forces massing in many different locations in the north. "Fewer refugees than last week, my lord, but that seems to be normal for this time of year. Everyone is more hopeful in spring."

"If the Prophet does lead the Red Swords out toward Kemeklos, we will not have to worry about Imperial attacks on our border," said General Erdis.

"Perhaps, but how long before the Imperial army responds? Nilin Ulim has grown strong these last months, if rumors are true. I suspect he will not hesitate to wage all-out war against the Red Swords. I fear for the Prophet and the Radiant Prince, but for now we have our own troubles to attend to."

The rest of the meeting consisted of details about food and weapons, which Sandun could make very little sense of due to unfamiliar words and units of measurement. Yet, through it all Lord Vaina seemed to have complete knowledge of all aspects of his government. Soon the meeting ended, and everyone bowed and filed out.

As Sandun and Sir Ako walked out of the large hall and down the short flight of steps, a small boy, around four years old, came running up to them. He was dressed in an embroidered tunic of green silk that was somewhat muddy near his feet. "You are *opmi* from Kel...Kel...Kelten? Yes?"

Sandun smiled. The boy looked rather like Lord Vaina, and he doubted too many other small boys would be found within the palace walls. "Indeed we are. This is Sir Ako, I am Master Sandun. And who might we have the honor of addressing?"

The small boy was suddenly serious as he said, "My name is Pavo. I am first son of the Lord of Kunhalvar. Are you really going to fight for us? Real *opmi*, in armor and with bows as big as a man?"

Sir Ako stepped forward and knelt down, looking the boy straight in the eye. "Yes. Yes, we are. And we will win."

The boy's eyes went round with wonder; he stayed silent, reading Sir Ako's face.

Lord Vaina appeared at the top of the steps and called the boy's name. The boy ran up the steps and hugged his father around his knees. "The boy has heard stories about *opmi* of Kelten, and he begged leave to see them when they next came to the palace. Why don't you join me for some tea? Pavo, go back to your mother now. You will see the *opmi* from Kelten another day."

The small boy ran off down the steps while Sandun, Sir Ako, and Valo Peli followed Lord Vaina and his two guards back into the audience chamber and from there to a smaller room with tea already steaming on a table with cups.

After drinking the aromatic tea in silence for a minute, Lord Vaina spoke.

"If things go as I expect, the Vasvar fleet will be here in a week. I have a special plan for you and your men, but no hint of it must reach Two-Swords Tuno, or it will fail. Not a word about this must leave your embassy."

Sandun nodded, as did the others. Lord Vaina then continued:

"There is a great lighthouse down near the harbor..."

Far to the north, in an army camp filled with soldiers of the Kitran Empire...

Nilin Ulim stepped out of his grand tent, clad in gaudily painted blue-and-green leather armor. His helmet with its long white horsetail plume made him seem even taller than he truly was, but even without the helm he towered over all of the guards who stood around his tent. The sentinels saluted him; the warriors in the huge camp all addressed him as *Hejman* when he walked past them on the way to the northern horse enclosure. The skin of his arms looked like dark leather from a lifetime spent riding across thousands of miles of the northlands. His legs even had the slight curve that was characteristic of the veteran Sogand warriors—those that lived long enough to see thirty or more summers, as he had.

And yet, for all the outward signs that here was a true Sogand warlord, leader of one of the Nine Hosts, Nilin knew that he was not one of them. And while he was out in the field, collecting tribute, defeating Red Sword rebels, slaughtering bandits, increasing the dominion of the Kitran Empire, planting the flag of the Sun Eagle in towns and villages across Serica, he was not wanted in Daka. He was not invited to sit with the ruling council of the War Eagles. His missives were read and discussed at the monthly planning meetings, or so his uncles assured him, but nothing ever changed. Always the orders were the same: suppress the rebels, increase the tributes collected, send all food and silver back to Daka as soon as it came into the camp.

As if you could suppress rebels by mere words! As if his host could conjure food and silver out of the ground, just by riding over it! No, the food came from farmers working the land, and the silver came from towns and cities through taxes. His father, Bolod Ulim, had told him of the days when the cities were rich and the monthly taxes from Kemeklos or Sasuvi were so great, they had to be carried on a wagon!

Now, as his host rode through the once-busy towns, he saw the empty streets and the abandoned houses roamed by packs of wild dogs that would tear children apart and eat them. Monthly taxes were now handfuls of silver coins, paper thin and no longer round, with pieces bitten out of them, bearing only a faint resemblance to the fresh, gleaming silver coins he had seen years ago, so bright in the sunlight that the design was nearly impossible to see. His father had given him one of those coins; he remembered the hour vividly, standing beside the great man at the mint in Daka, back in the days when it still minted coins. He still carried the coin inside his belt buckle, but it no longer shone as it had years ago; years of rain and dust had darkened the silver. Rather like the empire, he thought to himself grimly.

As Nilin rode his horse around the great ring, shooting arrows into man-shaped targets made of straw, he looked at Sogand warriors who had just recently come into the camp from the far north and were showing off their skills to the various regimental recruiters. Most were of the Gokiran tribe, a few Kitrans as well. Nilin reflected bitterly on the effortless skill the young Sogands had. They all seemed to ride without thinking, to guide their arrows to the target just by wishing. Whereas he had to work, every day, for hours, just to be considered "acceptable." To please his father, he had learned that every hour not spent on horseback or practicing on foot with the bow, the spear, or the sword, was an hour wasted. And all because he was not a Sogand.

Every day he felt it—the hidden glares, the hard eyes of his captains, the muttered jokes in the soldiers' native guttural tongue about fish pretending to ride or deer who thought they were wolves—as if he did not understand, as if he did not curse his parentage every day of his life. No matter how far he had climbed, no matter the victories he had won, nothing he did was ever good enough for the War Eagles back in Daka. And nothing he ever did would change things, because he was not a Kitran by birth.

"Only trueblood sons of the Heavenly Ruler, Beeshe Tem, can lead the Kitran." This phrase was repeated over and over, every time there was a new emperor, every time there was a parade down the streets of the capital with a host guarding the line of captives who were soon to be sacrificed to the Sun Eagle. "Only a Kitran can lead the Sogands."

His parents by blood had been servants in the household of Bolod Ulim. Natives of Serica, both of them. They had died of the plague when Nilin was very small. Bolod, a trueborn Kitran, blood relative of Beeshe Tem, had no children of his own and Nilin, tall even as a small boy, fearless and headstrong, had captured the great man's heart. Bolod raised him as his son, trained him in the Sogand ways, and took him on hunting trips and then on his campaigns. Had named him his heir at the age of fourteen, despite all the gainsaying from his brothers and cousins.

And so here Nilin was, at the front line of the empire, winning battles and taking back towns and cities that had fallen to the Red Swords and the Iron King and the Red Priest. And what, what exactly were the War Eagles doing while the empire fell into pieces under their horses' hooves? When was the Great Host going to assemble and sweep across Serica as it had in the past, making the earth tremble with the rumbling of a hundred thousand horses, filling the sky with enough dust to blot out the sun?

Nilin had only heard stories about the Great Host from his father. In his lifetime, the Great Host had never assembled. Even when the Red Priest's army had marched all the way to the outskirts of Daka and burned down the Palace of Boiling Waters, even then, the Great Host had not been summoned! Instead, a host was formed out of chaos, an uncoordinated mass of Sogand warriors: Kitrans, Gokirans, and Turans. Horsemen from all the great houses, they assembled in the central plaza over the course of a day. With only the barest hint of a battle plan, the Sogands rode out of Daka under the cover of night and charged the rabble army with the coming of the dawn.

He had been there with the thousand men who had remained loyal after his father's death, men who now formed the core of his host. Nilin knew that they had won the battle that day not through skill but through fear, the fear that the unbeatable Kitran army was attacking. The front ranks of the enemy had broken and run even before the first wave of the Kitran elite cavalry reached them.

Nilin and his men had swept around to come upon the rebels from the north, a flanking move that proved to be entirely unnecessary. But it gave him an eagle's-eye view of the battle from a hill above the plain, his father's chief commander, Fahjemon Orsbil, by his side. Throughout the morning, Orsbil acidly commented on the stupidity of the action and pointed out how a well-organized army would have shattered the Sogands' undisciplined charge and driven it off the field with heavy losses.

"Earthworks and firm spears would have broken that charge," Orsbil said to him. "Where is the circling fire? Where is the reserve? Where is the baited hook? Bah. These are boys down there, playing at being warriors."

Later, Orsbil had spoken slowly to him in his deep voice as they rode into the night, following a trail of dead and wounded Red Sword rebels who were fleeing back south the way the way they had come. "We should leave Daka, young lord. Take what remains of your father's host and go south. Avenge your father's death. Do not wait any longer for the Eagles to act. Go to the southern farmlands, pillage the land, and gather warriors to your banner. While the War Eagles drink and add to their fat bellies by eating soft meat, you must do the work they will not."

Nilin had thought about his father's death that night, as he had many times before. Bolod had gone to war, at the head of a vast army, with the permission—no, with the express orders—of the War Eagles. His army had skirted around Lake Rudohe, scattered the cavalry of Dombovar, and marched to the very walls of Naduva. But the walls were high and strong. True to his name, the Iron King had covered the bastions of his capital with sheets of iron. Thousands of men died assaulting Naduva, to no avail. The Kitran army settled in for a siege.

The siege had gone on for months. Dombovar was not beaten, the Red Swords to the west were not beaten. Attacks on the supply lines heading north were a weekly occurrence. Nilin spent most of his time leading detachments of fast horses up and down the road to Lake Rudohe. Smashed and burned wagons littered the road, accompanied by the stench of rotting corpses and dead oxen.

Gosta Feshti, the Iron King's younger brother, gained his reputation for daring in those months as he raided and harassed the Kitran army. The few times Nilin's men had seen Gosta's raiders, they had galloped away into the thickly forested hills only to reappear a day or two later, in a new location. And the siege dragged on.

After six months, three *bastiuanis* of Kitran imperial guard rode into the camp; at their head, imperious and arrogant, was Tolu Iefu, one of the War Eagles come to see for himself what progress was being made. Nilin showed the man to his father's campaign tent, decorated with captured weapons and ropes of hair from the heads of slain Dombovar warriors. Nilin could see his father was concerned.

"Report, war leader Ulim," Lord Iefu said, standing with his legs apart, his cloak of white fox fur swaying from side to side.

Bolod had explained the situation in detail, pointing out the problems they faced in every direction. Tolu Iefu snorted with disdain at all obstacles. Nilin could hardly contain his anger as he listened to Iefu belittling every difficulty they faced. Tolu Iefu seemed to think every Dombovar soldier was an infant lamb just waiting to die at the hands of a true Kitran warrior. Finally, his father had enough, and he stood with his nose right next to Lord Iefu's and demanded to know why the man had come.

"The War Eagles require your personal report on the siege of Naduva." Iefu's voice was like the crack of a whip. "You are to return to Daka immediately. In your absence, I will take charge of this army. I will follow the Sun Eagle to victory. Under his wings, Naduva will fall!"

After the meeting, Bolod's generals pleaded with him to reject Lord Iefu's command. "Ignore Tolu Iefu," said Orsbil. "This is the largest army for ten thousand tik. If the War Eagles want to help us take Naduva, they can summon the Great Host and bring it south. That would bring an end to this siege! What did Iefu bring? Two hundred of the Imperial Guard? His farts are just as useless against these walls. Phah!" He spat on the ground.

But his father trusted the War Eagles, and so, despite everyone's misgivings, he and Nilin and Orsbil and a hundred household warriors headed back north. The War Eagles in Daka listened politely to Bolod but dismissed him with talk of a future campaign directed at Kisvar. Six months later, Tolu Iefu himself returned to Daka, with no honors and no victory. Naduva remained unconquered.

Nilin could see that the army that rode behind Tolu Iefu was but a shadow of the army that had laid siege to the city. He learned from men who had stayed with the army that many warriors had deserted since Tolu Iefu took command, and that Tolu had to retreat in the face of the Iron King's superior numbers. The Iron King's brother, now called the Iron Duke, harried them all the way to the borders of Dombovar. Although the retreat had not turned into a rout, nevertheless, thousands of Sogands had died or disappeared along the trail. Tolu Iefu was a laughingstock in Daka, but the War Eagles did not remove him from command of the army.

Bolod Ulim died just two months later, shot through the eye by an archer outside of Somjarvi. Red Sword assassins, hired by the Iron King, was the story Nilin was told. So died the best war leader of the Kitran Empire, and what would have been a glorious victory over the Iron King was snatched away by political machinations. The most powerful army of the empire simply melted like frost on blades of grass in springtime.

So it was that as Nilin Ulim's small army pursued the broken and retreating Red Swords south, he swore to himself that he would regain his family's honor, avenge his father's death, subdue the Red Swords, and restore the Kitran Empire. In his heart, he thought: If the War Eagles would not rule the empire, why not him?

Spurred on by loot and easy prey, his men drove the remnants of the Red Priest's army like the wind blows chaff about the threshing yard. They plundered every village and town in their path. As the Serice had doubtless sided with the Red Priest, ruthlessness was required. Using some of the money he gathered, he sent riders to the northern lands of the Sogand tribes, recruiting warriors. Stories of riches, fighting, and slaves were spread through the camps of the north. His army grew steadily. In truth, despite the commands from the War Eagles, he sent very little back to the capital; most everything stayed with him as he rebuilt his army piece by piece. One year after he had ridden out of Daka, Nilin was in command of the largest Kitran army in Serica. He was, he told himself, the last hope of the empire.

After his hours of practice, he returned to his tent and ate a light lunch, following which he held his daily staff meeting. His spymaster, a sly criminal named Rini'i, had something juicy to report. Nilin could tell from the way the spy brushed his hands over his shaved head, something he did only when there was a secret in his possession that he was ready to reveal.

Following Kitran custom, the generals spoke first, and then came the spy report.

"Master Rini'i," said Nilin, "what news today? What do your ears hear?"

"My lord, we have confirmation that the Fire Toad, Arno Boethy, has joined the rebel lord of Kunhalvar." Rini'i smiled, revealing several missing teeth. The man was a former smuggler who should have been executed ten years past but was instead pardoned by Nilin's father in exchange for his services. "The Fire Toad travels under a new name, but it is assuredly Boethy."

While Nilin sat pondering the news and dredging up dim memories about the man, Fahjemon Orsbil said, "A dangerous adversary. We should have executed him when he said he was retiring to his home."

"That was not possible," said Mazy, Nilin's Serice advisor and paymaster. "Boethy's reputation for incorruptibility was no less than the truth." Mazy was a graying Serice scholar who had managed Bolod Ulim's estates for as long as Nilin could remember.

"Kitrans do not let wounds fester. We sear the wound with hot iron instead of waiting to see if it starts to weep green pus," Orsbil retorted.

"I remember him," Nilin said loudly. "My father respected him. He served the War Eagles loyally for more than a quarter of a century, and when he retired, rumor had it that he was gravely ill."

"Lies, rumors, the stratagems of the weak Serice!" said Orsbil heatedly. "A wolf on a leash may serve you, even fight for you, but let slip the rope around its neck and one day it will turn and attack."

"What of it, Orsbil? Arno Boethy is one old man. Will he come north on his aged horse and challenge our host? Without an army, he is a mole in the dirt." Nilin was hard pressed to see why this news mattered. He had lived in times of rapidly shifting loyalties—how many of the rebel soldiers they had defeated had once served under the Sun Eagle banner? And the Kitran, for all their talk of loyalty unto death, were little better. In his lifetime, three Golden Eagles had been assassinated, and the current "ruler" was just a boy, a pawn of the War Eagle council.

"If I may interrupt, Lord Nilin," Minister Mazy spoke slowly but deliberately "Arno Boethy is a threat, not so much in himself but in what he represents. If this report is true, Lord Boethy would be the highest-ranking minister to have switched sides since the rebellion began. Even the so-called Iron King has no one of his rank serving him. Boethy's support of the Boatman Ruler of Kunhalvar will be seen by many as a powerful sign of change." Minister Mazy paused and then continued: "It is hard to explain, but heed my words. This one old man's defection is a threat to the empire."

"Mazy, I don't see danger. Hasn't Boethy joined the weakest of our foes? The Red Priest, the Iron King, even King Borsos—are not all of these more dangerous than the contemptible Boatman of Kunhalvar? Haven't we deliberately been avoiding his lands because you counseled it? Ten foxes are easier to fight than two saber tigers—those are your words. What has changed?" asked Nilin.

Minister Mazy bit his lip and stared down at the ground. "I…I do not know, Lord Nilin. The Boatman's power grows, while the greater kings around him seem content to wait for his inevitable fall, and yet he does not fall. Lord Boethy could have joined anyone, yet he joins with the Boatman?" The minister's voice trailed off into silence.

"Then we kill Arno Boethy. We send a message no one will mistake. Kill him, kill his family. Those who betray the Sun Eagle must die." Nilin stared at his spy chief. "See to it. We have the gold. Hire fifty men."

"My master…once, hiring fifty men in Tokolas would have been easy, but now? If your army were closer, if men feared our swords at their throats, then they would be more eager to win favor with us. Can we not move toward Tokolas? Can we not attack them?" asked the spy chief.

"I agree," said Orsbil. "Time for us to move south. We may not be able to cross the river as yet, but we now have the strength to take everything from the Boatman that lies north of the river Mur."

Nilin made his decision swiftly. This was good; this was the Kitran way of war. "It is decided. The host moves south. We will cut off at least one leg of this fox. And see to Arno Boethy's death. If gold does not loosen daggers, there must be other reasons men would wish to see the old traitor dead."

For the next week, everyone was in a state of near frenzy. The Kelten expedition trained mostly at night and slept fitfully in the day.

Olef's baby was nearly due, and while she watched the others practice, she could not use her bow at full draw as her belly was in the way.

Lady Tuomi read some books on medicine and visited one of the hospitals where wounded soldiers were treated. She came back pale but resolute. "The blood is not something that makes me unhappy, but the screams of grown men…those are hard to listen to."

Ashala mostly fretted. "I do not understand why you are involved," she told Sandun. "Let these crazy Serice lords fight among themselves. Why should you pick sides? Traders come from Vasvar and Lakava to Gipu every year. They are no worse than the traders from Tokolas or Sasuvi." Sandun had no good answer for her, but the approaching battle had all the Keltens in a state of excitement.

Many of the men had fought at the battle of Agnefeld: Sandun, Basil, Sir Ako, Padan, and Farrel. They took turns telling stories about the fight, reassuring Damar, Gloval, and Wiyat and, truth be told, themselves as well.

"In a big battle, no man sees it all. Just do your part and trust that it will work out," said Sir Ako. "I'm not overly worried. If the reports are true, then ten thousand men—even supported by huge ballistas—cannot take this city. A direct assault on the capital city, held by the most loyal soldiers, defended by strong walls? I'm no general of thousands, but this seems like madness to me."

During the preparations, Valo Peli was in the cellar, making a special version of his thunder powder. He usually stank when he came upstairs. "Horse piss," he said in response to questions about the smell. "One of the key elements of thunder powder is horse piss. There are other compounds as well. The alchemists here have some skill, so my job is not so difficult."

Four days passed, and Lord Vaina came to visit. Rumors from the street vendors and the servants had it that the Lord of Kunhalvar never slept, that he was always appearing at one spot or another of the city, day and night. Sandun did not doubt it.

Lord Vaina came in like a whirlwind, asking questions, making suggestions, giving orders as his staff of scribes and messengers labored to keep up. He was like the fabled director at the mouth of a beehive: bees came in with legs coated with pollen, and other bees flew off in search of fresh flowers, with the bee king ordering all the others to their places. Here Lord Vaina was the center of information; messengers came in bearing morsels of knowledge, and he sent them back out with orders or instructions or the promise that he would look into it "soon."

"I have a request, not an order. You may decline. My advisors are opposed already," said Lord Vaina.

"Go on," said Sandun. They were down in the cellar; Valo Peli had just finished showing off his work. The smells and the smoke had driven nearly everyone else back upstairs.

"In two days, I will summon the first company from every regiment to the west market. I'll give a short speech to inspire the men, and then I want you to cut an iron bar in half. Very dramatic. Symbolic of our coming victory."

Sandun thought about that prospect, he imagined a vast crowd, all eyes directed on him; what if he stumbled? What if he failed to cut the bar? Beads of sweat suddenly appeared on his forehead.

"I'll do it," Sir Ako said. "With your permission, Master Sandun. I'll wear my armor. Everyone seems to want to see a Kelten knight. Might as well give them a show."

"Thank you, Sir Ako, I think that would be best." The relief Sandun felt was palpable.

Lord Vaina was surprised. "But will the sword work in your hands?"

"I don't see why not," said Sir Ako.

"Have you tried?"

"No."

Lord Vaina said, "The stories about these 'iron-cutting swords' are somewhat contradictory. Some say that the swords get old and lose their power with age. Others say that the swords only ever work for one man, and when that man dies, the sword becomes just an ordinary piece of metal."

"With Master Sandun's permission, I will try it first. If not, then he will handle the task." Sir Ako was quite matter-of-fact about the prospect of standing in front of a crowd of thousands of men. That was the sort of thing kings or great nobles did—not archivists, thought Sandun.

"I must go. Twenty things to do before sunset. I'll send word two hours before the rally." And with that, Lord Vaina was off, his staff following behind him, leaving an odd void in his wake.

That afternoon, Sandun, somewhat reluctantly, handed over the Piksie sword to Sir Ako in his room. A short iron bar as thick as a man's forearm had been obtained by Scribe Renieth. Sandun held one end, Kagne held the other. Sir Ako drew the sword from its sheath and, with some effort, pushed the blade down through the bar. The strange whine echoed through the room as the sword cut the bar into two pieces.

"This thing worries me," said Sir Ako, handing the blade back to Sandun.

"Me as well. It's unnatural, like a thing out of legend. Who am I to have such a thing? Are you sure you don't want it?"

"No. No. My sword, she is everything I ever wanted in a blade. You can tell your weapon was made by Piksies, not men. And anyone who knows its power can just use his shield to take its blows, making it less useful. Why don't you give it back to Basil?"

"He doesn't want it either."

"Do you know of any stories about Piksies making weapons like this?" said Sir Ako. "They always seemed mysterious and somewhat comical, but did they make iron-cutting swords?" Sir Ako's voice dropped, as if he thought the sword could hear him when he talked about it.

Sandun thought about that, and then a dim memory came up. "Once I read an old history of Kelten, full of tales about the years before the founding when the empire had shattered. The story of King Arktorus and the Lake Knights was briefly mentioned, and it said that Arktorus's sword, Chalris, was originally made by mighty smiths from deep within the earth. Perhaps that tale refers to Piksies?"

"Hmm. That puts a different light on the stories about Chalris, doesn't it? Not a holy weapon blessed by Saint Hurin but a Piksie blade? I wonder what King Pandion would say if you come back with your very own version of Chalris in hand? You could claim to be the new king of Kelten!"

"I could give it to the king."

"Aye, that you could. He might make you a baron instead of me." Sir Ako's face fell. "We will be lucky to bring the Piksie sword out of Serica after the big display in two days. Lord Vaina said we could decline his request, but I don't see how we can."

"That thought crossed my mind also. Perhaps I should be the one to cut the bar. We could tell Lord Vaina that he was right, and it does only work for one person. If the Serice believe that, there is much less incentive for anyone to steal it."

"That's true enough. Since you are going to become a knight, you need to learn how to perform before the public. I'll demonstrate. Everything I know about public performance, I learned from Sir Kerick."

"You know Sir Kerick? I mean, you've talked to him?" When Sandun was a young man, Sir Kerick had been perhaps the most famous knight in Kelten.

"I watched him carefully. He was the best jouster in the land when I was squire. Now, you can wear my helmet, and I think most of the upper body armor will fit you with some padding. Try this pose: chest out, chin up, as if you survey the world and find it lacking!"

Two days later, Sandun was riding through the crowded main street, accompanied by most of the Kelten expedition; Olef was not feeling up for travel, and Basil stayed with her.

He had been wearing most of Sir Ako's armor all day to get used to it. The armor was heavy, and it chafed despite the layers of clothing underneath it. But he felt safer with it on, as though the armor protected both body and spirit. The helmet Sir Ako had brought was light, and gaps in the visor were reasonably open so he could see well enough while wearing it…if it didn't slip in front of his face when he turned his head rapidly. He had learned to avoid that.

A crowd filled the market square, but a lane had been cleared so Sandun could reach a platform that had been erected near the salt note merchant's house. Sandun and the rest of the Archive Expedition stood behind the platform, surrounded by some of the Tokolas palace guards. Then Lord Vaina arrived, dressed in bright, silvery armor. He dismounted from his horse and walked past the front ranks of the soldiers, greeting many of the men by name, shaking hands with officers. Eventually, Lord Vaina climbed up onto the stage and quieted the crowd by holding his hands out, palms down.

Although Lord Vaina spoke in what seemed a normal tone of voice, his words echoed throughout the great plaza: "Soldiers of Kunhalvar! People of Tokolas! We are under attack. In a day or two, the fleet from Vasvar—commanded by General Two-Swords Tuno—will be here with an army of ten thousand. Why is this? By heaven, what has been the cause of this bloody breach of the peace between our two lands? For years, we have had peace with Vasvar. Indeed, more than peace; we have fought together, side by side against the Kitran. In years past, their ruler was a good man, King Borsos. Many called him the Gold King, or the Thrice Blessed.

"But now, he is dead. Most foully murdered by his former servant, Bloody Two-Swords Tuno. And now, General Tuno has sailed up the Great River with his fleet, and he demands—yes, he demands—that we submit to him and his rule. I do not wish to submit to this murderous traitor, but I asked my advisors."

Lord Vaina turned to General Erdis.

"General Erdis, you know Two-Swords Tuno. Do you think we should submit to him?"

General Erdis strode forward; his voice was angry. "Never! I would sooner cut off my right arm than submit to General Tuno!"

Lord Vaina continued: "I asked my chief minister: Would it be best for the city and people to submit to Two-Swords Tuno?" Lord Vaina lifted his hands out toward Minister Udek, as though asking for alms.

Minster Udek, dressed in his formal robes of office, stepped forward and gravely shook his head. "General Tuno has violated the duty of loyalty. He has behaved improperly. He is a savage, not a man fit to rule over Serica. We would be dishonored to surrender the city of Tokolas to such a man."

Lord Vaina now addressed the soldiers standing in ranks before him. "I ask you, representatives of our great army of Tokolas and Kunhalvar, should we submit to Two-Swords Tuno? Should we abase ourselves before the army of Vasvar? Should we let the spirits of our slain brothers go unavenged to avoid further bloodshed?"

Cries of "No" and "Never" rang out from the men. They stamped their feet, and the noise was like thunder.

"Very well. All are agreed. We will not submit. We will fight to defend our land and our city. We will fight to defend our honor. I tell you, heaven sees all and understands the hearts of all men. Heaven rewards virtue and punishes evil. Further, we have allies. The Red Swords to the north have begun a campaign to once again liberate the old capital of Kemeklos. Once established, the Radiant Prince will send help to us; he has not forgotten our aid in years past. And doughty warriors of far Kelten—though few in number, they too have seen the justness of our cause, and they will fight to defend Tokolas. Can you men of Tokolas do less? Can you sit idle while others defend your homes and family? Are you not warriors of Serica?"

This time, the yelling and shouting from the soldiers was louder than before. The noise lasted for several minutes before Lord Vaina quieted the men again.

"Together, we will beat the Vasvar fleet. My generals have devised brilliant stratagems certain to result in victory. Follow your orders. When the drums of retreat sound, obey with speed. When the horns of attack blow, press forward with courage. United, we will achieve a glorious victory."

At a command, two of the burly palace guards each carried out two large poles of iron, crudely shaped like Serice swords though made of dark, hammered metal. They held the mock swords at an angle, crossing each other about six feet above the stage. Sandun stepped forward and drew his Piksie sword; his heart was pounding as he tried to copy Sir Ako's style of walk. He lifted his sword over his head and with two hands, he brought it down on the mock swords held in front of him. Theatrically, he pretended great effort in cutting through the iron. Two guardsmen strained to keep the heavy iron bars steady. The tension built, and then he really did use his strength, and his sword sheared through both bars at the same time. The ends fell to the stage with heavy thuds.

A roar of surprise and excitement rose from the crowd. Sandun looked down at the sea of faces, and he held his sword high in the air. Suddenly he was surrounded by a sea of sparks and colored smoke that swirled around him and rose into the sky. He had been warned earlier in the day by Scribe Renieth that this would happen, but he was still quite surprised at the effect. Sir Ako's armor protected him from most of the sparks, but some came close to his face, so he closed his eyes to mere slits and held his breath. The noise around him was deafening, a nearly continuous series of sharp cracks, like hammers striking and breaking stones. He had no idea what it looked like, but it thankfully came to a stop before he had to breathe.

When the sparks and smoke died away, he found pandemonium in the plaza below him. It seemed like everyone was yelling and pointing up into the air. Lord Vaina waved at him, and so Sandun turned and walked back and down off the stage. It was then that he noticed the two *krasuth*, standing together and holding their hands up as if they were pushing against the sky. The tall one briefly caught Sandun's eye and nodded to him, nothing more.

Sir Ako and Kagne and the other scouts were laughing and shouting. They slapped Sandun on his back with big smiles on their faces. Apparently, the effect had been quite dramatic even from the back of the stage.

"Good job, Sir Sandun," said Sir Ako. "I doubt I could have done better myself."

"How did they do that?" shouted Kagne. "By the seven stars, that was a grand sight!"

Several minutes later, Lord Vaina came down from the stand and walked over to Sandun. First he shook Sandun's hand, and then he hugged him. "Thank you. I think the soldiers found that inspirational. I trust you are not burned?"

"I'm fine, Lord Vaina. The sparks all seemed to go past me and up into the sky."

Lord Vaina went to the two *krasuth* and gave a slight bow to them. They bowed back in return. "Thank you. That was most impressive."

The tall man replied, "We serve, as we serve."

"Your powers will be needed in the coming battle," said Lord Vaina.

"We will endeavor to protect you, Lord of Kunhalvar."

"Good. I count on you."

On the way back to the embassy, Valo Peli joined them. He was unusually jolly, happier than Sandun had ever seen him.

"I guess that the sparks and smoke were your doing, Valo Peli?"

"Not entirely, but yes, I had something to do with them. I must say, I have never seen anything like that before. That was…fun. Yes, honest pleasure. And no one was blown up, either. You seem to have come out intact. It would have been even better at night." He paused. "You know, they are calling you the 'Fire Sword.' I heard it repeated all around me as the crowd was breaking up. It did look rather like the sword was producing a great column of fire and smoke. A remarkable vision. Assuming we beat off the Vasvar fleet, people in Tokolas will be talking about this for a few months, at the very least."

Two days later, shortly after the third bell rang out, the Vasvar fleet appeared, black shapes against the gray water of the mighty Mur. Oars beating the waters, sails hoisted, the huge fleet came up the river toward the city.

All the Keltens woke from their short sleep and joined the throngs of people who were hurrying to the upper city walls to see. At the closest tower, guards recognized the Keltens and allowed them to climb up to the top.

Standing there with the wind blowing through his hair, Sandun looked and listened. He heard the faint calls of the river birds as they circled overhead, uncaring about the drama occurring far below. Clouds were building up in the east, but no rain was expected. Rain would be bad, but the wind was blowing out of the empty blue western sky.

Basil and Sir Ako passed their farseer glasses around. When Sandun looked through the farseer, he seemed to leap from the tower and fly like one of the white river birds. He could see the great boats of the Vasvar fleet, dim through the river haze but looming up, vast hulks dwarfing the other ships around them.

After an hour of watching, both with the farseers and without, a commotion below drew his attention away from the river and back to the tower he stood on.

First, two palace guards climbed up the ladder, and then Lord Vaina appeared, hardly winded, as though he climbed up ladders every day.

"Good view here?" Lord Vaina asked.

"We can see all twenty-seven of the enemy's big ships. See for yourself," said Sandun.

Farrel, who had one of the farseers, handed it to Sandun, who offered it to Lord Vaina.

The Lord of Kunhalvar looked at the tube skeptically, but he tried it out. He exclaimed, "This is better than a cat with an eel! It puts the crap tube we have been using for the last year in the shade!" Like a small boy with a new toy, he spent the next quarter of an hour examining the enemy fleet, and then his city, and then the surrounding lands.

Finally, a polite cough from a junior minister who had followed his lord up the ladder brought him back to the world.

"Time is pressing. More towers to visit. But how long have you had this marvel?"

Sandun explained, "This is the latest design from Kelten, Lord Vaina."

"But it is so much better than the one we have." Turning to the minister, he said, "Where is my looking glass?"

The minister searched in his satchel and drew out a long box. From within the box, he produced an old-fashioned farseer. Sandun had to fight back the urge to laugh; behind him he heard snorts of derision from the others. Kagne actually did start laughing, but a sharp jab to his side from Basil brought him up short.

"You have seen one of these before? I find that strange, because this came all the way from Budin, far to the east, and it was very expensive."

"May I examine your glass, Lord Vaina?"

"Take it."

Sandun looked at the tube. It was exactly what he thought: one of the oldest designs. He remembered seeing such a thing when he was still living with his family in Hepedion.

"This is an invention from Melnehlan, about fifteen years old. The early models were, as you aptly put it—crap. But artisans all over the Archipelago swiftly made improvements. Every year, it seemed a new design would sweep the old versions away. The farseers we brought across the Tiralas were nearly the latest models. The older models have become something of a joke."

"I see," said Lord Vaina. "Like when a man brings a reed boat and docks it next to one of the latest wooden sailing ships. That man can expect to be laughed at."

Sandun thought it best to say nothing.

"Trade with Kelten suddenly assumes an even greater importance. Your glowing orbs were very impressive, but this looking glass is astonishing. I'd like to buy this from you. Ussi, how much gold do we have left in the treasury?"

The young scribe said, "I can't tell you this instant, my lord, but I can say it is rapidly dwindling."

Lord Vaina looked hard at the young man and then laughed loudly. All the guards on the tower smiled at the exchange.

"Well, other than gold, what would you accept for this glass?"

Sandun replied, "Actually, it's not mine. It's Basil's. I'll ask him."

Sandun turned to Basil.

"Let me guess, he wants the farseer," Basil said. "Again. Why is it that no one wants your farseer, Sir Ako?"

"Yours is better. Mine was a hand-me-down from my older brother. It's years out of date," Sir Ako replied.

Basil said, "There is a fleet down there full of men who want to kill us, my woman is about to give birth to my child, and you are asking me to name a price to a lord of Serica for the farseer that you gave me in place of my own. I can't do it. Negotiating is your job, not mine."

Sandun turned to Sir Ako. "I don't have any good ideas, do you?"

"There is something I want, yes. I want armor for my men. Since they are to be knighted, assuming we live through this battle, I want them all with suits of armor. *All*. A man needs a suit of armor to be a knight. That seems like a fair trade to me."

Sandun made Sir Ako's offer to Lord Vaina, who agreed immediately.

"Yes. Excellent. After the battle, we can borrow *Opmi* Ako's armor and make copies. Add that task to my list of things to be done after the Vasvar fleet is defeated."

"Yes, my lord," replied the Scribe Ussi. "The list grows longer by the hour."

"Time to go." Lord Vaina went to Basil and shook his hand. "Thank you," he said in Kelten. Basil shook Lord Vaina's hand gravely and then saluted him.

As Lord Vaina was going down the ladder, he said to Sandun, "You will come when I call you? Yes? Be ready!"

"Yes, Lord Vaina. We will come."

After the lord left, Basil said to Sir Ako, "How much for your farseer? I keep losing mine to people far more important than I."

"Take it, Sir Basil. You had a generous heart when you could have asked for your weight in gold. We are blood brothers, yes? We have debts to each other that money cannot weigh."

As they walked down the street back to the embassy, Sandun remarked, "I find it amazing that an old farseer should have traveled nearly all the way around the world. It likely was made in Melnehlan and then traveled east, thousands of miles, from Maspan, across the sea to the Island of Ice maybe, and then across the great sea to Budin, and finally to Serica. Why, if we were to take it back to Melnehlan, it would have done something no man has ever done—gone completely around the world!"

"Sandun, no one is taking that old piece of junk back across the Tiralas to Kelten and then sailing it back to Melnehlan!" Basil shook his head in mock dismay.

The rest of the day dragged interminably. The Keltens kept to their embassy, sharpening weapons, refeathering arrows, praying. Sir Ako spent more than an hour in his room with Lady Tuomi. No one said anything when he came back down by himself.

Olef's time was nearly upon her. A midwife had been summoned, and a large room upstairs was now closed to the polluting influence of men. Basil sat silently, oiling his great bow so that it gleamed darkly in the dim light of the common room.

Kagne paced around, rather like a caged saber cat. He had been practicing with a shorter Serice bow, but he was still the worst shot of the group. Several times in the afternoon, he went out to the wall and then returned with the latest news.

The attack was proceeding largely as expected. The Vasvar ballistas had smashed the water gate rapidly. Small boats had sailed in through a rain of missiles thrown down from above, and soon the gate area was seized. The Tokolas soldiers had retreated, in good order, away from the invasion. Towers were defended, but not to the last man. By midafternoon, the Vasvar army had taken much of the port city at the river's side. Above the river, the gates of the inner wall that surrounded the main city of Tokolas had been shut fast.

The Vasvar commander, General Tuno, established two additional camps. One was on the north side of the river, perhaps to hold supplies, though it was impossible to see clearly with all the smoke in the air. The other camp was established upriver, a mile or more east of the Tokolas walls. That was unexpected but not without wisdom, for even the clumsiest spy would have learned that half the army of Kunhalvar was on its eastern border, fighting the Iron King's army. The eastern army was two weeks away by normal marching, though given enough boats, it could sail back to Tokolas in a week.

As the evening drew its hazy curtain across the sky, the Keltens moved restlessly around the courtyard. They were waiting, waiting for the summons from the palace. Around midnight, Kagne went to the wall and rapidly returned.

"The fires have mostly been put out. Everyone is on high alert, but nothing is happening other than more soldiers landing on the docks and the sounds of hammering on wood." Kagne was clearly excited, but the others were tense and irritable.

Sir Ako said, "The enemy commander is cautious. He fears a sudden assault when his troops are still unsettled and unfamiliar with the new land. If I were Lord Vaina, I would attack shortly before the coming dawn. But the command of thousands has not been my study. Perhaps my father would counsel waiting for a day or a week so to lull the enemy into a stupor. Right now, the enemy will strike at every shadow."

In the early hours of the morning, no word had come, and the men were all dozing in the dark room. Sandun was woken from a fitful dream by the sound of a woman crying out in pain upstairs. Sandun knew the sound; it was one he'd heard often echoing in the small, crowded town of Tebispoli.

"First born usually come with the dawn. May the light of Sho'Ash guide them all their days." Padan said this while looking up at the ceiling.

After a few minutes, the cries ended, and suddenly they heard the faint wails of a baby.

Lady Tuomi came down the stairs, looking unusually disheveled, and said to them, "It's a boy. Sir Basil has a new son. Olef is well enough. You can go see them." All the men stood up. "Just Basil!" she said.

Basil, with a big grin on his face, bounded up the stairs.

Sir Ako came over to the Lady Tuomi and held her; she rested her head on his chest for a minute, and then she straightened up. "This has been a day to remember. I think I'll lie down for a bit." Then she said something in her own language. "That's an old expression from my country. 'When the baby's born, the midwife sleeps, and the mother gives her milk.'" She smiled weakly and let Sir Ako lead her back to her room.

Basil came back down, and the men all slapped him on his back and congratulated him. "I named the boy Niksol Kol Vono. Kol for Tokolas."

Ashala came down half an hour later, carrying the newborn all wrapped up in clean cloth, and showed him around. She seemed remarkably happy, as though it was her child she was presenting.

Sir Ako returned and told the men to get some sleep. "Tomorrow night, perhaps."

Sandun awoke to find Ashala sleeping beside him. She must have come in after he'd fallen asleep. There was a strange, booming noise and then the faint sounds of yelling. He hurriedly put on his leather armor over his clothing and went outside to investigate. It was midmorning, high clouds above and below, smoke and dust in the air.

He asked one man running down the street what was happening, but the man just kept running. At the closest tower there were great jars of oil hanging above makeshift fire grates. The commander in charge told Sandun that the enemy were shooting huge arrows at the upper gate and the walls around it. "Sometimes they shoot at other towers as well. But they can't shoot this far, and many of the bolts just hit the earth!"

Sandun climbed up to the wall to survey the scene. The great ships of the Vasvar fleet each carried a ballista—what was essentially a huge crossbow. It was too far for him to see how exactly they were loaded, but every minute or so, a massive piece of wood, like a small tree trunk, would leap from one of the galleys and fly toward the upper walls of Tokolas. As he watched, one hit a wall and disintegrated into a shower of kindling and dust. The noise it made was somewhat like a great tree hitting the earth badly and shattering, only faster and louder. The wall he was standing on trembled, even though he was half a mile from the impact. Another flying tree trunk came up from the river, but this one fell short and smashed into an old shack that had been built precariously on the steep hill some way from the main road.

I wonder how long they can keep up this bombardment? Sandun thought to himself. *I wish I'd brought more farseers. I should have guessed they would be highly desired.* The enemy soldiers had not approached the walls yet, but they could be seen, lower down the slopes. They looked just like the Tokolas soldiers, with the same type of armor and weapons. *How do I tell them apart?*

Sandun asked the commander how he could identify the Vasvar soldiers. The man smiled and pointed to his left arm: a strip of dark-red cloth was tied around his upper arm. "They wear green. We are wearing red."

Back at the embassy, the Keltens were eating. Sandun suddenly felt ravenous and ate with them while he described what he'd seen. "I want to see this myself," said Sir Ako. About half the men went with him while the others stayed behind.

An hour later, he was back. "Impressive design. The galleys have remarkable stability on the river for making such shots. I would have taken those great ballistas off the boats and put them on shore—more accurate that way. Kelten warships use much smaller ballistas, no doubt because the ocean is usually too rough to make long shots with any hope of success." He paused. "Also, I noticed the lighthouse tower looks undamaged."

Sandun felt a tightness in his chest, but he did his best to pretend he felt nothing.

"Don't worry, Master Sandun. It's a crazy plan, and it will work brilliantly."

"Are you always so confident before a battle?" Sandun asked him earnestly.

"Always. As the Great Commander said, victory lies not in numbers but in men's hearts and minds. Devoted men and a good plan—that's all you need to conquer the world."

All that day, the bombardment continued. By evening, the gate area was reportedly a wreck, even though hundreds of strong men and stonemasons worked to shore up the wall with beams of wood and hasty brickwork.

Before dinner, Ashala took Sandun to their room and kissed him. "I know I should not care, but I do. Come back. I...I don't know what I will do if you don't come back."

Sandun hugged her and tried to reassure her, but his words rang hollow in his mind. "It will be all right. Don't worry. I'll come back."

After dinner, as the sun set, Sir Ako led them all in prayer. Olef, with little Niksol in her arms, came down to join them. Lady Tuomi sat at the end of the room and watched, her dark eyes intent on Sir Ako, as though she were fixing his image in her mind.

The long-anticipated messenger came an hour later. Everyone collected their gear and assembled in the courtyard. Sir Ako, in full armor, checked everyone to be sure. Valo Peli and Lathe came up from the cellar, bringing their special weapons, which were then loaded onto the steadiest of the Piksie rams. Then they headed up the streets to the by-now-familiar side entrance to the palace. Guards looked at Sir Ako, all dressed in his armor, and said, "Fire Sword," with some awe, and let them in. Sir Ako chuckled deep in his throat. "Not the first time I've been made famous for someone else's deeds." Sandun was too busy with his own thoughts to ask him what he meant.

They were escorted to the war room, which was strangely empty. Lord Vaina stood by himself, staring down at a large map. Aside from a few boys acting as messengers, only the captain of the guards and two other soldiers were with him.

"I am glad to see you. Everything is ready. The enemy ships are still in range. Do you have everything?"

Valo Peli said yes and listed the things he had brought.

"Then let's go."

Sandun expected to follow a messenger boy or one of the guards, but instead Lord Vaina himself headed out of the room and jogged down the steps. As he did, he tossed aside his elaborate robe and revealed a suit of plain and rather worn leather armor; some reddish paint could still be seen on the back of the arms.

"Are you coming with us, Lord Vaina?" asked Sandun.

"I am. Which is why I have sent nearly everyone away. This is my plan, my city, and I'm going to see it through. And if it turns out to be a shark on the line, we can always throw away the rod and row to shore."

They made their way to the center of the palace complex. At least a hundred of the palace guards were waiting there. The guards were not the great giants Sandun had seen before. These were a different group, and they greeted the Lord of Kunhalvar with an ease that come from long familiarity.

"Coming with us? Fish Guts, now we must worry about keeping you safe. I won't face Lady Osmo's wrath if you get hurt."

"Are you going to fight this time? Or just stand back and yell orders like always?"

One man, older than the others and shorter, had a bristling beard that stuck out stiffly from his face. He loudly said, "Just watch out for canoes!" and most of the men laughed, sharing some private joke.

Lord Vaina went up to the older man and poked him in the chest. "Old Bristle Face, if you get skewered by a Vasvar arrow, only fish will weep."

"Not so! The tea house girls on Silk Street will be crying their pretty little eyes out since the only real man in town will no longer be around to make them happy."

This provoked a chorus of jeers from the other men.

The two *krasuth* now appeared, escorted by one of the messenger boys. They had made no apparent effort to get ready for battle, save that they both carried long staffs. The tall one came up to Lord Vaina and bowed. "You summoned us, my lord."

"You are going to help with the attack and protect me."

"As your lordship commands."

Sandun watched as the *krasuth* swept his gaze over the assembled warriors; the man's face was almost masklike, concealing all thoughts behind his fixed expression. Sandun thought that the man was somehow being forced into this, but he didn't know how or why.

An old man with a handful of keys now opened a door to a nondescript building nearby. Inside was just one room with stacks of aromatic wood all along the walls. Large bags, some of which held roof tiles, filled most of the interior of the warehouse. Toward the back of one wall, a space had been recently cleared, and there was a trapdoor in the floor. The old man unlocked and opened it, revealing steps descending into darkness. Valo Peli distributed his explosives among the Kelten soldiers, who stored them in rucksacks they wore over their armor.

"This part is only a short way down," the old man said out loud to the people around him. Although he had long white hair, he was spry enough going down the steps. Some thirty feet down there was a tunnel lined with rock. It looked long unused. Many of the soldiers carried lanterns. Lord Vaina wore one of the glowing orbs from Kelten around his neck, as did his guard captain.

Soon they came to more stairs, leading down in a gentle spiral. Lord Vaina, who was walking just behind Sandun, said, "We are circling around the deep well that stands in the center of the palace. Most of our drinking water gets delivered from a stream outside of the city. This well water is used for cleaning and in case of siege."

The stairs went down and down. They were narrow, just wide enough for one man, and old. In places, the steps were quite slippery where moss or slime had grown, fed by some seeping water from the earth. The air became close, and the smell from the burning lamps carried by the guards ahead of him made Sandun cough. Everyone was silent as they wound their way down deep into the earth.

Finally, the stairs ended, and the men ahead slowly moved off the stairs and walked down a narrow tunnel and then stopped. The old man with the keys, who had been behind Lord Vaina, pushed forward, apologizing as he went past each man. Sandun couldn't see what he was doing at the end of the tunnel—too many people blocked the way.

He asked Lord Vaina, "Have you been down here before?"

Lord Vaina replied quietly, "Just once. A year after we took the city. This is one of the secret escape routes. The palace needs a water supply. But what is not known is that the water actually comes from the Mur." After a pause, he bellowed, "What's taking so long? Don't you know there is a war going on?"

"Sorry, my lord, sorry. The door is older than I am."

Lord Vaina whispered to Sandun, "This was built sometime during the Water Kingdom. It's likely two hundred years old now. Amazing that it is still intact."

With a grating noise, part of the stone wall at the end of passage opened out, and dank, cool air rushed into the passage. The torchlights flickered as the new air passed by like a wind. The soldiers rapidly exited, and soon Sandun found himself walking inside a low tunnel with a curved roof of stone close above his head. Cut into the floor and running the whole length of the tunnel was a stream of water. In the dim light, it seemed motionless, but he heard the faint sound of water falling behind him, presumably into the large cistern where water was stored at the bottom of the well. On either side of the small stream, there were two paths of stone. It was damp inside the tunnel, and there was moss in many places on the walls and on the flagstones beside the water.

Now the old key master led the way, followed by the palace guards, then the Keltens, and then Lord Vaina and the *krasuth* with a few more guards at the rear. The tunnel was long and straight.

"Strangely," Lord Vaina said, "through some feat of engineering, the tunnel does not flood when the river floods, or so the old key master tells me. I have no idea how that was done."

In the tunnel there was no sound but that of the warriors as they strode along on both stone paths. It seemed like an hour had passed, and Sandun was feeling both sweaty and chilled at the same time. Finally, the end of the tunnel was revealed at the edge of sight, and Lord Vaina called a halt.

"Leave the lanterns here. From this point on, the only light will be from the Kelten orbs. I want no smell of burning oil drifting up through invisible cracks and alerting the enemy to our presence. We are nearly under the lighthouse. There is a short flight of stairs that leads to another stone door. The key master will open the door; it should be easier than the last one. It opens to the basement of the lighthouse. With heaven's blessing, the basement will be empty, and we can assemble inside. If not, then the first man through will have a fight. Guard Captain Ferant has requested the honor of going first. Does anyone object?"

Lord Vaina paused. The guard captain loosened his sword in its sheath and glared at everyone around him. No one said anything.

"After we have secured the basement, we take the first floor and bar the door. Your job is that of a boat itself—hold back the water! No Vasvar soldier must enter the lighthouse. Not one. If there is a danger of losing the door, you must send word to me. I will be at the top of the tower with the Keltens. If you send word that the door will fall, then I will have to decide whether to retreat back the way we came or die here with you, but you must give me that choice!"

"You'll not die here, Lord of Kunhalvar," said the short man with the beard. "I'll drag you down the stairs myself if it comes to that."

"I am not afraid," said Lord Vaina. "The Vasvar army has fallen into my trap. Even now, General Erdis is attacking from the west, and General Kun is attacking from the east along with the cavalry from the eastern army. We will destroy Two-Sword Tuno's army and sink his ships, and our city will never be attacked again."

His guardsmen nodded and shook their fists in the air.

The key master, holding a glowing orb in one hand high over his head, went down the tunnel and then through an opening and up a newly revealed flight of stairs. Lord Vaina stood halfway up the stairs while the rest filed past him.

Despite Lord Vaina's promise, the door at the top proved equally hard to open. The old man struggled and cursed under his breath as he worried at the locking mechanism like a terrier with a large rat. Finally, it opened with a loud thunk.

Captain Ferant pushed through the door and was met with several spears, one of which he could not avoid. Mortally wounded, he killed two of the Vasvar soldiers before throwing himself on the third spearman, knocking him to the floor. In a minute or two, the room was cleared of living enemies, but Captain Ferant bled to death before anyone could help him.

The Tokolas guards wasted no time mourning for their commander but rushed up the stairs. On the ground floor, the fighting was vicious and in very close quarters. The palace guards proved to be deadly masters of hand-to-hand combat. The first floor was cleared in minutes with the Vasvar soldiers all butchered and the doorway to the outside locked and blocked.

While most of the guards ransacked the rooms and the cellar for things to buttress the doorway, a few of the guards led by "Old Bristle Face" headed upstairs toward the top of the tower. Sir Ako followed, leading the Kelten warriors, not rushing but rapidly. One man was found sleeping on the third level in a small alcove; he was captured and tied up for questioning. With Sir Ako now leading the way, they reached the top of the tower. Here there were three men. One appeared to be an officer of some rank. His two guards were totally surprised, and while they fumbled for their weapons, Sir Ako killed each of them with swift sword strokes.

The officer of the Vasvar army went to his knees and made no effort to fight. He asked, "How did you get here?" Old Bristle Face blindfolded him and then took him down the stairs for questioning.

The Keltens had made it to the top of the tower. Now it was their turn.

Kagne Areka looked out from the top of the lighthouse tower. The air was full of the noise of fighting. Kagne was not a trained soldier; he was, he told himself, a jack-of-all-trades. Before this year-long journey to Serica, his major jobs had been as a trader and herbmaster. Although he had killed at least ten men in his life, he liked to think of himself as a peaceful man who only killed when he or his clansmen were threatened. He took pride in the fact that he had resolved several disputes that could have erupted into near warfare between powerful rival clans.

But the fighting going on now…this was on a different scale from anything he had seen before. Ten thousand men in a single army? There weren't ten thousand men in all of northern Erimasran, counting the oldest graybeard to the youngest new man with his faint mustache. Kagne felt like a very small antelope in a huge herd, running through a sea of dust, and he didn't like it one little bit.

He rapidly oriented himself. The city walls of Tokolas were set upon a great ridge to the south, about a mile away. Directly to the north and reaching almost to the foot of the tower was the Mur. It was impossible to see the far shore of the river, even from the top of the tower. The Mur was like a vast, shimmering curtain, stretching both east and west into the night. Black shapes of boats could occasionally be seen on the water.

Looking at the sky, he guessed it was around midnight; the moon was rising, still close to the eastern shore. Kagne looked down upon the Tokolas harbor, which was filled with boats, just as Lord of Kunhalvar had predicted. The great ships of the Vasvar fleet had sailed into the harbor under the cover of night, and now they occasionally shot huge arrows at the walls of the city. When a giant ballista on a nearby ship fired, the missile made a roaring noise as it shot out into the sky and then vanished.

As Sir Ako pointed out targets, the Kelten scouts strung their great bows and looked down below.

"We hit the closest ship first and then work our way out," said Sir Ako. Their targets were the huge ships that now crowded the harbor.

Kagne thought the boats were a bit like sheep penned in at night—and now, the wolves were inside the fence.

Lord Vaina arrived at the tower top, accompanied by two guards, and then the two strange *krasuth* climbed up the stairs to join the men already there.

Kagne did not like either of the *krasuth*, and he did not know why they had come on this suicide mission. Looking at them now, he got the distinct impression they had even less desire to be here than he did.

Valo Peli and Lathe were laying out "fire arrows" on the stones beside the central iron grate of the lighthouse. In normal times, the grate held aloft a great fire that served to mark the entrance to the Tokolas harbor. Now the grate held nothing but cold ashes and bits of charred logs. Each archer picked up one of the arrows and waited while Valo Peli or Lathe lit the fuse, and then the archer rushed over to the edge of the tower and launched his fiery arrow at the targeted ship.

Kagne picked up a burning arrow and bounded over to the east wall. As he pulled the arrow back, it sent sparks and flame directly at his face. He knew he had to shoot the arrow rapidly, but he could not concentrate with the fire spitting into his eyes. He made his best guess as to the target and loosed his arrow, but the shot went wide of the mark, disappearing uselessly into the black water near the boat.

He watched as the other arrows landed more accurately on the boat, most of them directly on the main target: the giant ballista. Faint cries of surprise and alarm came from the boat, and a series of explosions erupted on the deck; fire broke out in many places.

Individually, the arrows didn't carry much of Valo Peli's *lopor*, or thunder powder, but ten or eleven arrows together produced a conflagration that looked like it would destroy the war machine and perhaps set the whole boat on fire.

Any sense of accomplishment he felt as the ballista burned was undermined by his own failure to hit the target. He threw his bow down in frustration. As he stood there, he saw Damar fire his arrow and then put his bow down and begin swatting his face, apparently burned by the sparks. Immediately, Kagne thought back to a day on the Erimasran plains when a large grass fire came toward his village. While the women and elders made ready to flee, the men had gone out to halt the fire. The older men had soaked strips of cloth in washtubs and then wrapped the cloths around their faces and hands. The Kelten archers could do the same; he just needed water and cloth.

Kagne hunted around for buckets of water. He was about ready to go down to the lower level when he found two buckets, both only a quarter full, near the woodpile. Success! Now for some cloth. Sandun usually planned ahead for injuries, and that meant he likely had some strips of cloth in his pack. Kagne rooted around in Sandun's pack and pulled out several pieces of clean cloth. He dunked the cloth in the water, lightly squeezed the excess out, and then offered one to the next man, who had come to pick up an arrow that Valo Peli had set alight.

"That's a good idea, Kagne!" Padan said. Taking one of the wet pieces of cloth, he wrapped it around his head. The other Keltens soon followed Padan's lead. Kagne ran out of rags, and two archers still needed them when Lathe came over with some extra pieces of cloth; it looked like he had torn off his sleeves to provide them.

That done, Kagne went back to the east side and saw three boats burning in the night. He watched as another arrow flew in a smooth curve down toward a new target. But then an arrow snapped and broke against the stone wall next to him; it had been fired from below. More arrows came up and then rained down. The arrows came down with little force and no accuracy, but they were annoying, and there was nothing that could be done about them...or so Kagne thought.

His attention was drawn to the two *krasuth*, who began a weird dance. After a few seconds, the hairs rose on Kagne's arms, and the air felt odd; he could not explain the sensation. Over the next minute, a thin haze grew into a thick fog that surrounded the top of the tower. Soon he could barely see the harbor, and the burning boats were just hazy outlines. Very few arrows made it through the fog, likely because the archers down below could no longer see the top of the tower.

But even as it protected them, the fog became an increasing hindrance to the Kelten archers. Basil shouted angrily, "I can't see the next target! Sho'Ash curse this fog!"

Kagne ran over to the two *krasuth* and said, in his broken Serice, "Clouds, too big! Archers not see boats." In response, the smaller of the two *krasuth* set his staff aside and went to the eastern edge of the tower, all the while making odd, choppy hand motions. The change in the fog on that side of the tower was rapid, and hard for Kagne to believe even as he saw it. In one place, where the smaller *krasuth* was standing, there was now a hole or a window, and the boats in the harbor became visible again. The fog thickened in all other directions, and the air grew bitterly cold, almost as if winter had come to the tower.

Now, the Keltens shot their burning arrows at an undamaged behemoth. Some of the flames vanished, likely extinguished by buckets of water, but others stubbornly resisted going out, and after a steady rain of exploding arrows, the fourth boat was burning brightly.

The sounds of fighting and yells came from below. Kagne went to the south side of the tower and looked down, through the fog. He could dimly see soldiers with torches advancing on the tower.

A terrible whistling noise, and Kagne turned to see a giant arrow flying over the tower. Then another arrow could be heard, this one lower, but it flew past and smashed into a building nearby. Then one great arrow crashed into the lower part of the tower, the stone floor they were standing on shook violently, and several Kelten archers were knocked to their knees.

"This is getting exciting," Kagne said to Sandun. Sandun grunted in response but seemed fixed on lighting the fire arrows for the other archers.

Kagne watched as Valo Peli took a grapefruit-sized package in one hand and applied fire to its fuse. Valo Peli then hurried over to the south wall and dropped the package down. Within seconds, there was a great flash of light and a booming noise, followed by a cacophony of cries and shrieks. Valo Peli saw that Kagne had observed this novel means of defense; Valo Peli picked up another package, set its fuse alight, and handed it to Kagne.

Holding the burning bag and knowing it would soon explode, Kagne ran to the tower's wall and threw the bag toward the largest collection of torches below. The bag of *lopor* vanished into the fog; a moment later, there was a sudden shouting followed by another flash of light and an unearthly roar. All the torches vanished, as if doused by a gale's gust or because the Vasvar soldiers had thrown them down. Kagne felt thrilled and then sickened to be the agent of such destruction.

In the quiet after the explosion, Kagne thought he heard the sound of fighting coming from farther west, near the city wall. He strained his eyes, but the fog was too thick to see through. A minute passed, and now the sounds were unmistakable: the yelling of men and the clashing of steel.

Behind him he heard Sandun say, "That is the last of the fire arrows."

Another great arrow hit the tower lower down. Kagne turned and saw that a section of the top wall had fallen away.

"We should get down from here!" Kagne shouted at Sandun. "Before this whole thing collapses underneath us!"

"Wait," said Sir Ako. "I think the boats are moving out of the harbor."

"That doesn't matter. They can still hit this tower from the river."

The Lord of Kunhalvar, who had been striding back and forth, stopped and said something to Sandun, and then he and one guard went down the stairs. The other guard was sitting down: an unlucky arrow had cut deeply into his arm, and he had bled out while stoically protecting his lord with his own shield. He had found a seat with his last strength.

The two *krasuth* were arguing with one another; the tall one seemed to be telling the smaller man to go down the stairs, while the latter shook his head and protested. Valo Peli and Lathe had collected their few remaining pouches of thunder powder and were heading down the stairs; the Kelten archers were ready to follow.

A minute later, everyone but the tall *krasuth* and Kagne had left the top. Another bolt had hit the tower, this time from the river side. The tower was swaying a little from the impact. Kagne wanted desperately to leave, but he felt he was being shown up by this strange man who had kept fog wrapped around the tower for more than an hour.

"Go down!" Kagne yelled at the man, pointing down the stairs.

The *krasuth* waved his hands around as if pointing to the fog and shook his head in refusal. Kagne now suspected that if the man went down the stairs, the fog would swiftly vanish, and then the tower would come under heavy fire from the remaining great ships. He didn't know how many of great boats had survived; he guessed at least fifteen of them. In the tower's weakened condition, it would not take long to bring the lighthouse down in a cataclysm of broken stone.

Suddenly the man stopped his strange dance and took Kagne's face with his two hands. Kagne tried to pull free, but the man's grip was strong. The man gazed at Kagne with his intense eyes, so dark they seemed to swallow the man's face in shadow. The *krasuth* spoke, and somehow Kagne understood him.

"I am Orinok. I do this at the behest of the True Master. 'Protect the Lord of Kunhalvar,' he said, and I obey. You too may learn to serve the True Master. Go north! Follow the call! Now leave!"

Kagne stumbled away from Orinok and headed down the stairs as he had been told. He seemed to hear Orinok's words echoing over and over in his mind. *Follow the call. I serve the True Master.* Kagne hardly noticed the bodies and the broken weapons on the ground floor or the last few palace guards who were still defending the doorway, bleeding, clutching broken pieces of weapons and covered in blood. Vaguely he noticed that one of the remaining defenders was a short man with a beard whose bristles were now stiff with blood.

Stones fell from above, and there was a choking dust of pulverized mortar in the air. Torches had been hurled into the room through the shattered doorway; some were still burning. Kagne paid little attention. He just kept going down to the cellar. He felt like he had been smoking dream weed for an hour, and he knew better than to fight the sensation. He was just going to do what seemed right without thinking it out.

At the narrow secret entrance, he found Valo Peli and Lathe doing something with their bags of *lopor*. He pushed past them and went down into the darkness. At the bottom of the stairs there were lanterns. Sandun was pulling at his arm and urging him to go down the long, endless tunnel. Valo Peli and Lathe came running down the stairs and collided with him; they both smelled of thunder powder and smoke.

There was a booming noise that was followed shortly by a growing rumble that shook the ground. Bits of stone and flakes of dry moss blew around them. Kagne saw the lanterns go out one by one down the tunnel. He found he was completely unworried by both the crashing sounds and the darkness.

When there was light again, he discovered Sandun was splashing his face with cold water, and he was recalled, for a time, from his waking dream. He was on his back, his left hand and arm hanging down in the waterway.

"Are you hurt?" Sandun asked. "The tower has collapsed, but the tunnel is still intact. Let's go!"

"Orinok is staying behind, doing the will of the True Master, and I must follow the call" Kagne replied. Sandun looked at him quizzically and then offered his hand to Kagne.

Kagne struggled to his feet and slowly headed down the tunnel, following Sandun. Two dark eyes seemed to be staring back at him from whichever direction he looked.

Climbing up the stairs, Sandun felt good, perhaps even elated. While Sir Ako stayed at the base of the stairs to let the other Keltens rest, Sandun followed Lord Vaina, who was eager to get back to the palace war room and find out what was going on. Behind them, the survivors of the palace guard were also climbing the steps.

"Did you see those boats running back downstream? I'll bet they keep going all the way to Fuseboni." Lord Vaina said this to Sandun as they both stopped for a breather after reaching the halfway point. "Your men performed wonderfully well. Fishcakes! I hope General Kun's soldiers are able to capture some of the great boats that were on fire in the harbor."

As they continued up the stairs, Sandun asked, "Lord Vaina, you said General Tuno and his fleet had fallen into your trap. Did you want them to attack?"

"Ha-ha, yes, I did. The army of the Radiant Prince in Sasuvi is still weak. Their losses last year were even greater than the rumors spoke of. We knew Two-Swords was building a fleet, and he was ambitious. I didn't trust him from the moment I first met him four years gone. I thought Tuno would either sail down to Buuk or sail north. Then, the size of his boats told me he was heading upriver."

"The mouth of the Mur is a huge swamp, or so our old maps say."

"Yes, very much a swamp. The river splits and splits again into a maze of shallow lakes. I've been there, once. Flat boats can sail all the way to Buuk, with a guide. Lots of bugs." Lord Vaina seemed to recall Buuk without much affection.

"So you felt if General Two-Swords attacked Sasuvi, he would take it?"

"Like an eel swallows a minnow. Growing his strength, putting Tokolas in between two large hostile enemies. We would be like a trout on the shore caught between two hungry cats. So my spies planted stories throughout Vasvar of our weakness, our disunity, even a highly placed traitor who was going to defect and bring his army with him. Hah! We magnified our losses and minimized those of the Radiant Prince. Also, Two-Swords Tuno has hated me for years."

"But the Radiant Prince attacked Kemeklos? Why would Sasuvi do that if they were weak?"

Lord Vaina stopped and faced Sandun. "The Radiant Prince is just a boy. The real leader in Sasuvi is the man we call the Red Prophet. I have great respect for the Prophet—he is a powerful speaker, an inspiration to all who hear him. But I never expected the Red Prophet to order his army out and attack Kemeklos, because it makes no sense! My people in Sasuvi think the Red Prophet's army has barely eight thousand men. And most are raw recruits. If General Two-Sword's fleet had continued north, he would have found no one to oppose him. He could have captured every city along the Nava river, from Sasuvi north to Hevravi. And without a fleet big enough to challenge him, there was little we could have done in response. No, we had to convince him to come to us."

Lord Vaina, his face illuminated by the glowing orb he wore around his neck, looked at Sandun closely. "I want you to be part of my council. You have proved worthy of my trust, and because you are from Kelten, you take warfare seriously. We have long known that Kelten is both a civilized land and one where warriors and generals are treated with respect. I believe we are just playing at war here in Serica these days. If Kunhalvar is going to triumph, I will need the best experts I can get. You and your men are the finest warriors I have ever seen. None of my soldiers could have done what your men did this evening."

Sandun looked up at Lord Vaina, who seemed so convincing, so earnest in his entreaty. A part of Sandun wanted to say yes, to not just read about the events of the past but actually be a part of decisions as they were made.

"My lord, we have been away from home for more than a year. We were sent here by King Pandion to see if it was possible to cross the Tirala Mountains and to set up trade relations. Our mission is not complete until we return."

Lord Vaina bore down on Sandun's argument. "You spent a year traveling to Serica. It will take nearly as long to return, yes? Why not spend a year here before returning? Stay here, learn about Serica. You came to set up trade? In a year, I can send you back with a rich caravan of goods and with an ambassador as well. But right now, I need you. With you and your men, we have a chance to change the course of history!"

Sandun hesitated.

Lord Vaina tried another tack. "More than one hundred years ago, Ors Divar, a Sogand warlord, the leader of the Turan tribe, met the Kelten army in battle, and you won." Sandun nodded his head. Lord Vaina was referring to Maklinos the Great; everyone in Kelten knew the story of his victory.

Lord Vaina continued, "The news of the defeat traveled all the way back to Serica, giving hope to the armies of the Water Kingdom that the Sogands could be overcome. People still remember that—one of the rare times the Sogands were ever beaten. The Kitran army is coming for us; I don't know when, but they will come. Your presence here would mean something far more than just numbers. Serice armies have been defeated so many times by the Kitran—by the Sogands—that my people don't believe they can be vanquished. They don't think Serice warriors can do it. Serice armies are overcome by fear before the fighting starts. But you don't think that way. You can show us the path to victory!"

This argument carried real weight with Sandun. In Kelten and throughout the Archipelago, the Sogands were believed to be in league with the Black Terror. Coming on this long journey and finding the land of Serica ravaged by Sogands reminded Sandun of the story of Sho'Ash.

It had long been taught that the story of Sho'Ash, his leaving his home and family and traveling on a great journey to overthrow the rule of the Black Terror, was a metaphor for everyone. For all of them, their expedition had become something more than just trade or exploration. It was more like a crusade.

"Very well, Lord Vaina. My men and I will stay for a year and help you."

"Thank you, Sandun. You won't regret this." Lord Vaina turned and started up the stairs again. "We are going to do great things together. You will see."

Back at the war room, there were a pile of messages and very visible relief on everyone's face when Lord Vaina appeared, unharmed. Quickly he put on his formal robe and then sat down. He motioned Sandun to sit on a chair beside him. The time was near dawn, and tea and food were brought to them as the lord listened to the reports.

General Kun, leading the eastern wing, had captured the Vasvar camp, and many of the Vasvar soldiers had switched sides after a personal appeal made by General Kun. The western wing, under General Erdis, had slowly driven the Vasvar soldiers back to the Tokolas harbor. For the last hour, the Vasvar army had been embarking onto their ships, but the situation around the harbor was chaotic. The surviving great boats, fourteen all counted, were miles downriver. No one had seen General Tuno, but Vasvar prisoners claimed he was on board one of the great boats.

The commander of the Tokolas navy asked for permission to advance down the river in pursuit, but Lord Vaina rejected that idea. "We have won a great victory, but their fleet is still larger than ours. I require you to use your ships to seal up the harbor entrance and stop any more Vasvar boats from escaping. That is enough for this day. Further, and to repeat: there is to be no execution of prisoners and no taking of heads. Many of the Vasvar soldiers will fight for Tokolas if they are treated justly."

Half an hour later, Sir Ako appeared, guided by one of the messenger boys. "I sent everyone back to the embassy, but this boy told me I could find you here."

"How are the men?" Sandun asked.

"Gloval has a bad wound to his left calf. It seemed minor at the time, but by the end of the climb we had to carry him up the stairs. Perhaps the arrow was poisoned? Valo Peli sent for a doctor when we reached the top, but there is a war going on. Also, Kagne acts like he took a blow to the head, but he seems uninjured. Perhaps he got too close to one of the explosions."

"Reports are that we destroyed twelve boats. Fourteen great boats were counted sailing down the river. One is unaccounted for. The Lord of Kunhalvar is very impressed."

Sir Ako smiled. "Is that why you are sitting here? Have you been promoted?"

"Yes, as a matter of fact. I've agreed that we will stay here for another year, and I've been invited to act as an advisor to Lord Vaina."

Sir Ako considered this for a bit and then nodded. "Makes sense to me. There is a war going on. I don't like our chances of getting home right now, even if we wanted to leave. And, to tell you true, burning those great ships down with Valo Peli's fire arrows was the most fun I've had in years." He laughed a deep, booming laugh and smacked his fist into the palm of his hand. "Watching those flaming arrows arc down and then blow up into great gouts of fire... may Sho'Ash blind me, but what a sight that was! The fifteen of us destroyed twelve great ships? That deserves a song, even if I have to write it myself."

The knight grabbed a bowl of tea and drained it. "Let me tell you something, Sandun. In war, usually victory or defeat is the result of a few men, the ones who stood their ground in the middle of the line or the ones who first panicked and ran. After the battle, it's usually impossible to say who those few men were. But we, we stood on top of a tower and rained fire and destruction down on the biggest damn ships in the world, and every man knew it was us—those bastards on the tower—who were doing the deeds. We won this battle, and we have lived to tell the tale."

He paused and then said, "For a warrior, it doesn't get any better than this. We are going to be famous in Kelten and in Serica as well."

Lord Vaina returned from an inner chamber with his face clean and his hair wet. He shook Sir Ako's hand, saying, "Armor for all your men. *Opmi of Serica!*"

Sir Ako saluted Lord Vaina, and then he and Sandun returned to the embassy to find everyone but Valo Peli asleep. Sandun congratulated Valo Peli on his amazing fire arrows, as did Sir Ako, who took off his armor and then headed upstairs.

"The Lord of Kunhalvar was very pleased, and he asked me to be one of his advisers. I have agreed that my men and I will stay here for another year to help him," said Sandun.

Valo Peli was not enthusiastic. "Don't you see? Lord Vaina is using you. You aren't from Serica. This isn't your fight. Why are you risking your lives for the Lord of Kunhalvar?"

Sandun had all manner of arguments. Since he had agreed to stay for a year, he felt compelled to defend the decision he had made just two hours earlier.

"Firstly, Kelten cannot trade with a nation in a civil war. For better or worse, we have picked a side, and we have to live with that choice."

Valo Peli was dismissive. "Trade? Trade is irrelevant. It is unworthy of a refined man."

"We don't think so. Kelten has gained much wealth and some measure of power through trade. We came here to reestablish trade relations. I freely admit that we all hope to be very wealthy men when we return home. Trade is good. That farseer glass, that was an invention out of one Melnehlan city that we traded for and improved. The nations of the Archipelago are constantly trading, at least when they aren't fighting with each other."

Sandun felt strangely energized; by rights he ought to have been dead on his feet, but since drinking the delicious tea, he'd felt his mind racing like a horse on the grass of the Hippodrome. "Serica used to trade. Serice stone-glass is worth a fortune in Kelten. The king himself has a beautiful white-and-blue Serice vase in his study. There are items like it for sale in the markets here. They were traded in the past. Why not again?"

Valo Peli sighed and put his fingers together. "You do not understand, and it would take days to explain. In short, those were gifts—inspirational, civilizing gifts. That those items ended up being bought and sold for money…well, it wasn't the intention of the Gold Kingdom. But I ask you as an educated man, did you agree to stay and help the Lord of Kunhalvar just for money?"

Sandun choose to deflect the question and responded instead with a question of his own. "Why are you so concerned? I'm now on Lord Vaina's council, and you are my advisor. I have no doubt that Lord Vaina wants your advice as much as he wants mine. You came here to help the Lord of Kunhalvar. Why aren't you happy?"

"Because as an advisor to a foreigner, I won't be remembered in the historical records. I came here for redemption, but I can't have it if I'm only working through someone else!"

"Speaking as a Master of the Kelten Archives, why do you care? Few in my country care what is written and stored in the Archives. Sho'Ash knows what I, and you, and everyone else has done. When you and I are dead, Sho'Ash will judge all of us according to our deeds. Why are you so concerned about what one man writes in a history that perhaps no one will ever read?"

"Because, Sandun, there is no Sho'Ash, or Eston, or Sky Eagle, and no Heavenly King." Valo Peli said this quietly but with a certainty that was, ironically, almost religious in its intensity. "There is nothing but the judgment of history. When I die, all I will leave behind are my children and my deeds as written in the annals."

Sandun suddenly felt pity for the older man. Clearly there were many aspects of Serice ways of thinking that he did not and perhaps never would understand. But he had met nonbelievers before. Not everyone followed Sho'Ash in Kelten, and a few people believed in no god at all.

"Valo Peli, my friend, you aren't dead yet. There is still plenty of time for you to improve in the opinion of future historians. If you don't blow yourself up mixing more of your *lopor*, you will become Lord Vaina's chief advisor. But you can't expect redemption to happen overnight. Have patience. And even though you don't believe in Sho'Ash, he sees you. He knows what you have done. You struck a righteous blow last night, one that will never be forgotten."

Sandun awoke as the door to his room was thrown open and Ashala came in like a hurricane. She was in such a state of excitement and worry that she just hugged him and then started crying.

Eventually Sandun pieced together her story. She and the other women in the embassy woke before dawn and heard stories about the brave men who were shooting flaming arrows at the Vasvar fleet from the top of the lighthouse and that the lighthouse had been destroyed. She and Lady Tuomi had walked to three different field hospitals inside Tokolas, but no one knew anything, and so they had returned to find all the men asleep and mostly uninjured.

After he reassured her that he was all right, Sandun and Ashala went down to find that the house was wide awake and several very pretty young women had appeared with plates of food. Rumors were spreading about what the Keltens had done last night, and their miraculous reappearance had caused all sorts of curious people to come by and see for themselves. Sandun ordered the doors closed and had one of the servants stand guard. The girls stayed.

Reliable reports from beyond their wall told of the retreat of the Vasvar fleet. This was deemed a suitable occasion for pouring out some stiff drinks.

However, there had been a great many deaths and injuries, not to mention an entire section of the city that had been captured and then recaptured. Thus, the people of Tokolas didn't fill the streets in celebration.

Inside the Kelten embassy, it was otherwise. The men of the expedition ate and drank and recounted their deeds of the previous night. Gloval, pale and unable to walk, was sitting by the fireplace, attended by a woman from one of the hospitals that the Lady Tuomi had visited.

Basil sat beside Olef, holding the baby, with his dog contentedly at his feet. The right side of his face was singed and swollen from close proximity to the fire arrows, but he seemed almost happy.

After an hour, Sandun thought this was a good time to break the news. "My friends," he said, "the Lord of Kunhalvar is most grateful for your heroic actions last night. As promised, you will all be made knights of Serica as soon as preparations are completed."

"Including suits of armor," interjected Sir Ako. "But you are all going to have to learn the rules of knighthood, and the ceremony will be done right and proper, including the vigil the night before. When we return to Kelten, no one will be able to look askance at your claims."

Sandun continued, "As you can imagine, this will take some time. Now, Lord Vaina has asked me to serve on his council of war, and I have agreed to stay and help him for one year, after which time he has promised to send us back to Kelten with a rich caravan of goods and an escort for the journey. I am asking you to stay here for an additional year before we return home. After all, we spent a year getting here. Would you return after just a month or two?"

Padan, with his left arm around one of the new girls and his right hand holding a glass, said, "Ah, but will we be staying here in Tokolas or going off to fight this lot that just attacked the city?"

"The Vasvar army has been properly whipped, and I doubt they will show their faces here again for some time to come. No, the Lord Vaina thinks the Sogands will attack next. He believes that we may be very useful in training his soldiers to fight the Sogands. To speak plainly, the Serice are afraid of the Sogands and we…we are not."

News of a possible Sogand attack shifted the mood inside the room. This was not some squabble between rival princes in a foreign land; this was a threat they all understood.

"As knights of Serica, it would be a matter of honor to oppose the Sogands." Sir Ako said this firmly, and the other men murmured agreement.

They'd been taught that the Sogands were the common enemy of all civilized men.

"Just so long as we aren't a part of Lord Vaina's army," said Damar.

"No, the knights of Serica will be like the knights of Saint Pellar," Sir Ako said firmly. "I will be the lord commander, in charge of military decisions. Master Sandun will be the high templar, in charge of diplomatic decisions."

"And what if you two don't agree—what then?" asked Farrel.

"Then the decision goes to a vote by all the knights, and majority rules."

This was greeted with shouts and cheers and toasts to the good health of Sir Ako and all the future knights of Serica.

While they were drinking, Sandun asked Sir Ako, "How much do you know about the knights of Saint Pellar? Because I know very little."

"Strange to say, but I know quite a bit. I was recruited by them after I won the tournament eight, no, nine years ago. An elderly gentleman from Akia came up to me during the king's banquet and asked me if I would consider joining their order. I didn't know much about them, just the stories we all hear in the temple. So I asked around: my father, other knights, and the queen. Queen Joaris, her younger brother had joined, so she knew what it was like from an outsider's perspective. As you can see, I chose not to join, but in later years I often wondered at that decision: travel to distant lands, live a life of adventure, be part of the most ancient knightly order. But here I am, in far Serica, and about to set up my own order of knights. I daresay rather more adventure than I would have seen if I had joined the Saint Pellars." Sir Ako drained his cup and placed it on the table with a solid thump. "I'll write up the rules of the order, a rough draft, and then you can see what you think."

"I noticed that you put yourself in charge."

"Yes, I did. You aren't the leader that I am. The men respect you, and you have knowledge and some measure of common sense, but you aren't the leader these men will follow into battle. I am."

Sandun felt deflated. Sir Ako's words were like a bucket of cold water poured over his head, but he knew in his heart what the knight said was true, at least for now.

"We are friends, yes. Brothers in arms?"

"Yes, my friend. Always and forever," Sir Ako said warmly.

Three weeks later, the preparations for the investiture ceremony were complete. A dozen blacksmiths had labored to create replicas of Sir Ako's armor, sized to fit each man. Sandun's armor was hung on a wooden stand in his room. Ashala and he had spent some hours learning how to put it on; it had become something of a game.

Basil complained about the way the shoulder piece interfered with the drawing of his great bow, and Sir Ako agreed that the shoulder pieces were not good copies of his pauldrons.

"The knights I know who specialize in the use of the war bow all wear only a helm and cuirass of metal," Sir Ako admitted. "I expect you and perhaps all the others will do the same in battle. But for ceremony and parades, the full suit is required."

There had been an afternoon of good-natured debate about the design of the symbol that all of them would wear. "A knightly order has only one coat of arms," Sir Ako stated with authority. All sorts of animals and weapons were proposed. The decision came down to a vote between a lion, standing while holding a great bow in its upraised paw, and a burning tower. Sandun liked the lion better than the tower, but the majority voted for the burning tower, which was Sir Ako's favored design.

All the men were going to go through the initiation ceremony and become the founding members of the "Knights of Serica." Sandun had asked Basil about it, but Basil was unconcerned. Kagne too was joining. He had recovered from whatever afflicted him on the tower, though he was somewhat withdrawn from the group. He had requested a map of the northern lands of Serica, which Sandun was able to provide.

The night before the vigil, Sandun and the others were all supposed to get extra sleep. However, Sandun could not quiet his mind. He lay in bed for several hours, thinking about the decision to form a new knightly order and his decision to join it and so pass the leadership of the expedition to Sir Ako. He worried about what would happen when—or if—they returned to Kelten. Would the king take offense at his decisions? Had he betrayed the king's trust by agreeing to serve Lord Vaina for a year?

He rose from his bed, leaving Ashala sleeping, and he went to the library. He wrote what he called "An Apologia" to explain what they were doing and why. After several hours, he felt he had gotten it all off his chest and was now ready to retire. He returned to his chambers, but just as he was closing the door, he heard a noise.

The sound was that of a grunt followed by a soft thud. Sandun was suddenly wide awake, and a cold thrill filled his body. He pushed open his door very slightly. He then heard the main door to the street creaking open. Given the late hour, there was just one plausible explanation: they were under attack.

He grabbed his new helm and his Piksie sword and yelled out into the atrium below: "Who goes there?" And then in Kelten he shouted, "Awake! Danger threatens!"

A group of masked men burst through the main door, armed with daggers and shortswords. There were cries of "Death to the traitor!" and "Kill everyone!"

Ashala, naked, pulled Sandun back into their room. She ran over to the armor stand and lifted off the gleaming metal cuirass. "Please, my lord, put this on. It will only take a moment."

Sandun agreed and stood there in mounting anxiety while Ashala buckled the straps behind his back.

"It's done," she said.

"You stay inside," he ordered, "and don't open the door until it is safe." Sandun opened the door again and went out with his sword in hand.

The attackers were easy enough to recognize with their masks and their weapons. It seemed several of the house staff who slept on the ground floor were already injured. There were shrieks and yells. A masked man came running up the stairs and threw himself at Sandun with a wild fury. Sandun tried to parry the attack, but the man dived low and tried to knock Sandun off his feet.

This was not an unexpected move; indeed, it was one Sir Ako had trained all the men on. Sandun just retreated back down the hallway, and his attacker ended up down on his hand and knees. Sandun leapt forward and kicked the man in the face. Then he retreated again as he heard a noise behind him. It was Padan, in his nightclothes and carrying a sword and shield. Their eyes met, and Padan turned and headed back the way he'd come, banging on the doors and shouting, "Kelten rises!"

The man wearing the mask got to his feet and came toward Sandun more cautiously, but then Basil's door flew open, and the attacker turned to face the new threat. Sandun leaped to attack and chopped deeply into the man's back. He cried out in agony and collapsed onto the floor. Basil was carrying a shortsword and dagger. From inside his room, the wailing of his new son was suddenly muffled.

"Get your bow; I'll go ahead," Sandun said to him. Basil looked around and then went back into his room. Sandun advanced to meet another attacker coming up the stairs. This man also attempted to grapple with Sandun; he sprang, and Sandun swung his sword, which bit deep into the man's left arm. But the man's other hand held a dagger. It plunged toward Sandun's chest, but the metal cuirass held firm, and all that the blow produced was a terrible grating noise. The man's surprise was short lived as Sandun's next blow came right at his face, and he went down in spray of dark blood.

The next man up the stairs got hit by an arrow right in his eye—from Basil, who had strung his bow and was now behind Sandun. The next attacker on the stairs had a dagger thrown into his neck; this came from Kagne, who was crouching low on the far side of the stairs. With the stairs held, Basil began picking off attackers who were below in the courtyard.

Hearing the sounds of Sir Ako's curses and yells from the ground floor, Sandun advanced down the stairs. One of the two cooks, a middle-aged woman, was slumped in a pool of blood near the doorway to the kitchen. With Kagne beside him, Sandun entered the dining room only to find Gloval's body near several overturned chairs.

Gloval's wound had not healed well; he found it difficult to climb the stairs to his room, so he had taken to sleeping at the end of the dining room, with screens around his bed. The masked intruders had found him early in the attack, and he'd been in no good condition to defend himself.

Kagne got down onto his knees and cradled Gloval's head. Gloval had been part of Kagne's herb team; normally a laconic cowherd, Gloval could curse with the best of them when he lost at cards.

Sandun left Kagne with Gloval's body and went out to the courtyard. There he saw Lathe fighting with a much larger man who was standing near the gate. At first, Sandun thought Lathe was fighting with his usual sticks, but then he saw the young man was using shortswords. Again, Sandun was amazed at Lathe's speed and physical agility. The bigger man's blows seemed to miss Lathe by feet, not inches. Lathe's swords cut the man in several places until blood was dripping down his arms. And then in a move too swift for Sandun to understand, Lathe was behind the big man and kicked him in the back of his head, sending the man to the ground.

"I want him alive," said Sir Ako to Lathe. Then he ran off to the sounds of more fighting in the back of the house. Lathe followed Sir Ako lightly on silent feet.

Sandun stood over the fallen attacker with his sword at the prone man's neck while Basil closed the gate and barred it. Kagne appeared with some cords and bound the man up like a bale of hay.

Valo Peli strode into view from out of the shadows, his bow in hand, looking pained. He had a piece of bloody cloth wrapped around his neck. He started examining the bodies in the courtyard in the faint starlight. One belonged to their gate guard, an old boatman with a bad leg. Around his neck was a silken cord.

"The attackers appear to be river men, by their style of dress and choice of weapons. I guess that some were soldiers of Vasvar who surrendered after the battle," said Valo Peli.

Sandun told him, "Gloval is dead. As is one of the kitchen servants."

"Since the fighting has died down, let us go examine them. There may be some hope. I expect the city watch will be here soon. Someone must let them in."

Kagne agreed to stay at the gate and keep an eye on the prisoner. Sandun led Valo Peli and Basil to the bodies.

Both the kitchen servant and Gloval were cold to the touch, and Valo Peli shook his head in dismay. They found a young servant girl hiding in a closet. As soon as she came out, she burst into tears and clutched at Valo Peli's legs.

He spoke to her sharply. "Go and heat some water! Many have been injured while you hid."

The young girl wiped her eyes and then bowed to them several times before going to the fireplace.

Of the intruders, they found eleven men dead and two injured. Ashala came out when Sandun called to her. She said to him, "Outside, toward the eastern market, I saw flames and heard the beating of the alarm."

Once she mentioned it, Sandun heard the noise as well.

"A coordinated arson and attack. No wonder the watch has not arrived," Valo Peli said thoughtfully.

Instead of the watch, the first people through the gate were members of the palace guard. Half an hour later, Lord Vaina appeared with more soldiers at his back.

As Valo Peli explained the situation, Lord Vaina looked around and then came up to the prisoners. He looked with a grim face at the three men on their knees in the torchlight.

"I know you," Lord Vaina said, his voice flat and hard, addressing the big man who had been knocked down by Lathe. "You were one of the officers of the Vasvar army who surrendered to General Kun. I saw you and your men two days after the battle. You swore to serve me then. Now you will tell me who you were trying to kill and how much you were to be paid."

The big man looked up and then back down at the ground. He was silent. The noise of the fire alarm had died away.

"Your death is foretold. The only question is, how many of your companions will die in addition to you. Ten? One hundred? One thousand? I offered you the hand of mercy, and you have repaid me with betrayal. Everyone you know will die!" Lord Vaina's voice was thick with a barely suppressed rage.

"Wait, wait, I will tell you everything. Just spare my men," said the big man.

"Speak, then. I promise nothing."

"A man I knew, a smuggler, from Virmakla, a week past. He offered me fifty strings, in silver, to kill Arno Boethy."

"Why?"

"He said Nilin Ulim wanted Arno Boethy dead and everyone with him. He said the Kitran army was coming, and their retribution would be the murderous thrashing of the riverbeast, but those who killed Boethy would be brought on board their mighty ship."

Lord Vaina drew his sword in fury and slashed it across the man's shoulder, drawing blood. "The Kitran are coming like the terrible riverbeast? You piece of fish shit, how is their army getting across the Mur? Will dragons carry them? Or were you and your traitorous friends going to steal my boats and present them to Nilin Ulim to save your miserable necks?"

The big man struggled in the grasp of two of the palace guards. "No! No! We never would have done that."

Lord Vaina told one of his officials to take the man and the two injured away for detailed questioning. "Find out everything they know; use every means. They die tomorrow along with a thousand of their compatriots. This one feared the wrath of the Kitran? Bah! He feared the wrong army. He should have feared me!"

He told a guard to take a message to General Kun, which he rapidly wrote on a portable writing desk carried by a scribe.

"Let me see your dead," Lord Vaina said heavily. Sandun led him to the dining room, followed by all the Keltens and Valo Peli.

Gloval's body had been laid back on his bed, covered by a sheet. Lord Vaina drew back the sheet, uncovering the man's face. Then he got to his knees and bowed down, his head nearly touching the floor.

The room was silent for a minute. A faint light from the eastern sky could be seen through the high, narrow windows.

"I am shamed," Lord Vaina said after rising to his feet. "I trusted soldiers of Vasvar, and they spat on my mercy. The city watch also failed in their duty to guard this embassy, and that failure will be punished severely."

Valo Peli got down on his knees and bowed. "Lord Vaina, the responsibility is mine. These assassins sought to kill me. I should have been living apart and not been here, drawing dangers to others."

"No, you were well hidden here. The Sogands have better spies than we imagined, given that your true name was known to only a few and you spent most of your days holed up here like badger in his den. However, I have heard some people connect the fire arrows from the battle with your name." Lord Vaina got up and helped Valo Peli to his feet. Addressing Sir Ako, Lord Vaina said, "Shall we continue the ceremony planned for tomorrow, or do you wish it delayed?"

"I wish no delay, Lord Vaina. I ask only that Gloval, Sir Gloval, be named as a knight of Serica along with us, his living companions."

"Certainly. That is a very Serice thing to do. We are not so different, Keltens and Serice."

The next evening, the Keltens marched over to the old temple of Sho'Ash, wearing their new burnished armor. Some work on the temple had already been completed: the dust was long gone, the old wooden statue of Sho'Ash was bound with strips of silver-plated copper. All night, they prayed and stood watch. At three times during the night, the old priest and his son recited sections of the ritual, the first from the beginning of the year, the second from the harvest, and the last, just at dawn, telling of Sho'Ash's death and ascension.

Then the Keltens, blessed by the priest, marched back again through the dawn-lit streets. A few of the early merchants saluted them, but the street sweepers ignored them and continued to collect the trash in the quiet morning.

Several hours' rest were followed by a grand procession to the palace. They were escorted by one of the regiments of Tokolas soldiers. Now the streets were crowded, and scattered cheers greeted them as they walked uphill. For the first time, the main gates to the palace, great heavy iron and wood doors painted with fresh green paint, were open to them.

They marched into the central plaza to find a large assembly of people, all dressed in elaborate costumes. On the one side were what looked like all the civilian officials, dressed in long robes decorated with animals and flowers. On the other side were the officers of the Kunhalvar army, all with their armor and carrying great spears and swords with silk banners hanging off the shafts.

"I didn't expect such a great crowd," Sir Ako said to Sandun as they walked in between the ranks of men.

"I think Lord Vaina is doing more than just knighting us."

Indeed, as they came before the Lord of Kunhalvar, who was seated on a richly carved and painted wooden throne, they found the other generals standing beside them: General Erdis, General Kun, and five other generals who Sandun did not know by name.

"I feel distinctly uncomfortable," Sandun whispered to Sir Ako.

"Try walking up to the king and all the nobles of the realm before the royal tournament, Sandun. Since you are a knight, you should learn to joust. You aren't too old!"

Sandun shook his head. He was not going to learn to joust.

The chief administrator now stood forth and invoked the blessing of heaven and the spirits. Musicians holding strangely shaped instruments played an odd, atonal music. Women in striped gowns danced a spinning dance where they changed places on a geometric grid.

Silks with painted symbols in gold ink were tossed into the braziers that stood on either side of the stage. Many of the words the old man used were unfamiliar to Sandun, and he saw that Lord Vaina looked somewhat puzzled himself at times. But then Lord Vaina rose and nodded to his advisor. When the lord spoke in his commanding voice, it boomed across the great open space and echoed faintly off the walls. White river birds, startled off their perches on the roof, wheeled about the sky, calling out to each other in tones like low trumpets.

"A great state needs more than wise administrators. A state needs men both brave and skilled in battle. In every age, the people are beset by enemies who bring war and death to the land, even to our capital itself. We give our leaders ranks in the army, but we can do more. It is written that in the days of the Fire Kingdom, the great heroes of the land were known by titles of honor. These titles told all the people that the men before them were not just officers in the military but men of worth, men raised up by heaven as examples to everyone of bravery, exemplars of justice. Today, I honor these men who have demonstrated their worth through years of service to their people, to their homeland, and to me."

Lord Vaina drew his sword; it flashed in the sunlight. Sandun could see sweat dripping down the lord's face under his heavy hat of state.

"General Pojo Erdis and General Esko Kun, step forward. I, the Ruler of Kunhalvar, Commander of Tokolas, the Duke of Divine Repose, name both of you *rakeg*, for you and for your family. Bear the title with honor."

Both men stepped forward, and Lord Vaina presented to each of them a heavy necklace of gold with a tiger medallion in the center. He then named the other generals to different titles that Sandun had never heard before.

Turning now to the Keltens standing before him, Lord Vaina spoke in a quieter voice.

"Rarely in our long history have foreigners come to Serica and found us so inhospitable as at present. Our nation is divided, this city, attacked. As the Lord of Kunhalvar, I suffer because I have been unable to uphold the duty a ruler of Serica owes to his guests. But you have overlooked my shortcomings. You have repaid our small welcome with mighty deeds. Never before have ambassadors from a distant nation done so much to help us in our hour of need.

"It shall be recorded in the annals of our state and remembered from this time forward, that together we stood atop the lighthouse tower and rained destruction on the fleet of our enemies. Although the tower has crumbled, Tuno's ships have been taken or fled. You men of Kelten—standing before me—are unbroken heroes. As the Ruler of Kunhalvar, as the Duke of Divine Repose, I now proclaim that you are each granted the title *Opmi* of Serica. Let it be known throughout my lands that *Opmi* of Serica are men of boundless courage, that they are men of honor, and that they are men of virtue."

He now signaled to Sir Ako to come forward.

"I now appoint Sir Ako as Master of the Opmi of Serica." Sir Ako knelt, and Lord Vaina hung around his neck a silver necklace with a palm-sized amulet, covered in gold and figured with the design of a flaming tower.

Lord Vaina then called for Sandun, and Basil, and Kagne, and all the rest, ending with Wiyat. Each man was given a medallion, covered in silver, bearing the same image of the burning tower. One more necklace was brought forward and given to Sir Ako. "In memory of *Opmi* Gloval. His valor will never be challenged, his honor, never lessened.

"Rise now, *Opmi* of Serica!"

Sandun stood up and looked around. The light was somehow brighter, and it seemed as though the world was more clear and also that a nimbus of color lay behind the people standing around him. He shook hands with the other Keltens, calling them brothers. Waves of cheering broke out, and the soldiers in the square beat upon their shields with spears and swords.

Sandun felt as though he had grown a foot, as though he were standing in great boots intended for a giant.

Together, the men of the Archives Expedition turned and walked out of the palace grounds and into the city.

EPILOGUE

They had been drinking for hours. The dining room was filled with bowls of food and bottles of many shapes and colors. Despite the noise, little Niksol was sleeping in Olef's arms, while she rested her head on Basil's shoulder. The other women sat beside their men, smiling and laughing behind their hands.

Sandun was talking freely with Sir Ako, his head filled with more than a dozen confused thoughts.

"Did you hear that strange music they played during the ceremony?" Sir Ako said, and then shook his head as if to clear it. "Horns, drums, bells, things I've never seen before. All playing at the same time without rhythm or melody. I didn't know what to make of it."

"It sounded old to me. Like music out of the past. What say you, Valo Peli? Had you heard such music before?"

Valo Peli, his eyes notably bloodshot, clapped his hands together and told them, "It is very old music and yes, I've heard it before. Once. In Sasuvi, after I completed my studies and passed their test."

"Does anyone like it? What does it mean?"

"I think a few people like it. In the days of the Water Kingdom, the writers described sages drinking tea and listening to refined music. That doesn't happen often now." He coughed and drank from his teacup. "As to what it means, that I can tell you."

Valo Peli proceeded to talk for five or ten minutes, using many words that none of his listeners understood. Stupefied by the alcohol and unwilling to interrupt the older man's soliloquy, Sandun and Sir Ako just nodded their heads and drank. Finally, Valo Peli looked at the two men and the women sitting beside them and tilted his head. "Did that make any sense?" he asked quizzically.

"You said it has to do with keeping the world in balance?" said Sandun.

Russu Tuomi said, "Isn't it about creating harmony in the hearts of the listeners?"

Valo Peli shrugged. "I don't really understand it, although I have memorized the Book of Ritual and the Book of Songs. The Kitrans who rule in Daka never play the music. They have ruled for nearly one hundred years, so perhaps it doesn't matter."

Russu said proudly, "Back home, we play that music once a year. We haven't abandoned the old traditions."

"Do you? Then I salute you. Rakeved grows in my estimation." Valo Peli raised his cup to Russu.

Finally, Sandun's thoughts crystallized on the question that he had pushed aside for the last forty-eight hours. "Valo Peli, who is Nilin Ulim, and why does he want you dead?"

The Serice scholar gave a long sigh and put his hands into the large sleeves of his silken robe.

"That is a topic unsuited for today's happy celebration. But I will say this much: Nilin Ulim is a powerful and dangerous man. I could not ask for a deadlier enemy. Yesterday, I sent a messenger back to the land of my birth, asking for aid. Perhaps some of my clansmen will join me here. You Keltens have a reputation for seeking out challenges. In taking me on, you seem to have acquired more troubles than anyone could have guessed. Defeating Nilin Ulim is a true test and one that I would not have sought. Ah well, time enough for that in days to come."

AFTERWORD

Thanks for reading the book. I hope you enjoyed it.

There is another book being written, titled *The Lord of Shadows*. It continues the stories of Sandun, Sir Ako, Basil, Kagne, Valo Peli, the Lord of Kunhalvar, and more. A third book, tentatively titled *The Lake on Fire*, is waiting out in the future, like a cloud.

Personal Note

As an historian, one of my great joys has been discovering unlikely events and subtle connections that had profound effects on the course of human history.

But real history is messy. Important things happen, sometimes for no discernible reason or for reasons that are trivial compared to the monumental consequences. This book is not a history, but it takes place in a world much like our own with people, cultures, and stories that are similar to Earth's.

About me, I will say this: I am an American, and I have lived most of my life in California though I have travelled widely. I have been married, and I have three children. Professionally, I have held several jobs, including developing commercial software, technical writing, and teaching.

The following people have been the literary and philosophical inspirations in my life:

J. R. R. Tolkien
Gene Wolfe
Aristotle
Confucius
Lord Dunsany
Roger Zelazny
William Shakespeare
Philip Jose Farmer

E. R. Eddison
F. W. Mote
Richard Feynman
John von Neumann
And, Publius (Alexander Hamilton and James Madison)

ABOUT THE AUTHOR

Colin Glassey has driven across the United States four times and has traveled extensively throughout Europe and east Asia. He has degrees in History, Computer Science, and Law. He has worked for many years as a technical writer, a software engineer, and an attorney. He presently resides in California.

Made in the USA
San Bernardino, CA
21 April 2017